AMANDA

ALSO BY

H. S. CROSS

Grievous
Wilberforce

H. S. Cross

AMANDA

Europa Editions
27 Union Square West, Suite 302
New York NY 10003
www.europaeditions.com
info@europaeditions.com

First publication 2025 by Europa Editions

Library of Congress Cataloging in Publication Data is available
ISBN 979-8-88966-135-1

Cross, H. S.
Amanda

Jacket image: Dame Laura Knight, *At the Edge of the Cliff*, British School, 19th Century/Alamy Stock Photo

Cover design by Ginevra Rapisardi

Prepress by Grafica Punto Print – Rome

Printed in Canada

CONTENTS

If you’re reading this, hope is real.

AMANDA

London

If you would know the flavor of gooseberries, you must go where they are found and pull them off the bushes. She pulsed with shame to think of the poems she'd once written thinking they were deep. Thinking was a vain act.

She had come to London to disappear, which was her specialty, never to see or think of any of them again, and in time to become a different person. She had not yet hit upon the name for this new girl, but when she heard it, she would know. The plan had cracked immediately, as did all ideas when forced to spend a day in reality. The hostel made her expect knives, and after only two days, Nigel at reception had offered her a drink and touched the small of her back.

Resolutions were vain things and people should be ashamed to make them. She had resolved never to write anyone from Oxford or the press, but by week's end she had escaped Nigel's nicotine tongue and written to Artemis from the table in the post-office hall. The next day she climbed out the hostel window and carted her Gladstone bag across town to Artemis's flat. Artemis—now called Diana—promised never to mention her return to England to anyone at the press, not that Diana had much to do with them now, living in London, going by her legal name, and married to Bernard, but still. Her own former self, called by the name that couldn't be said, no longer existed. She must stop living in fear. Firm chats to oneself in the looking glass were vanity. They sounded full of conviction but always made one feel absurd and never arrested the mad slide.

She'd since left off staying at Diana's flat, but this afternoon, as if they smelled her on the wind, the ogres of Erin threw their nets across the bog.

She was with the children at the British Museum waiting to meet Diana. They'd taken an omnibus, it was hot, they'd complained. Inside the Egypt Hall, cool and tall, she set them copying designs from the sides of a sarcophagus. She stepped away to discourage their questions, and there, on the other side of the case: Emma.

—Mary? Emma said. Marion McDonagh, is it you?

She never thought to have dyed her hair, but now she wished she had. She behaved to Emma as she'd seen Diana do last week encountering a friend from childhood, pretending it was ordinary and delightful. Emma had been in the class above her at school, and after getting the civil service exam, Emma had gone to work in the Galway Post Office. Now, eight years later, Emma claimed to be in London on an advanced course for the overseas desk.

—Of the Post Office?

—No, silly goose, the Foreign Office.

Emma regarded her as one would an injured animal. How many times had she imagined running across someone from home? Eloping with Lovelace was one thing, but vanishing when he turned up dead could not be explained in a museum.

—Oh, Emma said. You don't know, or do you?

The old fear pricked, that more of them were dead now, even her mother dead of a broken heart as she'd always said would happen if—

—I'm married, Emma said.

She extended her hand to show a ring with a red jewel.

—And . . .

Emma touched her flat stomach. She kissed Emma's cheek and asked who was the lucky man.

—You'll hate me, Emma said, but he's English. My parents were fierce, but it's all right now.

Emma returned her hand to her stomach as if that apologized for everything. She saw then that Emma's hair was cut stylishly and that her frock looked new, or at least not adapted from an old one, and she thought of how Emma's house had always been a sty when she would play there, kitchen table grimy, cobwebs and spiders everywhere. Yet here was Emma, fingernails varnished, lips rouged, married to a Black and Tan and wearing a ring that came dear.

—But what happened to you? Emma demanded. After Professor Laighléis, your people—

—When did you leave?

Emma said it had been nearly two years.

—Ah, that explains it, it does.

All bluffs were helped by distraction; she called to the children. Emma's face came over surprised, and she could see Emma assuming the children were hers. There was no way of explaining, even if she wanted, why she thought of Laighléis as Lovelace and how she'd been made a widow so fast.

—When Laighléis died, I had to go away. Then the boys died in France and . . .

She could say this and have a shred of hope she'd be believed because Emma had married the Englishman and left the kitchen table behind.

—I couldn't go back, you see.

Emma still looked confused.

—Oh, no! she said to the children, I've forgotten all about your lesson!

—What lesson?

—We must fly!

—But Marion—

She kissed Emma again, stuffed pencils and boards into her bag, and rushed with the children down the stairs, asking them to play along.

—Why, Marion? Clive whined.

She promised him a new puzzle and Felicity a dress for her doll if they made it to the park without being caught by the spies.

—What spies?

—The spies of the exiled Tsar.

—Oo-ooh!

—They've found us in hiding and if they catch us—

—Off with our heads?

—Don't even say it!

They'd fled the museum before her appointment with Diana, and now she'd have to tell another lie. She only ever told Diana half the truth at most, but still.

—Who's that? Clive asked.

They ducked behind a pillar and peered down the street at a line of carriages and policemen on horses.

—Someone important.

—The King? asked Clive.

—The Tsar? asked Felicity.

—The Tsar's murdered to death, you ninny.

—But his spies.

The children fell to bickering as the carriages rolled into the park.

—Can the King pardon anyone of any crime? Clive asked.

She said she supposed he could.

—So if you did something horribly wicked, like killing your husband and children—

—Murdering them to death!

—He could pardon you?

—Yes, she said, but the King's pardon doesn't mean everything.

—It does! Felicity protested.

—What's more, Marion? What's more?

Shortly the Irish whisper circuits would hear of her existence and tell all Galway where she now dwelt. She didn't think

Irish detectives would ever speak to Scotland Yard, but you never knew for sure.

Midnight, parlor, Chesterfield sticky in the heat, her employer—Mother—gassed about her night at the orchestra. The woman imagined the ladies of London disdained her for her frocks, which she feared looked northern and marked her as provincial. Pinched between her employer's complaints and loudening voices from Ireland, she began to sing as she did to the children:

—*When the red red robin comes bob bob bobbin' along, along! there'll be no more sobbin' when he starts throbbin' his old, sweet song—*

—Dear Marion.

—How was the *rest* of the evening? Did you walk in the park or get an ice at—

She named a popular place for the late night sets, and Mother launched into a description of peach sherbets. When the woman looked bright enough to go to bed and not annoy her husband with melancholy, she steered her into the corridor, but there the woman halted, as if on the verge of tears:

—You've a great well of kindness, Marion.

—Oh now.

—I feel it, dear. I feel it!

—I'm just a kid again, doing what I did again, singing a song . . .

Mother hummed as they climbed the stairs.

—When the red red robin comes bob bob bobbin'—

Intermittent visions of being captured, tracked by the kinds of men who tracked people across the Continent, these were as chilling as stories told after dark in the big bed with Daniel and Teddy and Joe. They served to frighten and distract her from the present incursion. Emma hadn't smelled of a turf fire, but her voice had conjured that island eight years after she'd escaped on the night ship to Holyhead and the boltholes where Daniel's friends had taken her. She never dreamed she wouldn't see Daniel again, or Teddy and Joe, never dreamed her brothers wouldn't even have graves, only fields across the channel covered in poppies. Nor had she ever dreamed anything would happen to the jars in her childhood fairy circle after she filched them from the back of the airing cupboard and took them to the place where she kept her drawings scrolled into ginger beer bottles, the buttons she stole from Daniel's collection, and the lock of hair cut off her grandmother's corpse when no one was looking. One day she found the jars empty of their perfumed ointments. A chill had come upon her, and she'd taken everything straight back to the house and found new hiding places for the buttons and hair and drawings. Maybe the fairies would track her, maybe not. Once they had something of yours, they'd steal from you forever unless you got away, and you had to get far away, not just over the garden wall or the River Shannon, but all the way across the sea, off the whole magic-pocked landmass that was their miserable home.

She didn't have a weapon. If someone came at her in the street, she had only her handbag and her teeth. No one had yet come at her, but she wished she could fight like a man. She had Clive down for boxing lessons even though Mother had been against it. The woman considered boxing nasty, but she managed to convince her that he'd need to dodge punches once he started school.

—But I'd never want him fighting!

—Certainly not.

She described her brothers as all having had boxing lessons that taught them to outstep every fisticuff bullies tried. Mother believed her, and that was when she'd realized how to manage the woman.

She took them to the Center Wednesdays and Saturdays, not only for ballet and boxing but for free play in the garden afterwards, all of which gave her nearly three hours if she dropped them early.

—You must have enough time to put your things in their place and to take your breath, she told them.

Tuesdays, Aunt Philomena fetched them at eleven and kept them until teatime. On Mondays and Thursdays she took them to the Institute for their music lessons and told them how important it was to listen to other people's practice from the corridor.

—To master a musical instrument, you must take your breath in it.

—It's boring, Clive insisted.

She bought him a booklet of puzzles and kept a special pencil sharpened in her bag for the occasion. Felicity, though younger, was more easily entertained if she were allowed to bring her doll and a pocket of sweets. She couldn't get away for more than ninety minutes from the Institute, but it was something. She sat in the square when it was fine and the café when it wasn't.

She could stab a man with Clive's pencil if she stashed it in her chignon. She didn't have a particular attacker in mind, but when she'd been sleeping on Artemis's—*Diana's*—settee, gazing at Bernard's shirts above the stove, she'd thought how you could snap a wet singlet at someone's eye, toss salt at their face, kick them between the legs, and if she could ever manage to grow out her nails, she could claw someone, though the men near Diana's flat looked too big to dent. She wanted a knife, the kind you wore up your skirt and whipped out in a blink. She never told Diana of her thoughts, but it was a relief for many reasons—Bernard's snoring, the sour smell of him—when after her first fortnight giving Clive and Felicity language lessons from two to three o'clock, Mother confessed she was just done in arranging their studies by herself. She had thought she could manage until September when Clive started his school and

Felicity her dear little nursery, but her nerves simply couldn't take it. Oh, why couldn't they be as ordinary people, live in one place, have a nanny who didn't quit? Why must everything be an arduous exception for them, but she was rattling on and what would Miss Marion think?

—That you could do with more than a French and German tutor?

Oh, she could, she really could. She hated herself for her failure—

—Why must it be failure? I could—

—I know, dear. I saw at once that you're worth ten of me.

—Nothing's worth more than a mother.

—Dear Marion, I'd hand it all over to you in a heartbeat, but you'd have to live in, and there's only the little room at the top of the house.

She plunged into her story: she'd been looking for fixed accommodation since arriving from the Chalet School. She'd no family of her own—

—Oh, my dear, I hadn't realized!

But it was nothing to be sad for. She'd been raised by her aunt and uncle, and when her uncle died, her aunt had sent her to the Chalet School. Then her aunt died, and she became a teacher there. The girls had loved her, but then this spring her friend, her dearest oldest friend, had begged her to come to London, told her she could stay as long as she liked—

—Was this Fraulien Lina, who wrote us about you?

You had to keep your wits when you were making up stories you'd have to live with.

—Lina is my Swiss friend, the famous poetess?

—Of course, of course.

—My English friend is Diana.

—What a lovely name.

—The kindest friend you'd ever know, not a nasty bone in her body—

—I adore her already.

Diana was desperately lonely, knew no one in town but her husband, and perhaps Mother would not mind if she were slightly indiscreet—

—Tell Mother everything.

Diana's husband was a dear man, lost a leg in the war but she adored him, and although he was employed, their accommodation was very spare and the part of town—

—But Marion, dear, you must come here, now, tonight.

—And they've a baby on the way.

—Oh, my dear!

Mother embraced her fiercely, and as soon as Father came home, they agreed she must bring her things tomorrow; she must take a taxi and they'd pay the driver. The children were overjoyed, and she had a room with a door and three afternoons mostly to herself. Also, it was only until September. She didn't have to become an actual governess or get used to children. She could decide on her new life and new name, and no one would know to look for her in Kensington.

With a prolonged and surprisingly tough series of snips, the nail scissors cut through the hair. Thankfully, Felicity had a lot of it. She called her Morgan le Fay, the secret name she'd given the girl to go with Clive's name, Finn McCool the Irish giant.

—Now, Morgan, you mustn't make that face, and you must do everything in your power, your ancient well-drawn power, not to let on about these few missing locks.

—Because Mummy will be cross?

—Because a sorceress never admits to losing anything.

—Will it weaken my powers?

She raked through the blond locks for the last of the chewing gum:

—Only temporarily, but once it's grown back, you'll be stronger than ever.

The girl looked doubtful.

—Sometimes in Ireland a sorceress will cut her hair on purpose just to give her powers a boost. My grandmama cut hers all off.

—*All* off?

—Like a boy with nits.

The lovely family's house in Kensington smelled of paint and wallpaper sizing; they'd never smelled peat in their lives, but every idea she had for how to treat them she drew from shadows they couldn't see.

If her own mother had been any kind of mother, she would have dragged her home by the hair and locked her up until she quit being such a fool. *Who are you, Miss Marion McDonagh, so high and mighty? Marry me to save my soul? I never heard such bog-bottom blarney all my days and that's the truth. You tell this Laighléis*—But her mother was never any sort of mother, not to any of them once they crawled off and found ideas in their heads that weren't hers. Once you saw her with your own eyes, once she told you to take the look off your face, you weren't long for her arms. She'd get another one and carry it in her belly, and you could just see to the tea for the little ones and nip down Mrs. Shea's for some sugar, she'll have pity she will, and fetch your father home while you're at it, *milis*.

The trouble with Lovelace was that he'd read so many books, the only person besides her father to have read more than she had. His lecture on Christina Rossetti made her feel faint. That was a euphemism. Boys were forever committing impure acts, but she didn't think under the blanket counted as the same thing, at least, she couldn't imagine how to say it in confession, but when he read them "Goblin Market," it made her feel how she felt under the blanket, and that was only his second lecture. He had rooms in the college where he received pupils to answer their questions. She almost didn't go, even after writing her name on the paper, because what if he could see by her face what his lectures did to her places? He had a warm, kind voice and a beautiful soft accent that was hardly any accent at all, the way books sounded in their true sound. When she told him about their spaniel pup drowning, his face turned grave and he put his hand on top of hers and said, *Oh, I am sorry,* the warmest sorry she'd ever heard. He could find a poem for anything, and when he said things, they sounded like the truth.

—Marion, *qu'est ce que c'est*?

—*C'est un mégot. Donne-le-moi*, Morgan.

—Do you *mégoter*?

—*Fumez-vous les cigarettes? Et non, je ne fume pas* and neither should you.

—What's the worst thing you can say *en français*?

She tried to teach them useful phrases. *Je mange un toad dans le hole. J'adore le candy floss.* Her French was passable, and she'd got some German, but Lina had composed three references on Swiss paper that said she was lovely with children and a wizard with languages. Lina's letters with their crests and foreign postmarks had twiddled the lovely family into offering her a position sight unseen. If she didn't know a French or German word, she'd make it up and say it was dialect, and who knew if that wasn't how dialects got started after all.

—*Sacré bleu* is the very worst.

—*Sacré bleu*!

—Marion, *qu'est-ce que c'est*?

—*Mon doigt. Doigt, main*, remember?

—No, *qu'est-ce que c'est*?

—*C'est un bleu.*

—*Sacré bleu*!

—Cook has one and Mother says it's from cigarettes.

—*C'est possible. Mais celle-ci* is from when I had to fight off *un chien.*

—What *chien*?

—It was gigantic and mostly friendly but sometimes . . .

—*Sacré bleu*!

She blamed Emily Dickinson for addling her brain when she was impressionable. Thanks to that recluse, she'd grown up thinking Boanerges was a horse. She used to draw pictures of him on the endpapers of books, a steed that rode the skies faster than trains, a half-dragon who'd breathe fire over the Connemara hills and alight beyond their back garden in the place she went when she didn't want to be found. He would nuzzle against her like a horse-sized wolfhound, rubbing his nose along her cheek because only she could soothe him.

She blamed Padraig O'Brien for the rest of it. If he hadn't been so beautiful and clever and tall, she never would have begun hanging about the *Píob Mhór*, and she never would have rubbed his mickey to get him to show her how to use the press; she never would have snuck out to help them sift through the mess in the back of the Pearl & Oyster, all the sorts that had been strewn into the bay by the Black and Tans and fished out again by bold boys who'd do anything for a penny; she wouldn't have broken out in rashes cleaning rusty sorts, wouldn't have got metal splinters trying to repair the 72-point P for the masthead Padraig wanted after the Easter Rising, and later, in Oxford, it wouldn't have seemed so natural to try to do for Gutenberg what she'd done for Padraig, so Gute would give her work until the boys came home, tending the sorts and then the presses and most especially tending Boanerges, without which Gute would never have printed anything special, and certainly not the Arabian book. And then when the war ended and the boys did come home, Gute never got round to sacking her because no one else could make Boanerges run, soothe his frothy flanks, oil his gears, make his drums roll true so the ink pressed smooth into the papers, across the sorts she'd coaxed back to form, and lap out page after page, from her giant hound, son-of-thunder pet.

Gute never did expect things from her, not when he took her on, not when he got her lodgings at the Gorgon's and paid for them until she'd earned enough to pay for herself, not even during salons. She assumed he was a poof until Artemis told her everything. Artemis lodged at the Gorgon's, too. She worked at the press answering the telephone and delivering messages, so she was up on things. She knew the latest from every front. She knew what they'd ration next and what the Americans were saying. She knew how to introduce Gutenberg (*He's called Gute, rhymes with lute*); she knew the proofreader, Adonis, had almost been pinched for forgery, that the illustrator, Thalia, was carrying on with three soldiers at once, that the typesetter, Pangloss, owed Gute a scandalous sum of money, and that Gute was a Jew whose parents came from the shtetl. A shtetl, Artemis explained, was a Russian potato-famine farm, and the only difference between the Jews and the Irish was that the Irish drank like fish and the Jews saved up money. She herself had never met a Jew before Gute and couldn't say what marked him as one. His accent sounded like Chaplin's, and Chaplin had spent his whole life before the press in the same stretch of Cheapside. Gute drank moderately and ate like the English. He seemed to have enough money for the press and for small assistance to his employees and friends, but he never bought luxuries, not even those things that had become luxuries since the war. He observed no holy days. The press closed Sundays, but Gute could always be found at his desk. He was a rationalist, he said. He'd never seen evidence of God, but if proof were found, he would examine it under a loupe.

Now, in London, she ached for Boanerges, abandoned to unskilled hands, if indeed Gute used him any longer. It wasn't easy to throw off the old world. Pangloss once said that when you woke up to reality, you could see that everything you'd believed before was a lie, and then, he said, the old ideas became so light, like weeds turned to dust, that it took only one gust to sweep them away. Pangloss believed in history and dialectic and the power of the proletariat, but the trouble with Pangloss was he didn't know many proletarians. He'd never watched an Irish priest despoil a parish. He'd never sat at the back of a mildewed church where the priest dished out the sacrament with dirty fingernails, interested only in who would have him to lunch and how good the roast would be, if there was a roast. The priest so-called who'd married her to Lovelace had only done it for the cash, and Lovelace hadn't even given him much.

If she'd been an atheist then, she never would have believed Lovelace when he asked her to save him. She thought she was saving him from Hell, or worse, from a barren, living damnation. She thought that if she loved him enough, he would abandon his unbelief. You couldn't speak uncut atheism and have any kind of public work in Ireland, and he didn't, but once you knew him, his skepticism was plain to see, and later his grubby scorn. But he loved her purity, he said, by which he meant he loved her mind and her innermost self, untouched by the rubbish of the world—he, who could have any woman, whose mind and heart spanned time and space.

One day they'd been arguing theology, and he'd said that if he could be saved, then she could do it. And so she'd begun praying for him each hour of the day, later waking herself in the night to pray for him with all her heart and all her soul and all her strength and all her mind. And just because her parents were locked in a medieval past, that didn't mean she shouldn't marry Lovelace and help him attain to great things. He was already the most brilliant, talented, vibrating-with-energy human she knew, and if she could open his prison door—

The Talkers talked more that week than they ever had before. The male, whose voice had been urging her to make her vows to the sisters, said he too saw purity in her and that she must decide her vocation at once. When he said that, she had come over shaking and fallen to the floor of the pew, but then the louder voice, the woman like the Holy Mother herself, whom she was just imploring to pray for her, that woman said that taking to the convent was the easy path, the light yoke, whereas Lovelace, saving him—

How many people were seized during the Angelus, shaken to the point of falling, bruised where she'd felt heat and light? Daft Mrs. Lacey, who believed in fairy folk, said the Talkers were the Holy Spirit, but even though Mrs. Lacey was not the full shilling, it didn't make her wrong. When she was shaking on the floor, the Holy Mother had said *Marry him* and the Archangel trumped *Yes, Yes!* and she tasted blood down the back of her throat and her head raged in pain. No one said it would hurt so much to hear from Heaven, and after that she knew she had to do it. Of course she had a choice, even the Holy Mother had a choice, but she didn't *want* to say no. She wanted *yes* more than she'd ever wanted anything, and when Lovelace asked her again, in the library that night, asked her for the third time to come away with him, he said words the Holy Mother had used: *Would you damn me to this coldness*?

Later, after the lorry and the cart and the man who said he was a priest even though he didn't wear a collar, after the ring and the place they went in Cork, he flew into a rage when he heard her praying for him. Was it two days later? Three? She was still sore from the bold thing even though he said it would soon feel different. But then his rage turned to laughter, and she knew in a flood how night-and-day, hot-and-cold, dead-and-quick stupid she was: he never meant save him like that. *Save my balls freezing off, Mary mine. Ah, don't look that way. You know I need saving from this whole wicked world.*

He kissed her, quoted Dante, and said his life's project was salvation, but through reason and art, not superstition. He wanted saving one-hundred-percent awake. Intuition he knew and loved in its own way. Sure, what were poets for? She was pure intuition, he pure reason. Together they would make a generation that married both in ecstasy.

When they'd left Galway in the night, they could take only one suitcase each, but once in Cork he began bringing home crates of old books. She fashioned shelves from the bits she found behind the privy, and they read to each other as they had in the library when he took her through the doors you weren't supposed to open and handed her books she'd never heard of and sat on the stone floor and read them to her.

His drunken criticism of women he always disavowed in the morning, at least in regards to her. *Sure, you aren't women. You're my own Mary, aren't you, a stór?* He, like her family, called her Mary, and when he was gay-drunk, he sang a tuneless song with a refrain: *I'm a-going to marry Mary I am, I'm a-marrying Mary am I.* The trouble with him, besides the library, was that he was so very handsome and his beard so very smart. The day they married, she wore a frock he bought her from the shop. It was pink, not white, but it looked a dream on her, he said. He wore his good suit, but they were in such a rush that he hadn't time to polish his shoes.

Any kind of person would have seen him for the scoundrel he was, but he was so affecting with his dark eyes that always smiled, and the teasing pout he used only towards her, and his pianist hands that one time played Ravel in the empty lecture hall so it sounded inside her. *You incomparable girl, I'd have you save my soul all night long*, he said on top of her, and when he spent, he would call out to God and even Jesus, and she didn't know if it was blasphemy or if in some way she really was saving him. If he put his seed inside her, could he not also be changed? *You'll have to persist with me. I'm a far ways gone, Mary-mine, and I'll take a world of saving, I will.*

He'd left his position at the college, but he had a plan, he said, one that would smooth it over with her family and the chancellor. When they ran, it had poured for days, as if the old gods of Ireland were staging a rear-guard maneuver. They rode south in the cab of a lorry, and she looked out at the swimming burren, exuberant to have got away and in thrall of the real life beginning. She felt she had never been truly happy until that hour, yet the sodden fields had given her a sense that the old gods were weeping, weeping to lose her, a daughter of Galway Bay, where the mild wet weather blew in from the Atlantic smelling of Canada and America and the great sargasso seaweed patch that floated, they said, invisible to sailors.

At the cottage in Cork, he grew cagey. He would go out to place a telephone call, to further the Master Plan. Whatever questions she asked about his aims or their future, he told her to trust in the Master. She thought, now, that it was possible he'd never had a real plan, but he'd talked the way artists surely talked of their paintings, a vision they could see entire even if everyone else saw only splotches.

After days of his disappearing hours at a time, she followed him. The village had three public houses, and she found him in the cellar of the farthest playing cards with four men who looked as though they could rearrange a face without losing their breath. She called out cheerfully, but he startled from his chair and had her halfway up the cellar stairs before she knew where she was, and when he came home near dawn—

She thought now that it all must have been about money. One time he came home without his pocket watch and jacket, and she'd been too afraid to ask about it.

He had a cousin in Canada and said they'd take a ship there. Her brothers would never find them. Sometimes at night he'd pretend they were already there. They'd bundle against the cold and he'd speak of *Canadia* and Indians, and he'd go at the bottle longer and show her what a man of the frontier was made of, and when she told him to stop—

The worst was getting out of the bath and seeing the marks in the mirror. She tried not to look, and her hat was large, but there was the morning she couldn't go down to the shop for the things because there was no way to hide it, and then when he came back and she didn't have the things—

There was the part in *Oliver Twist* with Bill and Nancy where it all went too far, and she wondered what it would feel like to come that close. How many nights in Canadia until it happened? And when the last night came, there wouldn't be anyone describing things as Dickens did, making them beautiful and tragic.

One morning she heard voices in the next room, except the flat on the other side of the wall was empty because the lady and her children had gone to the poor house and the landlord hadn't got anyone else in. She could hear two men and a woman, not her old Talkers but new ones. One of the men didn't like Lovelace, but the woman did. How many girls could get a man at all, she said, let alone one who knew as much as he did? Look at Mary McGuire age of twenty-six and still no one would have her. Who could frown at a man like Lovelace, a man of learning who promised to take her away and then did, a man who wasn't in the bloody church? One of the men said things from the bold book Lovelace made her read, but the one who didn't like him scared her in the womb. There was the morning she cadged a ride to the next town and found the church and confessional and asked the priest about what the Talkers were saying. She didn't tell him everything, there wasn't time because right away they started mithering and she couldn't hear herself speak. She stumbled out of the place, blood dripping from her nose, and when she got back to the cottage, he was there and asked where she'd been. Things got broken, but at least that always stopped the Talkers. The only real silence was when he was thrusting, and she wouldn't have minded if he split her open because it shut them up and stopped the fear in her womb that it might be God doing the talking, or the devil. Lovelace said that was all rot, the kind of drivel that kept the Irish in chains, but he didn't have Talkers, and he didn't actually know everything.

—Marion!

—Why are you out of bed, Clive?

She was tidying the schoolroom. She'd never been a tidy person, but at the lovely people's house, her head would start to ache if she came down in the morning to books on the table or puzzle pieces on the carpet.

—It's there again, Clive said, where I said it would be.

—Did you say what we practiced?

—I tried.

—Tell me everything.

She sat with him on the window seat so he wouldn't cry. Stumblingly he narrated his confrontation with the outsize demon squirrel that occupied the rocking chair. He told it to go away, tend to its nuts, hurry back to its tree which was even now being sawed down.

—It said it was done with trees. It said it wanted my bed.

—Did you tell it you had a powerful sorceress for a sister?

He burst into tears, and she put her arms around him. Whenever he tried to tell her the worst, sobs exploded.

—Now now, I believe I know a spell to use against this . . . what's its name?

—The Squirrel King!

If it had been up to her, she might have gone with Lovelace to Canadia, but there was the day in the market when she heard her name and saw her brother Daniel dressed as a soldier. He pulled her down an alley into a backhouse, and the Talkers, who'd started hissing, shut up with the click of the latch. She didn't have to say anything because Daniel always knew, but she started shaking and her nose bled and he crushed her in his arms and said it would be all right. He went away without anyone knowing he'd been there, and then, a fortnight to the day—

—He . . . he . . .

The boy had hiccoughs now:

—He said he'd stuff my mouth full of mashed potatoes, and choke me to death, and run through the city with my . . . my . . .

—Oh, dear.

—Raw corpse!

Clive's nightmares overwhelmed him as hers once did, but he had no Talkers. Though what if he had and didn't know how to tell her? What if he was pretending to nightmares as a way to speak of them? Daniel would have been able to tell. The world lost a weapon against demoniacs when Daniel left, shot dead by a German bullet in a stupid war fought by the English for no reason but pride.

Gute always said they'd fought the war for money, that it had been brought on by men making themselves rich with munitions. Recently, she'd begun to think he was right. Malevolent people controlled the world from the shadows, pouring more and more into their own sagging pockets, using other people as so much fodder, not only for cannons but for lusts. They all spoke the same language in latinate diction. The hoping and wishing of her youth had been an illusion. Life was only the bad, and the very bad, and the less bad than average.

Clive wanted to be an aeroplane pilot and Felicity a ballerina with five children like the Bastables but less naughty. They asked her often what she would be when she grew up.

—I am grown up.

—But grown up all the way.

She never told them what she used to wish, and she never would tell anyone again because never again would she believe such rubbish. Even after Lovelace, she believed. She believed she would be a poet, and she imagined that one day when he was very old, Gute would give her the press and she would publish the best poets and the best books, enough to fill the houses of every child who ever wished to live in a library.

She wished nothing now. The children were not hers. She would not become one of those exhausted, wet-eyed lady teachers. She would not write poems. She could make presses run. She could clean the floors of a chalet in fifty-four minutes flat. She could talk boys out of nightmares. Daniel deserved life more than she ever could.

She'd not been sure until afterwards that she'd been pregnant. The curse had never been reliable with her, but she assumed she'd get a baby as soon as she married him. Wasn't that why they scared you senseless? Mary Kilkenny said you could get a baby from kissing a boy with your mouth open for more than a minute. Her curse never came in the four months with Lovelace, and the whole time she'd hoped it was because of a baby. She even, curse her stupid self, imagined a baby would change him. Then after the night in the pub, the horror of everything made her sick, and she hoped it would make her sick enough to kill it if there was one inside her. And then when she got over to England, and the Mulligan boys carried her down to the first place, and the other man took her to Gute's, then she prayed every hour that there not be anything inside her. Every day those first weeks at the press, she would look at herself in the glass to see if she was changing, but the girl that stared back was so distressing to look at that she had to ask Gute for something strong to start the day.

At home there were women who knew things, and if you went and gave a thing and did a thing, things could stop. At least that's what Mary Kilkenny said. She swore in her prayers that if the Almighty made one grow in her, she'd strangle its first breath she would. But once she swore, she'd been so afraid of herself that she'd had to ask Gute for something strong again. In the end came the day like knives, and there it was, not even noticeably a thing, but more than the curse.

She cried because it was the first reprieve to have happened to her, and she cried because it meant her prayer to take it away had been answered, just when she'd worked herself up to Lovelace's position on God. You could say it was prayer or you could say it was nature, but once you'd prayed hard enough and had the prayer come true, it took trenches of blood to go back to trusting nature.

Back home they knew that anyone who wasn't Catholic was going to Hell. Lovelace, whatever he professed, was Catholic, baptized and confirmed. If you mixed with the English, you'd find Protestants, and Mary Kilkenny claimed to have met a Jew in Dublin, a doctor, rich, and sure a nice enough man so she said, but they were all heretics. The Irish might not have anything else, but at least they weren't heretics.

English people didn't understand the way you looked at them. If they knew where you came from, if you let it show in your voice, they'd think you no better than mud. They thought the look on your face was longing for the old country, angry and ignorant. They didn't know you were looking down on them, pitying them because they didn't know right from wrong and sure were going to Hell. The fact that she didn't believe it didn't stop her looking down.

Then came the hour when that terrible hand reached into her womb a second time, like a child poking its finger into a tulip, squishing and playing with the jelly inside, until—Vivid faces in her dreams. She knew what her mother would say, *visitations from the dead,* but she knew dreams, and these were clearer and more still-standing than that. Last night in her room atop the lovely people's house, her brother Daniel stood by the bed, flecks of gray in the blue of his eyes, as if he knew not only everything that he'd known when alive but everything since and how deep the roots had grown.

Roots didn't go anywhere without a plant, which needed ground and a seed. And if there was a seed, then somewhere was a sower even if it was only the wind. Who made the air and moved it? Even if you accepted fronts and evaporating seawater, who made the sea? Who prepared the dry lands? Who made the firmament and breathed across the face of the waters? Plants had no choice of ground. They could live or die, send roots or wither. But even when the ground was as poor as this, you'd be gobsmacked at what would grow.

Clive had received a concussion. There was no blood, or not much, but as she was examining the back of his head, he was sick all over the schoolroom rug. There had been a long period of quiet after a morning of ceaseless chatter. She hadn't thought they were climbing the spiral stairs, imitating the boy in the story she'd told who climbed like a monkey to escape the place he was held captive.

—You're being very brave, Finn.

His sister started crying, and she told her sharply to hush. If they'd been home in Ireland, she would have bound up his head with cold bandages and put him to bed in a dim room, and everyone from her mother to the milkman would know such things happened to boys and the best you could hope was he'd recover and not be stupider than before. But the lovely people would not take this line. They'd dwell on how it happened. They'd take testimony from the children, and she'd be out by nightfall without her wages. She ought to be alerting someone, but instead she put his head on her knee and hummed a tune that came from nowhere and went nowhere.

—Marion, you won't leave, will you?

—Shh.

—Say you won't.

—*My young love said to me, your mother won't mind . . .*

She was thinking as she sang how she would explain the accident—*Poor Clive had a bit of a spill*—and in the bass clef ran the part of her mind that was always making plans, the kind you had for emergencies or sudden possibilities like a book of matches on the mantlepiece, an innocent, everyday object, but to a mind like hers—

—Your brothers won't slight me for my lack of kind . . .

The night it happened, Daniel told her to stay in the pub. She wasn't to go outside, not even for the jacks. The most important thing, Dan said, was that everyone should see her. She must go to the pub with her husband and never leave people's sight. She did as he said, but as the night wore on, all she could think of was needing a piss, and then the men came in from the back and they were helping Lovelace walk, except he wasn't walking and his coat was wet and his trousers were spoiled and when they laid him on a table, the fiddles stopped and she wet herself and someone shouted for a doctor, and they said *can't you see*? and someone shushed them because she was there, right there seeing his eyes rolled back, and a woman was praying to our Lady and another to our Father, and the blood was draining out and he was already in the past.

They searched the back and found nothing. Whatever did it was bigger than a kitchen knife, they said. They'd found him face down in the jacks, trousers still up. One boy thought the Hun had invaded at last, but they told him what, and he shut his lip.

She was to go no later than the morning and make sure no one saw her. She was to take this packet, that train, this ship, and the Mulligan boys would meet her at Holyhead with word from Daniel. The word, when she got there, was a postcard in Daniel's hand: *He moved through the fair*. That was when she knew for certain Daniel had done it, and knowing was like another knife because until those words, which conjured that song, she'd made herself believe he'd got someone else to end Lovelace, that he hadn't actually taken the knife in his hands, taken a life and damned himself forever. She hadn't asked for murder, but Daniel had done it, to deliver her from evil.

The Mulligans said Daniel, Joe, and Teddy had shipped out

to France, but Daniel had told them to take her to a place, and someone else would take her on from there so they wouldn't ever know where she went. She stayed in the first place a fortnight waiting for word, and then one morning Daniel came to her by the jacks, finger over his mouth, but when she got close, he was gone. That afternoon, the Mulligan boys brought the news about Joe and Teddy. There was no word of Daniel, but she knew. That night a man took her away on the train, and she paid him as you paid a man, not the whole thing on a train but enough to show she was grateful, and he took what she offered and was kind and bought her coffee and took her to Oxford, to Gute and the press, and that night she tried to show Gute she was grateful but he said, *another time*. He told her to sleep but someone kept whistling in the corner, and she knew it was Dan but didn't look because she didn't want him to leave again, but when she got to whistling herself, the lady called Olga gave her a hot drink with bromide, to make traveling easier, and then she was gone for years, felt like.

—Teach us that song, please Marion?

—Sure it's no song at all.

The one time someone sang it at a salon, she was sick in the garden, and when Gute found out, no one sang it again. She had other songs at the ready, and if someone asked for that one, she'd give them *Toora Loora* or *Skibbereen* or even *Bluebells of Scotland*. The Irish had the worst songs, all sad and sappy like drinking one last pint for the old country. She hated fiddles and hated the harp and as for the pipes, they were enough to make you break your head, and the time the tinker came to the press with his old clothes on his back and the music rolled up in his wooden leg, and Gute asked her to sing it so he could hear how it went, she missed home so much it was like a knife to her belly, cutting out her sausage guts like Lovelace when the man tried to shove them back inside even though it was too late.

—You won't leave, Marion. Promise you won't.

—I promise.

You had to lie to children, more than you'd think.

Lina always said the earth would be better as a matriarchy, males kept as slaves but kindly. She herself had nothing against men per se. She was long rid of Lovelace, and as for the other one, Diana had been perplexed in the extreme when she'd insisted with violent finality that the name Jasper never be mentioned. Diana didn't look happy about it, but she agreed. They visited the museum twice a week, and as the children sketched, she'd hear what news Diana possessed, not only concerning their erstwhile family at the press, but also the miners, the strikes, the forecast, the Grand Prix next month at Brooklands. Today, the children drew Roman coins and totted up their value as Diana chattered.

—This governessing suits you, Diana said. I swear you've never looked more a dish.

Her hair needed cutting, she hadn't rouged her lips in weeks, her frock was an old one Mother had given her, and her fingernails were chewed to the quick. Diana advised sticking plaster against nail biting and said every woman looked more beautiful during the time she could easiest get a baby. You longed for a man more then, or so said the midwife in the flat below Diana's.

—People say you have to do it all the time if you want a baby, but really it's only that time.

Diana and Bernard had tried for eight months, but after befriending the midwife, she'd got a baby straight away.

—Do you mean to say that if you *don't* want one, you have to avoid it when you want it most and are prettiest?

Diana always thought she knew things, and it was infuriating when she was right. Without rhyme or reason, she would start longing for Jasper, and she'd feel so alone that it seemed like a sign. Now to hear it was nothing to do with fate but only the working of her own body, designed by some vile engineer to make her want what she couldn't have.

—Don't take my head off, Diana said, please, and I won't say his name, but you must know he dogged us like mad after—

—Don't.

—Gute told him nothing, *of course*, but even months later, he kept writing. He sent me a Christmas card.

—Gute?

—*Him.*

—Is he still writing to you?

Felicity tugged her hand:

—Marion, Clive says I haven't enough to buy the makeup box, but I have so.

—Your arithmetic is pathetic! her brother declared.

She helped the girl count the coins and then made her a loan of several more, drawing them herself and promising they would indeed pay for the faience box in case four. Once they'd run off to the drinking fountain, she turned her cold fear on Diana:

—He is writing, isn't he?

Diana colored.

—And you've been writing back. You didn't tell him about me, did you?

—I'd no idea at first—

The walls of the gallery smelled of blood and salt. She called her a four-letter word in German.

—I never dreamed you wouldn't want him to know.

If they weren't in public, she'd have bloodied her nose, like she did to Mary Kilkenny before she'd learned to suppress the savage answers her brothers taught her.

—Marion, please, I've put him off. I told him nothing except that you're back.

Diana rattled on: she'd sent Jasper a note after learning she was back in England. Since promising to keep her secret, she'd told him only that Marion was well and would never see him again. She slaved to kill his hopes. She'd never betray her secret, or the lovely children.

—Honestly, M, if only you'd read—
—Stop.
—He's driving himself mad for you, even after a year.

Oh the mind, the mind has mountains, and what mountains did he have. Tell the truth, she was always thinking of him, but when she noticed, she set to thinking something else: His education was oversold. He was a man so knew nothing of reality. He was born with the silver spoon. So on and on.

He seemed the kind of boy every girl wanted, fair, charming, un-maimed and alive. But he was so much not what he seemed. Gute said she had a penchant for older men who were tutors, and she supposed she did though she tried not to. He wasn't much older, wasn't a tutor, and when he threw the drink at her that first night after the reading, pretending to spill it, she could have walked right off as she had from so many. Had she wanted someone like him all along and not known it?

She had a way of testing boys. She might toss a rude gesture across the room, as she'd done to the barman that night of the spilled drink. Jasper saw it, and with a mirthful tone he said:

—How strangely a human voice clangs on one's ears.

He was quoting something, but she didn't want to give him the satisfaction of asking what. Later, she tested him again with questions. She'd met boys who were cagey or lying, but most men would talk on and on if you gave them your beautiful attention. He, by contrast, absorbed each question as if running it through a translation service, to the point that she wondered if her accent was slipping. After answering several of her queries, he rubbed out his cigarette, cast himself into her gaze, and asked if she'd ever found herself in the open air unable to breathe. He asked in full sincerity, like a scientist undertaking an investigation. Or like herself the time she'd slept out with her friend Jenny in the back garden, watching the shooting stars and then, much later when the house had gone dark, asking Jenny if she'd ever put her finger there and made it feel like—

—Yes, she told him. Have you?

He nodded as though they knew each other already. His hand fluttered near hers, but he didn't do the flirt's thing of brushing against her finger.

—Tell me?

She said one time at a pub they'd brought in a man who'd been stabbed and laid him on the table and a strong breeze rushed in the windows.

—My hair was blowing in my eyes. Papers flew across the floor.

—And the man?

—His stomach was falling out like sausages. I couldn't tie my ribbon because my hands weren't working, and someone looked through the window and asked *Now what, eh*? And a sentence ran in my head.

—What sentence?

His voice made her feel she could walk into the mountains and never have to come back.

—A few passers-by watched with dispassionate interest.

He didn't ask if that was the sentence; he only took it into the great translation machine.

—The poem you read tonight, he said, the part about the rowboat and the nightingale?

Her face tingled.

—A great deal of time, he said, and pains. In the rowboat.

—And you?

He didn't ask her to clarify because he already understood her, that she was asking about breathing.

—People were drowning.

—In the sea?

—In the gas.

She asked what he wrote. He looked surprised though it was a question everyone asked at readings such as this.

—Not poems.

—What then?

He looked as though he could see vanished glades. She decided he was a famous author incognito. It was the only explanation for why he wasn't trying to show his writings. All men wanted you to be their mother, to read their awful compositions and tell them well done.

—Do you think, he said, that everything is different since the war?

—Different how?

—Oh, he said, *you* know. Is it true, say you?

—Finn threw my flower in the river!

—Stop caterwauling. The park is full of them.

You tried to be patient, but sometimes—

—My special flower! With my fortune in the petals!

Clive kicked along the banks, your man who'd done a low thing and pretended not to care.

—Flowers are only practice, she said. A real sorceress reads kismet.

—What's that?

—Better than fortune.

—I can't read.

—You read a whole page in the primer this morning.

The girl was still crying, but her heart wasn't in it.

—If you want to know kismet, the first thing you must do is take a book from off the shelf.

—What sort of book?

—Oh, any one at all at all, the first your finger touches.

—Any one at all at all.

She took the primer from her bag, and the girl curled against her hip.

—Then, you open the book at random.

—How's that?

—Wherever it falls.

The girl traced the letters on the cover:

—Wherever it falls at all at all.

—And the first sentence you see is your kismet for the day.

They tried it, her finger beneath the words the girl sounded out:

—*Jack will come some other day*. But what does it *mean*?

—You've got to ponder it, along the limeretty hillhockers.

She pointed to the path, and the girl ran off.

The sun was burning her nose, but she pulled her cardigan closed. If she were to think with clarity instead of feelings, she would know that since miracles weren't real, neither was kismet. You couldn't evict religion and put fate in its place. That was going backwards, and if you were serious about reality, you had to settle for nothing doing the job of a god.

Before, when she would argue with Jasper, he would say kismet wasn't rational. He'd beg her to explain her reasons for believing it. She couldn't, and she knew that his demand for reasons was only his masculine weapon, because that's all they did, those university boys, talk around you and down to you and say it proved them right. But now her thinking was cutting through like new teeth, and though she could remember the vague miasma of those feelings, she saw as if from a bluff looking across other people's lives that on this point at least he had been right. She'd devoured more books than he'd ever touched. He'd barely read before the war by his own admission, and though he got his degree, that only took reading a few books and saying what they expected at exams, all of which he did with easy confidence and a veneer of logic. He knew bits of Shakespeare, but he'd never read a single American poet, not even Emily Dickinson. He didn't know that Little Nell wasn't one of her sisters until she explained, and he'd never read a word of Baudelaire despite having French. She was better educated in all the ways that counted, so why was she only now beginning to reason? Why did he think with the power of a steam train while she was more or less on the level of a kettle? He'd spent months in mud and bullets and might even have run across one of her brothers without knowing it, but he'd never seen Ireland or Switzerland, he didn't know what eucalyptus was or how it smelled, and he'd never had that hand put life in him and grow it.

It was a fact that women were more powerful than men, and this was so intolerable for the men that they had to change definitions and say that because they were taller with bigger muscles, they were stronger, on and on, the perpetual swindle. People like Lina and Diana could talk of the sexes until they were hoarse, but their philosophy didn't show you how to earn money and not be at someone's mercy. It didn't tell you if you were right or wrong to leave your desperate family. It didn't tell you how to make the dead alive.

She was too young to have a crisis. But there was something—not in her head, *shut up*, not there—something in her *thought* that popped out like the cuckoos in the chalet clocks, never quite at the same time. Now the cuckoo was going on and on as she slept, rose, took care of children, listened to impractical plans for a holiday, and mended the sole of her shoe where it had split. People were made to do more than think. Before, with Jas, every day had power, better than the old gods ever knew.

The first time she pulled him into her, his cheeks went red and he didn't know what was happening to him. She felt him then, felt what actually happened when a man did it, because it happened so fast. With Lovelace there had been so much doing that she never knew what had happened until he pulled away and she saw the seed. At the place in Wales with Jas, they lay under a feather blanket, his body thin and mostly smooth, smelling of soap, his mouth sweet from the sultana piece in his tooth. He put his hands all over her, his tongue in her ear, and when he put his mouth on her, she gasped and pulled him into her again. She wanted to say *Oh, God*, but instead she said his name, his real name, over and over as she pulled him in, and she wanted all of life to be this, but then it was over and she began to cry. He was afraid he'd hurt her and she said no no, but the sobs were bitter even though there was no bitterness for him, not even in the hurtiest fights.

He always snatched victory from the jaws of defeat. Gas? Survived. Capture by the Hun? He sat out the rest of the war in the citadel of Mainz making friends with people who to this day, she supposed, would come when he whistled. People such as the Frenchman, whose poems they'd published at the press on his introduction. He knew famous writers, too, like the one who wrote about the citadel but was too snooty for the press. Anyone who survived the war and didn't wind up a tramp qualified for victory. Even Bernard had come out ahead because he'd finally settled down to the paying job and convinced Artemis to revert to Diana and marry him. With two legs, he would have wasted his life dreaming of the Olympic Games. Diana said he could still dance, but only a little at home to the gramophone.

Jas could dance. At his Scottish school they'd had it as an extra, and even though he didn't want it because his father insisted, it turned out fantastically because at the end of term they went to a dance with girls from a nearby school, and since he didn't have to think about the steps, he'd been able to flirt the whole time. Or so he said as he steered her around the dance floor, his hand warm through the thin fabric of her frock and chemise set. He put his mouth near her ear and pushed them in swirls around the well-heeled girls and Oxford men, whispering the things he'd like to do if they were alone, and she said things back. They could touch only in a dance pose, hearts racing, and at the punch table they stood apart, he setting a chair before his heliotrope trousers. She fetched her purse-bag from the table where the other girls had slung theirs and joined the crush for the ladies', feeling something though she wasn't expecting it, worried for her pale yellow dress.

The ladies' wallpaper was all exotic birds, and soft rolls of paper hung beside the toilets. It was blood after all, but she'd nothing in her bag. At the vanity, she dabbed her eyes where the makeup had smeared, but then she poked herself and cried, and the old woman attendant gave her another towel. Girls cuddled round and said not to let any boy treat her wrong, and then the woman came back with a tin of sweets, except they weren't sweets but little white lipsticks. Then the woman said it wasn't lipstick, and a girl showed her how to use it as a thing. It felt strange, and when they started to dance again, it felt stranger still, and she knew more than ever that life was decided by bodies and that all men's talk of weapons and politics and poets was nothing to the cologne-scented pull of his fingers through the swoops of the waltz, her body beneath her frock, and his, once you took the trousers off him.

On the way home from the park, Clive insisted they go inside the shop whose window always entranced him. It sold shaving things, and as he fingered the brushes enviously, she asked if they made razors for a child. The clerk looked as though she'd suggested chocolate knives. In defiance, she lingered longer than she would have, tickling Felicity with the biggest brush and opening the shaving soaps. That was when the scent hit her, the way smells did when you weren't prepared, summoning Jasper nearly to the flesh. She wanted to hurry away, and she wanted to buy the jar so she could keep smelling the leather scotch whisky with herbs in a window box after the rain.

—Please, may we buy it? Clive said when he'd smelled the soap. I'll pay you back from my money box. Please?

She didn't want to give the snooty man their custom, but now Felicity too begged for the soap.

—I need it for enchanting!

—You don't put shaving soap behind your ears, silly.

—I do!

The man scowled down his nose, so she had to buy it, tossing her money on the counter and not waiting for the ticket.

—I've got a whisker coming, Clive announced as they bundled through the door.

—No, you haven't!

He snatched the package from his sister.

—I have, haven't I, Marion? Feel it.

Later, after she'd put them to bed and was having a bath herself, the room breathed with it. Was it possible to assimilate a scent? She'd been wearing his scent when they got back from Scotland the second time, the last time. She'd stopped at the press to fetch her umbrella and found a salon in progress. She hadn't come to the last one because she didn't want to be touched by anyone but Jas, and now after Scotland she doubly didn't want to. But Gute was so happy to see her, as though she'd done him the kind of favor a girl could do her old father to make his heart warm, and so she said she'd come as a surprise.

She decided as Gute was pouring the first glass that she wouldn't let anyone inside her. Other things didn't count, and if she refused to do that, then what happened in Scotland could grow into realness.

All Gute's rooms had people in them, some she'd met before, including the very louche Spanish boy who was like an African explorer with his tongue. There was also a famous actress, who made her breath catch, and a beautiful woman from Lucerne. In the red room, girls lounged on the leopard rug and most of their clothes had already come off.

Later she stretched across the blue pillow, glad to be wearing her good slip and the stockings with no ladders. The sip in the glasses had made her mouth numb, and the Spanish boy had a tongue like a warm bath.

Later she was crying on Gute's knee, and he called her *dear Mandy* and handed her to the beautiful woman from Lucerne while the Spanish boy sergeant majored him and Artemis bit his neck, and the beautiful, beautiful woman from Lucerne took her to the blue room and wiped her face with a handkerchief soaked in wine and told her she was a goddess. The woman kissed her throat, but it felt of nothing, just as everything felt except Jas.

Later the curtains rang across the rail, and Artemis put her head into the crook of her arm. *There was a man from Milton Keynes*, Artemis said. *He mesmerized me and made me into a monkey.* The man had a foreign name and only one of them, and he had tried to mesmerize her too, but Gute told him not to.

Later, the next day, she walked Rory along the hill. He was feeling better and scampered ahead to see about a squirrel. They cut across to a place they'd never been, and that was when she heard the church bell. You could hear bells everywhere in Oxford, clanging like a cutlery drawer every minute of the day, but this bell smelled of turf, and it rang right there and it rang in the past, and that was when she saw the little girl, her hair a thousand tangles, needing to wash her face. At first the girl wouldn't speak, but when she saw Rory, she lit up like a sodium lamp: Was he a wolfhound? What was he called? Could she stroke him? Would he bite? Rory licked her face, and she took the girl's hand, told her she was grand, told her she knew, told her Rory loved her, they'd be her friends, and she'd comb her hair so's it wouldn't hurt. It was just for a spell, a beautiful spell, but she mustn't pinch Sheena that way with her just a baby who couldn't talk, and she mustn't let Daniel go off to war, and if she ever met a man called Laighléis, she must run and never look back.

When she checked to see if the children were asleep, Clive was standing on his head.

—You'll scramble your dreams that way. Get under the covers.

—But I need a glass of milk.

—You've cleaned your teeth.

—It's still light through the curtains.

—If I close my eyes, Felicity said, I can see into your mind, with magic.

—No doubt, but remember, when you're looking into someone else's mind, they can see into yours.

When Jasper had swaggered up and spilled his drink on her, she'd thought, *Here's another one I don't care if I ever see again.* Almost as a novelty she'd decided that everything she said to him that night would be true. And then she did it again the next time. And the next.

—If you're married, Felicity asked, can you see your husband's mind?

—What do you think?

—No! Clive said. I don't want any girl seeing into my mind.

—I can, said his sister.

—You can't. And I don't want to look at any girl's thoughts either, thank you very much.

At last she climbed to her hot room overlooking the rooftops. It had been warm, too, when they met, when they'd walked so much that she had to buy new shoes. She'd been living in Oxford four years but had never walked the places he led her. Some were forbidden to all but college residents, the lengths of lawn as lush as the fields where you waited for the last trumpet. Once he expressed a wish to take a rucksack and walk all day, sleeping under the stars as he'd done in France, the fine nights when it seemed the mud and guns could never be true, only the crickets and the firmament and the stars shooting across it. At the place in Wales, she'd wished all of life could be the cottage, the cliffs, and him in the bath by the coal fire. Then later when they went to Scotland, both times, she'd wished they could stay there forever sheltered from the world by the glens, the stag, the tugboat filling the silence with its bell, their breath beading up the windows of the bedroom.

If she were to depart the waiting room that was her life with the lovely people, she would have to choose between two essential acts: either she must row back out to the loneliness she'd known before she met him, or she must go to him and show him everything. The loneliness would be harrowing since she now knew its opposite, but facing him would end in loneliness, too, because once he knew everything, the cottages could never shelter them again.

—What will the Tsar do if he catches us?

She raised her brow, and Clive pulled the sheets to his chin.

—He never will catch us, she said, because we're runagates.

—Outlaws?

—Only technically.

She told them of Jean Valjean, how even though he broke the law, he wasn't wicked, and when he told his story to a bishop, the bishop gave him silver.

—Rings and tiaras?

—Rings and tiaras, which he couldn't wear himself, but he kept in a pouch in case he ever had a daughter as runagate as he.

—Can I be a runagate when I grow up?

—A ballerina runagate?

She talked until they fell asleep, about an old forgotten lane down an old sludged-up canal, and an old forgotten cottage, turf burning in the grate, where lived a grandmother who had once, in the last century, made the playhouse that she discovered as a girl in the forest where she would go to get away from the people who had bought her.

—People bought you?

—From an orphan asylum?

—It's only a story. Close your eyes.

Now she was grown, the asylum closed, the people gone, and still she roamed, a runagate until the night she happened on the old forgotten cottage down the old forgotten path. It was dark and wet, she was fevered and fainting, and the grandmother took her in and sat her by the fire. And on this long, dark night on the old forgotten path, her grandmother would ask nothing, and she'd start wherever she started, telling one thing then another into the turf, and her grandmother would give her bread with butter—brown bread with real butter, not English ugliness—and when the telling got to the worst, she would pour cordial into a little glass, and she'd stir the fire and bring in the cat and a wet setter would lay his head on her knee and lick her hand where tears fell, and at the end of the long, forgotten night, when the windows faded milky white and the setter scratched to go out and the cat brought them a dead mouse, then everything would be different, and her grandmother might tell her to stop being a runagate, to find him, make a family, and they could all of them come back in the summer and their children could play in the playhouse and nothing would have to be kept apart because the winter was past. And they'd go out to the canal, and the turtles would be calling, and the young boatman would have poled up the banks so he could take her back, and she would cry to leave her grandmother, but her grandmother would kiss her with dry kisses and give her an orchid, which would be her token back; she was to keep it alive and whenever she needed, she would give it to the boatman and he would bring her.

Every morning she awoke in the garret of the lovely house, and beside the chalet, edelweiss grew in the grass. She knew exactly where and could return with railway tickets. The only way it would ever be forgotten would be if she died and never told anyone.

Last year when Rory died, it was cold and empty and she didn't feel a thing. After staggering around the press all morning, he lay down suddenly in the garden. His eyes glazed over as she stood beside him, thinking this was how it must have been with the apostles. They thought he'd be with them much longer, but then after the out-fling at the temple, the soldiers in the night, the horrible day, all they had was his corpse. Later, when Gute made her come inside and she started saying things she didn't mean to say, she thought of her granny's sister who'd been put in an asylum at the age of twenty-three. Reason: she was thrawn. Once you went into an asylum, you never came out, and whatever was the matter at the start got worse, and if nothing was the matter, they wrecked you anyway. Even if your family came for you only a month later, you'd be a shell when they saw you, simply a shell, and soon they'd forget you and cut your name out of the family Bible so your mother wouldn't cry every time she opened it.

Jas came to see her after hearing the pup had died, but she couldn't go downstairs because she couldn't see out of her eyes because they'd swole shut and any hour she knew her heart would stop because that was the only thing that could happen. Artemis tried to tell her he was only a dog, and it hurt more than Rory looking at her while he was falling over the last time, just a pup who couldn't understand, and if only she'd known, she would have buried her face in his ear and he might not have given up the ghost. He always was and always would be more than a dog, and she had to take the mixture the Gorgon gave her to sleep.

Mary? Mary! Moonlight cut the floor. *Well, I don't know, Mary*! Whispers in the passage, loud enough to bring the Gorgon. It hurt to get up, but when she finally opened the door, the passage was empty. Then the cold came and she started to hiccough.

In her room, worse. She stirred the mixture double strength

and had it chalky and sour. Her heart tried to burst, but she watched like a separate person as the mixture bloomed blood in her gums and made the Talkers clearer, like tuning a wireless. She had been hoping they were new ones, but they spoke like old friends:

Dear Mary, we came when we heard.

Poor dear Rory, what a thing!

I saw him only an hour ago, happy and romping and saying he'll see you soon.

And you mustn't worry, Mary.

He's happy and romping.

Dear Mary.

They talked until the hurt flattened, still there but not spiking her, talking of Daniel and Artemis and then Jas, except instead of that name, they called him Knox.

—That isn't his name!

It was one of his names, but she hated their saying it, especially the man because he made it sound like Beelzebub.

Knox has knocked, hasn't he, Mary? He's knocked and knocked and come and come.

—Shut your stupid lip.

Oh, but everyone knows. Everyone knows what he—

It wasn't the same as what Lovelace used to do, but once she'd drawn blood and cracked the plaster, her head hurt loud enough to shut them up for a window. She fetched her papers and coins, wrapped Rory's collar around her wrist, and went out to the empty street. Her footsteps smacked louder than the blood in her head, and at Gute's it took only three pulls of the bell to wake him.

As he bathed her head, they came back a-chatter and she began to shake. He took her in his arms and squeezed her very tight and asked what it was and who did her this way. When she asked if someone was talking in the other room, he took her face between his hands and said words in a foreign tongue. He said she must tell him, and even though her nose was bleeding, he didn't let go or even wipe the blood.

—It's Talkers—

A roar—he squeezed her again and sang the foreign note and she knew he understood and that with his note he was putting up a charm, like a fairy circle here on English soil, and when she stopped crying and started to breathe steady, he asked her what she wanted to do.

—Not an asylum!

The gabble bubbled over, and he had to speak the note again until she could breathe.

—No, he said, not that. Never that.

And her arms were around him and she called him *Papa*, and tears ran down his face and into her ears, and he said he knew, he knew. Did she want to get away?

—Away away, Papa.

Across the water where no one could find her. He gave her something strong and sweet and sang the note again, and when the windows whitened, he opened the door to a lady dressed in tweeds. Her scent was French and her hat a man's, in the band an early rose. This was Fraulien Lina. She'd nursed in the war and knew many things, but now she was a poetess returning to Switzerland. Lina could take her to a fortress in the mountains and find her work as long as she wanted.

On the boat she had to hang over the railings because the channel made her so sick. Fraulien Lina said it was common, but the sea was flat and no one else was sick.

On one of the trains, after she'd gone between the cars for the third time, Fraulien Lina asked the question no one had asked. The Talkers got loud and told her to sew her ugly lip about what was inside her, and her nose began to bleed and she couldn't stand up, but when she fell and the windowsill hit her, they shut up long enough for her to say, *yes*. Fraulien Lina said that explained why she was sick, but they were going to a chalet where no one could find them and she knew someone who could help her with the thing. She didn't know if Lina meant the thing in her womb or the things in her head, but you had to hold on to something, any hand, any thing.

—I've had a letter, Diana said as the children tried to draw the pocket watches in case three.

—You promised not to—

—It came to me here at the museum, and inside was a note for you. Not from him.

Diana must know his script by now, but it was queer to think of Jas writing other people.

—What's the stamp?

—English.

—Male or female?

Diana rummaged in her Morocco bag:

—Why don't you?

The envelope felt expensive, like those Gute used for Christmas letters, but the hand wasn't Gute's, wasn't Jasper's, wasn't one she'd ever seen. It was addressed to Miss Marion Amanda McDonagh.

—I didn't know that was your middle name.

She crammed it into her bag.

—It isn't.

The children had just begun to draw, but mercifully a tour group arrived for Diana. She bought the children sandwiches in the café and then led them back along Oxford Street, allowing them to look into all the windows. She didn't dare touch the envelope in public, but the memory of its script teased her eyes, hinting at taste, tact. No one had ever addressed her that way, and the name struck her as beautiful, and then sad because she knew she could never be called it.

—Why can't we go in the fountain? Clive whined as they entered Hyde Park.

—I'm melting, Marion!

Day upon day, the heatwave built. Everyone agreed it had never been so hot. The lovely family spoke longingly of a holiday. Last summer they'd taken a cottage in Cornwall, and the children told her many times of the games they played in the sand and rocks, buffeted by the surf. Cornwall was an old place, she told them, where the other world came close enough to touch. They'd found a tunnel to a lead mine, but their father had forbidden them to go down it. This year, she could go with them and teach them French words for mines, and German stories of pirates and druids. She doubted her dictionaries would cover German druids, but the brothers Grimm would do in a pinch.

—Can we buy some matches from that soldier?

—I don't like his mask, Felicity said.

—His face is all blown off underneath!

Felicity burst into tears, and she had to tell Clive off. He sulked and dragged, but his frustration lifted his sister's spirits.

—Marion, she said, when we go to the seaside, will you teach me to swim? Properly?

She put them in the bath as soon as they got home.

—It's like the sea, she told them, but better because there's no sand and no bits.

—I don't like bits.

—Close your eyes and try to float.

She stepped into the corridor and took out the letter. The flap opened with a pop of the wax, and the page slid easily out. The signature made her burn, but she couldn't stop reading even though she wanted to drop it in the bath.

My dear Miss McDonagh,

It continued in that beautiful hand, assured and sensitive, more refined than his son's. You never doubted that Jas thought a lot of himself, but his father seemed so assured that cockiness melted into generous ease. He asked if she might do him the favor of lunching with him at his club. She'd only to name the day, and he would arrange it. He took care to let her know they would not be joined by what he called *other parties*, though they both knew what he meant. He meant, *my son will not accost you*; he meant, *my daughters, who are witches, will keep far away*. She had always understood this father as a tyrant. From the beginning, four long years, she had loathed him even more than his son did. Of course she knew that underneath, his son didn't loathe him at all but abjectly hungered for his approval despite everything he did to show he didn't care. She had despised the man for his hold over his son, for his putrid views and occupation, and later for empowering his vile daughters. Now, his letter between her fingers, she realized that she had piled onto the man every resentment she'd ever felt. She imagined writing a reply and actually going to lunch, an act that would surely scandalize his club as much as it scandalized her own heart.

—Marion! Marion!

—Stop shouting.

—She's drowning!

The girl clung to the edge of the bath, choking.

—Now, she said scooping her into a towel, you've passed the test.

—What test?

—Trial by water. That means you'll be able to swim like a fish before you know it.

—I don't want to swim anymore.

She set the girl back in the bath:

—First you must learn to put your face in the water, then you must learn to blow bubbles, then you must learn to open your eyes, and then, my little truckely howl, you'll have the whole lot, only just to go on practicing.

Mother burst into the bathroom:

—Marvelous news, my darlings! It's too good to wait!

The children shrank at the invasion.

—What? Clive growled.

—Don't say, don't say! I'll guess it with my mind!

—Don't wrinkle your face like that, Felicity dear.

She rustled them out of the bath as Mother revealed that their hopes for the place in Cornwall had fallen through, like other hopes before them. It was too late in July, it seemed, and everything at the seaside was spoken for.

—You said it was good news.

—Oh, but it is!

As she mopped the water the children had splashed, Mother unveiled the marvelous plan: they would go to the Alsace, to the lodge of a friend from the firm. It had woods, and the children would play outdoors, and most important, Marion would speak French and German for them. Mother knew only schoolgirl French, Father mostly Latin—

—I speak French *and* German! Clive declared.

How fortunate they were to have Miss Marion, and on their holiday she could be governess to them all after a fashion, helping them with the trains and the shops and whatever else the Alsace might demand.

As soon as the children were in bed, she found Mother and Father in the drawing room and launched an assault against this monstrosity. The dialects of German to which she'd been exposed where nothing like what they spoke in Alsace, she told them. That dialect was unique, unintelligible to anyone not native. Even the French was peculiar.

—Oh, Father, we'll be lost!

But she was too modest, as usual. Father was certain she'd be able to converse with the people there. After all, she knew two languages in addition to English, and surely with some assemblage of words she would show herself friend to the natives, and then—oh, Mother—she'd help the children befriend the local young. She needed to start having *confidence* in herself.

She was a very capable girl, the children had come miles since she'd arrived, and Felicity was already talking about her wish to go to boarding school in Switzerland when she was old enough, in a chalet like the one where Mademoiselle Marion had taught.

She tripped up to her room and its little bed, where the heat skulked despite the open window that let in the flies. The grubby truth, the one that would kill you: she missed him. If she had succeeded in killing him off in her heart, would Alsace press with such hazard? Diana said he had a new position someplace, and at the end of August he would leave London forever. This was why he dogged her. This was why he wanted nothing so much as an address to write. And this, surely, was why his father had invited her to lunch.

The man hadn't referred to Jasper directly, not as *my son*, and not by any of the names his family used for him. He was called different things by his father, sisters, and friends, and only when they were entirely alone did she pull out the names she used towards him. He was all of them, of course, but when his family was marking him as their own, he would play out a cord to her so they wouldn't pull him under again. That's what it meant, he said, when they spoke of leaving your family and becoming one flesh with another. He'd never asked her to marry him because he knew she didn't believe in marriage. She'd explained it was a vile thing made to keep women under. You erased your name and were nothing before the law except as you pertained to the man, who owned everything, even the child that came out of you. It was an ancient scheme to make slaves of women, and there was no way to explain why it had gone on so long.

He saw her as no one ever did, not even Daniel. *I couldn't have dreamed you up*, he said. He didn't come inside her mind, but sometimes he had a way of knowing about people, even though he never told her everything he saw. Once, a couple of months before the end, they'd been eating breakfast. They'd gone back to Scotland the second time, and everything was changing. When he came into her, he was an animal and so was she, and it wasn't a bad thing but a true thing, and they were there inside it, and when the wave was crashing, there was light between them and they weren't two, but one, caught up in a *yes*, and her body was her own and not her own, and she knew this was what they were for.

At breakfast she remembered the thing that had been standing between them since Christmas. It came up like heartburn. He was reading a book, his eyes blackened and large from how little they'd slept. Her own felt swollen still from how much she'd cried. And she was filled with envy at the two men he'd broken his promise for. She'd known after Christmas that something was wrong, and when he told her, he treated it as nothing. He had said he didn't see Tim and Malcolm any more, said he'd given up the thing he called the Business except with her. He didn't want to do it any more, he said, except with her. He didn't want anything except with her. But then he admitted that he had seen them one day during the holiday. They'd done the usual. He refused to admit that he'd broken any promise. Boys mucked about, he said. It wasn't love, wasn't even sex. He wouldn't even have seen them if things hadn't been so desperate at home and if she hadn't been away with everyone from the press. She said he could have written her, but he said he was afraid his nerves were going sideways again. The row lasted days, and she'd been physically sick—not at the picture of it, which in a certain light was alluring—but at the betrayal. It was betrayal, she finally made him understand, to let her have one idea and then to kick her in the teeth with a legal argument. Did everything need to be spelled out like a contract? Of course it didn't, he relented, and once he saw her crying, he fell on his knees and held her and stroked her hair and said he was sorry. Later he asked her—not on his knees but it felt like it—if she would forgive him. She had been surprised into silence. When people asked you to forgive them, it was a demand, at least they made you feel you'd be mean not to. Her father specialized in requests you couldn't refuse. Laighléis always asked her to forgive him afterwards, and she always did because she wanted it to vanish even more than he did. But Jas asked like a petitioner before a king, in hope but not confidence. He asked putting his heart into her hands. She could have said yes, but she didn't mean it yet, and his asking was so true that she couldn't say yes until it was just as true.

At breakfast in Scotland, her eyes swollen from animal tears, the forgiveness still between them, it came upon her that what he'd done with Tim and Malcolm didn't matter any more; something had overshadowed her and him, and that something was already rewriting categories. And she saw that whatever her ideas about the Irish and the English, about women and men, the cloud around them in the night was older and deeper and truer.

—About the thing, she said.

He looked up from his book, eyes strained.

—The thing you asked me to forgive you.

He sat up straight.

—I forgive you, she said.

He blinked, breathed in, and reached for her:

—Thank you, he said. Thank you.

It felt so old and petty to raise it, but when he said that, it felt like the most important thing in the world. His eyes got bigger and she thought he might cry, but he didn't. She thought he might kiss her, but he only held her hand. They sat at the table, almost bruising each other's fingers, and everything past was gone forever, even Daniel she didn't mourn anymore. It was just the two of them and Rory, who got up from the hearth and snuffed their plates and then poked her arm until she let go to pet him.

Did there come a point when you'd gone so far that you could never come home because the truth was lost to you, or you were lost to it, when you'd taken yourself into exile and damned yourself so you never deserved to come back? She had broken his heart when she left, he said in a letter to Diana. He had hoped his nerves would give way so he could go into the asylum and never come out. His nerves hadn't, and damn them, if they didn't then, they never would again. If she were to ask after him in Oxford, they'd tell quite a story, he wrote Diana. He'd finished the degree and taken Vincent's post, and now he'd taken another, and because people loved to talk rot, they would make him sound like the young god she used to call him in mockery. But the truth was she'd broken his heart and it was worse than anything the war had done. He wasn't a man anymore but a machine, and if she saw him she'd know he was a ghost without her.

It was probably true. At least, he believed it. But when you went far enough along a road, footpaths closed behind you. The girl who broke his heart was a closed path. She didn't know if she'd left that girl back in the rot-smelling room in Berne, or if she'd been dumped in an asylum, records burned. There was no way to tell him what happened to her because she didn't exist anymore.

But—Jesus!—she missed him, even if he was nearly a ghost. Before she had thought it possible, he had seen her and known her, and then he kept seeing and knowing, and even battier, started loving her, even *after* he saw. And honestly, *honestly*, couldn't she have run to him instead of Gute? Couldn't she have told *him* about the Talkers? Would he have turned her away? And honestly, really honestly, hadn't there been a tiny whirl of smoke in her mind that she *could* run to him? She couldn't run to him in the night because his college gates were locked, but if she could have stood the Talkers until morning, she could have gone to him. She could even have gone to Gute and later to him, but once Gute started singing the note to make the Talkers stop, she had got swept up.

But even that wasn't quite true. The heat that made her choose the sweeping up was like a furnace you backed up against even though you knew it would burn you. She knew there was a light place in the cloud, and she wanted to trust in the cloud, trust it could overshadow them so much that the Talkers couldn't poison them. But the Talkers were so strong and so heavy, and if she were to trust in the cloud and then find it weak against them, then she would be like the flame at the end of a cheap candle that flickered until the great finger pinched it out.

So she went to the furnace she knew, even though Gute had no hell in him and did his heart's best. She could have refused Fraulien Lina, she could have said *wait*, she could have done anything at all except run away when she wanted to run *to* him and pray to whatever he prayed that it would shadow them and mercy them and make true what she'd seen in his animal, make true everything she was scared to believe. Instead she got swept up by her own giant broom, swept onto the train and the boat and the other trains, swept into Fraulien Lina's ideas and the person she found to help her in the low room in Berne.

She wished sometimes that she'd taken that mixture, but she'd been afraid then, too. Not of the pain, but of the flesh she could smell, and she knew that even after Laighléis had his stomach pour out like sausages, even after Dan and Joe and Teddy died in foreign mud, she had never known evil until this: the deep-voiced woman telling her the choice was hers, telling her she could be rid of it, telling her the world was too wicked to bring it in, that they didn't have to give themselves to whatever a man put inside them. Everything sounded calm and wise, and if the mixture didn't work, there was another way, but the woman reeked of rot, the room was ice, and stuck in her mouth was a certainty worse than fear that this was a tempter she never wanted to touch.

She let it grow, and it made her not herself anymore. They

called her Marianne at the chalet, and this was happening to Marianne, not to her. Long out of money, she earned her bare keep cleaning the chalet, and she would have to work longer after it came to pay for two. But then Lina found a Frau, and the Frau said she'd take it when it came, not only take it but pay her for it. She couldn't understand why anyone would pay for a baby when they were born every day in their thousands, but the Frau was like a guardian angel, and the offer meant she wouldn't have to live years as a slave, suckling it and paying its keep, and she wouldn't have to go into a Magdalene home or suffer the even worse things they did to you in that vile island of her people.

When the time came, she thought she would die. It took almost two days, and things were coming out of every part of her long before it came. There was a blizzard so they couldn't send for anyone, and when it came, they wrapped it up, and when she saw its eyes, they were his eyes, and a sound came out that she'd never before made, not even when it was coming, and she knew she couldn't let her go and she'd never let her go and she'd pay the Frau no matter how long it took. They said she was a German word that meant out of her head from birthing, and she suckled her until the Frau could get through the snow. She didn't have a name because it wasn't decided if she was hers or the Frau's, and then she woke in the night to suckle her but the baby was hot, and before she thought to wake someone, she was wheezing and then she wasn't.

When the snow stopped and the Frau arrived, there was nothing the Frau could do because she was under the ground. The Frau didn't make her tell what happened during the wheezing, how instead of calling for someone, she had reached her finger into the glass of water at the bedside, how she'd dragged the finger across her head and said the words that made it true, *Amanda Sebastian, I baptize thee in the name of the father and of the son . . .* She thought the wheezing stopped before she finished. She promised then, to the one in her arms and to the one in the water, that she would keep this between them, they three, and if she did that, then he'd take her, wouldn't he? And love her like he loved Rory, but more, even more than the sand on the seashore, and if he would do this, he could have *everything*, he could have her life and whatever else there was, more even more than the stars in the sky, more than every sand, from now and until the sea rose up and swallowed them.

Yorkshire

Foreign smells were overrunning him. Aftershave conquered the carriage, and even in the train corridor, scents occupied his nose and mouth—musty study last night, orange squash, manured fields—until he didn't know who he was anymore. He'd been in foreign lands, and now he was going home not the way he'd come but with luggage and via his father's house, as if back to the start, back to the years before the war, the years with John, who yesterday reappeared without a breath of warning, crashing back into the world, dry bones given flesh by three hours' cricket.

Words played inside his ear as if a distant wireless broadcast the plea: *Da rober, fer auxilium*. He could hear the Christ Church choristers singing it over the Oxford walls. He could hear it being chanted at the Vale by his godfather's theological students. He could hear himself whispering it as he tramped the banks of the Isis the night he learned she was gone, walking until darkness faded and he found his heel was bleeding.

The aftershave emanated from the one with whom he shared the first-class carriage, a seventeen-year-old public school boy who by all accounts excelled at messes, to the point that he'd been all but expelled, and Jamie was, absurdly, delivering him to his father—Jamie's, not the boy's—for sorting out. The comic irony had been painted with broad strokes, so obvious a cretin could see it. There was a way the Old Boy had of abandoning the divine nudge and taking up a stick until he had your undivided attention.

Of *course*, he hadn't simply gone to Yorkshire as respite from thinking about her and inadvertently wound up headmaster of a failing school. That might be how one would narrate it to the Set, but his father wouldn't buy it. It would be hewing closer to the truth to say he'd been ensnared by the place, or that through a series of rash improvisations he had disrupted its complacency. His own life was a litany of disruptions, lately intensified in nature and frequency. During the war, they'd struck roughly twice a year, but he seemed to have reached a point where he'd be lucky to confine the bombs to once a week.

The train emerged from a cutting, and the morning sun blared into the carriage. He hadn't expected an ambush from the school any more than he had really imagined being captured by the Boche before it happened. He wasn't even sure when the ambush began. Was it the first, uncertain glimpse of John across the St. Stephen's chapel? The extended observing of him on the pitch? Something must have happened during the cricket because by the time the match had run to its surprising conclusion, Jamie's defenses were down, and once he and John had an actual conversation, he had already crossed the flood—ought he call it the Rubicon, the Tiber, the Jordan, or the Styx? One assent had altered his life, and he still couldn't explain even to himself why he'd taken the post.

He couldn't guess why his father had agreed to meet this gangly wolfhound of a boy sitting across from him in the carriage. There hadn't been any resentment in his voice that Jamie could detect last night, though the man never engaged in argument across a telephone line. His style was to corner one in the study and go to work on one's nerves. Once he heard the whole saga of Yorkshire—morning chapel, afternoon cricket, and at sunset a change of career—his father would never brook Jamie's moving north, out of reach, and he would feel nothing but betrayal at Jamie's abandonment of the choir school, his father's long-cherished project Jamie had agreed to head in a year's time.

But that was a conversation for the evening. Now, he faced a protracted journey to London followed by a trundle across the city and another journey up the line to his father's, all in the company of this wolfhound puppy who had lost the battle with sleep and now sprawled in his seat, mouth open, feet splayed, oblivious to surroundings and growing with every breath. But if he wished to make it through this day with his composure intact, analogies must cease; this boy was nothing like Rory the pup, and the last thing anyone needed was to resurrect that episode, another ruin caused by oblivious good intentions.

Though how could he have *known* the hound would die so young? And even if he had known, he never could have left it where he found it, in that man's barn, scarcely fed, growing out of its skin, escaping to kill lambs and be shot at by other farmers. At least he'd bought the pup out of bondage, for too steep a price, but still. He hadn't been able to rescue the litter-mates, who were shot before he could get there but he had rescued the pup, and she had called him Rory. The pup, rangy and half-starved, had loved her right away, entire and sloppy with the strength of a hero, and she had slept with her wolfhound on the counterpane, kept warm by him, calming him at thunderstorms. She had never been as happy as she was then, she said, her giant hound at her side, walking the towpaths with Jamie. It was absurd that he should mourn a dog as if the very muscle of his heart would tear. Perhaps he wouldn't have been so bereaved if Amanda had not acted as though, with Rory's death, her own child had been ripped in pieces from her womb. He still didn't know how much his anguish had been entirely his own and how much the torment of her suffering.

He had just about got used to the idea that he would never see her again when Diana's letter brought its vandal news. All his efforts to resume contact had been thwarted by Diana, and though term time at Marlborough was in full crush and his duties as housemaster taxed him, he hadn't slept a full night since hearing Amanda had returned. Now, twenty-four hours after embarking on a supposed holiday to Yorkshire, he'd punched through to yet another foreign vista.

The tea trolley woke the boy. He looked less bilious than he had, so Jamie risked food.

—Sir, the boy said after downing half a sandwich, are you a Corpus man?

—Whyever do you ask?

The boy gestured to his cuff links. The boy's brother-in-law, it emerged, had also been at Corpus Christi, though before the war so Jamie had never encountered him. It emerged, too, that the boy, like Jamie, was the only son in a family of elder sisters. He felt a wash of sympathy.

—That knuckle has split open, he observed.

The boy stammered as he wrapped a handkerchief around a hand that had seen obvious action the day before, and not at cricket.

—Stop speaking.

Exhaustion ringed the boy's eyes, nicotine stained his finger, and a sunburn reddened his face. She hadn't looked so different the first time he saw her, though her knuckles hadn't been broken. It was June, and an angry sunburn covered her nose and the strip of her cheeks below her eyes. Her blouse was closed at the neck, so he hadn't been able to see if her chest was burned, too. Once she spoke, he forgot everything else. She had the kind of voice that stirred him in his root. She smoked as she read her poem in that cellar of the Egg and Ostrich, her voice animating the words in a way that could slay the hardest heart, revive the deadest mind, hurt the bravest organ. He had never been able to think of oars and nightingales the same way again. He'd taken her for a student at one of the ladies' colleges, perhaps a radical (the knit crimson hat?), but when she came to the end of the poem, to the bit about songs echoing in darkness, he knew without understanding how that she was a person, possibly the only person, who'd felt the suffering and desire that plagued him.

He couldn't decide if she was closer to sixteen or thirty. Weeks later, when he'd earned her trust, she told him her age, three years younger than he. Her irregular papers weren't as unusual as they might have been before the war. It hadn't been easy, she said, but she had been able to get documents testifying to her legal name (Marion McDonagh), birthplace (Galway town, Co. Galway, Ireland), age (twenty-one), marital status (unmarried), and residence (Oxford).

After she'd stepped off the stage that first night, Jamie had been seized with an unfamiliar urgency. He had never imagined there could be a person of the female sex capable of knowing and loving his most private aspects. His sisters always behaved as if they knew him better than he could ever know himself. They had been alive longer and could remember things he was too young to recall (including so many embarrassing episodes that he suspected them of inventing to humiliate him), and so they presumed to know him. They didn't know him. His father didn't know him. There was no person living who knew him, but suddenly, in a gesture of cosmic surprise, here was one who could.

She was flirting with a boy behind the bar. Jamie bought a drink and proceeded to spill it down the front of her mustard-colored cardigan. She didn't shriek or jump off her stool, but she turned on him an evil eye that disordered his pulse, there in the suffocating cellar.

—Bugger.

—I beg your pardon?

—Sorry, sir, I meant—Oh . . .

The boy was pressing a handkerchief to his nose, but blood had already dripped onto his trousers.

—For heaven's sake, Wilberforce, what have you done now?

Jamie offered his own handkerchief and noticed color under the boy's left eye.

—I thought you said the other boy hadn't landed any blows, Jamie said.

—Oh, he didn't but . . .

Jamie raised a brow and Wilberforce dried up, unwilling to add anything to the confession he'd offered the evening before, one that had ranged from fornication with a local girl to sending a younger boy to the sanatorium with broken nose and rib.

—That's quite enough blood, Jamie said, wrapping the soiled handkerchiefs in newspaper and stashing them in the outside pocket of his case.

Wilberforce appraised him:

—Sir, did you . . . last night after I left the room . . . ?

Jamie let him flounder. He thought it best not to give an impression of companionship despite his growing urge to question the boy about the school, its pupils and staff, about—

—I only wondered if Mr. Grieves said anything about me.

—He said a good deal about you.

Wilberforce looked paler.

—The lavatory is two cars down, Jamie said. Sort yourself out, if you can do it without tripping into more trouble.

The boy left more flustered than he'd been.

John was Mr. Grieves to them, a name Jamie associated exclusively with John's late father, yet when pronounced by Wilberforce with such obvious feeling, one that stirred Jamie in ways he didn't care to catalogue. And surely the point was the miracle of it all: if John could materialize after twelve years, was it so much to ask after only twelve months to see her again in the flesh?

The fields of Lincolnshire rolled by, and he could almost imagine this was an ordinary train journey where the miles whipped past as you unwound a great many thoughts in your mind. The carriage still smelled of Wilberforce's aftershave, and his hands felt sticky from the boy's blood. The things they both had said the night before jumbled in his mind with the things other people had said, and as usual he wished he could revise his lines. Something had happened in Yorkshire, something he didn't understand. The day seemed now as though it had been a battle for St. Stephen's Academy. He had little idea what St. Stephen's truly was, but he imagined that in some way—whimsical but not necessarily unreal—the school had whispered to him. He saw it almost as a hostage, one disguised as a servant boy, the kind to whom horrifying things were being done below stairs and who above stairs, as he served, whispered for rescue. But this was metaphor, and St. Stephen's was a school, not a hostage.

And yet it was hostage to a manifestly long habit of sloth, to insensate barbarism, to the worst parts of public schools and none of the glory. There he was at the place, and after a third-rate luncheon, there had been the violent, astonishing cricket played by John with a force that confused times and made Jamie glad for the lawn chair beneath him. He'd had to swap out his drink for an orange squash, but this only stacked time up even more, and he was back at Marlborough, not the school he'd left just that morning employed as a housemaster, but the school as it had been in his day, when he himself wore flannels and clothing that never fit properly because he was forever growing into it or out of it or both at the same time; and it was not June of 1926 but the last golden summer before the war, those days after he'd converted John but before he'd blown the whole thing to pieces, those days when it was always fine, when the sun scarcely set, when lessons were a pleasing torment of minutes without John, when the cricket stretched on as if they would always be playing it, John always bowling fast, himself always watching, orange squash in his hand, the tang on his lips, thinking of the taste of John and the heat and dust of the boxroom, the dead flies they swept aside, and the way they seemed not to have slept the whole time, unless passing out in lessons counted. And then yesterday there they stood in wild moorland, and the sun was blazing again, and they were men. Their clothing fit, the orange squash tasted flatter, and John bowled at Wilberforce with surgical severity. Why John should have singled out Wilberforce, Jamie couldn't fathom. The boy had begun tentatively (John having just sent another batsman off with an injured foot), and Jamie had a nasty feeling John was trying to eliminate the weakest point of the side while he could. He wondered if time's stacking up was a mirage, that this John was not the John he had known but rather a brute honed by war and by schoolmastering in a place captive to something distinct from but just as abominable as the things they'd seen across the channel.

But then as they were changing ends, John spoke to the boy with a flash in his grimace, and Jamie saw he was not grinding the boy to powder but trying him by friendly fire. The boy looked no less rattled, but Jamie knew then that the boy was in John's hands and that John's hands were good hands, that he was attempting to haul him across some Rubicon, as he had so many others. And later, in Burton-Lee's study, John had seemed so out of sorts that time stacked up all over again, and John fought for the boy even as he fought against him, and even though Jamie had dived headlong into the mess without knowing why, he had been drafted, it now seemed to him, for the Big Push, the spring offensive, the decisive battle in a war they at St. Stephen's had been waging for years, he in the role of the Americans, fresh, healthy, waltzing into the mire to show everyone how it was done.

When had the school spoken to him in the secret mental shaft where his wooden cart ran, that tunnel beneath the glimmering tracks where his public self carried on witty conversations? Had the hostage spoken in St. Stephen's chapel, so diminished but potent? In the cloisters, which seemed to say they had once held off the world? In the hand-to-hand of the cricket, or the knife fight of the study? Was it when John, having discovered Wilberforce in the midst of his crimes, made him admit them, or was it when Burton-Lee, wielding a professional technique Jamie yearned to study, elicited the real confession, against all logic of what any boy should disclose? These two men, John Grieves and Burton-Lee, had fought for the truth, for justice, and somehow even for that wretched boy, despite the fact that the place had turned to mud around them. The walls could have come down and they would have continued to battle both the strangling vines and each other, to save what they loved. Was this the cry of the hostage? Or merely a siren? There were troubled boys in his own house at Marlborough, and his mentor, Vincent, had walked him through plenty of sticky maneuvers as he found his feet as housemaster, but at Marlborough he was a speck, in history and in weight.

Without precisely deciding, he had joined the battle for St. Stephen's, and now he had charge of the battalion though he'd no merit. The entire war, of course, had been fought by men without merit. The best fighters had been on the German side, men with ingenuity and daring and ruthless flexibility of mind. It defied logic that they'd lost, and if they hadn't been tempted into Russia, they never would have. The Russians themselves were turncoats loyal only to themselves—though rumor had it Stalin was killing his own people; why, Jamie couldn't imagine. He'd heard a story of Russian soldiers so hungry they roasted dogs over a fire, the dogs howling as they burned. But he had to stop thinking such things or he'd cry himself into the asylum.

He hated the way people talked about what kind of war they'd had, as if it were an ocean crossing. *What kind of war did you have, old sport? Oh, stormy in the main but several first-rate days, bit of skirt, more luck than not, but Hell, you know.* His war had been arse-first, thumbs-backwards, nothing according to plan. It took ages to join, and then when he was finally sent forward, his unit never fought in the heart of it. The first year he'd spent weeks at Rouen with Trench Fever during the thick of fighting. The second year he earned enough trust from his CO to take his men behind enemy lines, only to be felled by gas in no-man's-land. Instead of dying as they did, he survived and, after a month in field hospitals and four more back home at Kardleigh's war hospital, recovered. Having finally been boarded, he was given two weeks' leave, most of which he spent in London at the club, drinking to blackout. When they allowed him back to France, it wasn't to his old unit, which was extinct. The Russians had released the Hun from the eastern front, and now the brutes were preparing their assault. The Americans were said to be on the way, but Jamie didn't hold out much hope. In any case, none of it was up to him.

His orders attached him to a machine gun unit, and he spent weeks tramping here and there, tasked chiefly with tending machinery. No one knew where the line was, where anything was. They spent a good deal of time encamped in dugouts awaiting orders that never came, or came but made no sense. The last day began as any other. There were bombardments over the hill, but their orders were to stay in place with the gun. By late afternoon, the gray coats had cut them off, and then his war became a ludicrous game of Bedlams except there were no cans to kick and he was locked up with a cadre of public school men until the whole thing ended and prisoners could be exchanged.

Life in a German prison camp was scarcely worse than Kardleigh's hospital. He'd been sent to one for officers so was treated civilly, and although they were very hungry, so were the guards. He'd never been much of a reader, but that was all there was to do unless you were good at cards. He read what there was, which ended up being quite a bit of Dostoyevsky, and entertained himself imagining what his father would say to it all.

When the war finally ended and he announced his intention

to stay in the army in hopes of an overseas commission, his father reacted badly. Not even three days had he been home, a war hero, and his father was berating him like the boy he no longer was. His godfather was called to the Rectory to prevail upon him. They even attempted to enlist the support of Jamie's old housemaster. Jamie was forced to decamp in the night, go down to town, and establish himself at the club.

It was farcical to come closest to death once the guns had stopped. His sisters opined that it served him right to contract the Influenza after running himself into the ground with dissolute living. What did he expect with his lungs already weakened by gas and his body by starvation in prison? Reminding them that hunger was not starvation did nothing to blunt the force of their chiding. None of it would have come to the point it did if he hadn't been so furious with his father's telegram (*COME HOME DIRECTLY*—the rest was unrepeatable). If he hadn't been so angry, he never would have conceived the mad idea of going to Oxford Street at Christmastime, in the state he was in, his temperature being what it was, and then surely the rest of it would never have happened, the crush of people and the crush of the trench, the squeezing in his lungs, the pitching of pavement, until he wound up where he did, scarcely alive when they found him, or so his sisters said. The height of absurdity to contract both Influenza and shell shock in the middle of Christmas shopping when the war was well and truly over.

He survived the Influenza, which at the time he took as spite, death refusing him its ticket no matter how much he deserved it and how many others, more needed than he, were being cut down where they stood. The London hospital sent him back to Kardleigh, a failed, un-prodigal son. He'd lost track of the days while ill, and he did everything possible to continue ignoring them at Kardleigh's hospital.

When the tulips poked up around the croquet grounds, his father and his physician began to contend over him. The chief battleground, Jamie gathered, was terminological. Kardleigh said his lungs were normal. He couldn't expect to run a hare and hounds without careful retraining, but as for civilian life, *moderate* civilian life, he was fit. Walking, fit. Cycling round Oxford, fit. Cricket, fit. Golfing, fit. Pleasure boating, fit. Football unfit six months, ditto boxing, but then he could train if he was sensible about it. He should avoid cigarettes and cover his mouth in the cold.

If this appraisal were true, his father argued, then why was he so easily fatigued after so little exertion? Why was his memory destroyed, his concentration so poor? His father did not believe in neurasthenia, nor DAH nor Effort Syndrome, nor any of the other mendacious terms the War Office approved. If his son were debilitated, and now upon conclusion of the conflict when he hadn't been before, then the explanation had to be the war. He had suffered gas, and then malnutrition during which he'd lost a stone and a half when he hadn't any to lose, and finally the Influenza. It was plain as day that his lungs and heart had been compromised.

It did seem so, Kardleigh allowed, but it wasn't quite the case. True, he did go the whole war with no sign of mental weakness. He'd spent four months recovering from the gas; he'd had trench fever, trench foot (unusually, not venereal disease); he'd been a prisoner for seven months; in a weakened state, he'd almost died of the Influenza but he'd never had any mental symptoms until the Oxford Street episode. Now, five months later, his pulmonary health restored, now he was suffering neurasthenia. His father hit the ceiling: his son did not have shell shock. Kardleigh agreed: the term had been banned. They actually shouted over each other. Jamie could hear them down the corridor. His father's view was a choice of opposites: either his son was an invalid damaged by gas, or he'd lost his moral fiber and bearings. In either case, the best place for him was home at the Rectory, where his father could restore him to the person he knew him to be.

This was when his godfather was called back in. Kardleigh's mention of Uncle Mark incensed his father, who could never stand being upstaged, but one day without announcement, Mark arrived with a tin of biscuits and consulted at length with his physician. Kardleigh later admitted that Mark had given him the third degree. *Anyone who thinks they're all lace and incense at the Vale hasn't met Father Mars.* Without consulting Jamie, Mark began to broker the peace, proposing removal to the Vale and light secretarial duty to build his mental stamina. Kardleigh, Mark, and his father agreed he was in no state to take up studies, and the Army gratified his father by rejecting Jamie for further service. Truce arranged, Kardleigh had him boarded and discharged. And so the month, and then the year, at his godfather's theological college began.

Wilberforce slid open the sticky door and tripped into the compartment, treading Jamie's foot in the process. Awkwardness was becoming such a part of their brief acquaintance that Jamie longed to cut off the boy's apologies with *Let's take it as read.* Wilberforce had cleaned his hands and face, rearranged his tie, scrubbed the blood from his trouser knee leaving a wet patch, and from the subtle relaxation around his eyes had likely relieved himself in more ways than one.

—Haven't you a cousin? Jamie asked.

—Sir?

—Male cousin.

Wilberforce confessed to girl cousins years older, and some distant male relations he'd met only at funerals.

—A friend, then? Someone at university perhaps?

The boy regarded him baffled and embarrassed.

—Someone you can talk to about intricate matters.

The penny dropped.

—No, sir.

—No one?

—*No*, sir.

He said it with bitterness, as one who'd endured years in the wilderness. An iron door divided them, and the tides of feeling that had lapped at Jamie all day—one moment bathing him in the pleasure of obeying a call, the next crashing with dread at what he had done—those tides reminded him that if he had not all but usurped the role of headmaster, he might be free to advise this boy, to share frankly his wisdom such as it was, perhaps even to confide in him. Instead, he was bound by adulthood. He could not say for instance, *Look here, Wilberforce, everyone knows fornication is wrong, but to be perfectly honest I've only just begun to discover why*. He couldn't say, *At your age I'd already been expelled once and was sailing close to a second.* He certainly couldn't put the boy's transgression into perspective by confiding the shame and despair he had felt at twenty-one knowing he'd never put himself in a woman; how when he went with the others in his unit to visit girls in the villages, he could never do what he had paid to do; how the part of him that hardened in every inapt circumstance (including when shells were falling), that part refused its duty, played dead as it were. The girls were invariably kind and said it happened all the time, and afterwards, he'd say things that made everyone assume he had done it. His father assumed it. His godfather assumed it, and Jamie never got round to contradicting him since Mark had offered blanket reconciliation for sins committed across the channel.

Jamie assumed that once he was home and returned to himself, everything would go back to how it had been before the war, when he would have thrown himself at any girl and impregnated her given half a chance. Providentially, he was never given the chance. What would this Wilberforce think to know how he'd lusted after his sisters' friends, how even at fifteen he'd carried on with Lucy's friend Thomasina, called Tommy. Was it the boyish name or flat figure that made her so intoxicating? He hadn't a notion of what he was doing, and one holiday they had come as close to trouble as it was possible to come without actual scandal.

After her abrupt departure (just as she'd learned what to do with him), there had been a clash with his father so bitter that Jamie repaired to school and immediately got into an even worse mess with MacAvoy (two years younger and a day boy at that). Result: expulsion, shipped back to the Rectory before half term.

Yes, the same Rectory to which they were headed, and this, he would explain to Wilberforce, was the point at which his godfather was recruited for more than Christmas gifts. His father, having outdone himself over Thomasina, farmed the whole MacAvoy affair off to Uncle Mark. Jamie was dispatched to Oxford, and Mark took a stab at what was to become their mature relationship. The difference between himself and Wilberforce was that he'd never actually fornicated with Thomasina, and he'd never beaten anyone as Wilberforce had beaten that boy. He'd never nursed bloody knuckles, and the only bruises his face had ever suffered came from the scrum. Even in the war, he'd fired rifles into fog and thrown grenades, but never had he watched a man die at his hands. Had he truly been more innocent than this Wilberforce, or was the world now more savage than it had been in 1914?

After his expulsion, his father moved mountains to get him a place at Marlborough—yes, the same Marlborough where he was now a housemaster, and yes the same father to whom he was bringing Wilberforce. From his father's perspective, Marlborough was close enough to keep Jamie under his thumb. To Jamie, anything was an improvement on freezing Scotland. But even more (and sometimes Jamie wondered if he hadn't got expelled for this purpose), John was at Marlborough, a year ahead, about to make prefect. Jamie was placed in John's house and found his childhood friend not a dour swot, but a captivating athlete and something of a social god.

—Mr. Grieves has taken an interest in you, I gather, Jamie said.

Wilberforce scowled in response.

—Don't suppose you'd care to tell me about it?

—Whatever interest he's taken I pretty much shot in a ditch yesterday, sir.

Oh, bring back the hound, the graceless schoolboy, anything but this tight, flat sorrow!

—Did you know Mr. Grieves at university, sir?

—At school.

Wilberforce looked caught between curiosity and scandal.

—I suppose you were clever, sir.

—No.

—Was Mr. Grieves?

—What do you think?

The boy cracked a smile, and Jamie allowed himself to describe John's last days at school, the slew of prizes he won, things Jamie could never dream of winning, the history medal, the English essay, the fencing plaque, the bowling belt, and that wasn't counting the way John won back the cricket cup after it had languished two years in the house of their bitter rivals. Wilberforce listened, animated and expansive, crackling with zest as John had that last term. Of course, Jamie was censoring his account, but was it entirely mad to imagine this boy might understand those seventeen days that eclipsed ten years of chaste childhood friendship? John's utter surprise the first time, his pureness and naïveté and then his tears, as though the act of release was so strong that it cut loose something inside him. Jamie could see now what he couldn't then, that when you unleash feeling in a heart as bound as John's, you ought to take care. You ought not bounce it into the next thrill.

But thrill and change were coursing through everything that month. Term was ending. The papers buzzed of coming war, in Ireland he assumed. The Irish had plagued them for centuries, he declared to amused listeners in the houseroom, and if they wanted war, they could have it. Better, Jamie averred, they accept Swift's modest proposal. The houseroom laughed and circulated his quips. Of course, one was supposed to feel grave concern for world affairs, all the enormous snore of adults who insisted on upbraiding the young for their vivaciousness, heroism, and daring. When Jamie, home for the summer holidays, complained of being too young to enjoy the war, his father accused him of callousness. Jamie penned his rebuttal in a letter to John: Young men had always been thus. This was how the human race advanced. Without Jamie and his so-called vices, how would poles be reached, women wooed, children begat, cathedrals imagined, electric lighting invented, indeed how would anything of verve come to pass?

His defense to John exceeded his father's rebuke, mutely apologizing for the way things had ended between them. John ignored not only his letter but also numerous invitations to the Rectory that summer. Jamie told himself that John's silence was to be expected; he would be making arrangements to defer his scholarship and to take whatever qualifications would be needed for his commission. Jamie was sixteen and headed back to school whether he wanted to or not, but for John and for the other lucky ones already eighteen, the incomparable romance of war beckoned. John would have no time to answer his letters, full as they were of provincial life, Lucy's ongoing threat to cross the Tiber, his father's difficulties having lost six curates and an archdeacon to the front, the Middlesex Kent match, the dancing tea with Lucy's friends, Agnes's enrollment in the nurses' training course so that she could stand ready, bandages in hand, to fall upon whatever handsome, desperate soldiers returned from battle. Jamie's self-deception fired so wildly that he believed it was all for the best that he hadn't been able to make amends with John. It was the kind of chat, he decided, best not had directly but rather allowed to fade into the past.

When they did see each other again, the whole kerfuffle would look vanishingly small.

In a way, it was true. That whole time belonged to the world before the war. His last view of John had been as their fathers shook hands and John gazed blankly into the Marlborough quad. They'd neither seen nor heard from John in the intervening twelve years—estranged or dead, they didn't know—but yesterday at St. Stephen's, he had materialized. He'd spoken civilly, been forthright, and even accepted, in the end, the outlandish prospect of Jamie's becoming his employer. Amanda had been lost only one year, and although Jamie never stopped rehearsing the weeks before her disappearance, he could think of no injury he might have inflicted to cause her to flee. That brain-addling uncertainty followed by the shock of recovering John had pummeled his nerves so that the current moment, despite its veneer of mastery, felt like the summer of 1919 after leaving Kardleigh's hospital for the Vale, when he'd felt he had no skin.

That year, in his godfather's study, he held back none of his vitriol or his newfound atheism. He railed against people's triumphalism, their high-handed theories and self-pitying grief. He deplored the way they blamed the war for everything. The price of milk? Ah, the war. Girls' hemlines? War. Unemployment? Shrinking wages? The difficulty of finding good servants? Radio towers, chewing gum, jazz music, motorcars, lax liturgy, any confusion in the body politic were all attributed to the war. Mark warned against nihilism and insisted that the trenches had not been a moral or spiritual no-man's-land, where good and evil ceased to contend for them, where no eye saw, no mind recalled. Mark had said a good many things during those months of the abyss, when Jamie performed secretarial work for the college but remained aloof from its seminarians. When he could recall himself enough to joke, he'd refer to the place as the Vale of Tears.

Eventually, Mark judged it time for him the leave and sorted out his arrangements at Corpus. Once Jamie had matriculated, Mark had him back to the Vale once a week for dinner and to hear whatever confession he offered. He knew Mark expected him to fall into error with girls, but he railed against them too. He abhorred English girls, he declared so often that he felt Mark must have suspected him of preferring English boys. Girls today were self-satisfied and naïve. His friends in the Set agreed. While they men had been swallowed by Leviathan, these girls had stayed home boosting a fraudulent morale. They had felt heroic pelting un-uniformed men with white feathers. They had believed themselves valiant, working in munitions factories and hospitals while Jamie and every boy of his acquaintance had faced a wall of savage futility. Mark had pulled him eventually from that cauldron of ingratitude, but the first November in 1919, when the King decreed that *all locomotion should cease so that in perfect stillness the thoughts of everyone may be concentrated on the glorious dead*, Jamie had scarcely been able to endure the two minutes amidst red-eyed women and maimed young men, the silence shrieking with the names read out before the bells, slowly over more than a quarter of an hour, Jamie standing there a mental wreck perhaps, but physically robust, intact, virile, capable theoretically of anything.

As he forced himself through his first year at Oxford, the girls he met seemed alternately to bemoan the shortage of husbands or to hurl themselves into antic gaiety. They who had gone nowhere before the war without chaperones now claimed to possess banking accounts and even flats. They attended parties and restaurants on their own recognizance. Their self-abandon always struck him as more fervent and vicious than a man's. After two years' acquaintance, Jamie wanted nothing more to do with them.

Mark had negotiated, as part of the Oxford accord, that he might read history rather than pursue ordination as his father expected. He'd finished his undergraduate course in two years, which wasn't as unusual as his father thought given the numbers who'd delayed degrees for the war. In his last term, the looming standoff arrived: What would he do next? The official options were to begin a DPhil in theology, which would keep the door open for an occupation acceptable to his father, or to sit the Foreign Service exam and go abroad. The latter gave his father apoplexy, so Jamie had to pretend to be more wedded to it than he really was. Just as it seemed Jamie would have to accept exile in the colonies to defeat his father, Mark produced a third option: do the doctorate and then assist with his father's newest project, opening a school.

—That is the very last thing I will ever do!

Mark told him to calm down and explained about the choir school. His father had long wished for one at the cathedral, and now it appeared, through a flood that had providentially made the ramshackle Bishop's Palace uninhabitable, that the Palace would have to be either torn down or rebuilt. Funds had been secured to refit the building as a choir school, and when it was ready, the Bishop hoped that his son would serve as headmaster.

—But I've never even taught! I'm literally the least qualified person for such nonsense.

—Unqualified now, Mark said. And I'm sure it hasn't escaped you that you're still letting your father dictate to you, if only in the negative.

He didn't, then, believe in prayer as an effective act. At any rate, the only thing that could release him from the cage—take his father's route, which he wanted for its own sake but not for his father's, or his own route, which he didn't want at all—was his own self. He sat the Service exam. He awaited the results. And then, in his ongoing exploration of pubs undergraduates didn't patronize, he wandered into the cave.

His father never knew the real reason he gave in. Mark told him that Jamie had warmed to the Reverend Kirk as supervisor for his DPhil. For a time Mark even believed it, but Jamie couldn't keep the truth from his godfather, and once he began haltingly to speak of her, everything opened in the sunlight of Mark's clarity and compassion. It was the girl he'd seen first in that pub, reading her poem. She was the reason he wanted to stay.

—I thought you detested English girls, Mark said.

Jamie had blushed so deeply he feared Mark would know everything at a glance.

—Ah, he said, she's Irish.

Her Irishness was one of her secrets. For the most part, Amanda used an accent that marked her as a decently educated English girl. Only when she was very tired and they were quite alone did she let the drapery slip. There were certain phrases guaranteed to tighten his trousers, and when she learned what they were, she would sometimes whisper them while they were in public.

Once Mark had died and she had vanished, he came to understand how alone he was in the world. Mark was not even so old as his father, but his heart had stopped one afternoon in Lent. Jamie had received a note upon returning from his tutorial with Kirk, the one in which they'd finally hashed out the crucial chapter of his thesis. When he got to the Vale, they were collecting the body. His godfather didn't look like men had looked in the mud. He looked less dead, but then at the funeral he looked more dead. In his own life, nothing visible changed once Mark was gone, but when she left too, there was no one to look out for him, no one he'd permit to hold him to account, no one he could fully trust.

—You take the cases, Jamie told Wilberforce as the train jerked into the London terminus. Wait there.

He pointed to a pillar.

—I'll see about your trunk.

At least the boy was strong, so the cramming of items into

and out of the cab, onto and up from another platform at Waterloo, the steps, the overhead racks, all was accomplished without Jamie's having to break a sweat. Their compartment leaving London was full, which at least cushioned him from the naked force of Wilberforce's attention. As they clacked through the ugly outskirts of town, Wilberforce's stomach began audibly to growl, to the point that an interfering spinster-aunt shot the boy looks. There was no tea trolly, and Jamie hadn't thought to feed the boy at the station. When a mother and child produced sandwiches, bringing further protests from Wilberforce's digestion, Jamie unfolded the evening paper and erected columns of print as bulwark. When he eventually lowered it, the sandwiches had disembarked, the spinster-aunt was dozing, and Wilberforce had finally opened the book Jamie had offered at the beginning of the journey.

Other people could not read his mind. He could sit in a railway carriage with a pupil, an employer, or the King himself and think whatever he chose. The fact that no one could know or judge his thoughts was a cardinal aspect of his freedom as a human being. He could recall what he pleased, imagine what he pleased, feel what he pleased, and speak to himself in ways that concerned no one else on earth. He could in moments of strain, such as this, recall scenes he would give fortunes to live again, not because he wished to change them but because the memory and the hope of them made the rest endurable.

Sometimes one could realize when one was in the middle of such a scene; he'd realized it the fourth time they met, when they'd walked the towpaths and then lain in the meadow. He'd said to himself then, in the wooden cart of his mind, *This is life changing forever*. To her he had said, *I like to listen*. She had been bubbling with words—he didn't know where she was drawing her breath—rippling along about the landlord of the pub pursuing a liaison with someone, a friend of hers called Artemis. Now as he leaned against the window of the slow afternoon train, his mind raced faster than her words ever had, sometimes getting caught in the repetition of a phrase—hers, his own—sometimes recalling parts of conversations—last night, last year—or imagining future ones—with her, with John, even with this Wilberforce, around whom he most especially must maintain iron boundaries of discretion—being carried downstream in a current of all night glissades, through which no one could emerge in firm grip of his sanity.

Or what? Her tongue at his ear. It was beyond imprudent to allow the memory of her into the railway carriage with this boy and the wrinkled woman who snored in the corner. *Or what*? The party was a crush, roiling and boiling, and she'd teased him almost beyond endurance, taking pleasure in it. The music throbbed and so did he as he pressed her against the wall: *Just you stop. Stop it now*. Her breath on his neck: *Or what*? He had the upper hand, then and only then, more experience, more age. She provoked him on purpose, or what, *or what*? She knew the things he got up to. He'd answered her questions lying beside her in the meadow, fully dressed, not touching in the June evening sun. *Tell me everything. Start with the first.* The grass tickled his neck, and her voice sounded in his ear like a telephone without static.

—The first was Phil.

—Phil?

—Solicitor from the City come down at weekends.

Phil's accent testified to a public school education, and his manner the first time showed he'd been a prefect, or whatever they were called at his school. The name Phil was so unlikely, but no more than the one Jamie had given: Jasper Knox.

He and Phil met in a distant pub, and when last orders were called, Phil produced a pocket notebook and a gold-plated pencil. They had been speaking of test matches and gazing at the bottles behind the bar, the relaxed, easy state of an evening at the local.

—Stick? Phil said like a fist punching through plaster. First time?

He nodded mutely.

—One goes easy.

His heart was beating in his jaw:

—I wouldn't . . . go easy.

Phil wrote in the notebook, tore out a page, and passed it to him. Before he could unfold it, Phil shrugged on his coat and left.

It was only a small piece of paper. The phrase repeated inanely in his mind. *A small piece of paper. Here is a small piece of paper. I thought I asked you for a small piece of paper.* It gave an address and said, *Knox minor, Report 1600h, Clarke.*

He'd never felt more at a loss for what to wear. He examined his drawers and was dismayed to find they all had holes. He chose the cleanest looking, mended the hole, polished his shoes, brushed his trousers, cleaned his fingernails, and emptied his pockets of everything except a handkerchief and the small piece of paper.

The sky was cloudy but glaring. Phil had said, *first time*, and now the words had the power of a wrecking ball. They declared that what he was walking through the streets to meet, a thing he could not fully imagine let alone understand, was something actual, something other people took part in regularly. And it occurred to him that Phil had conducted himself as if following a method. The seemingly idle conversation had been deliberate, its purpose to take his measure. The questions, so impossibly abridged, had been professional. Over a pint and cricket scores, Phil discerned everything he needed to know. He had not seemed to find him unusual, even calling himself Knox. The appointment Phil had written on the small piece of paper—for which he had needed whisky even to leave his rooms—would to Phil be routine. Far from the shadowy corner of his mind only thought of in bed and the bath, this time—to him the first, to

Phil uncounted—belonged to a world other men knew and in which they practiced.

He had to wait to cross the road, and he realized he was shaking, not as bad as at the hospital, but getting there. He could turn around. He could simply not turn up. He'd no call to visit that pub again. If he ever encountered the distant acquaintance who had passed him the thing called *The Staff*, he would claim to have forgotten about the magazine, not to have read its eight sewn-together pages, certainly not rung one of the exchanges on page seven and spoken the phrase written beside it.

The place was a flat with its own bell. Building works across the road filled everything with their noise. He could feel the vines tightening. This wasn't why he'd come, not to bring on the crush—

—You're late, Phil said opening the door.

He was seven minutes early; he'd set his watch before leaving his rooms. He apologized, and Phil locked the door behind them. They climbed the narrow stairs to the first floor and then a narrower set to the second, where Phil admitted him to a flat.

The room was bare except for a table, two mismatched chairs, and two lit lamps. The curtains had been drawn, heavy blackout fabric. He could still hear the building works, but muffled. Whatever happened, he realized it wouldn't be heard.

Phil was wearing tails, a brocade waistcoat, and bright green socks. His hair was slicked severely back. He wasn't actually taller, but it felt like it.

—Knox minor, Phil said disdainfully. Just what do you have to say for yourself?

Not even in no-man's-land had he felt so lost. The only thing that came to him was *Sorry*.

—Sorry, what?

—Sorry, Clarke.

Phil beckoned him forward and then circled slowly, pulling back his collar with a fingertip, snapping his fingers so he'd hold out his hands, snapping them again so he'd turn them over. They were still shaking, but Phil pointed to his trousers:

—Those creases are a disgrace.

He didn't know if he was expected to apologize again, but it seemed abject, so he didn't.

Having completed his inspection, Phil produced the notebook with its small pieces of paper, adding something with the pencil.

—So, he said at last, you're sorry, are you?

—Yes, Clarke.

—You mike off afternoon school, you break bounds, you go fishing in the Earl's pond, and then you speak that way to the Earl when you're caught?

—I didn't know he was the Earl. He looked like a gardener.

—Of course he looks like a gardener, and if you didn't know that, then you'd no business poaching his carp.

—Have you poached his carp?

A blow to his ear.

—You're a good deal too cheeky, Knox minor. You can count yourself lucky he didn't ring the Head.

Phil began to pace, his shoes clacking like shots. He rustled with the drapes at the far end of the room. When he came back, he was carrying a cane:

—It's your first report, so you get the choice, though God knows you don't deserve it. Six-hundred lines or six of the best.

His mouth was dry. It had never happened like this in real life.

—I . . .

He was stammering.

—I don't want the lines.

Phil appraised him.

—Right, Phil said, let's get it over with.

And like that, almost like that, he was on the other side. His jacket was off and so was Phil's. He was doing what Phil told him, and Phil was pacing, swishing the air (meant to frighten you, and working), standing beside him, tapping the target, and almost as an afterthought, pulling his shirttail out of his trousers.

—Why? she asked.

She'd been silent on the grass, but now her voice had edge.

—At the time, I'd no idea.

—Was he bent?

—No.

—Then?

—Layers of protection.

He could feel the questions sprouting in her mind.

—Do you want me to go on?

She took his hand, interlacing their fingers. His heart beat as it had in that room, muffled by the blackout curtains.

—Hold still, Phil had said, and count these out.

The first took his breath. He'd forgotten how much it hurt.

—How much? she asked.

—Not the worst.

Not by a long shot. Her thumb brushed a circle in the center of his palm.

—Well? Phil said.

—One, Clarke.

—Late. We'll start again.

By the end, it had been ten, not six, but he could have stood it longer if he'd had to. As they shook hands and as he gave the customary thank you, the sensation continued to grow. He remembered that it used to, but unlike then, no shame attended. It was sore and would be sorer in the morning; Phil had given it full strength with a free hand for so-called extras, which you'd never get in a real school; yet, in every way including the bodily, it was better, more toothsome, vital.

As he arranged himself, Phil inscribed another small piece of paper. For his housemaster, Phil said, proof of his Report. Then he was standing in the road and squinting at the light, and the lock was clicking behind him, and a bell began to ring. He'd been there less than fifteen minutes by the clocks of Oxford, but by other measures . . . ? He unfolded the small piece of paper, hands now as firm as rock. Phil had written an exchange and beside it a three-word phrase. That was all. The first time was over. Nothing at all when you added it up, but he was there, on the other side.

—The other side, she repeated, kissing the palm of his hand.

Was it true you got only one shot at innocence? Logic all but demanded it, for how could things ever be that free again, when he talked into her ear and the rain began to fall, when they hadn't yet grown into each other? He felt bludgeoned by the mere idea of falling in with another girl. True, he was not yet thirty, and people such as his father and Vincent and even Kirk called him *very young*, but one couldn't send down roots time and again. He couldn't erase his education, couldn't undo the war, and he couldn't pull up the tendrils he'd sent into her and then worm them down into someone else. And if she were taken permanently from him—passive voice, concealing the actor—it would be a monstrous violation of the deal. Yes, deal. *Listen. You sent her. You sent me, into the heart of the labyrinth. And I was going. I was going*!

He knew it was pointless to contend with the Old Boy. Where were you when I made the stars? Can you hold Leviathan in your hand? He had a thorough training in matters philosophical, theological, moral, and even practical. And yet here he was, in the heat of a midsummer railway carriage, under more duress than he'd been in some time, his only stronghold the cloud of her chatter. *Say anything, anything, walk along the river and talk to me like the sea, my eyes will wash my face and I'll never look your way. I'll be like Orpheus should have been, like Lot and not his wife, just speak, speak—*

—Sir?

—What?

—Our stop?

—*What*?

The whistle was blowing.

—Guard! Hold! We've a trunk in the—

His father's new fragility alarmed him. Certainly, the man had improved since Jamie saw him last, in hospital. Now he wore a summer hat as he clipped roses from the trellis. Jamie mentally composed a report for his sisters (up and about, steady on his feet, good color) and tried to squash his trepidation. Had his self-absorption extended so far that he expected his father to have recovered his full vigor simply because Jamie needed him? The desperate dread he'd felt arriving at the hospital returned as he saw his father's shrunken frame in place of his usual coiled strength, these slow movements in place of a vast nervous energy.

Once they began to speak, in the garden and then in the conservatory, the man he knew surfaced. Jamie collected himself over supper, which his father conducted in customary silence. The boy ate like the wolfhound puppy he was, to the point that his father accused Jamie of starving him. The barb restored his equilibrium (had it been delivered for the purpose?), and he settled into the comfortable posture of rebel son. When at last Wilberforce was dispatched for the night, the paternal glare settled on him.

Rather than brace himself for a tick-off, Jamie barked commands to his nerves: *Hold the line*. If his father wanted to look into him with the knowing, let him. Let him see Jamie's refusal to be handled as a child. Twenty-four hours ago he had been the object of every man's esteem. The aid he needed now was not—repeat, *not*—on his own behalf, but on behalf of an entire institution, one that had engaged him and offered him some presumably shabby salary (he would be ashamed if forced to admit they had never discussed details).

—Tell me, his father said.

The warmth in that voice disarmed him and unloosed his tongue, as doubtless it was meant to.

—It's the biggest mess you've ever seen, he said of the school. Boys barely middling, chapel moribund, music none. I assumed Overall was putting a gloss on the place.

—Board Chairmen will do that.

—But you should have seen it, middle of exactly nowhere, rutted lanes, reckless cricket, vile conduct, and the staff . . .

There seemed no way to present the welter of impressions that beset him yesterday and bloomed within him last night and on the train. The previous evening when Jamie had telephoned to ask for help with Wilberforce, his father had opened the conversation by asking if he was at St. Stephen's, a place Jamie had never mentioned to his family. Now, pleasure showed in the man's turned-down mouth, which was where he kept all his secrets until he was ready to deploy them against you.

—I did mean to tell you I was going, Jamie said, but I didn't think, that is, I didn't expect—

—You only went with Overall to put an end to the question and then found things taking rather a different turn.

—Quite. Only I'd find it a mercy if you didn't finish my sentences for me.

Jamie crossed his legs and waited for the snap in return, but his father's gaze drifted to the gurgling conservatory pool. Jamie tried to summon the list of problems as he'd composed it in his mind.

—I can't think what to say to Vincent.

His father nodded. Jamie stumbled on: no one at Marlborough had an inkling that he was considering another post, certainly not after everything they'd done to encourage him. Vincent most especially had put himself out for Jamie, was depending on him.

—Just as I know you—that is, the choir school, which I said I'd—

—Oh, that wasn't never going to work out, was it?

His father's tone spread like a balm, not even faintly bitter, and amidst his surprise, Jamie felt an airy joy: *That's the end of it. You don't have to do it. He never expected you to do it.* Perhaps his father had known months or even years ago that collaborating on the choir school would never have worked, that everything between them would suppurate, and that no matter how much either of them labored, they would never be able to escape mutual vexation.

—It would have been a catastrophe, Jamie said.

His father laughed.

—Perhaps, Jamie continued, we ought to make a pact never to undertake a project together unless there are at least a hundred miles of railway between us.

—Oh, his father said, I'm sure it isn't necessary to make a pact.

Jamie wasn't sure how to take his father's mildness.

—Vincent is extraordinarily fond of you, his father continued. I'm sure he'll be disappointed when you tell him of your resignation, which of course you must do face-to-face before you submit your letter.

Jamie realized his father was right. His former housemaster, now mentor—Ali as he was generally known, Vincent as he'd asked Jamie to call him—had devoted untold hours since September listening to Jamie's questions, his complaints, his half-baked strategies, all in a scheme so elaborate that only Vincent could have sold it to the headmaster: install Jamie as master of a smaller house and allow Vincent to train him in post so that Jamie could take on Vincent's own house at the end of the following year, when the man intended to retire. Only after such a molding could Vincent trust any hands with his boys, his world.

—How can I do it? Jamie said. How can I leave Vincent after everything he's done?

—He has a year to make other arrangements, hasn't he?

—It isn't the same.

—Of course, you can always tell Overall you've changed your mind. There's still time for him to find another man before September. You could be excused having been swept along by it all.

His father's words brought another breath of air, like gas blown off: to set down St. Stephen's, not to have to solve its gorgon knots, not to have to wound Vincent, free to spend the summer holidays refreshing his lessons for the next year, and—crucially!—free to devote himself to recovering *her*.

—Perhaps I should.

—Perhaps.

And *yet*. Upstairs somewhere, in onc of the girls' bedrooms or even his own, the gangly wolfhound Wilberforce lay as if washed up by the tides, a boy whose fate and future Jamie had seized when he brought him here to the Rectory. How could he say to this Wilberforce, *Sorry, change of plan, off you go home and good luck to you*. Jamie knew that the boy trusted him, trusted him perhaps as any orphaned pup trusted someone who gave him a meal, but trusted him completely nonetheless. As for the pit of vipers at St. Stephen's, he would not like to let down the man Burton-Lee, as irascible as the codger was. Burton-Lee had installed himself, Jamie was realizing, as someone whose esteem he wished to earn. But beyond Burton-Lee, how could he after all these years and after the most blatant intervention of the Holy Spirit, how could he abandon John?

—It's never pleasant to let people down, his father said, but sometimes it's necessary, and decent people, who wish for your good, will see that. Vincent is a resourceful man. He'll conceive another way once he sees the matter clearly.

—Meaning?

—Oh, you know as well as I do what this is.

—I haven't the slightest idea what you think it is, Jamie retorted. I'm not a telepathist.

His father raised his brow:

—If he call thee, thou shalt say Speak, Lord, for thy servant hearest.

—I haven't said anything of the kind.

His father gave him the look that said his words were too frivolous to contradict.

—The choice is yours, his father said, but decide tonight and resign in the morning, whichever it's to be. Don't sit down to luncheon with two employers.

He nodded as if the suggestion were obvious though really he'd been expecting to knock it around the tracks of his mind a bit longer. A fortnight remained to the term, and this he'd supposed was his margin. Now he saw his margin was vanishing, that he'd have to decide before he went to sleep so he could confirm the decision in the morning, which would be early as he had a lesson first thing. But if he could have a closet in which to think, impossible with his father seated across from him, he would know that only one option remained.

His father's housekeeper appeared and caught his eye. There was much he needed to turn over with his father, much he abruptly found he longed to discuss, but he had to catch his train. There was no margin, actually, at all.

—I've rung for the cab, she said.

—You aren't staying the night?

He said he was expected back, and if he slept out, explanations would be needed that he shouldn't want to give, though in the morning—

—Tell me about the staff, his father said.

Jamie evaluated six matrices at once and then gave a thumbnail sketch of the men he'd met. He described his impression, garnered obliquely from Wilberforce, of pupils at once over-disciplined and lawless, brutalized and brutalizing, sheltered in their views yet run wild. Academically, again if Wilberforce were an accurate gauge, tending to the deplorable even by public school standards. Spiritually . . .

—There wasn't any nonsense at least, and the chapel was attractive. Your friends from the *Ecclesiologist* would approve. There's an organ though it wasn't used. According to Overall, all it needs is a bit of sticking plaster and someone who can play it.

—Good, his father said, but?

He had a picture of savages overrunning the forest of Arden.

—Moldable?

—If it is, that's the only reason for hope.

—Now, now, his father said. Hope abounds for this Academy of yours.

He flushed at the assertion that the place spoke for him and was somehow, already, a part of him. But then the doorbell was ringing, his father was standing, and Jamie was fumbling with his jacket, frustrated to bursting that they couldn't continue.

—One thing at a time, his father said. Concentrate on ending well where you are. When term is finished, we'll speak again.

The man looked as though he wanted to clap him across the arm.

—Your first task will be the staffing, obviously, despite Overall's wish for slow change. Explain afterwards, not before. You're good at that.

Jamie bit back a grimace.

—As for the boys, leave young Wilberforce to me.

—I shall be glad to hear what you make of him.

—I'm sure, his father replied, but don't expect me to break his confidence.

Jamie dismissed the suggestion though he realized he had been hoping for it.

—I suppose it's a project after all, he said wryly.

The housekeeper appeared and handed him his hat.

—Don't worry, his father said, there will be something like three hundred railway miles between us, a safe distance, even with the Flying Scotsman.

The train was late and the platform steamed after a cloudburst. Early summer always promised reprieve, but tonight he had a crick in his neck and three more railway segments before he could collapse across his bed. He'd given up the Business more than a year ago, but its thick allure returned as he fretted on the platform. Sweat trickled under his collar as it had the first time with Tim and Malcolm, some months after Phil. Trinity Term, preparing for his Mods, he'd corresponded with them for more than a fortnight. They'd written in the first person plural, hinting at elaborate experience.

Birch spray or apple rod? they queried.

Not sure, can you advise?

A treatise followed, history of each with anecdotes. One more watery, the other thwackier. Area weapon versus point weapon. When he arrived that first, hot afternoon, he discovered Tim, short and middle aged, and Malcolm, a once-tall man in the mold of retired headmaster. They always worked together, so you'd get the two-hander. Usually it was school, and indeed this variety of the Business appeared to be Malcolm's vocation. Every now and then when they wanted to sing through lesser-used parts of their repertoire, they'd give you Borstal or the Navy. It had never before crossed his mind how many implements could be cherished and used. They arranged the first outing in an anonymous flat out by the Morris factory, but after two meetings, thrilling and compatible, they invited him to their house, though perhaps it was only Malcolm's. Here were a variety of rooms given over to the Business, one a lumber room kitted out for leisurely experiments with birches. Afterwards, instead of the abrupt tearing from one world and thrusting into another, one collected oneself, used the cloakroom, and joined them in the drawing room for tea, or if it was evening, drinks. He'd never been offered a meal, but he had spent several hours in mufti chatting with them and being shown sketches from Malcolm's prodigious collection.

They were less cagey than some, and more professional. Rather than small pieces of paper in a pub, you'd correspond poste restante. The Business for Malcolm was an art. He insisted on fresh canvas, so there was always the tension between wanting more but knowing that the more you took, the longer it would take for the marks to disappear, and the longer you'd have to wait before seeing them again. In a way, it imposed a veil of temperance. As a distraction, Jamie would plunge himself into his studies, and the time after a visit could be vitally productive. Once the marks had faded, canvas nearly restored, it was permissible to send a note and begin the next preliminaries.

While Malcolm curated history and implements, Tim specialized in the surprises of the scenes themselves. He had a way of tossing you into a scenario, giving you just enough to play with and then incorporating anything you said. With Tim more than anyone, it felt not-pretend, and later, when he'd stopped seeing them, he would catch himself yearning not for Malcolm's implements but for Tim's power to enchant, to erect the conceit with sheer force of personality so that it felt more real than the rest of his life.

He worked his way through the exchanges in *The Staff*, and eventually it became clear that everyone knew one another. When he met Mad Mick, Mick revealed he had heard of him, Knox. Jamie had been surprised and flattered, thinking he'd earned a reputation for taking a lot, but later, once he'd reached a level of friendship with Tim and Malcolm, Malcolm had said in his off-the-cuff mumbling way, *My dear boy, don't be absurd, it's those effortless good looks of yours*. He knew that his looks had a certain power, but even though Malcolm didn't say so directly, he was crushed to be told that his idea of himself as heroically tough was just that, an idea, and that compared with others they had known, he was memorable chiefly for his appearance.

If he'd met Tim and Malcolm earlier, he could have saved himself experiences he'd rather have avoided. But if he'd never known the others, even Claude, he never would have realized how exceptional Tim and Malcolm were, how rare their talent, their taste and stability. Claude had been knocking around for a while, they said. He'd be arrested any day, along with anyone foolish enough to be found with him. As for Phil, they rated it likely he'd end up killing someone by mistake. Jamie believed it. Phil's drinking frightened him. It had increased over the months and reached its apex in a rash scene with a cold bath. The fact that he didn't get injured beyond what he was there for, he took as a slap the morning after a binge. It was always up to the recipient to make first contact, so in the end it was as easy as not ringing Phil again. There were others, less chancy than Phil but more interested in the follow-on, which was by no means assumed as part of the enterprise. Jamie wasn't opposed theoretically, but he didn't fancy most of them, especially if they had poor stage sense or, worse, poor technique during the main event.

Claude had been younger than the others, close to his own age. He was good looking, but in a way Jamie couldn't put his finger on, Claude repelled him. Claude had a passion for plimsolls, and he accomplished a lot the one time they met. In the follow-on, Claude had been more adept than anyone he'd encountered, and he began to think that the one-note area weapon might become tolerable if such technique were to follow. The initial sense of distaste had passed, and they were smoking and contemplating a second round when Claude's gossipy patter, which had roved across a wide range of lechery, wandered into an anecdote about a choirboy who'd been surprised by two older boys in a church vestry. Claude described the boy's ravishment with professional eye. His cries, Claude claimed, had been drowned out by the organ, and the affair had been enough to give the boy a rupture.

Jamie didn't think he had scruples, but he discovered this was one. And he discovered in that instant that he had a power to see people, and he saw that Claude not only was telling a true story but also had been a participant, and not the choirboy. And as he buttoned himself up, he saw that there was something fiendish about Claude, something not touched by his five senses but nevertheless known, and as he walked and then hurried away from the place, he knew truly for the first time in his life, more certainly than he'd known in no-man's-land, that he had touched evil, something too potent to be called by old names but something categorically encroaching and malignant.

He'd never been able to bring himself to repeat the story to Malcolm and Tim, except to say that Claude had chilled him to the bone and that after Claude, he had given up ringing exchanges in *The Staff.* They'd corresponded with Claude but had never agreed to a meeting. Something happened when one stepped into the room, Tim explained with deadly seriousness. One took on and one stripped off. Every customary defense was left outside, and if one wasn't careful about the people one let into the room, one might find oneself disarmed by something better left alone. It could get in even with the best safeguards, which was why it paid to go in with someone experienced, preferably with two others. The one time Tim regretted had been when he was starting out and met someone alone. Little could be more dangerous, Tim said, than being alone with one other person, knowing you wouldn't be disturbed.

Later, at Fishguard, in the week he had alone with her in Wales, knowing they wouldn't be disturbed, Tim crossed his mind. First he thought how wrong Tim had been, that the highest pleasure and satisfaction he'd ever known had come from being alone with her, and that Tim's philosophy explained why he was a bachelor. But there was a moment that week when he'd felt that Tim was right. Nothing could be more dangerous than this. Nothing more real. Nothing more perilous and alive.

If Kardleigh had known about the Business, he would have hit the roof, but Jamie didn't tell him about it, or about relapsing into the weakness halfway through his first year at Oxford. He had been managing his studies, stamina returning like weeds after rain, but after Christmas—tremors, short breath, an inability to remember the lecture he had just attended. Kardleigh was the only person he could have admitted it to, but Kardleigh was then at the asylum in charge of true madmen. He'd heard of faradism but was too much of a coward to put his finger in a socket. He didn't ring exchanges in *The Staff* with any of this in mind, but after the first time with Phil, feeling calmer than he had in years, he realized the Business was better than anything they'd tried in the hospital or after.

It became routine that year to introduce himself as Knox when in places students were forbidden or discouraged from going. He felt different, too, as Knox. Knox had face, nerve, moved confidently in any society, the cock fights, the illegal distilleries, the card tables, the Belgians, the Jews, the Pekingese. His French was fine, and his German had come along in Mainz. He lost money regularly to the Russians but gained a taste for their vodka and a knack for bidding and swearing as in Petersburg. (Anyone who called it Petrograd got held down and punched.) When he bluffed well, they called him Knox the Fox, and when he lost, it was Hard Knox. No one asked his Christian name before Amanda.

He returned to the cellar where he'd first seen her, but the barman claimed no memory. Eventually Jamie showed enough coin that the man summoned one of the girls. Did she know the poet in the crimson hat? Jamie asked. From the versifying Friday last?

—Ariadne, said the girl.

—*Ariadne*?

—Not her real name.

—Indeed.

He could feel the girl responding to his looks, and to the hint of accent he was letting show. He usually roughed it up as Knox unless he was meeting men from *The Staff*, in which case he used it neat. It didn't take long before he'd got the girl to tell him where to find Ariadne, Thursday week at the Turned-Up Horn. The name of the place was legitimate for a change, and he found it at the top of the Headington Road. He was spending too much money on batteries for his bicycle lamp and was forced to explain the expense (to his father, begging funds) as punctures incurred on the parlous roads of Oxford.

A band was on stage when he arrived, and the man playing the horn was coal black. He didn't see her anywhere, neither Ariadne nor his informant. Later when the musicians stepped down, a consumptive youth drifted onstage to recite a dreary poem, and then a Russian read a story that degenerated into nonsense when the tram driver turned into a wolf and the devil offered the narrator a cherry glacé. Jamie was thinking about the long ride home in the dark when she stepped onto the stage wearing a working man's suit, her hair still curling around the edges of her red beret. Instantly he was hard, and it only got worse as she swished to the music stand, cocksure as a Turk, struck a pose—*waiting for you lot to shut up*—and then, when the noise lessened and someone had called for Ariadne to spin her web, gave a cheeky grin and unfolded her paper.

The first poem told of gooseberries and the steppe and being lost beneath the ice. The second was a rude, jaunty thing that sounded at some moments like a nursery rhyme, at others like the limericks in Malcolm's broadsides. She had a way of pronouncing the word *country* that was profane. Ditto *pistol* and *rapier*. Finally, and without the slightest hint that she was changing tone, she read a sonnet, English, meter broken only once when asylum turned to refuge, and he wanted to shout and he wanted to weep and more than anything he wanted to be inside her.

Later, when he'd managed to buy her a drink, she admitted to remembering him and begged him keep a steady hand with his glass.

—Ariadne is your nom de plume, he said with a smile, but what's your name?

She replied by asking his, and when he said Knox, she demanded more.

—Jasper.

He put a finger on her wrist, lightly so he could take it away if she objected, and then fell into his real accent, speaking so only she could hear:

—Quid pro quo, Miss Ariadne.

Her neck flushed. His mouth watered.

—Amanda, she said.

Her name was Amanda. Even though it never appeared on her papers, it remained her name, her true name, no matter what she might claim later.

The American jazz music resumed, and to keep her on the line, he mentioned that he wrote as well. Her response was indifferent:

—Poetry?

—Prose.

—Published?

—Oh, no.

He'd never been one for writing when he didn't have to, but the habit-forming nature of the Business combined with the necessity of spreading it out over time led him to try stories. He'd read enough of the genre in *The Staff* to know he could never write that way. As much as those tales made him hard, they were nevertheless dross. His first effort, a short narrative called *The Earl's Pond*, read like a bland dispatch from the Front. Later when he showed it to Tim and Malcolm, they said he should submit it to *The Staff*. He disparaged the suggestion. The style of that rag was too pant-pant-slurp, he declared, an adjective that made them erupt with laughter. It was true, they agreed, most of that literature was mere wank-fodder; there were some greats, of course, and Tim nursed a fondness for *Lesbia Brandon*, even to the point of wishing to stage the scene at the shore somehow, but when it came to writing, neither of them cared to do it, and none of their other friends in the Business had the taste to tell wank-fodder from art.

The Earl's Pond. Pouring Rain. The Old Mill. Faust. Knox developed a body of work. If Tim and Malcolm ever started a journal, he said, they could publish his oeuvre. Some evenings they would bask in the warm afterglow of the Business and discuss the theoretical gazette as if it were a going concern. So long as they never allowed modernists, Malcolm averred, he didn't mind what went into it. Tim thought there ought to be drama as well, perhaps an opera, though how opera could be presented in a literary journal, they never bothered to explore. Their favorite pastime was thinking of names for it. *A Gentleman's Guide. Lashings*. Or simply, as Jamie always advocated, *The Business*.

—Do you do recitations, she asked, like tonight?

—Heavens no, he said. What I write . . . it's rubbish.

—I'll be the judge of that.

He wanted to get down on a knee and ask her to be the judge of all of him.

—Meet me tomorrow afternoon, he said.

She finished her drink and refused another. She would meet him again, but not until next week. She was not free in the daytime. Later he learned this wasn't true, but it was a wise enough thing to tell a boy she'd seen only twice. She wrote the name of a pub on the back of her poem and gave it to him; he half-expected there to be an exchange for him to ring. She'd be there Tuesday after ten. He could come if he wanted, but if he expected her to let him buy her a drink, he would have to bring a token.

Of love?

—Of work. We'll read this Jasper Knox and see what he's made of.

The wait until Tuesday drove him to distraction. He fell behind with his work. He tried to write a story in response to her sonnet, but after several aborted attempts, he had to accept that he didn't have the skill. His only talent, such as it was, lay in the academic essay and in clinical accounts of the Business. In the end he put *The Earl's Pond* in his satchel. She didn't know his real name. She knew nothing about him. If the story repulsed her, so be it; at least he'd be able to concentrate again. She could take Jasper Knox in all his vices, or she could biff off where she'd come from and leave him to his peace.

She was sitting at the bar when he arrived. He set the pages beside her and excused himself to the jakes. The yard smelled of petrol. A rat scurried out of the privy. He smoked a cigarette and listened to a couple arguing out a window. When he returned, she had folded his manuscript under an ashtray. He gave his order and stood beside her, fiddling with his signet ring. He resolved to count to three hundred by threes. If she said nothing, he would take his papers and leave.

Six, nine, twelve. She didn't know his tutor, his college, his father. *Thirty-six, thirty-nine*, good things were a mirage. *Sixty-three, sixty-six*, if he left now, he could get in a night's revision. *A hundred and two, a hundred and five*, no one in the Business so upset his equilibrium. It would be better, surely, to put her behind him, to erase from his record this nothing of a pub—

—Was everyone at the school as vile as this Clarke?

Her fingers tapped the rim of her glass.

—I wouldn't call him vile.

—But the school was vile. Eton, I suppose?

He glanced at her, a swamp of misunderstanding.

—No! he said. It isn't *real.*

—I see.

She was humoring him, thinking he'd written truth disguised as fiction. He had, of course, but not the way she thought.

—This happened last year, he said.

When she asked how old he was, he told her, and her face resolved into a scowl. He asked if she'd ever done any drama.

—No.

—Or make believe, when you were small?

—Of course.

—It's like that.

Last orders had been called, and the pub was closing. She agreed to a walk. Along the river in the night air, he grasped for words to describe the Business, the realness of their pretending, the play behind the surface ordeal, how the encounters were both more true and consequential, yet less . . . he couldn't think of a word to summarize the fist of life. At last they reached a passageway that would take them back to the road; he stopped, his words a cloud of gnats:

—In any case, it doesn't matter. One only does it for a lark. The story's nothing, rubbish, as I said.

She took hold of his wrist and then his neck, and her mouth was on his and he was being kissed, and he was kissing back and no one could stop him. It was perfectly legal and if anyone objected, they could tell it to the river because he was twenty-four years old and they ought to be grateful he wasn't ill, mad, or bent.

She said she had to get back to her lodging. Her landlady locked the door. When they emerged into the High Street, a clock began to toll. His college gates had already closed, he said, and to avoid knocking in, he'd have to climb through the window of a boy called Stoat, whose rooms gave onto the garden. He let everyone use his window and in return was kept in gin. Her route, she claimed, was a dustbin to a window that the

Gorgon couldn't hear. He thought she was joking calling her landlady the Gorgon, but that was before he met her friends and discovered that everyone in her life went by nicknames—Gutenberg, Artemis, Pangloss, Lovelace. Not a single one could be found in a tax register.

—Tomorrow, she said, at four.

He was supposed to see his tutor. She told him a place and disappeared down the lane.

The Dog and Duck was a working man's pub, no whiff of literature or music. The next afternoon, she handed him a poem and vanished while he read it. *Tell the Truth but Tell it Slant*, twelve verses sketching an encounter in the vein of *The Earl's Pond.* She wrote with a force he'd never encountered, but when it came to the Business, she didn't know what she was talking about. He felt an urge to throw her into the sea right then, to invite her to Tim and Malcolm's bolt by the Morris factory and educate her senses across an afternoon. When she returned, she was blushing all the way down her neck even though her hands played the indifferent man-of-the-world with her cigarette. She was wearing Oxford bags, a blazer, and the kind of flowing tie they wore before the war. She'd slicked her hair back and pinned the pieces down; with the right hat, she'd have passed for a boy. She was making him uncomfortably hard, but he knew all at once to be cool with her. She showed promise, he said. With a certain education, something might be made of her. Rage flashed: she had an education and not just a woman's one. He smiled in a way that said, *Lay down your arms*. He said he knew that, said it was obvious. He meant a *certain* education, and then he smiled again and she blushed some more.

Before he knew it, they'd abandoned the pub, sprawled side by side in the meadow, and he was telling her every detail of the Business. It had never occurred to him that a woman could bear hearing. When it began to rain, they fled under a tree. Her eyes were darting everywhere, and he realized he'd spoken too boldly.

—My viva's the week after next, he said. I won't be free for a while.

She said she, too, was not free. The press had a special print run for a book by an Arabian.

—Will you write to me? he asked. Poste restante?

The suggestion intrigued her, and he could see things fizzing in her mind. The next afternoon, a letter awaited him at the post office, a flamboyant ramble, absent much punctuation, about characters in literature (or so he supposed, recognizing only a few), what she thought of them and what each needed in terms of the Business. She signed herself Amanda Dunhill, a surname surely lifted from the cigarettes they'd smoked in the meadow. He had a vision of Malcolm's study, the two of them in school uniform hauled up for smoking. *Dunhill and Knox minor, what do you have to say for yourselves*? He penned a reply as well as he could given that he had a fraction of her reading. Something in her letter struck him as the overeager pupil; he addressed her as Dunhill and delivered a playful ticking off. She had a modicum of intelligence, he said, but showing off would get her nowhere.

Her reply seared. He could take his pompous black-and-tan snout and shove it where . . . he'd never heard such idiom. She'd missed his tone entirely, thought he was lording his education over her when he'd meant to convey awe at her mind. She cursed him in colorful terms and said she was sure he'd be happier with Tim and Malcolm, trading tales that only men could tell. She'd signed herself AD and told him to go to hell.

He walked all the way to Swinford and back. He went to hall and listened to the dinner conversation, suddenly aware that he was an imposter. He dressed the undergraduate, talked the undergraduate, drank, smoked, and laughed the undergraduate, but in the part of his mind she'd already moved into, there he knew his life had changed more deeply than ever before and certainly in a better way than he'd ever thought possible. She had told him to go to hell, but during his walk, the future showed itself to his eye.

That evening as he sat in Stoat's rooms drinking gin and smoking with the Set, the urge to write grew so strong that he felt compelled to resist it. He pilled with the others, egging on Grady's passion for Caravaggio, Stoat's for *Gawain and the Green Knight*, Dunham's for Bolshevism. When the Set retired, he resisted even longer by listening to Stoat's tale of woe, the girl he loved having accepted the proposal of an oiler he'd thought a friend. Jamie commiserated, and later, when Stoat turned maudlin, Jamie even recast the Thomasina episode as something recent, a piquant association that might have developed further if his father weren't such a nightmare. Everyone knew his father at least by reputation, so Jamie's accounts of the man's tyranny not only increased his own bona fides but also fit perfectly their understanding of Victorians and everything the war had exposed. Finally, Stoat fell into a stupor, and Jamie repaired to his rooms more sober than he was used to being at such an hour.

He finished the story as the sun broke across his desk, an adventure of Dunhill and Knox, barely mentioning the Business. He titled it *Quid Pro Quo*, addressed it to her, and took it down to the outgoing post. When he lay down under the covers, still in his clothes, it felt like the transport ship where he'd rocked in a medical haze, only now he was spun by something greater than war, greater than fate, something setting his course for however long his life would last.

The whistle screeched as the train pulled into Marlborough station, wisps of pink still brushing the sky. He dragged his case down from the rack and carted it back to school. Stepping into the house and its drowning concerns, he knew that his longings for the past were merely a distraction from what could not be changed. Time moved in one direction, and some mistakes, more than you'd think, could never be recovered, no matter how much hope you drank to soften the knowledge.

He took a cold bath and scrubbed from himself every whiff of the journey. In the morning, he would break it to Vincent. He would spend the summer holidays embroiled in St. Stephen's. Of course, he would try to reach her, but no amount of wishing would change facts: She had left him. She had vanished. Now she had returned and wanted nothing to do with him. He lay in his iron bed, no less narrow for being a housemaster's. He had a life anyone would envy. Why did it all feel so much like a coffin?

When he came to himself in the foxhole that was the advanced field station—and by came to himself, he meant became aware that he *was*, that he had thoughts and a body, that something was wrong with it—he was face down and vomiting. He regarded himself as an illustration in a book, his mind the author of captions. *Anyway, I was alive, which is always a good start.* Someone threw sawdust beneath him. Foundations shook, mud fell. Later—were they moving?—later was it night, liquid down his throat and up again, burning. Was he blind? Groans all around, but later, quiet. Had his ears blown out? Later, gasping, lungs of a flea, later, later, Beth beside him, felt not seen, tracing his palm as only a sister could. Later, his father's hand blessing him. He wanted to tell him that prayers had no power. *It's all a play, don't you see? The book, the words, the bread, the wine, none of it true. Can't you see what we've wakened to*? He wanted to tell him the truth he had learned. *Father*, he would say, *you don't need to be good. The darkness is too strong. You can't resist it, Father, no matter what you do. It swept in as a ghost, and it was swift, Father, an instant they fell and much longer they drowned, and Father, I fell and later, later . . .*

No one could tell him why he had a later. Why had the breeze blown the gas away, sparing only him? Because he alone was wiser than the others? Because he was more important, more favored by fate? Because he had something that *earned* him a later—class, taste, effortless good looks?

Choking awake in his housemaster's bed, he was ashamed of the thoughts he'd had then. The smell of furniture polish fished him into the present, the windows lightening, birds making a racket. In a few hours he would tell Vincent he was leaving and blow up everything the man had labored to arrange. Was there no way to close his eyes again and awaken to Oxford and those days preparing for his viva after the earthquake of meeting her, drinking hope more potent than morphine? In the span of that fortnight, he'd been destroyed and remade, and hope loomed so large he couldn't stop himself from preaching it. He lived three years in that hope, but when she vanished, he knew destruction had only been biding its time, waiting for him to err as it had in no-man's-land. Later, when he could no longer pretend to Grady that she'd left any trail to follow, he'd declared that he'd marry her if only she would send him one word on a card.

—What? Grady scoffed. You'd marry her out of embarrassment? Yes, Jass, embarrassment. She left you naked. You haven't the first idea where she went or why because you hadn't the first idea of *her*. You lived an illusion, and now you've woken up. You're embarrassed because of how wrong you were.

In the silent light of the present day, he dressed in his housemaster's suit. He drank black tea, greeted boys in the house, and taught his first lesson, casuistry to the sixth. His matron assailed him afterwards with a stack of problems that had arisen in his absence. He hacked away at them until the morning break, but nothing could save him from a reckoning with his mentor.

—You've made an upstart out of me, he said to Vincent by way of introduction.

They'd only quarter of an hour in the break, nowhere near what the operation required, though why drag it out if twelve minutes could punch through to the other side?

—Oh, yes? Vincent said. Young Rawlston's coming apart, by the way.

—Again?

—He's cribbed all term, and yesterday he had the front to do it during the exam. I couldn't overlook it, I'm afraid.

As alarmed as Jamie was by what this news portended for his student, he told himself to hold the line.

—There's something else I need to turn over with you, he said. It's slightly urgent.

Vincent set down the books he'd been collecting.

—You aren't going to like it.

—Aren't I?

—And, listen, I'm most awfully sorry about it.

Vincent sat with the tolerant ease he had turned to each of Jamie's felt crises, none of which had constituted a personal betrayal.

—I'll never be able to repay you for everything you've done.

It sounded soppy, but he couldn't think how to rephrase it.

—Going somewhere? Vincent said at last.

—I didn't mean to. I never would have sought it out, and even when I went, I hadn't the faintest intention, it's only that Overall—he knew Mark, you see—

—That man who came to supper the other week?

—Yes—

—He knew your godfather?

—Yes, and he wouldn't leave off no matter what I said, so I thought, especially since we had the Remembrance malarky here, that I'd just go see the place to end it once and for all. I would have told you if I'd thought it was anything.

Vincent looked grave.

—The place is another school?

—Yes.

—Rugby?

—It's called St. Stephen's.

Vincent was now thoroughly confused:

—I'm afraid you're going to have to fill in the details, old boy. Am I to understand you mean to leave us?

He couldn't say it. Vincent pressed: Was he unhappy at Marlborough? Was his scope too small? Was it so long to wait for Vincent's house? Had he been mistreated? Was it money?

The bell rang. He could propose continuing after lunch, but as he'd already done the damage, nothing would be gained from plowing on with it.

It was a third-rate school in the middle of nowhere, he explained. A disaster, he'd been kidnapped by it, and it was a very long story but they couldn't do without him and even though the last thing he ever wanted was to disappoint Vincent, he had to do it. It was breaking his heart, so to speak.

—No need to drag sentiment into it.

Vincent was recovering himself with the icy manner.

—Will you have a house there?

—Not really, Jamie admitted. They've made me headmaster.

Vincent for once was at a loss for words.

—Upstart, you see. It's all your fault.

When they met again after his viva, he was determined to show her he wasn't illiterate.

—Have you any idea what it's like growing up in Cloisterham? he asked.

Partly, he was hoping she'd commiserate. This was before he knew of her atheism and of the feral Irish Catholicism behind it. By Cloisterham, he explained, he meant not murders and opium but the seething cliché of an English cathedral town. Not quite Barchester Towers or the absolutely wet warden in that book his father loved so very much, but Cloisterham, the late-Dickens creation, a world of complacency, vain ambition, and a hidden heart. John Jasper was a cad and worse, he told her, but didn't Jamie know him?

—Is that where you got the name Jasper?

—Oh, no. Not intentionally anyhow.

—I'd have pegged you for Drood.

—The blind, unbridled boy who treats the world as his plaything?

—The very one.

They laughed over it and used it from then as a joke. Now in his final days at Marlborough, the connection to John Jasper seemed gravely apt, both of them having their niches handed to them, unencumbered by matrimony, stunted by unrequited love. The fact that Dickens had ended his earthly course before he could end the story seemed to Jamie ominous for himself. As to the author of his own story, how were the two of them to get on together?

Oh, he understood perfectly well the knock on the head that had been St. Stephen's, and he didn't need the Right Reverend Bishop of Cloisterham dropping coy hints about vocation. The swarm of problems that arrived with each day's post concerning St. Stephen's, these he could conquer eventually. But (and this was the point he wished to make to the Old Boy) did Jamie exist merely to work and obey? Certainly he wished to serve, but did that of necessity mean always feeling a slave? What about his *heart*? Where was the providence in Diana's writing breathlessly of Amanda's return and then refusing to say more? He pressed his correspondence with the woman, measuring the lines he played out to her, inducing her to flirt with him and hunger for his replies. The psychological battlefield mattered, and if he could get Diana to meet him in town when term was over, surely he could prevail upon her to tell him where Amanda resided.

His own headmaster was stunned at his resignation, but once the man got over the shock, he decided that the news reflected brightly on his regime: here was the kind of man Marlborough produced, war hero (ha), youngest housemaster in a generation, now headmaster of his own school at twenty-eight. As it happened, St. Stephen's was known to the Head. He had a glancing acquaintance with its previous headmaster, a man the St. Stephen's prospectus called Saltford-Kent but whom everyone else referred to as S-K. The Head hadn't seen S-K in years, regretted to hear of his ill-health, but recalled him as a decent man, quixotic perhaps but not foolish or misled, a bit stiff in his moral joints but then it suited a monastic little school in Yorkshire. Were the pupils all poor? No? But no People went there, did they? Jamie had to plead ignorance. In the end, the Head gave his imprimatur, and everyone was forced to treat his appointment as a triumph. Things never returned to normal with Vincent, but mercifully only a fortnight remained.

He resumed his old habit of writing to the Old Boy in an exercise book before getting out of bed in the morning. No response had been forthcoming so far, but he persevered out of desperation. He had erred in countless ways, he wrote, but to start with one proximate, it was probably wrong—all right, it was wrong full stop—to have fornicated with her. That act was set aside for man and wife and the possibility of children, but he'd used it and used her for his own gratification. To be fair, she'd also used him, and he wasn't sure he regretted it absolutely, but he could see that fornication was less than ideal.

Who could live to ideals, though? Not even one raised in Cloisterham! The truth—and even if it was wrong, wasn't he supposed to be honest before his creator?—he missed sleeping in a bed with her. How many times had they ever slept together? When he thought of it, he thought mostly of the first time, the week they spent in Fishguard at the cottage of a friend in the Set. Jamie had borrowed Stoat's motorcar and collected her down the lane behind her landlady's house. Their cases had barely fit, and when they stopped outside Fishguard to buy coal, she had to sit on the sack the last few miles.

The place was a caretaker's cottage down the track from the

Big House, where his friend's family stayed at holidays. Upon arrival, as he fussed over the fire, she prepared their supper. He'd never quite confronted the fact that she could cook, but she dug out a stone and set to sharpening the kitchen's blunt knives until they were sharp enough to draw blood, and did, as he took a turn slicing the carrots. She by contrast diced her onions with some geometric legerdemain that accomplished the task in seconds and without tears.

There was a tin tub, and one had to draw water from the well to bathe before the fire. She washed his hair and demanded he teach her how to shave him. They walked along the cliffs and down to the coves. And they played.

She was serious about play, he discovered. You weren't to say no to the other person, meaning you weren't to deny the conceit they proposed. If you didn't like being bounced into a scene—as he'd been one morning returning from the shops to find not Amanda but Aunt Agatha, furious with him for filching coins from her purse—if he didn't like being bounced in, he could take it up with management later, but for now, there they were. When he thought back on the week in Fishguard, it seemed he'd lived many lives. They'd both shed tears as more than one person. Had he ever wept as much? As if every sorrow were being collected and expelled through the others.

Above the kitchen, one reached the bed via a ladder. Atop the feather mattress, pressed against the softness that was her skin, Jamie felt as he imagined it would be in the womb. There they took refuge, abandoning play, stripped to their skins. There words ceased, sight dimmed, the silence of the countryside broken only by the ticking of Jamie's wristwatch on the bedside table. The third day he forgot to wind it, and it fell silent.

He'd been afraid he'd fail with her even though he'd imagined the act countless times in the months since they'd met. In the end it happened before he realized: she had him in hand,

and he was there, her legs pulling and holding him as her fingernails clawed his back where it was sore.

As the week neared its end, their playing grew outlandish. He hadn't even considered the danger when he, under threat from That Woman, the one he saw that night only, had slid the lit candle under the wooden cupboards and burnt them. Later, the remembrance filled him with dread; they could have burnt down the house.

They didn't burn down the house, and that woman didn't kill him. After she exited up to the Big House, Amanda returned in her own clothing and came to him in the bed. He was shaking, and she stripped off to warm him skin to skin. She'd been afraid, then. Of his ire? Of what she'd unleashed? He'd reacted badly, but later, back in Oxford, he longed in a haunted fashion for that woman and the extremities to which she led him. Amanda said that woman would never come back. She hadn't even been there to begin with. It had only been a nightmare, she said. But he wanted that woman back sometimes, and he wished he hadn't acted as he had in the aftermath.

He paid to have the kitchen cupboards repaired and sent the friend a case of champagne, but it was agony returning to ordinary life. If he'd known how wrenching it would be to have to sleep alone again, to look into her eyes in public and see one of her other selves, to catch their expressions in her face, to hear her say one of the phrases significant only to them and not be at liberty to reply with his whole self—if he'd known the torment, would he have gone to Fishguard at all? He supposed the Old Boy would have preferred him to pursue a chaste courtship.

But never to have had Fishguard? No one would ever know what passed between them in that cottage and under those feathers. No one would ever know what passed between them anywhere they were alone. The day return to the sea that summer was recorded in his diary as *walk at Bournemouth, mist, shipyard.* She would never speak of it either, not even in her poems. The salty air, the petrol fumes, the rat or mouse droppings, the force of her tongue, the strength of his arms, and a hand—so it seemed for a minute—as unrelenting as death. These people, the people they shared almost as a family, no one would ever know them, and if one day he died and someone found the letters they wrote one another—he still had the notes from Charlie, from little Mae, Aunt Agatha, Marie—they would believe they'd come upon a bundle from a second hand shop, correspondence in different hands and idioms, kept in his childhood strongbox. Only she knew and remembered. And if she were to vanish forever, it would be as if Fishguard had never happened, as if none of it had happened. He would be like an amputated widower the rest of his days. If his father had ever loved his mother, truly loved her as Jamie was just beginning to understand love—the kind that hit you like a minenwerfer and began creating the world all over again—if his father had loved like that, how could he have survived without her?

He introduced Amanda to the Set in the autumn after Fishguard. With the exception of Grady, who'd gone to work for the museum in London, the rest of the Set had dispersed to other colleges for their graduate studies. They met Thursdays at the Anvil, the table in the snug always held for them, drinks and food brought without asking. Amanda knew enough about politics and philosophy to earn their respect (except Dunham, who respected only Lenin), and sometimes she joined them. The Set assumed that he'd done it with her, but it amused him to insist that they had gone to Wales to discuss Kant. For her part, she enjoyed frustrating their expectations and boggling their attempts to classify her if only by changing up her accent.

The first time she invited him to the press, it was for supper after a long and late printing, a punch run they called it. Gutenberg had premises behind the press rooms. People were drinking beer and vodka as Gute tended pots on a stove. An opera was playing on the gramophone, and some men, whose names Jamie couldn't retain but whom she called the Latvians, were weeping into their beards at it. Her friend Artemis was having a drinking contest with a cockney boy, and an older woman called Olga huddled over a table and spooned red soup into her mouth like an orphan at a workhouse. He'd felt an itch inside his shirt, and even when he'd rolled up his sleeve and scratched it red, the itch remained. She had persuaded him to stay all night since it would end too late to climb through Stoat's window, but once the opera began to play and the goulash was served, she behaved as though he were just another member of the press, part of a crowd and not special to her. She was louder there. They laughed at her risqué jokes and treated her as one would treat a batman who could repair a broken-down motor. She showed him the machines and the one she called Boanerges. He'd never felt more a stranger in his own land.

Trysts were possible, and they arranged them, but after the excitement of the stolen hour wore off, he began to understand that he didn't want trysts. He wanted to be alone with her, undisturbed for days on end. Holidays were the worst. His family expected him at the Rectory, and when he asserted the privilege as doctoral student of staying behind in Oxford to work, one of them seemed always to drop by unannounced to take him to lunch. A stroke of luck arrived several months after Fishguard when Uncle Mark announced a trip to Rome and invited Jamie to accompany him as secretary. Jamie did want to see Rome, but he'd reached the point that he couldn't bear more than a week away from her. Providentially, Grady saw things in a different light. Rome was the top of his lust list, as he called it, and that spring Grady's only holiday prospect was to pack a case full of books and mooch around his grandfather's hunting lodge in Wester Ross, where at least you could get good fish even if you had to catch it yourself.

It didn't take the knowing to see a solution, not when it stripped off before him like a boy before a swimming pond. He presented Grady to Mark as a friend from Corpus, professional in London, and passionate aficionado of religious art. Grady was his most charming self, and by the end of lunch, not only was it arranged that he would accompany Mark to Rome, but he'd also given his card to three of Mark's seminarians, who looked just as eager to be seduced as Grady looked to lead them astray.

Jamie and Amanda took the night train to Fort William and were collected by a caretaker. Amanda had felt unwell on the train, and once their things had been loaded into the caretaker's car, she fell asleep across Jamie's knee, even though the road to Applecross was atrocious. He had bought two cheap rings from a pawnbroker, and they were wearing them, which let people believe them man and wife. By the time they'd weaved past Lochcarron, climbed up a pass and wound down through moorland again, he could feel she was not simply feverish but burning up. The man got their things into the so-called lodge, really a croft overlooking the sound, and Jamie, having settled her onto the settee was forced to ask for a doctor. Her throat was swollen now, and she could barely talk. The caretaker had Scottish words to describe her condition, none of them good. He went away and came back with a woman, who examined her. It wasn't the diphtheria, the woman said, but a putrid throat was serious. She sent the man for her things and settled in for the night. They kept Amanda close to the fire, and on the fourth day, the fever broke and Mrs. McKyle went home. On the sixth day, Amanda was swallowing without pain. Just as it was time for them to leave Applecross, she was walking with him down to the shore. Mrs. McKyle said she had made the quickest putrid-throat recovery she'd ever seen. They shared the upstairs bed the last two nights, but she couldn't do anything but sleep. If Dante had been charged with designing a holiday in the last detail to punish his concupiscence, he could not have tormented him worse.

—Marlborough nine five, he said into the telephone.

—Jamie! Is everything all right?

—You've rung *me*, Beth.

—So I did.

He put his hand across the mouthpiece and pretended to speak to a boy. He was alone in his Marlborough study, but his sister's tone, not to mention her artifice, called for an escape route.

—How's Father? he asked.

He'd avoided a relapse, Beth reported, but everyone was desperately worried. She paused for him to ask why, but he let the line crackle.

—I've met this pupil of yours, she said at last. He has quite a touch with the boys at our school.

By which she meant the village school she patronized. His sisters had been to dinner at the Rectory, he learned. Wilberforce had made an impression.

—I hope you aren't expecting me to apologize for him, Jamie said. I've spent all of twelve hours in his company.

—But why *on earth* did you drag Father into it?

—Do you really want to have this out over a telephone, Beth?

He knew her complaint wasn't the boy. Her complaint was he himself, his failure to help sufficiently with their father, his disloyalty in accepting St. Stephen's, his—cue list of deficiencies going back and back.

—Put your hackles down, she said. I'm quite fond of young Wilberforce, and so are Robert and the children.

—Your children?

—Your nieces, who miss you. As do your sisters.

—I've a lesson in a moment.

—I only wish, she said, you would patch it up with Lucy.

—Oh, for heaven's sake!

Of course, this was why Beth was disturbing him of a Tuesday afternoon. Poor Lucy was desperately upset, she gushed, and so was Agnes.

—What do you expect *me* to do about it?

—Jamie.

—She hit me first.

—This isn't school. This is your *family*.

Beth continued until she'd worn him down and won his promise to apologize. He should have rung off when she mentioned Lucy, but Beth had a knack for making him feel she was on his side and then entangling him all over again; the fact that she was the most reasonable of his sisters always left him unprepared. Everyone considered Agnes the most difficult, but they hadn't had to grow up an Irish twin to Lucy, who had their father wrapped around her finger from the instant she was born though no one accused *her* of being spoilt.

He hadn't behaved as he ought that evening last month, though who but his sisters would have expected it? They were all snapping under the strain of their father's crisis. It was difficult enough to manage the man, his physician, and the hospital before factoring in the raw fear the whole episode caused. When Beth had them all to supper, he ought to have spotted the ambush, but then the nature of ambush was that one never spotted it.

He'd used language unbecoming. He'd been churlish and sarcastic and everything he thought he'd left behind. They'd never even *met* Amanda, except Lucy of course, and in the intervening months when Jamie had supposed they'd forgotten all about her, Lucy had been gossiping and nattering and whatever sisters did until the girls had universally turned against her. They'd kept their hotly developed opinions to themselves, naturally, until the sudden and unexpected occasion of Amanda's rumored return.

The night of the ambush, they had just sat down to eat—Jamie, Beth, Agnes, and Lucy—when Agnes barged into it: just what were his intentions with that woman?

—What woman?

—You know perfectly well! Lucy snapped.

—I don't see that my private life is any of your concern.

If he hadn't been so blindsided by Diana's initial letter—the content of it but also its arrival mere days after his father's brush with death—he never would have rung Grady, begged him to come to Marlborough for the night, and then unloaded the hours-long thread of his hopes and fears. He realized too late that he ought to have sworn Grady to silence. Grady never would have told his sisters, but clearly he'd told Lucy's husband, Michael, with whom Grady lunched every Saturday since Michael had sponsored his crossing the Tiber the year before.

—This is typical of you, just typical! Lucy vented when he refused to discuss Amanda. You're always storing up secrets, not thinking for a *second* whether they affect anyone but yourself.

—I don't answer to Jesuit whisper circuits.

Sometimes when he opened a skirmish with one of his sisters, the others could be diverted into taking sides, but that night, they refused to break rank. His private life was very much their concern, Agnes insisted, as it affected the family and would certainly affect their father. He rejected such assertions, but they badgered and needled, carting it all out, even things Jamie didn't realize they knew: She was Irish. Amanda wasn't her real name. What else had she lied about? Her unsavory associates. Her class. Her lack of people. And what about Marlborough? (This was before St. Stephen's even entered the picture.) How would he carry on with a girl like that while housemaster at a public school?

—I'm going to marry her, if you must know.

—You aren't!

—And I don't care what any of you think.

Their harridan vomit spewed everywhere. What about her year-long desertion? Where had she gone and with whom? Why had she returned? What was she after? What about her temper? (Lucy had more than asked for it when they met.) Her vulgar, libertine, cadging harlotry—

—I'm leaving.

He threw his napkin onto his dinner plate and thrust back his chair.

—It's all very well for you, Beth said hotly, but what about Father?

—If you marry her, you'll have to tell him everything.

—If you don't, he'll find it out.

—Perhaps things you don't even know yourself, said Lucy.

—I swear you're growing more insufferable by the month.

—Do you think his heart can take a strain like that?

—At least I won't break it by defecting to Rome and making his grandchildren bloody papists.

This was when Lucy hit him. He slapped her back, her fists flew, and they shouted bitterly, their first wale-on scuffle since he was nine. In the end, Agnes and Beth had to pull them apart, and the next morning he explained a blackening eye to his colleagues as an encounter with a garden rake.

Even if he could find Amanda, even if he could learn to call her Marion, even if he could cross the desert that separated them, how could he bring her into this family, with these vipers and their viper master in bishop's clothing? He didn't want their tentacles to touch her. He wanted to lie by the river and listen to her words rippling like the water, her mouth by his ear as they watched the clouds part, her speech breathless and racing.

He awoke coughing again, hurled from his housemaster's bed by liquid in his lungs. He'd been dreaming of the attack, the same dream for eight years yet different each time. One minute you're all there together shin-deep in mud, creeping over the top for the raid, danger of course, danger always, but you and the others still one, a single body. Wire-cutters at the belt, rifle in hand, you advance without the usual clamor—one could say like ghosts, but there were so many ghosts that the comparison had lost its meaning—silently in this never-quiet war, until even more silently, cloud slips through cloud on the edge of a breeze that moments earlier you praised for masking your approach. And then it's happening, the thing you've all heard about, without warning or whistle, and it's cutting you down, they've fallen already, writhing and—what was the point of rehearsing it again?—they've fallen, you too are falling except the wind comes and the swimming-baths whirl away as if a finger has been drawn across everyone but you, and you're alone with them, unable to help the dying because you can hardly breathe yourself, and you know—they've told you this back in a command tent—that the gas collected down the places where they fell, and if you went there, you'd be unable to help them or yourself.

When he overcame the dream-induced choking, he saw it was just past four though dawn had already broken. And he felt the vibration of another dream, the one before the gas, a dream of John but as he'd been at school, wearing fencing kit and darting down the strip looking cloaked for righteousness. If the war had been fought on fencing mats, John would have decided it for them. In the dream they fenced, and John knew his secret places, thrusting his point into them one by one. Then Jamie's shirt was red with blood, John's face red with feeling, and Jamie fell to the ground sobbing, *Forgive me, please, I want to be better.* Could they not return, he asked, to summers at the Rectory, when Jamie invented their games and John took them to extremes? *We must eat it raw, we're castaways,* John would say of the fish they caught above the weir. Jamie must be bound with rope to be keelhauled under the rowboat. They must fast two days as prisoners, singe the soles of their feet as martyrs, and as monks copy long passages from foreign books with chicken feathers for quills. The summer Jamie was thirteen, they'd spent a month in Coverdale at the home of a distant relation. There John had rejected the strictures of time, and they'd stayed out full days and sometimes nights roaming the moors and dales, talking endlessly or not at all, entirely candid, entirely free of supervision.

Could it be true that he was being given a second chance, with John at least? Gas had come in the fog, and wind had blown it off, the same wind, he imagined, that had rushed into the upper room and made the apostles speak other tongues. Those fearful men became fiery evangelists, in a day, a moment. Had something happened to him, too, at St. Stephen's, or was he merely trying to make his muddle look coherent? *There's so much we must tell each other*, Jamie said to John in the dream. *Please, please tell me. What happened when you died? I never knew, you see. But now you're back, and I mean to be better. To think I don't have to talk to you in my dreams any longer.*

He'd written John twice since the day at St. Stephen's but received only a cursory reply: *Term's a crush. Thanks for report of Wilberforce.* It would take time before he could speak with John as freely as he used to. It had been so long since he'd been candid with another human being.

Had he ever been as candid with anyone, though, as he'd been with Amanda along the river, in letters, in Scotland, at Fishguard? Even with his godfather, he had lacked candor. He'd wanted to be truthful with Mark, but sometimes the story was so intricate, the effort of deciding what pertained so vast, that he considered it more or less in the interests of health to give a précis or skip it altogether. He could imagine what Mark would say about the Business, for instance: dangerous, foolhardy, illegal. But if Mark truly understood it—the artful practice of English vice in a program of self-regulation and fellowship—then Mark would have to condone it as nothing worse than a discreet hobby.

There had been an experiment his second year at Oxford

when Mark had proposed someone else hear his confession. He'd been stung by the suggestion and in reply had provided mind-crushing detail about a party the Set had given. Mark, after absolving him and telling him to abstain from drinking for a week, explained that wasn't what he meant. No one expected him to stay under his godfather's wing forever; he was a man, and perhaps it was time he unburden himself to someone less intimately involved. Despite the lingering sense of failure, Jamie warmed to the idea. Imagine being able to tell absolutely everything to a stranger. He often wished for a Catholic confessional, where you could whisper everything to a screen as often as you wished, and all you had to do in exchange was tailor your admissions to one of the thousand and one sins on the Catholic list. Mark gave him three names, including that of a Sister, who he said wasn't Roman but a proper English nun. Jamie had the sense that Mark was trying to offer him a mother. It was one of Mark's ideas that his missing mother was at the root of something, and it was no good explaining that it wasn't. How could he miss what he'd never had? In the mud, men had often called for their mothers. When he had been delirious with trench fever, they said he had called for Beth, and he had to explain that Beth was his sister.

He chose the curate Mark claimed not to know personally. Their first meeting, he tried the man out with a few light transgressions: drinking to excess, blasphemy, pinching gin from a shop for the thrill of it. The man listened carefully and then asked if that was all. Smiling, he said he could try harder next time. The man proceeded to counsel him as if he were only just beginning to examine his conscience. He grew so vexed that he admitted the God business out of spite.

—Do you mean to say you don't believe at all?

—Not a whit, he said, atheist through and through.

It was clear he'd made the man think harder than he was used to thinking. Why, the man asked, had he come to a clergyman for confession if he didn't believe in God? Jamie rushed to assure him he wasn't mocking. He found confession good for his mental regulation, and because of, well, his nerves, which started after . . .

—Ah, the man said cottoning on at last, say no more.

He could see perfectly well why Jamie might wish to attend to mental regulation even if they never quite saw eye to eye on the God question. The man obviously viewed him as a challenge and his atheism as a war wound—to be cured by a curate! The trouble was he grew so very bored with the man, and the man seemed so fundamentally innocent that Jamie couldn't bring himself to divulge the bulk of it. He stopped seeing him but let Mark believe he hadn't.

At the same time, Hilary Term of his second year, he began to tire of the Set. He attributed his feelings to the strain of his studies, but when he went home for Easter, the real strain began. In the brutal slog of Holy Week with his father, he yearned for Stoat's gin and Dunham's Bolshevik harangues. Through the interminable Easter liturgies, he mentally debunked each theological claim he heard, recollecting what certain philosophers had already said to leave the enterprise in the dust. By Good Friday, it was in the dust all right, but then he wished only to rake through the books on Dunham's shelves for the precise argument that would extinguish the thing once and for all.

He exchanged long letters with Stoat and Grady. Stoat considered theological questions best ignored. *Starve them of oxygen and they'll float on their merry way* was his position. Stoat's letters teemed with discussions of the nature of time, broken only by descriptions of the dazzling, delightful girls he fell in love with every time he came up for air. These were all called Edith or Vera, and despite Stoat's high excitement, they bored Jamie senseless. Grady was a more satisfying correspondent on the God front in the years before his conversion. That Easter he wrote Jamie from Vienna, where he was chaperoning a maiden aunt, and eventually Jamie realized the majority of Grady's pages had been given over to describing religious art, and not in a spirit of criticism. He made a wager with himself, written down and sealed in an envelope with a guinea, that Grady would go over to Rome before he was thirty. If Grady could be allowed to study representations of the Virgin Mary while entertaining a steady stream of seminarians unhindered, he would have found his niche.

When Jamie returned for Trinity term that year, the Set were sharp and bursting with ambition. Dunham unfolded his plan for a Communist guild and demanded they all enlist. The next morning, Jamie found it impossible to get out of bed. He had no fever, his lungs were fine, but he was so physically enervated, he lay in bed two days. He had something already arranged with Tim and Malcolm, set up during the holiday, hungry and desperate, but when the appointment came, he accepted every out they offered and wound up taking scarcely anything at all. Tim warmed some broth, and they made him have it with toast and tea. They asked if he was quite well. They suggested he might wish to refresh his acquaintances. The Set seemed to them dreary, and the Business, as stimulating as it was, should always, they felt, be extracurricular. He ought to take up a second hobby, Malcolm advised. Jamie laughed it off, and they passed the evening making jokes at the expense of model yachtsmen and photographers, stamp collectors and lawn tennis players.

Sometimes when the weather was fine, he read out on the grass, and at a certain time of day, strains of the choir would waft over the walls from Christ Church. Once, he heard a piece he remembered from school. He hadn't been to an evensong since leaving the Vale, but suddenly he felt it would be an amusingly transgressive thing to do and that if any of the Set found out, it would stoke their ire for evenings on end. Unless they assumed he'd gone to study the enemy, which he supposed could be true.

He strode through the gates of Christ Church with the insolence of the socialist he professed himself to be, slouched in to the chapel, declined to reverence anything, and sat as far from the choir as possible. The candles had been lit, and even before they started to sing, while only the prelude hummed from the organ, he felt weak everywhere he could be weak. He didn't recognize the things they sang, but the sound shot into his ears like uncut medicine and he wanted to lie down on the floor and feel it vibrate through him.

Despite what he'd told the curate, he wasn't an atheist. Even the Set knew it. They believed him a promising agnostic who would soon abandon childhood attachments and wake fully to reality. At one point Dunham had subjected him to an inquisition, pressing him on why he did not cut ties with his father, and more important with his wretched godfather, who persisted to the point of running a theological college. The fact that the Vale had opened its doors to Russians during the war and become known briefly as an Orthodox college was a distinction of no interest to Dunham. It was all religion, a lie and a scam.

Evensong was an aesthetic experience, he maintained, yet in the wooden track of his mind, he knew it was his mother tongue: this music, this prayerbook, this English. When he was small, he had thought of God as one might a magician. He would say his prayers a certain number of times as he lay in bed, and if he could get through the prescribed set before falling asleep, it would bring good luck. (He should have been a Catholic after all and at least had the rosary.) Yet despite his childhood superstitions (and his father would have thundered if he'd known), there was also in the dark bed a fervent love, a true fear, an unguarded trust that God was God, a tangible presence as his mind escaped his command and his prayers disintegrated into sleep.

Attending evensong, he wondered whether those childhood experiences could have been true. The well-oiled mainline track rehearsed the logic of the Set, but the wooden-cart rattled, *the more you say it, the more desperate you look.*

Then, that spring, the wind rushed in, she rushed in, the rest as dust.

Three days before the end of his Marlborough career, a letter arrived from Diana: *You win, I relent! Thursday the fifteenth, eleven o'clock, the Egypt hall. British Museum, in case you haven't worked out where.* It was the seventh of July in the year of our Lord 1926 and people could still surprise you. In one week, time would begin to move again.

The breakthrough with Diana sent his mind into a whirlwind about St. Stephen's, as if removing one stumbling block had dispatched the Hun to the other front. He'd been corresponding about the school since June, but never to the point of sitting up past midnight, filling page after page with the wild, disjointed thoughts that assailed him. A systematic person would have invented codes to categorize them, staffing, curricula, discipline, religious life, sport, leisure, funding. Overall had given him a pre-war yearbook as well as a leaflet-cum-prospectus from last year. As far as Jamie could tell, little variety graced their lives at St. Stephen's. No music. No theater or art. He supposed photography might count, but he was not disposed towards it given what he knew could go on in darkrooms and given his impression of the housemaster who supervised the club. Overall had urged him not to be hasty in making changes to staff, particularly the housemasters who had served the Academy for so long. Change, Overall said, was better incremental.

He needed a confidant, someone unentagled who could think strategically and ruthlessly about matters most essential. Halfway down a list of questions about the chapel, a thought came to him, unexpected and unexpectedly calming: Kardleigh. The last time he'd confided in his physician had been the night Jamie told him about the knowing. They'd been having fish pie and porter to celebrate his passing his Mods when he mentioned that sometimes he knew things without being told.

—Never anything useful. No exam questions, no winning bets.

No secrets a person might pay him to keep. Kardleigh asked a few pointed questions and suggested he stop thinking of it as an occult talent.

—I do no such thing.

—I think you do, Kardleigh said. All that's happening is that you're heightening your sense of observation, translating into your conscious mind a constellation of details you haven't realized you're perceiving.

—Like some burnt-out Sherlock Holmes?

—Minus cocaine and misanthropy, one hopes.

—Ha, ha.

—You aren't, are you?

—What?

—Cocaine.

Jamie assured Kardleigh he'd never touched the stuff, to Kardleigh's visible relief. Jamie confessed that his father had the same ability in spades. On countless occasions his father had read his mind, always at the most inconvenient junctures and never when he wished his father would understand. Kardleigh viewed such claims with suspicion.

—The thing is, Jamie said, I can't think of its ever happening before OC.

A silence developed at the mention of his collapse in Oxford Circus. Kardleigh lit a cigarette. He asked if Jamie suspected a return of neurasthenia. Jamie denied it though the weakness had certainly crossed his mind. He asked if Kardleigh had heard of any neurasthenia patients who had developed abilities after their nerves collapsed. Kardleigh couldn't think of any, and he didn't think Jamie's so-called knowing was an example either.

—I'm sure you won't like hearing this, Kardleigh said, but it's probably a simple matter of maturity.

—When I was a child, I thought as a child?

He lit one of Kardleigh's cigarettes even though his own were in his pocket.

—I thought I told you not to smoke, Kardleigh said. You can be as ironic as you like, but it's perfectly natural to reach a mental breakthrough at your age. You can read and understand things you couldn't before, can't you?

Jamie said he supposed that was the point of his studies. The conversation went round from there, Kardleigh expositing on cognitive leaps and Jamie feeling once again like a child.

Later, after they'd settled the bill and were finishing the last pint, his emotions drained away and he found himself asking Kardleigh what had happened back at the asylum. He asked it in the perfect tense, as if Kardleigh had already mentioned it. Kardleigh confessed that he didn't know how long he was good for it. The men he'd learned from in the war, the men he admired and looked to, had emigrated, left the field, or died. This week, one of his patients had been out on leave and killed someone. The patient's mother, as it happened. Kardleigh had thought him fit, so in a sense he had killed her. Jamie lit two cigarettes and gave one to his physician, who took it with an unsteady hand. He felt a dull dread at the thought of losing Kardleigh, and then before the year was out, Kardleigh had resigned from the asylum and gone to London to study music. Jamie hadn't seen him since.

Frogs were croaking in the fountain outside his study window, piercing the warm Marlborough night with their courtship. Jamie closed his St. Stephen's notebook and riffled through his filing cabinet for the Christmas card Kardleigh had sent last year. He'd no idea if the man was still in London. For all Jamie knew, he could have fled to America like his mentor or taken a post sounding some organ in Aberdeenshire. Nevertheless, he penned a note to his former physician. He told him he was coming to town and asked him to dinner. Dropping the envelope in the basket for the morning post, he felt a tranquil certainty that it would reach Kardleigh and that the man would accept. Kardleigh knew nothing of schools, but he listened. And he'd worked miracles before.

When the knowing first happened with Amanda, he'd been too overwhelmed to grasp what was happening. Could you blame him? There they were, in a distant pub some days after he'd sent her *Quid Pro Quo*. She had written back, speaking of herself in the third person. *Amanda sat on the tiles of the w.c. sobbing like a banshee except the noise of Boanerges drownded it out so's no one could hear and she wanted to shout, Who is this Jasper*? Later, at the pub, they played the game he'd invented in his story, trading questions; the more candid your answer, the better the question you were allowed to ask next. He heard something break into her accent and asked where she'd been born.

—Galway.

—Catholic?

She uttered a profanity and said she didn't believe rubbish. When he told her he, too, was an atheist, an expression came across her face, only for an instant, not even as long as her accent had slipped. But then she began to talk of Nietzsche, and he knew her unbelief wasn't true however much she might want it to be. And he knew, like a second wave of nausea after a bout of drunken vomiting, that his atheism wasn't true either. And he was so unnerved by both realizations that he hadn't recognized the knowing.

Two years later, on that demented night when he'd left Amanda at her lodgings after the disastrous introduction to Lucy, he'd had to summon all his strength because Lucy had been so horrible to her, and she had been so difficult back, and he couldn't see how to knit her into his family. He returned to his rooms at Corpus and was gazing at his bookshelves, hands shaking, when it came to him: he was going to marry her. What's more, he didn't have to do anything. Things were simply going to line up eventually. And he was so overwhelmed by the earth-shattering good news that he fell across the footstool, saying *Thank you, thank you.* He was in hands much bigger than his own, sobbing with thanksgiving for her and with shame that he had been so stiff-necked all these years. He was angry, was he? He resented surviving the war without so much as a bullet wound, felt guilty for spending the final months cozy in Mainz, for languishing in hospital with trench fever during most of the Somme, for languishing again from the gas and missing Passchendaele, all this after he'd been too young when it started so missed the first waves of killing? He had been saved, and for what? So he could slouch around Oxford for a year and then let in with the Set? So he could tempt the darkest elements by dabbling in the Business when he'd no idea what was what? So he could blaspheme on a daily basis, lie to himself and others, and contribute nothing to the common weal beyond some effortless good looks, now surely fading? All this had filled his docket, and still mercy broke him open across that footstool, like shrapnel but bloodless. No penance, no punishment, not even a purging wound, but *this*, radical, warrantless good dropped onto his head from so far up that it fell like a 5.9. He was the last person to deserve anything good, and yet here she was, the most mysterious, difficult, perfect, wonderful person he had ever known—*I couldn't have dreamed you up*! She didn't realize it, but she knew his heart and now he knew hers. And he knew two other things, as if the knowing came in threes, and who knew maybe it did, he knew it was time to stop pretending, to stop his childish strop. It felt—and the image came to him as it was happening—as if he had been picked up by the scruff of his neck, given a smacking both kindly and firm, and told distinctly that enough was enough. The eternal patience for such a performance had run out because more important work was at hand. Jamie wondered for a moment if the work referred to his doctorate, which was interesting but not earth-shattering. He imagined receiving another smack, the sort you'd give a cheeky boy to remind him what you could do if he tried it on again. No, not his doctorate. *Concentrate, boy.*

He saw a labyrinth. He saw her inside, a little girl with tangled hair who needed to wash her face, calling for someone, for Boanerges (but that was what she called the printing press—*concentrate*), calling for someone to find her, to lead her out again, to save her.

—You're joking if you think I'm that person.

We often joke, but we aren't joking now.

Term at Marlborough ended at last. Prizes were given, speeches delivered, the assistant master in Jamie's house, Neils, was promoted. The boys had grown affectionate towards him in his final days, but he knew they preferred Neils. The only person to withhold his warmth was Vincent.

Jamie warded off the sound of burning dogs by concentrating on his appointment the next afternoon with Diana, an event he considered the commencement of the Big Push, though without the sordid outcomes of France—please! Neils was leaving early in the morning to catch a ferry and offered Jamie a lift in his motorcar since the main branch station was on the way. As they packed the motorcar at dawn, Neils overflowing with magnanimity, Jamie explained that he needed to make a quick detour to collect a young man, a project of his father's who needed escort back to town.

—You're a chaperone now?

—At Father's beck and call, as ever.

Neils commiserated and then feigned chagrin at his own promotion to housemaster. It was jolly unfair for Jamie to swan off and leave the mess to him, he said. Jamie consoled him with a description of the housemaster's wine-cellar, which was small but contained some expensive vintages that Jamie had restrained himself from opening. Neils declared he'd endure what he must.

They arrived at the Rectory as the sun was breaking through the trees. Wilberforce folded himself into the back of the motorcar looking as though he had sat up all night, had too much to drink, or both. His father's housekeeper handed him an address in Chelsea and declared Mr. Wilberforce expected his son at half past four in the afternoon. What he was meant to do with Wilberforce all day, the woman did not say.

Neils left them at the station, and thankfully the boy fell asleep as soon as they boarded the train, leaving Jamie to consider his options: he could take the boy home straight away and hope someone would take custody, but this risked making himself look foolish if no one were there. It also risked derailing the timetable, which possessed very little margin. He scoured his mind for places he could deposit the boy while he went to the museum, but given the boy's impaired state, Jamie couldn't see leaving him. He would have to cart the boy along, though he supposed it might make him look more plausible to Diana. He was not a jilted lover; he was headmaster of a public school tackling a myriad of difficulties, beginning with this hapless if good-looking young man. He had not booked into his club so he could moon over a woman who had left him; he had come to town to conduct business, to recruit staff, and to make more arrangements than he could enumerate. His timetable was thoroughly overcrowded, but he had made time amidst this busy day with the boy to pop in at the museum and consult Diana.

He'd made the mistake of drinking coffee from the trolley and knew that if he didn't take exercise, he risked a bad interval. They arrived on schedule, which mercifully left time to walk briskly to the club. After refreshing himself in the cloakroom,

Jamie realized he would have to feed the puppy. The boy declared himself not hungry, however, so after getting a cup of tea inside him, Jamie led them on another march, this time to the museum. There, he purchased a leaflet for the boy and scanned the staircase for Diana. He wasn't sure he'd recognize her, but he didn't think he had changed much. A school party bubbled into the gallery, and behind them a woman waved: Artemis. *Diana*. She looked as he remembered, but her hair was pulled back, her frock less flattering. He left Wilberforce examining hieroglyphics and went to meet her.

—Diana, he said leaning in to kiss her cheek, though I suppose I ought to call you Mrs. Porter?

—Don't. It sounds queer.

—You're called it, though, aren't you?

—Yes, but not by you.

He kissed her other cheek, and she called him Jas.

—Perhaps you'd like to be called something else, though?

—Not at all, he said.

She was looking over his shoulder at the boy.

—I didn't know you had a brother.

He explained: his pupil, chaperoning, in the midst of arrangements for the school whose helm he would shortly take.

—What about Marlborough?

Time was expiring as they slogged through unnecessary details of his career.

—Please, he said, Amanda.

—Marion. One isn't allowed to use the other name anymore.

—Very well.

—Not even privately.

His face prickled:

—Why not?

—It's the first thing she made me promise, never to say that name again.

The party of schoolgirls was making a racket. Diana led him

around the back of a case where it was quieter. Marion had been abroad, she said.

—Where?

Abroad, and now she was working as governess to a lovely family in town. Marion had no inclination to leave the family or return to the press, and, before he asked, she wasn't married and had no man in her acquaintance.

—But when can I see her?

His heart was working hard. He'd take the boy home and be with her after lunch. He would set eyes upon her, and whatever he'd done to push her away, he would renounce forever. He had all week in town even if she were only free a short time each day. He would agree to anything. If only she would speak to him, he could make them as they were, and the odd creature Diana was describing would melt away beneath the flame.

—Oh, Diana said with a giggle, but you can't *see* her.

—What do you mean?

—I promised I'd tell no one she was back.

Most especially Diana had promised not to tell him.

—But you *have* told me.

—Yes, and you mustn't, *mustn't* give me away. I couldn't bear it.

Then to the astonishment on his face:

—She's my only friend. You must promise you won't spoil it.

—But . . .

—And you know *her*. It'll come right in the end, I'm sure, but for the moment you must let her alone.

—But . . . ?

Why had he come if only to hear that he was barred from seeing Amanda—who, unaccountably, must be called now by the name she'd always detested?

—Why did you ask me here? he demanded.

—Oh, she said shyly, I felt ever so sorry for you.

She was toying with him. He'd never paid her much attention

in Oxford because even though she was Amanda's friend, he didn't believe Amanda confided anything of substance to her. But as they stood beside a case containing jars with mummified organs, Jamie knew all at once that she had envied Amanda and, despite being married herself, still did. She rattled on about her husband, Bernard this, Bernard that, implicitly lording it over Amanda, a stubbornly single woman occupied entirely with minding children that weren't hers, whereas Diana was expecting, she hoped it wasn't vulgar or bad luck to say, but she was, in the new year. It didn't show yet but that was her figure for you, slim the year round no matter what you did with it.

He couldn't turn her flirtation to his advantage. She wanted to continue collecting his letters and bringing them home to her sad little flat to read while Bernard beavered away at his job and his medical studies. Another school party swarmed the gallery, and the long-awaited interview came fruitlessly to an end.

As he and Wilberforce ate lunch back at the club, Jamie's thoughts began to sort themselves into pigeonholes. Diana hadn't said where Amanda's lovely family lived, but she had let slip—he realized with growing excitement as he recalled each turn of the maddening conversation—that she'd once met Amanda with her charges in the park behind the Victoria & Albert, where they were wont to go looking at the toy collection as they learned corresponding words in French and German. Previously, Amanda had not had any German, only French. She'd been in Germany, then. She'd gone, evidently, where Jamie had always refused to go, but he had to concentrate because the main course was arriving and he was going to have to dismantle the unexploded bomb of this puppy (oh, when would his metaphors sort themselves like his thoughts?). Wilberforce had got into some kind of mess at the museum, and he had to deal with it before the boy became an even bigger problem.

The rest of the afternoon banished Diana from his mind, and once he'd met the boy's father, learned what else Wilberforce had been up to, restrained the man from striking his son, conducted a hairy negotiation with his own father across the telephone to win Wilberforce's return to the Rectory, and finally put Wilberforce back on the train, tipping the guard and begging him to keep the boy out of trouble, he felt himself firing on all cylinders, as the saying went.

Sleep was impossible after such a day. Walking the streets of London at night wasn't as carefree as tramping the fields in Yorkshire, though one would think a captain in his majesty's terrestrial forces, even an ex-captain, would shrug at an urban foe. The men he glimpsed sleeping rough in the park may have once answered to military discipline, but they probably didn't have the strength to kill anything larger than a rat, perhaps not even that if it moved fast and bit hard.

If she frequented the V&A, why could not he? He imagined falling at her feet, but the vision had all the substance of a memory from childhood, as if she and the past occupied the same cosmos, equally longed for, equally unattainable. He turned into Regent's Park, keeping to the wide, lit paths. Men slept in the shadows there, as if amidst ghosts of the fallen. In some way it seemed she resided there too, just as aloof as Marsen and Thorpe and Billings and the rest of his men who would never rise until the last day (provided it was true). (Sorry, flippant! God of love, let it be true!) Those men he would never again see in this life, and even though it hadn't been nearly so long since she'd vanished, her absence felt possibly just as lasting. At first he'd thought she would turn up any day. On his birthday last October, he'd been sure he would hear from her. Eventually he'd disciplined himself to stop looking for her handwriting in the post. Mercifully, the whirlwind of Marlborough had caught him up just as he supposed actual children, when they filled your home, eclipsed other concerns. Now, the Marlborough maelstrom had been replaced by the sinking ocean liner that was St. Stephen's.

Diana had referred to his sojourn in town as his holiday, as if he were there for pleasure. He told her he hadn't had a holiday since [insert fumbling over Amanda's name] and couldn't imagine ever having one without her. Diana had plainly thought him overwrought and suggested he take in the theater to give his mind a rest. He'd met Americans who spoke of holidays as vacations. Returning to the club after midnight and collapsing across the bed, he hungered for an American vacation, a span of time when he simply vacated his thoughts, his position, his family, his clothing. He pictured himself lying nude on an Italian verandah, gazing at the scenery, thinking absolutely nothing at all.

For the next two days, he threw himself into preparations for St. Stephen's. He'd wake near noon, take lunch, and then spend the afternoon and evening with his correspondence. When other people were getting into bed, alone or together, he would take to the streets and to the paths of Regent's Park. Twice he'd encountered a man along the path, mutilated face exposed in the moonlight. Twice Jamie had avoided him, but tonight, pressed by guilt, Jamie stepped off the path and sat on a rock a few feet away. When the man did not protest, Jamie offered a cigarette. There was a sound like a wheeze, and an arm sprang out to accept it.

They smoked. Using the language one used towards another man who'd been in it, they played out line to one another. Where they'd been and when. What regiments. The man's voice rasped, barely there; the shell had landed as he had been crawling out of the gas. He wished now it had done its office. The man wheezed on about everything and nothing, and in the wooden-cart track, Jamie began to wonder if he couldn't help this man. Doyle he was called. Could his father not find a situation for him minding some door of the cathedral? Doyle came from Dublin town. He'd joined up in '15, partly for the adventure, he said, partly for the money, but mostly to escape his father's fist. All this, he gestured vaguely to his face, hadn't happened until the last year of it. They'd fitted him with a mask, though not the best. Some were true works of art they were, like the one he'd seen on an officer, a living portrait. His had been plain, but it covered the monster. Jamie didn't ask if he meant how he looked or what he'd done. When Jamie asked to see the mask, Doyle said he'd hocked it. When Jamie asked if he needed money to get home to Dublin, Doyle laughed bitterly. Oh, he'd been back to the devil town all right, as soon as they dismissed him from hospital. They'd given him a ticket home, a lump of cash, and the promise of a pension.

Jamie passed cigarettes to Doyle and to the other two men who arrived while Doyle was talking. They knew Doyle, had also been in it, also were Irish. Surely, he thought, here in the dark, in the circle of the war, someone could shed light on Amanda and on that island so many fled with wounds too deep to name.

Ah, that's how it was, the oldest man said in a leisurely drawl as though they'd closed the doors of the pub for the night so they could play the pipes and the fiddles and the other things she told him they did against the law. *First you must learn of the truckely howl*, she would say, mimicking her uncle Feidhelm. His name was like exams, she said, you pass 'em or you fail 'em.

—Ah, that's how it was, said the man like Uncle Fail 'em.

Lord Kirshner wanted you for his army, he a Kerry man himself so your mam didn't mind as much, but sure they were glad of the coin.

—They were glad of his coin when he came wearing the mask they were, said young Fail 'em.

—Leave it in the ground, Doyle graveled.

But Fail 'em wouldn't leave it, in the ground or in the air:

—When you come back, with your mask or not—

—You looked as pretty as the day you left.

—Ah, back you come, and instead of a parade, what do you think?

Jamie hadn't a notion.

—Now you'd taken the King's shilling, and what with your mother's cousin shot in the Rising, you couldn't show your face on Parnell Street.

—Because you'd fought alongside the English?

—They come round Doyle's with pistols and told him if he weren't gone in the morning, they'd shoot him through, and his sisters too.

—His own mother wouldn't take him in.

Similar things had happened to all of them, so they'd returned to England. Fail 'em junior and senior had tried to re-enlist, but their injuries prevented it, so they'd filled the streets like the rest, selling what they could, living off their pensions, which didn't go far, not far at all when you hadn't a home to go to.

When the cigarettes were gone, they asked if he'd any money, anything at all, and they asked where he lived and what he was, how much his pension was, how much he earned. He gave them all the cash in his pockets, but even then they pressed: could he find them a place at his school? What was it called? Where would you find it? The night was dark, the moon not rising. He invented someone who expected him, his uncle, yes even at this hour. They were still talking, still hurling questions at him, then curses as he walked away as quickly as he could without seeming to run.

When he gained the thoroughfare, he slowed. The pain in his chest was only mental. It was heartbreaking what they described. If it hadn't been the middle of the night, he would have rung his father. Surely something could be done. Surely Doyle and the Fail 'ems could be put to some employ and kept simply in some church property?

But as he returned to the familiar streets and the shop windows displaying waterproof jackets, the hunting costumes for him and her, the bottles of champagne set amongst the cut glass display and the watercolors of gay young people dancing as they used to at the parties where he'd go with Amanda, as he walked past all the other clubs to the welcoming steps of his own, a nasty sensation dawned: They'd worked together, the three of them. He'd nearly been set upon. The Irish were full of lies, and they knew a devil town when they saw one because that's where they'd spawned. Perhaps they hadn't been servicemen at all but demons, three of them come to put him off her trail. A chill ran across him. With their blarney, they had stirred the old suspicion that when it came to the Irish, there could be no friendship because they hated you to the core, for your Protestantism and your Englishness and every other chip they carried on their useless drunken shoulders. Now they were turning on their own, expelling any son of Erin who'd dared fight alongside the likes of Jamie to punish the Boche for their industrial gluttony and Teutonic pride. He'd heard that the Irish lost more per capita than the English or even the Scots. Ireland hadn't had conscription, but Irish regiments were feared across the channel. Weren't the Connaught Rangers the bane of the German command? Such had been the rumor at the citadel.

He'd never untangle the truth of the Irish, the Fail 'ems and Doyle, any of them except her. Given another chance, a *binding* chance, he could across a lifespan untangle and love the truth of her. She abhorred her people with the strength of burning coals. She hated them for Lovelace, for the boys who beat Roddy O'Hannah in the barn until he was dead so that every man and woman was frightened into helping the rebels and sabotaging the English. She said those boys went to the Continent and joined up with the Germans so they could wipe the English from the face of the earth. But after they'd killed Roddy O'Hannah, her brothers went to Lord Kirshner even though Daniel and Teddy weren't yet seventeen, never mind nineteen. *Go have a wee walk*, the recruiting officer had told them, *and be nineteen when you come back.*

Back at the club, he drew a lukewarm bath. He was so very incapable of managing anything of substance. He couldn't reach Amanda, could by no means take on a school, and could not even, in the middle of the night, distinguish a broken soldier from an Irish devil sent to keep him from his path. Kirk always said they must confidently expect the working of the Holy Spirit and must unhesitatingly identify it when it appeared. If only his head weren't so full of cotton wool, tonight and all the time, perhaps he would begin to sense it.

The morning brought a telephone message to the breakfast table, not as he feared from his father with complaints about Wilberforce, but from the bursar at Marlborough. When he rang back, the man insisted he remove his belongings directly rather than at the end of the holidays as Jamie had planned. Refurbishments had been approved, his former rooms were to be knocked out like rotten teeth, and the only possible time for the tradesmen to begin was tomorrow.

—We could have someone box your things if you prefer, the man said, though you'd have to explain what's yours.

In a shiver of horror at the thought of anyone going through his things, Jamie declared he'd come down himself that morning. He rang St. Stephen's to make arrangements and finished his breakfast in a state of resentment. Just as he'd met Diana in the flesh, here he was obliged to return to Marlborough, as though the place refused to give him his liberty. Packing for an overnight journey, he lost a cufflink behind the dresser and then pinched his finger in the clasp of his case.

The cab to the station took the edge off his vexation. Perhaps the inconvenience would work in his favor. He'd woken that morning with no fresh ideas for finding Amanda, and despite the relentless urgency, he had to admit that returning to pester Diana so soon would get him nowhere and might even paint him as a disturbed hanger-on. He needed time to conceive his next move, and if he exercised a shred of patience, perhaps the knowing would even grace him with its presence.

He always found empty schools eerie and sad, but his house at Marlborough looked positively sacked. Servants had piled all his furniture in the houseroom, leaving dust and detritus in their wake. He owned none of it except the hat stand, and once he'd disposed of old papers and clothes that were too shabby or juvenile, he was able to fit the rest into two trunks. The Albert Rose tea service she'd given him two Christmases ago, by way of Gute he suspected, he cushioned in a crate. He was driven to the station and his things loaded onto the train. In London, they were carried off the train, into a cab, across the city—stopped by traffic men to let horses, trams, and omnibuses pass before them—out of the cab, into the luggage car of the northern train, and at York into the vehicle driven by St. Stephen's porter, who smelled strongly of tobacco and motor oil. By the time the man had helped him haul it all into the rooms assigned him, he felt thoroughly a fraud, thoroughly unnerved, and less at home than he could remember feeling, even on the first night in a new school.

The next morning, he was awakened by the woman who was to serve as his housekeeper, a Mrs. Sparks. She brought him tea in bed and later served him breakfast in the headmaster's dining room, hovering as he ate. When he'd finished, she gave him a brief, awkward tour of the headmaster's quarters. Unlike his disemboweled rooms at Marlborough, these burst with paraphernalia belonging to the previous inhabitant. He informed her that his train back to London left before noon and that when his quarters were ready for him, he would return.

Mrs. Sparks stood before him baffled and flustered: she understood he had come to establish himself, or at the very least to stay until affairs had been set in order for the new term. He explained: urgent business in town, full confidence in her management.

She stopped rolling the hem of her apron and faced him resolutely.

—What is it?

The woman drew a breath. She was very sorry, she was very pained, but she wished to tender her resignation.

—What? *Why*?

She launched into a prepared speech (nothing against him personally, a matter of conscience, duty divided her heart); when he failed to protest, she expanded into autobiography (no husband, no children, her life was the school) and, as the hour for his departure came and went, into an unabridged narration of the Life and Times of Saltford-Kent: his founding of the school, Mrs. Sparks's employment from the beginning, S-K's wife, the woman's death, the son who'd gone bad, S-K's health crisis, his subsequent withdrawal to hospital and now convalescent home in Scarborough. Gradually Jamie perceived the morass. No arrangements had been made for S-K's things. Mrs. Sparks had been fretting for weeks, not only over the wrenching decision to *abandon the boys* so she could *stand by* S-K, but over the dastardly Board, which had refused to believe the man would ever recover.

The only way to stop the woman's tortured recital was to accept her resignation and encourage her to go to S-K as soon as possible. Teary with relief, she kissed both his cheeks, set out cold ham for his lunch, and telephoned the removers. That very afternoon she and the porter began boxing up S-K's belongings. She begged Jamie to stay so he could decide which fixtures he wished to keep and which he wished to have taken away before the new term.

Jamie took refuge in a classroom as they worked, returning to his lists and correspondence. He'd left Oxford for Marlborough in a similar flurry only twelve months previous. There had been no word from or of Amanda, and as the spires receded behind his brother-in-law's motorcar, so did the life they'd led in that city, the evenings no longer marked by Old Tom's tolling, the paths along the rivers forgetting their footsteps, the city's magic poured upon others.

At first he'd assumed she'd left on an emergency to do with someone in her family. Perhaps one of her brothers had turned up not-dead. Perhaps one of her sisters had fallen under the sway of another Lovelace. Perhaps one of her parents was on the point of death. Only something earth-shattering could have taken her away without a word, he thought.

Days had passed, a fortnight, no word. Should the constabulary be called? he asked Gute. Had she been taken against her will? Gutenberg refused such suggestions. She had gone under her own steam and of her own will. That was all he would say. He advised Jamie to forget her.

Such an idea was worse than ludicrous. Gutenberg had no idea what had passed between them just a few weeks earlier in Applecross. And then after the dog died, how he'd gone round to the Gorgon's day and night. When people asked if he'd any inkling that something was the matter with her, he insisted he hadn't, but in fact there had been those days, the Friday, the Saturday, the Sunday and cruel Monday. She was ill, the Gorgon had said. She had the Flu, Artemis told him. Something was dangerously wrong, but he'd resolved not to panic. He'd left her notes, two a day, three on the Sunday. If only he'd known she was slipping through his fingers.

Did he actually want to see her again now that she'd returned? The question intruded on his familiar meditation. Of course he wanted to see her. He wanted nothing else! And yet, if he were to start loitering near her haunts, would he not be putting himself in the way of the annihilating possibility that she'd never cared for him? That he had been a game to her, that she'd got what she wanted from Oxford, the press, and him, and had moved on before her tricks came to light. And if that proved true, then all the hopes he cherished in the secret shaft with the wooden cart, all those hopes would be well and truly dead. He'd be left without love, without hope of any future love, surrounded only by a stupid school with stupid people, problems upon problems, but not by her, the person he wanted for the mother of his children, for his playmate, for now and when they grew creaky and forgetful.

—Let's grow old together, he'd said on the shore at Applecross.

He'd meant *Marry me* but hadn't said it. She'd put her arms around him, and he'd felt the warm drip of her tears on his back. That night under the covers, she'd replied:

—Can we really grow old together?

—We've already begun. My hairs are gray already.

—I don't see them.

—One day you'll wake up and I'll be an old man.

If you found someone to grow old with, what were you meant to do with your heart if the plan were suddenly cancelled? It had happened to his father. He was thirty-nine when she died, not even slightly gray. It couldn't be that he and his father were in the same boat.

—Headmaster?

Mrs. Sparks tapped at the classroom door.

—Matron's here for you.

—Matron?

He'd been given to understand the school's matron was on holiday.

—Just returned, Mrs. Sparks reported. She's asked to see you.

Feeling like a boy in hot water, he followed Mrs. Sparks to the courtyard. There he encountered Matron, substantial, double-chinned, nearly as tall as he. She showed no sign of having encountered the sun on her holiday and had already divested herself of traveling clothes and donned what he presumed to be her uniform, starched apron, blue pinstripe blouse, white sleeve guards, and net around her graying chignon.

—Thank you, Caroline, Matron said curtly dismissing Mrs. Sparks.

Jamie introduced himself and extended his hand.

—Indeed, Matron said as though introductions were unnecessary.

She'd returned, she said, expressly to speak with him. She wished to comprehend his intentions.

Jamie sidestepped the demand by asking her to show him the areas of the school under her purview. She gave him a tour of the four boarding houses and showered him with more information than he was able to retain. Her responsibilities, in addition to the sanatorium, appeared far-reaching. In essence, every boy was her charge, every adult subject to her advice; there seemed nothing in the school over which she did not claim authority.

At last they passed through a wooden door at the base of a tower, a structure known actually as the Tower. A flight of stone steps conveyed them to a landing, and they emerged into a bright room at the level of the garrets. This she called the day room, this next the sanatorium ward, this the bathroom, and these her modest sitting room and monastic bedchamber. He'd never seen Kardleigh's quarters, but hers were not a type to seduce anyone up to Yorkshire. Even in July, the stone held a chill.

Matron bade him sit in the lumpy armchair while she prepared tea. She had been brusque with him all along, which he had assumed was her manner, but once the tea had been poured, she grew expansive.

Unlike the porter and Mrs. Sparks, Matron spoke properly. He pegged her for a clergyman's daughter. She began by sketching her employment, how long she had been at St. Stephen's (like Mrs. Sparks, from the beginning), under what circumstances S-K had engaged her (he knew her father, a vicar in the Chilterns—point to Jamie), how she had come and stayed on, never once entertaining suitors, never once taking steps to form a family of her own, though she would have liked children, very much so, and still would if fate would have it (this possibility he rated zero). She had stuck by S-K through everything, and she meant *everything.*

—Everything?

When Victoria died (the wife, he gleaned, not the Queen), there had been a stretch when none of them were quite sure he'd carry on. But she had stood by him, prayed with him nightly (nightly?), shared with him poetry and philosophy, arranged for carefully selected boys to consult him on matters of spiritual concern. In short, she had orchestrated his slow but steady rehabilitation after that too-young blow. She had thought he might choose another wife, but it was to be that instead he redoubled his devotion to the boys, and rightly so. Then, some years later, there had been the second blow of his son.

—Do I understand the son ran off?

The son, with whose name she would not sully her lips, put Eli's and Samuel's sons to shame. He went up to Cambridge and fell in with a set that she still prayed would be cut down where they stood and go to the devil. She assured him this was no idle profanity but her sincere prayer.

—I believe you.

Could he could imagine the grief such a development had inflicted on a devoted father such as S-K? And it fell to her again to minister to his mind and body (*body*?), which at the time weakened and then contracted a very stubborn catarrh that laid him up for the entire Lenten term, to the point that his physician, who knew less than he imagined, the quack, pressed him to retire (at the age of fifty-one!) and remove himself to Italy or any climate more healthful than theirs. This illness and its underlying grief she also assisted him in overcoming.

Jamie was growing uncomfortable the more she revealed,

and she was on a tear now, like a train stoked to full power on a straight with no junctions in sight. *Just how many women had loved this headmaster*?

And then, just as S-K ought to have been enjoying the prime of his life, the peak of his powers and the Academy's ascendency, then had come the *war*.

—Yes, Jamie said.

She remembered the tea in her cup. Finding it cold or unpalatable she poured it into a potted fern.

—Did St. Stephen's lose many?

A vain question, he added. They all had. Corpus had lost nearly a quarter, the waste beyond comprehension. Certainly they'd lost Old Boys, she resumed, and that was bad enough. His uneasiness flared. What was worse than losing a quarter of your Old Boys?

S-K might have borne the war, she said. It wasn't the first. They'd lost Old Boys to the Boers after all. She was circling the subject, and he didn't interrupt. She made a fresh pot, rattling on about the boys. He couldn't keep any of them straight, but the more she talked, the more he realized he could never dismiss her. She'd won his admiration not only for her poised devotion but also for her encyclopedic knowledge of the boys, which struck him prima facie as penetrating.

While she clinked around the makeshift kitchenette, he examined the knickknacks in her sitting room: tryptic from Compostela, a photograph of her and boys dated the previous year, cabinet card with family group forty years previous judging by the costume, and a collection of postcards from Lyme, Edinburgh, Paris, Florence, all addressed to Antonia from Andrew.

—He never would have taken a holiday if I hadn't insisted.

She returned with a tea tray that bore the additional ominous (or hopeful) sign of whisky.

—Against the Influenza, she said tapping her chest.

She poured them both a dram but did not broach her subject. He returned to the postcards:

—S-K, do you mean? Did he write these?

She nodded.

—To you?

She nodded.

—Does anyone ever call you anything but Matron?

She colored.

—He did.

—Did?

—Does.

—Have you seen him since . . . ?

This subject, Matron would not brook. He would not divert her so easily, she said. If he meant to take on the Academy (they all used this name for the school, never St. Stephen's), someone had to give him straight facts.

—I'd be very much obliged.

He came in '91, and what a naughty boy he had been. The father had died, and the mother, silly calf hadn't the first idea what to do with him. A year younger than the youngest boys, he won them with charm and daring. If she and Andrew hadn't taken him quite literally in hand, he would have ended up in Borstal.

She continued to describe this boy, whom she called Gordon, surname or Christian name unclear, a boy who stayed at the Academy seven years, half-adopted by S-K in that he spent holidays there when his mother became too ill to care for him, and then when she expired, he became their de facto ward. He left at eighteen, a fine, fine, fellow, to Balliol where he earned a first in Greats. He returned to them nearly every holiday, and then when he'd come down, S-K offered him a position. The Common Room was full then, and Gordon was happy to serve as undermaster in Clement's house. The boys loved him, and he loved them. He was born to play rugby football and made the boys love it too. There had been a moment when S-K thought they ought to try association football as well, if only as an experiment, but Gordon had defeated the idea before anyone had time to procure the other kind of ball.

His unease grew as she wandered into the weeds with Gordon's war service. Presumably, he had died in it and S-K had taken it hard. Gordon had clearly filled the place abandoned by the black sheep son, not only in S-K's heart but in hers. Was it possible that they viewed him as a surrogate, joint child? Dear Lord, let him not become so warped by the business of schoolmastering that he lost his allegiance to the most essential social unit, the family.

—There's no sense in any of it, she said. It was a day like any other. No one guessed it. A boy found him, and that boy was never the same again.

—Gordon?

(Had an accident? Took his life?)

—With his service revolver, inside those woods there. You never forget the way they look. You wished you'd never seen, but then of course you have.

—Yes.

She became increasingly elliptical, not to conceal, he thought, but more that she had admitted Jamie so far into her confidence that she'd lost track of what needed to be said aloud. The long and short of it was that S-K had never recovered from the tragedy. Gordon had been found by the pupil in the woods, and soon afterwards the Armistice had come. The connection between the suicide and the war, indeed Gordon's experiences in the war, Jamie never ascertained, but he felt cut to the quick. It was maudlin, he knew, to exercise one's heart over an individual tragedy when they as a civilization had been cut down so far; yet they lived as individuals, and the individual tragedy was all they could feel. They, he, any human.

The sun had come out, and Jamie needed air. He located

his hat and a pair of Wellington boots and took himself to the playing fields. The pitches wanted refurbishment, or at least cutting more energetically from the moorland. The goal posts would stand another fifty years with a coat of paint. There was a peeling shed, which he thought on the day had been used as a cricket pavilion. But ticking through plans for the school did nothing to dispel his apprehension. Matron, Antonia, needed a husband and children of her own. She needed better tea, new stockings, a holiday in the Aegean, and a wiser man than he to rehabilitate her school. He, meanwhile, needed not to admire her as much as he did. He needed Amanda. He needed John. He also needed Kardleigh, for his own sanity if nothing else, but for Kardleigh to serve as the school's physician, Matron would have to go. He was beginning to see why Overall told him to change things slowly.

He rounded the hedgerow and climbed up the common until the school dropped from view. He felt his mind open, and as he navigated sheep and their droppings, he wondered if he might stumble upon the barn that had figured so prominently in Wilberforce's confession last month, the barn whose black and white interior he had seen in the pages of *The Daily Mail* back in March. In that distant innocence, pre-Overall, pre-paternal-heart-attack, pre-Amanda's-return, he'd been vaguely soothed by the scandal in the way that one felt mild relief when disasters happened to people of one's distant acquaintance, because it used up one of the randomly occurring misfortunes fate assigned to every circle. Such a view was not justifiable by Christian theology, but there you were.

He saw a structure ahead, and it gave him a pain in his stomach. *The Mail* had told of a track from the road to the barn, and here was such a track. The place looked derelict enough. He had to force the door.

Inside, the old, musty smell that accompanied so many trysts. Fallen lumber, fatal beam? Who would bring a girl to this ill and eerie place? As for the loft looming above, it looked ready to brain him.

He went outside. Sunshine burned through the clouds and made him squint. He strode down the track to the narrow road, enclosed like the lane in France where his first batman had been run down by one of their own vehicles because they didn't see him in time. He wanted to go straight to the station and board a train home.

Home where, though? Marlborough was no longer his. The Rectory contained the noxious Wilberforce. The Club was only an hotel. He, James Alger Stires Sebastian, had been relegated to a haunted pocket of Yorkshire, having previously accepted a call, which was . . . ? Rebuilding a school gone to ruin? Breathing order from chaos? What about the girl in the labyrinth?

Mrs. Sparks served him tea in the headmaster's garden, a walled enclosure where he imagined S-K retreating from the buzz of the school or conducting pastoral interviews with boys. White roses overwhelmed a wrought-iron bench, and pungent things sprawled from untended containers. Amanda didn't garden, as far as he knew, but she'd kept herbs in a box behind the press. He fancied this gone-to-ruin cloister had once obeyed the thumb of S-K's wife. The sun had warmed the bricks, and now as it set, it painted the walls honey red, as beautiful as the strawberries were sweet. Finches twittered, flycatchers tsipped, and a skylark swooped in the cloud-swept sky. *He rises and begins to round, he drops the silver chain of sound . . .* He couldn't remember much of Meredith's poem, but she had memorized the whole thing after hearing "The Lark Ascending." They'd gone up to town for the concert, and for the first time since he'd begun taking her to recitals, she'd shed tears. He imagined her reclined in the garden chair opposite, gazing into the sky, reciting the poem as though she were composing it: *And you shall hear the herb and tree, the better heart of men shall see, shall feel celestially as long, as you crave nothing save the song.* He listened for the memory of her voice, of the woodwind, of the violin humming as her tears wet the back of his hand. Everything he wanted to tell her shriveled when he reached for words. But music? Could it not open the access and passage to remorse, in her as it had in him across the years of his ignorance? Over the walls, in the pews, music had softened his heart, shaped his mind, called him out of the dark.

And wasn't that the aim of education? he imagined telling her. How could he ever reform the boys of this school without music and the love it expressed? One could discipline them with routines and rules, one could reach their bodies with sport and pain, one could train their minds in classroom and chapel, but how was he to cut through the rime of their cynicism, stir the soil of their hearts, plant seeds of divine truth (*any* truth), tug away the weeds of coarseness and self-will? They needed music, real music, produced by someone with courage and skill. They needed it every day. They didn't even need to care. It would work on them, as it had worked on him.

Beth's husband made his living drawing up wills, but he could play the pianoforte in a different way entirely to how Beth played it. She'd tinkle out your Chopin and your Anna Magdalena's Notebook, but Robert played as if he'd learned to speak on the bench. The things he conjured came not from sheet music but from some invisible river he stood in up to his waist. Beth said he went straight to the piano upon returning home, and the children had been trained not to speak in the conservatory when their father was playing, but to sit silently on the settee or curl around the piano legs as he poured the language of centuries from his fingers. On occasion, Jamie had felt that he, too, could sprawl on the floor as the man soft-pedaled his way through Jamie's entire fortress.

The next morning, Mrs. Sparks served him a hot breakfast, and after introducing him to the slow-looking girl who would attend him until he'd engaged a new housekeeper, she climbed into a cab and rattled away through the gates. He felt a wistful envy that she would soon be breathing salt air, free to bathe in the sea and leave the school's problems behind.

Embarking on a more critical survey of the headmaster's house, he noted the dingy upholstery, the faded patches on the walls where pictures had been removed, the empty bookshelves, the very miscellaneous glassware and crockery. The headmaster's study he found only slightly less cluttered than it had been. The filing cabinets heaved with papers and the drawers with paraphernalia whose worth he could not judge. The previous day he had asked Mrs. Sparks to show him around the room and point out the records of import. She'd declared the study the headmaster's *sanctorum* and gave him to understand that she never entered it. Standing now in the dustheap, he realized he was going to have to go through everything by hand.

He opened a window. Not everything was impossible. Even if it took days, he could conquer this room. He could get to the bottom of his predecessor's affairs. He'd booked his dinner with Kardleigh, and even though John had refused to come to London, claiming complete absorption with family duties, he was answering Jamie's letters.

Bells rang in the quad every hour as surely others tolled near the house where she lived. Their tones she would hear as she woke, as she brushed her hair, as she wiped children's faces, as she dropped letters into a pillar box—

Sometimes the heart pumped goblets all at once.

He went in search of Fardley and discovered him amidst piles of old newspaper in the hovel that served as a gate house.

—I don't suppose you've such a thing as a postal directory? Jamie asked.

Fardley grunted, but after shuffling through newspapers and dragging out baskets full of coal, rusting metal, biscuit wrappers, and animal traps, the man produced a damp volume. Jamie took it back to S-K's study—*his* study—and peeled apart the pages for central London and its post offices. The Royal Mail had graced their first days . . .

Bells in the fog, such were the lines he wrote her, six identical copies sent poste restante to six post offices near the museum she frequented. Whenever the fog fell over Oxford and he lost his bearings in the fields, he'd listen for the college bells. Old Tom tolled Oxford time, and if the rest of the world kept other hours, it didn't matter because your rooms and your books and your teacups and the girl who destroyed the life you once had, all were fixed in Oxford time. You needed three points to reckon your location. He had Kardleigh's assent and John's letters from Saffron Walden. It wasn't enough.

The following afternoon, the girl delivered a telegram with his tea. It had come in the morning, he learned, but on account of everything being at sixes and sevens—the girl broke down in tears.

It wasn't from Amanda but from his father, declaring that the man would arrive with Wilberforce after tea, to St. Stephen's that very day, reason not provided, duration unspecified. Jamie suggested that the girl redeem herself by arranging bedrooms for their guests.

His sisters would tear down the walls if they heard their father was taking railway journeys across the country. Some hours later, Jamie received a breathless telephone call from York Minster's verger reporting that his father had fainted in a chapel, had been revived, and was en route in a cab. He needed nerves of steel, but those he had were dough.

When the pair arrived, his father tried to divert attention from his health by making it clear that through Wilberforce he had learned of John's re-appearance, indeed of his present employment at St. Stephen's. Jamie had no choice but to dispatch Wilberforce to bed and grab the thistle that was John Grieves:

—I wasn't purposely keeping it from you.

—Could you do me the mercy of skipping all this? his father said weakly.

—Father, I insist on ringing a doctor.

A hollow stand to take since he didn't know any in the area, but someone somewhere must know what to do, to steady the man's heart and restore its function, to tether him to life. *Years*. He needed years longer.

—James, his father said gently. Sit down, won't you.

—Father—

—I'm not dying. Not today.

—Father—

—You look peaked. Have you eaten?

He'd had an egg at breakfast, but . . .

—The honey is quite nice, his father said passing him a slice of bread slathered with it.

He concentrated on the bread's softness, the pulsing in his mouth as the flavors hit his throat, the ballasting of nerves, the cut of the tea. Again, sunset washed the walls, again the garden sheltered, and he grew one day more into the things that had been happening in that spot since before he was born.

—You can't imagine how it was finding him here, Jamie said still not meeting his father's eye.

—Took you by surprise?

—I thought he was dead!

His father didn't mention the last time they'd spoken of the Grieveses, when John's father turned up in an obituary, the summer Jamie met Amanda. Grieves senior had been survived by two sisters, the obit said, no mention of John. Jamie had been incensed at the omission, and his father, who had maintained some ties with Grieves senior, had expressed his regret that father and son had never reconciled even after the war and that the disowning of John had extended even to the obituary. *What makes you think John is alive*? he'd demanded. His father had no evidence one way or the other but reasoned that the son's death would have changed the color of grief in the father. Jamie had never accepted the theory, not least because believing that he was dead made the memory of his final days with John less of a torment.

—It seems he's very much alive, his father said, and a force to be reckoned with if young Wilberforce is any judge.

Jamie focused on eating.

—My dear boy, his father said at last.

Jamie clenched his jaw, but his father offered no acerbic observations, such as how useful it would have been to know of John when tackling Wilberforce, or how John's presence altered the entire project, or even how humane it might have been to share the good news. Instead, Jamie sensed that his father understood not only the wild mercy of finding John at St. Stephen's but also the reason Jamie's life was now hostage to the place.

—John fought for Wilberforce the day I came, he said. He'd been taking an interest in the boy for years. The mess that day was tearing him apart.

His father stared into the middle distance as he did when adjusting his opinion.

—He's been here since the Armistice, Jamie continued. It seems the previous head was the only one who'd employ him.

—Dear boy.

—He's the only person here I can trust without question. I asked him to meet me at the club, but he won't.

—Whyever not?

Jamie catalogued John's evasions.

—I'm not surprised, his father said. He's always been awkward. You'll have to go to him. He was always more reasonable once one got him alone in a quiet room.

Jamie appreciated anew that his father had in some sense raised John in those summers when John was deposited at the Rectory. His father's knowledge of John, then, was like Jamie's knowledge of the boys in his house, like the knowledge he hoped soon to have of St. Stephen's boys.

He expected the third degree from his father, but the conversation drifted instead into what Jamie had learned of the school and of S-K, of Mrs. Sparks and Matron Antonia. He explained his bind with the last, wanting to dismiss her so he could recruit Kardleigh yet wanting to retain her and give scope to her talents. He explained that he needed a proper housekeeper, as was obvious from the girl attending them.

—I intended to ask around Marlborough, but everyone's on holiday.

—You need someone now, his father said, someone reliable and preferably local.

—I know! I'm in a bind.

—I could inquire at York if you like.

A feeling of relief dissolved his humiliation, and he wondered if he and his father had indeed commenced a new chapter together. But then he remembered his sisters and their shrill concern.

—You ought to be in bed, he told his father.

—Yes.

—Can I have anything brought to you?

—I don't think so, thank you.

—An aspirin? Milk?

—Jamie.

His father's hand on his, its cushiony assurance. They didn't move, and he could feel the shadow of the unsaid. He couldn't escape it much longer, and now in the watery night he didn't want to.

—She's come back.

His father's hand heavier, more sure, more safe.

—I can't . . . I don't want to . . .

His father said nothing, but the hand said *yes*.

—There's no life without her.

Two days later, he saw his father and Wilberforce onto the train in York. Wilberforce appeared to have transformed from a project into a member of the family. Beth and her brood were to take a place at the seaside and had arranged for his father and Wilberforce to join them. The whole thing was unorthodox, but Jamie felt a measure of comfort that his father would be amongst family and, given Beth's persuasive powers, would be induced to rest.

He rang the club every day in case there had been a reply to his broad-cast letters. There hadn't. On the upside, Diana had invited him back to the museum mid-week. He filled an exercise book with his arguments, why she must give him Amanda's address, the urgency, the . . . it all went round in circles. Meantime, he'd got as far as anyone could with the wretched study, and his dinner with Kardleigh was approaching. He packed his case for a fortnight.

They used to talk in the dark of going to America, that vast unpeopled continent where they could live miles from humanity, huts in the forest, tents on the plain, free to do whatever they wished as loudly as they wished whenever they wished until they were well and fully sated, until they had rescued each other and grown into a state where the world could be borne. If he couldn't have America and couldn't have the cottage in Applecross, was it so unsatisfactory to offer her a school in the middle of nowhere to be a home for all the things they didn't need to say any longer? Wouldn't she join him in that walled garden, that shell of another man's dream, where they could live outside precedent, hidden from the clubs and the accents and the people who'd known each other back and back to the Doomsday book?

His train screeched into King's Cross just before four, and when he finally reached the club, he needed a bath. The oil painting in his room bore a stain that reminded him of vomit. Upon examination, he discovered mildew, easily scratched off with a fingernail. Since becoming a housemaster, he'd taken to minor acts of ordering, straightening frames he found askew, picking up detritus, aligning desks, even tightening screws if a penknife could accomplish it. The painting depicted ruins that reminded him of Riveaux, or of the rubble villages they marched through on the way to Mainz. What really was the difference? He was getting uselessly philosophical when he needed to arrange his mind for the assault on Kardleigh. The man's Christian name, he learned after years of knowing him, was Terrance, but Jamie had never heard anyone use it. Surely, though, if they were to go forward together, they'd have to get beyond surnames? Kardleigh called him Jass, as everyone had in the army and at Oxford. If only Kardleigh knew who else had called him that—not his initials JASS, but Jas, short for Jasper, which—*essential points*.

When he came downstairs, Kardleigh was waiting in the lobby looking uncharacteristically suntanned. They discussed trifling things as one did when getting used to the presence of someone with whom one had previously been intimate. Once the G & T's had taken the edge off the day and his nerves, Jamie broached the revolution in Kardleigh's life purpose:

—What's the scope of this music degree?

With characteristic sobriety and zest, Kardleigh described his program at the Royal College of Music, to be followed by a doctorate if he could find a place that would employ him as organist.

—I'm at St. Edward the Martyr's at the moment, Kardleigh said, but in September their man returns.

London was full of churches, more of them than organ students, Jamie would have thought.

—But you're still practicing?

—Every day.

—Medicine, I mean.

Kardleigh laughed:

—One keeps one's hand in. And landlords must be paid.

—Don't tell me you've gone over to Yellen.

Jamie said it jokingly, referring to the notorious London physician whose methods with the shell-shocked Kardleigh had always deplored.

—Oh, said Kardleigh awkwardly. I did ring him up, on the telephone you know, just to see what was going. The man had infernal nerve.

—Did he?

—*Terrance*, he said, *I was just about to ring you.*

Yellen had said it for shock value, and evidently it had worked, for Kardleigh revealed he was now seeing patients at Queens three days a week, though explicitly not under Yellen.

—War? Jamie asked.

—Some, though the war office isn't paying any longer.

The more they spoke of Kardleigh's circumstances, the flat in Richmond, the patients, the bicycle riding to this organ and that lecture or lesson, the more distant Jamie's purpose became. The proposal he had to make—leave London, come to the arse end of Yorkshire—simply had no place in this reality. He couldn't find the words even to propose it.

They went through to the dining room, and Jamie ordered hock. If he had to sit in a stifling room full of clerics and half-wit literary types, his shirt already soaking through, he needed more to drink. The hock wasn't good, but enough of it might open his mind.

He summarized his change of employment, emphasizing the adventure and playing down the impulsive disorder of the last month. Kardleigh regarded him with skepticism rather than the interest he'd hoped to pique.

—I suppose we're both striking out for new lands.

He wished he could be walking, even through the heat, even in the rain, anything but sitting still and fighting a hopeless campaign. When the roast arrived, Jamie ordered claret. He was beginning at last to feel unbound, like a parcel whose string had been cut.

—Listen, he said, I haven't the strength for this.

—For what?

His throat tightened:

—I tried to organize everything, the whole argument with logic and rhetoric, affecting details and charm.

—We all know about you and the charm.

—Yes, and I'm telling you I can't. People expect one to keep serving it up. You've no idea what it was like, the day they gave me the wretched post.

—Which you accepted.

—Which I didn't refuse.

—Because?

—The point is I can't anymore, not with you.

As if in demonstration, he unbuttoned his collar and loosened his necktie, club be damned.

—Now, now, Kardleigh said, don't be rash.

The man smiled, but Jamie didn't.

—I need you, he said. It matters.

Kardleigh had the mercy to set down his knife and fork. Jamie began to explain, haltingly at first, but gaining confidence as Kardleigh held him in his gaze. One detail led to another, and when he finally reached the end of it, Kardleigh had finished eating.

—Jass, Kardleigh said, I'd help if I could. You know that.

—I don't know it.

—I would. And who knows, if things don't work out here, I might need a position in a few years' time.

—I need you *now*.

Kardleigh consulted the second menu and ordered a lemon posset. Jamie asked for strawberries.

—It seems to me, Kardleigh said, that what you really need is a secretary, someone to sort through that study and tame details.

—I need that, too. But secretaries—

—Wait, Kardleigh said. Oh dear, you're not.

—What?

—You intend to confront Miss McDonagh?

—Not confront.

—Your hope, though, is *entente*?

—Yes.

—As in matrimony?

—What's wrong with that?

—Nothing, but you can't ask her to be your secretary.

—I wasn't going to.

—You must have a man.

He could think of no retort, and as the coffee was poured, he understood Kardleigh was right.

—And as it happens, Kardleigh continued, I know someone.

—You do?

They took their coffee to the smoking room, but it too was stifling. Jamie proposed a stroll to the underground station, and as they stepped into the sluggish evening streets, Kardleigh revealed that the secretary he had in mind was in fact a patient, someone down on his luck but full of potential.

—I thought you were serious, Jamie protested.

—I'm perfectly serious.

Kardleigh described a captain wounded in the war, a man who like so many had been unable to find employment since.

—It's a school, not a charity, Terrance.

—I'm aware of that, James.

Kardleigh pestered all the way to the station, and in the end Jamie agreed to meet the man. It seemed the easiest way to win the luxury of going to bed.

The next day, Kardleigh led him through the doors, corridors, archways, and gratings that controlled comings and goings in the hospital. He'd forgotten the smell of such places, their boiled antiseptic sadness. Had that time at the war hospital, which he remembered as refuge, actually been as small and life-wasting as the rooms they passed through here? Outside in the patients' garden, plane trees held off the heat of the day, and Jamie pressed his fingernails into his palms to recall himself to the present.

—Ah, said Kardleigh, here we are.

A rail-thin man in a wheelchair bent over a lap tray. He was rubbing out an answer in the crossword puzzle, and when he turned the chair to greet Kardleigh, Jamie saw he had no legs. Kardleigh introduced Jamie as his friend, jovially heaping pity upon him for having been left holding the bag at a boys' school. The legless man replied to the banter in near whispers, nervously rolling his rubber against the tray as they debated school food versus hospital food, crossword puzzles versus Patience, and dance bands versus orchestras as heard on the evening wireless. Kardleigh kept the conversation light, but Jamie felt the unspoken accusation: he'd been even more of a wreck once, though able-bodied, and Kardleigh had spared nothing to recall him from the abyss. Jamie felt caught by both shame and impotent anger; he'd come begging Kardleigh's aid and now was being told to pull his own weight and the weight of this man, who could with a breath of the Holy Ghost have been him.

Eventually they got round to exchanging war credentials, units, locations. The man disclosed a grammar school education.

—He wouldn't need much salary, Kardleigh whispered as they stepped away to fetch lemonade. Just room, board, steady hours, patience.

Kardleigh believed in the man, so much that Jamie felt that refusing him would put an end to his own campaign.

—The position's temporary, Jamie told the man. Through the summer, primary objective to organize accounts.

—I could manage that, the man said uncertainly.

They continued an almost comical interview, Jamie sketching

the position's undesirable aspects, the man emphasizing the limits of his abilities.

—When can he begin? Kardleigh interrupted.

Diana was expecting him in an hour. The hospital was getting on his nerves. He offered the man a token salary and suggested they journey down at the weekend.

—I can get you settled and show you the rat's nest, but I won't be able to stay.

—Right.

—I'll collect you first thing Saturday.

The man looked terrified. Jamie completed his performance and made an exit.

—I'm sure we'll get on splendidly, Lewis. You're doing me a favor.

Diana had nothing new to tell him. As he feared, she only wanted to flirt, but after ten minutes faffing about, she let slip that Amanda—*Marion*—had spoken of going abroad.

—*Abroad*?

—With the lovely family. The city's a furnace. I don't know how long I can bear it.

Diana touched her stomach, and he left before he said something he regretted.

The heat made everything less real, and truly he was losing his grip. Not content with having wandered unlit city parks, having fraternized with Irish tramps, now he'd abandoned self-restraint and begged his former physician to help him with St. Stephen's, only to find himself cornered into engaging a *mutilé de guerre* just when Amanda was slipping through his grasp. *Marion*. At least Captain Lewis wasn't Irish.

He was going to have to lie in wait for her, and the V&A remained the most promising location. If he could catch sight of her, he could learn where she was living and dispense with the multiple postes restantes. To follow her undetected, however, he needed a disguise, not monocle and beard, but something that would guarantee no one would regard him. If only he had a chair like Lewis's and a tray of matches to hock. He could just imagine Grady, introducing him to some friend at the opera to be dressed from the costume collection. But Grady had departed for the Aegean, monasteries and Trebizond, return uncertain. He still had his army uniform—in the back of a wardrobe at the Rectory—but if he wished to be invisible, he ought to feign a missing limb, or two.

Nervous energy coursed through him as he strode up Tower Hill towards Petticoat Lane. The barrows there offered everything that could be had second hand. Several carried uniforms, and one proprietress offered creative advice when he presented himself as costumer for a motion picture being filmed in London by an American (the great Failem O'Hannah, did she know him? A great talent). After hearing his description of the costume required (the actor was essentially his size), she proposed to immobilize his knee and ankle with rattan and puttees to give the impression of a wooden leg. Having accomplished this, she found uniform pieces to fit and even tracked down a lead mask to complete the portrait of *mutilé de guerre*. The ensemble plus a pair of crutches cost him less than a new shirt from his tailor.

Back at the club, he tried on the costume. The mask, which had been designed to cover a mutilated nose and cheek, was heavy and smelled of dust. Traversing the club in costume was out of the question, but he made arrangements to use the service entrance, explaining himself vaguely and allowing the porter to suspect him of espionage.

Next morning he took a cab to the Oratory and approached the V&A along the gardens with aid of the crutches. He couldn't enter the museum itself; he looked too rough, even with the unmoving elegance of the mask, with its real-hair mustache and aquiline nose. Thus, he decided to loiter in the East Lawn and read a newspaper. Was it wrong to feel a sense of adventure and even fun dressed in a dead man's clothes, with another man's face atop his own, waiting to surveil someone in perhaps the most consequential campaign of his life?

He sat on a bench all morning. A few women made his breath catch, but none were Amanda. Mid-day it began to sprinkle, pulling soot from the air and depositing it on the pavement. He'd left his umbrella behind in favor of the crutches, but when the rain began to demonstrate its sincerity, he had to resign for the day or risk the mask's mustache.

The next day, he came armed with umbrella and cigarettes, which he sold loose. Again he did not see her. Nothing said he was even in the right park, or that she hadn't already gone abroad with her charges. Surely she couldn't have changed so much that he wouldn't recognize her? He sweated freely in the woolen costume, and that evening his body sported various rashes. Soaking in the bath, he fought for mastery over his nerves. He was fed up with this person, this man who needed Epsom salts and scotch to keep himself from doing something desperate. Was it true what some said, that fear was a demonic attack? If so, it signaled battles he must on no account surrender. He knew these assaults. Really, he knew them. They made you think you couldn't trust your own mind; they made you think everything was a lie; they made you think the world was falling to pieces and all you could do was hide and wait for the smoke to clear.

Hadn't he known her in Applecross when she forgave him, when the bed caught them up into something that tingled, when they stood knee-deep in the sea and imagined growing old together? The last night of their holiday they walked in Wellington boots, wolfhound at their side, around the point to the village. The Royal Stag served food and welcomed the hound, but Rory started whining as soon as they went inside.

—I told you he doesn't like people, she scolded.

The pup had been more fretful than usual, off his food, panting even though it was cold, lying down twice on the trek over. He should never have cajoled her into pushing as far as they had. When they got back to the cottage an hour and a half later, soaked to the skin, Rory curled in front of the fire, filling the room with the smell of wet dog. He refused food and water, refused to move. Jamie brought out the scotch. When she looked up from her place on the floor beside the pup, he couldn't sift her resentment from her fear. He didn't know what could be wrong with the dog. He wasn't yet even four.

—Here, he said handing her a glass.

—Do you think it would bring him round?

He shrugged helplessly. She dipped her finger in the scotch and offered it to Rory. When the pup turned his head away, she buried her face in his ears:

—I can't stand it!

Six weeks later, he'd been in tutorial. Kirk had been hauling him across the coals for the sloppiness in his most recent chapter. The tick-off was deserved, and he'd gone to the press afterwards, smarting, to see her. He could still remember standing in an outer room, where customers were entertained, and having to wait for Gute.

—What's wrong? he'd demanded of the Latvians.

They'd been evasive.

—Stop putting me off, he'd said unsteadily. You're making me think something's happened to her.

When Gute finally arrived, he was blunt:

—The dog has died. She's gone home. Don't follow.

Jamie remembered not being able to look at Gutenberg but only at the repulsive porcelain figurines in the window. He went out to the garden to see the dog covered in a blanket, looking as though he was sleeping. When he asked how it had happened, Gute said she'd taken the pup out and come back ice cold. He wasn't sure he believed Gute but thought he'd learn it from her later. On the sickening walk to her lodgings, his imagination leapt frivolously to getting another pup, this time a mutt that would live until they were fifty. At the flat, the Gorgon refused him entry. They exchanged hot words, but then Artemis came down and promised she'd watch Amanda. Jamie felt he should arrange a wake, but you didn't have a funeral for a dog, even if he was their child.

The next day he returned to her lodgings when he knew the Gorgon would be out and let himself in using the latch-key Artemis lent him. The house was quiet, but in the passage outside her door, he heard her speaking to someone. When he knocked, she fell silent. Her door was locked. Nothing he said received an answer.

He'd replayed the scene countless times. Should he have broken the door? Scaled the drainpipe and forced the window? Should he have said more or much less than he had? He'd left thinking he try again later, try the Gorgon later, talk to Artemis. And so began the burning of his city, an arson that went on and on. Could she really have fled in grief? Maybe for days, but a year? It was possible that she was more disordered than he'd ever guessed, even more than he was himself. But he knew, outside his reason, that it wasn't true. He'd been to Applecross with her. He knew her. He knew more of her than ever had been or would be known.

His third day in costume, she appeared, wearing a yellow dress and a modest straw hat. Two children, aged he guessed five and eight, prattled at her side; she clutched their hands, spinning when they tried to pull away, groaning as if they were tearing her limbs. They passed some twenty yards from him, and he recognized her brown laced shoes. Then they crossed the street and went into the museum, the children still holding her hands, still smelling her scent, still hearing her wit.

She was not a ghost. Her hair was longer and gathered back from her face, but she hadn't changed. She was alive, vibrantly, at home in the streets of the city, engaged with people he did not know, living a life entirely divorced from the one he had known her to live.

His heart raced and his face itched beneath the heavy mask. He could hear Kardleigh's voice, feel his influence undiminished as he went through the routines to calm himself. Still, the carts in his mind careened down their paths, the loudest as jaded as a sixth former: *That's the girl, then*?

It was.

All this carrying-on, the moth-eaten disguise, the macabre portrait mask, and she passed just like that, forty-five seconds, done and dusted?

She would come out, though. He'd see her again.

Was this the peak of his sad excitement, stalking this glorified nanny like The Man who was Thursday? *Would he break into the home of her charges to confront her*?

He hadn't got so far as thinking what he'd do when he found out where she lived, but the train was racing, the engineer had piled on all the coal, the brake-men had passed out, and nothing could stop it now.

An hour later, she emerged with the children. They were irritable, and so was she. The girl she tried to humor, but the boy, more stubborn, she told off and yanked along. Was this what it had been like back home with so many brothers and sisters? She'd always portrayed herself as the one who would comfort the little ones when their mother's temper turned vile. She was tired now, he saw as he followed, her temper short. Did she ever let them hear her real accent? How had she presented herself to the family?

Soon they arrived at a tall white house. Before ringing the bell, she knelt to comfort the stroppy boy, offering them each a sweet from her pocket, kissing them and saying things to make the boy smile, though he tried to wipe it from his face. After tidying their clothing, she pulled the bell. A uniformed maid let them inside. The door closed.

That night he dreamed he was back at Oxford in his second-year rooms. A tragedy had occurred, he realized. His daughter had died, his elder daughter. She had been six. It all came back to him in the dream—he and Amanda and the two girls had been wading at the banks of a river, and the elder girl had been swept away. He'd physically collapsed, weeping. Their beautiful girl, now old enough to read and converse and guide her younger sister, she was drowned, dashed upon the rocks. Her sister, still lisping in curls, would be ruined without her. And Amanda! He staggered to the other room to find her, afraid she'd do herself harm. As he leaned over a wash basin, keening, she stood beside him. *We must have more children*, she said. They needed more so their remaining daughter wouldn't be alone, wouldn't grow up lost in the world. He wanted at least seven, but the sick unbearable pain wracked him: their daughter pulled under, afraid, crushed, alone.

A crow's cry tore him from sleep, and dimly he realized that the looming, tragic feeling belonged to the dream. As the sour grief drained from his limbs, as relief dawned, as the bedroom of a London club arranged itself around him, a new discomfort emerged, this time from the back of his neck, and with it the knowledge of his own self-deception: he hadn't lived in denial of any child's death, but had he not allowed himself to lounge in an easy state of martyrdom? She wouldn't see him, she ignored his existence, her refusals were wrecking his sanity. Cue orchestra, cue bathos, cue his impotence before poetic obstacles. But he had been walking the coward's path. He had been holding back the last of himself, of his need and daring. He like all cowards had pretended noble reasons for his restraint—not to frighten her, not to hurt her, not to coerce her—but in truth he had held back for fear of her final, snuffing rejection. To this point she had spurned him, but how hard? Had she not in some sense encouraged him through Diana, or by such private means as God communicated with his followers?

He'd come around to sacrilege, and if he had indeed made an idol of her, it would explain his failure and unhappiness. Didn't they worship idols because they were afraid to trust the real thing, those poor sods languishing in the desert? Their maniac leader who'd split the sea for them was A.W.O.L., last seen heading up a mountain to be savaged by God or beasts. The desert, the future, and indeed their contentious present were too menacing to entrust to a god they could no longer see, and so cowards that they were—and yes, they *all* were—they put their hopes in a golden statue. You could read in black and white how it worked out for them. The coward's path always ended in disaster. At least in literature.

In life, though? Had he not taken the coward's path countless times and survived? He always thought of himself as a maverick, not an outright rebel but the kind of boy who broke rules to prove he could. He knew people thought him self-willed, refusing to speak the language of ought. But such was only his public lie. The truth, he was a coward in everything of consequence, most especially in the thing that mattered most to his heart. Fully escaped from his dream, having shaved, having let his eyes un-puff from the tears he'd evidently shed, he knew that his current conduct answered the moment as mist satisfied a parched man. They must have children, many children. They must join together in their one purpose. He must see her and keep on seeing her until their vain purgatory ended. Whatever happened, he could not allow the torture pit of the dream to overtake the only life he had.

The Sea

She lay in the bath thinking of the tramp they'd seen outside the V&A and two other times since. She supposed he mustn't be called a tramp but a broken soldier, but they were so creepy with their masks over their hollow faces that it was hard not to see them as tramps who'd stolen pieces from a theater. She thought of the song she'd been singing with the children two days earlier. *K-k-k-Katy, beautiful Katy.* Felicity liked it because it was catchy and there weren't many s's in it. Then yesterday as she was returning with the children from the Institute, the same broken soldier had been begging just inside the Marble Arch, whistling the song they'd sung two days before. And she remembered the joke she had with Jas when they would write each other during the holidays, the joke that ended *k-k-k-kitchen door* and the letter w in parentheses, a code they developed early on to signify a wink and avoid rows because no one could read tone in letters and the things they needed to write had so much more color and play than your stuffed shirt copperplate. So there was (w) and also (i), which meant irony.

She flushed in the cool bath—was the tramp tracking her, sent by someone from the chalet, from Ireland, someone in the list of someones who'd pay to see her suffer?

He kept copious, some would say demented, notes about everything that robbed him of sleep and peace, everything but this: following her from the museum the first day; following her to the Serpentine two days later and watching her play with the children; following her yesterday to an imposing building where she left the children, to a café where she nursed a glass, to the building again for the children, and home through the park. He recorded none of these movements.

He'd thought finding her would slay the final ogre, but in fact it was only the beginning of his difficulties. If he were to confront her, he would have to remove his mask (the actual one on his face), and she would have to contend not only with seeing him, but also with the macabre disguise. If, on the other hand, he trailed her as himself, she might flee before he could speak. Confronting her in the presence of her charges would compromise her at the exact moment he needed to win her trust. He could imagine disasters all the day long, but although yes, an observer might accuse him of clinging to the coward's path, in reality he had not lost his nerve. He knew exactly where she was, he could confront her at any time (though he had to find a better word than *confront*), and it was in fact his steel nerve that prevented him from making a pig's dinner of the whole thing.

The heat was stifling, and even lying atop the sheets naked, club windows open wide, he sweated all night. Today he had to journey by train to Scarborough, where God willing it would be cooler, for the interview he'd been granted with Saltford-Kent to ask St. Stephen's previous headmaster the questions no one else would answer. When he'd made the arrangements with Mrs. Sparks ten days earlier, it had seemed impossible that he would not have spoken to Amanda by now. Saturday last, having just clapped eyes on her, he had been obliged to traipse back to Yorkshire to install Lewis and interview a housekeeping candidate. He and Lewis had talked the whole journey (a respite from self-reproach at his failure to ring her doorbell) and arrived at the school in time for lunch. Their conversation touched only vaguely on the war, which Jamie flippantly likened to a deadly camping expedition among those not of one's class. Lewis had laughed and proved less helpless than Jamie had feared. He even appeared invigorated by the chaos of S-K's study.

The housekeeping candidate, a Miss Meyers, presented sterling references, but Jamie was taken aback by her youth. She looked no more than fifteen, though she claimed nineteen. She all but begged him to give her a chance, and he remembered Mrs. Sparks having been with S-K from the beginning. He left them at teatime and caught the train back to town, feeling an unexpected assurance and an odd warmth hearing the kindly tone Lewis had adopted with the girl.

Now, the heat of a London dawn chased any hope of falling back to sleep. It was too early to dress, so he repaired to a bathroom and drew a tepid tub, which at least took the edge off early morning arousal. Ever since setting eyes on her, he felt he could, without one iota of enticement, tear off all her clothes. Perhaps not tear, but he would relieve her of whatever hat she was wearing. He would reach across slowly so as not to startle her and slide it from her head. Even if she sat erect at the bar of a pub, he would run his fingers through her hair, or perhaps if there were hairpins, he'd remove the ironmongery before exploring her collar and . . . Oh, what use? It was torture to think of it.

He understood now the appeal of black magic, any magic, and were it not for his agreements with the Old Boy, he would seek out gypsies versed in cards or totem dolls. He did still possess a lock of her hair, and the gypsy would require it before casting enchantment deep into the earth, calling upon all the powers people denied to their folly. She would enlist them, and then, to the peril of their souls, the gypsy would reach into her sleep, take hold of her unguarded heart, and force her to see who'd brought the hair and the coin.

He plunged his face into the water to rinse off the last of the shaving foam before pulling the plug on the bath. He would not treat with gypsies. He would wait for one of his letters to be collected, just one, and then—*Listen, Old Boy! If there ever was a time for you to incline your Holy ear, this is it*!

He put on a fresh shirt, but his suit had seen better days. He supposed he should be grateful he hadn't got plump like Grady and that his clothes fit as well as the day they were made. He still felt embarrassed about the fact that the first thing he'd done upon arriving in London after the long, uncertain journey from Mainz, even before wiring his father, was to take a taxi to his tailor. He'd conceived the idea in France while waiting for the ferry in view of the rubble and the *mutilés de guerre*; he'd calmed his nerves by telling himself that when there was no way to influence the world for the better, one could always visit one's tailor. He was relieved to find the man still in business, and the smell of the shop announced that ordinary life in some sense continued contra mundum. As his tailor updated measurements on his card, Jamie felt that the man had perceived not only his shrunken body but also the incurable illness of his self.

That day after the war, he'd ordered a new suit and taken a ready-made shirt and trousers to the club. He ordered two more suits once he regained his proper weight, and another upon beginning at Marlborough. He wasn't the sort of man to thrill over clothing, unlike Grady who always spoke rapturously about shirt cloth, not to mention his notorious Oxford bags, which once made headlines for their width. Jamie agreed with his father that a gentleman required at most four good suits for ordinary occasions.

The club's breakfast hadn't yet begun when Jamie came down, but he fortified himself with a cup of coffee before stepping out to the radiant street. Today he must not indulge the confused, forlorn youth in himself; today he must have his hands on all the ropes, and just as he had needed the art of his tailor to transform him from prisoner to man, patient to undergraduate, graduate to housemaster, so did he need the force of serge now.

Hear me out, he said to the image of his bank manager, a figure who looked like his father in banker's suit. *I require, and by require I mean require, two new suits: one for summer and one for the start of term. And when I say suits, I mean the whole parcel, shirts, collars, socks, underwear, and a pair of shoes to last twenty years and take resoling. Second, hear me out, I really, and by really I mean in all prudence, require a motor car. Have you seen the to-ing and fro-ing this madness requires? How economical is it to be paying taxi drivers and train fares and organizing precious moments around the lunatic timetables of a score of railway firms? If you—you stars—mean to rain your dust until I burn or prevail, if I am to have a chance, then these things I require*!

His conjured bank manager explained the fact of his limited bank balance, one that would not bear such expenditures even when the paltry headmaster's salary had been deposited. He needed . . . a loan? A legacy? He needed access to the small sum he was due from his mother's estate in two years' time. Surely the present juncture was more pivotal than anything he'd face after thirty? Because, *listen you stars, listen you eternal immoveable ear*, he had indeed found her, found her alive and well, but he needed more. He needed to become that man, the man who would tear the curtain away, the man who would fall at her feet, implore her mercy, and *convince* her to have him.

No one ever told him that becoming a man was something you had to do again and again.

Little yellow flowers in the grass made her throat hurt. It was easy enough to choke a feeling when the children were near, but alone on her free afternoon, passing the place where the church bells played like someone's piano practice, she felt how it was to feel things. She wasn't one of those women Lina used to tell her about, those up-kept Fraus and Frauliens in Vienna who suffered muteness because of walled-off memories; they needed doctors with secret lusts to crash through the masonry until they remembered things again, and the things were always awful. She didn't need doctors. She knew the flowers had not been scattered but had grown on their own, that they weren't the same kind she'd scattered in the snow when they put her in the ground. She could, if she stopped and breathed, regard the flowers here and think of the flowers there. She could stand in a London square and call up in her mind the Austrians at the chalet and the apple schnapps they gave her every time, from their schloss where they worshipped Egyptian gods and the sun and the devil. She could, on her way to meet a man who was a bishop, think of her broken contract with the Frau, and the Austrians she endured to pay her debt and how it got so bad that—

Here was the trouble with time and life, especially if you had a memory fresh as the day things happened: memories could seem real as anything, but you couldn't be *in* them anymore; you couldn't touch them or change them.

Lina had got her away from the Austrians; Lina had written Diana for her, found the lovely people, convinced them to engage her, and then taken her across France to the boat for England. Lina told her to make a new start in London. She was too young for regrets, Lina said. Her whole life lay ahead, and despite some mean turns, there was every reason for her to be happy as a free woman in the modern age. Lina held daft political views and nursed bitter attitudes towards men, but she did also write poems that were true, so she wasn't entirely a beautiful vacant hole.

The last time they made love, at the place in Scotland, she kept saying his name with every wave. She'd insisted that Jas be the name she called him, but in Scotland it kept coming out of her, *Jamie, Jamie, Jamie*, as if she were saying *God, God, God.* It would never be that way again if he learned what she had done. But even if she agreed to meet him, (and why was she slogging through the heat to lunch with his father if this wasn't secretly her aim?) she could never let him inside her again unless she lay out the truth.

Sometime, sometime, when the time wasn't this time, when she was on the other side of thirty, she'd be living a life that forgot this one, even the lovely parts with the children who would never be hers. For all she knew she'd be Catholic again, that's how much she wouldn't know herself.

Here was the trouble with futures: she didn't want any of them. Everyone saw her as a modern girl, but all she wanted was a coin that would buy what she couldn't have, the time again in the cottage by the shore, pup still nosing the table, him inside her and the cloud pulling them both up inside it as she said his name, *Jamie, Jamie*. She wanted the days and nights in the chalet after the snowstorm, her tiny fingers, her smell, her eyes that looked like his. If anyone used that name again, it would paint and paper over the night she put the water on her and gave her the name and made the bargain, and over all those months in the dark, in her tears, when she said the name again and again.

She wanted to move forward in time like other people, watching her child grow out of frocks and turn fresh and need her hair brushed watching him love her as he'd never loved a thing, not even the pup, whom he'd loved even more than she had, it seemed, because he'd bought him out of bondage and taken him from the farmer and made him happy with them, happy, until he walked crooked and—

Here was the trouble with heatwaves: they wrecked the flowers first, your hair second, face powder third, and not until you'd fallen into a constant state of hot irritation and forgotten what it was to have a crisp, coherent thought did the weeds give over and die. Her shoe was rubbing where it never had before, she didn't have a plaster in her handbag, and she'd come too far to turn back. She didn't know if it would be cooler at his club, but they had to have a drink of water.

The address the man had written in his careful Victorian hand was just ahead. She squinted at the facade, white and pillared, letting everyone know it had stood through reigns of kings. The heat pressed until she felt it inside her head, and her thoughts made no more sense than Felicity when she spun in circles singing to the birds on her nightdress. She almost wished she were the fainting type, though it had to be a nuisance if you couldn't choose when to do it.

She would go inside and find a glass of water. She would tell the man nothing. The club would smell of old men and English snobs, but soon she would come out. She couldn't walk back and she couldn't afford a taxi, but there had to be breeze on the top of an omnibus.

She climbed the steps, and the door opened without her touching it. No sooner had she passed inside than a man pounced, offering to assist her in the sharp, polite tone servants used to let you know you had no business there.

—I'm meeting someone.

—Yes, madam?

When she spoke the man's name, the servant looked doubtful and bid her wait. The hall held coolness like a cellar. She hated it for its imperious conceit, and for its beauty.

Presently a man emerged through an archway. Though gray and slightly stooped, he had his son's eyes, active and slate blue, his son's cheekbones, his son's smile. He wore a pearl-gray linen suit and dusty-rose necktie.

—You've come, he said.

He looked more surprised than he could mute with manners, but his hand, when she took it, sensed the pressure of hers and matched it. He addressed her as Miss McDonagh. She said that Miss McDonagh was what the lovely family called her before she came to live with them. Now they called her Miss Marion. This family employed her, she explained as he guided her to a room with gold molding and red curtains. A servant showed them to a table near a long window that gave onto the park. They sat, and he gazed at her as if studying a painting.

—There are two children, she babbled, a boy and a girl.

The boy sometimes demanded they play Robin Hood, and on such occasions she would be Maid Marion.

—They must be very fond of you, Miss McDonagh.

The warmth in his voice made her forget her porcelain face for an instant.

—Do you dislike being called that?

She said she didn't care. He could call her Miss whatever-he-liked, or he could call her Marion, or Mary if he must.

—I must call you only what you wish.

He said it like he meant it, like Gute when he'd asked her in the beginning what name she wished to be called. She didn't know how to address this man, having greeted him first with *Good afternoon*. Now at the table, the not-knowing boxed her in, and she hadn't come to be boxed anywhere. He wasn't wearing a priest's collar or a bishop's gaiters. Protestants could get away with anything, but did he expect her to kowtow to his profession even when he wasn't wearing it?

—Do people call you Father?

—These days only my children.

He had a smile that looked sad.

—How are you supposed to talk to a bishop anyhow?

Her tone sounded fresh. A waiter handed them menu cards:

—My lord. Miss.

—Do you expect me to call you *that*? she balked.

The smile again, an abyss of loneliness:

—Please call me Archie.

She cast her gaze into the menu. It had never occurred to

her to wonder about the man's Christian name. She'd imagined him always formal, but now he'd called himself Archie. A kind name. A broad name. A name for a man with a life you couldn't guess.

She ordered the fish. The waiter brought hock, cold and quenching. Archie sipped as though discovering flavor for the first time. She hadn't put anything into her mouth since the cheese and toast last night, but she could hold drink.

He'd heard about the Arabian book the press had done and asked what she knew of the author. He asked how the press had come to do it and what went into such a project. Was he right to think it a triumph for them to have published it when the University Press got nearly all the books there were to do?

—Yes, she said. You've no idea.

—Tell me.

His hands looked as though you wouldn't mind one set on top of yours for assurance. His fingernails were neat, not ridged and awful like so many old men's or stained with nicotine like her own. His face had wrinkles but no liver spots, and a nice color as if he'd spent a week at the seaside.

When the fish came, it wasn't what she'd hoped, and when she tried to eat it, she couldn't. He put the smallest morsel of his own onto his fork and lifted it to his mouth as if each bite were an experiment.

Talk of the Arab turned to other books the press had done. Shockingly, he'd heard of Lina.

—You read *poetry*?

—I read the Literary Supplement, he said with a laugh.

She wasn't sure if this marked him as cultured or philistine, but his son never even read the supplement. He asked about the poem he'd seen there, and she told him about the opera a German composer wanted to make out of it. She described Lina's circle in Berne, and the circle from Vienna that summered at the lake.

He asked the waiter for bread and butter, and when it came, he had them place it beside her and take the uneaten fish away. He began to speak of travels, places he had been and places he longed to visit but did not at his age hope to see.

—New York, he said, now that would be a place.

—You could still go, so long as you didn't try the crossing in winter.

—There comes a point, my dear, when the possibilities left to one fit in the palm of a hand.

The warm room inched warmer, the needles harder.

—Oh, I didn't mean that, he said. I haven't asked you here because I'm dying.

The question rang between them, too obvious to voice. He cut his lettuce with a knife and nibbled it uncertainly. His interest in the press now struck her as pointed. Had he written some furtive manuscript and hoped to have it published? He hadn't mentioned his son. She'd expected at least, *My son sends his regards*. Or perhaps an unprompted resumé of his son's activities. She expected the lunch to feel contrived, or dramatic like the operas that boomed through the press whenever Gute received bad news from abroad. She had retained her hat when they'd offered to take it and was prepared to depart on a coin if he trespassed on her privacy. But he'd treated her easily, as a particular guest, letting her know the gratitude was all on his side. He'd discerned her indigestion though she tried to conceal it. Now he began to banter about detective stories, whether she preferred Chesterton, Christie, or Conan Doyle. Whether she'd known a Miss Sayers in Oxford who'd just published a detection novel of her own. She'd managed a piece of bread, and when the orange ices arrived, she let the tangy lump melt on her tongue before swallowing.

—Forgive me for asking, he said in an undertone, but are you being treated quite well?

Fever swept across her, and she wished to whatever ear

would hear that he wouldn't slip the mask, wouldn't speak of his son—

—By your employers.

She had to put her hands in her lap.

—If there were ever anything you might require or wish for . . .

His voice trailed off and his eyes looked like the old forgotten cottage.

Her employers were lovely, she said. She wanted for nothing, except an end to the godforsaken heat.

He grimaced. Plunging his spoon into the ice, he asked how the press had managed paper shortages during the war. Her chest unclenched, and she described her work with Gute, from reducing the size of sheet music to making Boanerges run. Her chatter entertained him, which only made her chatter more, the government contract for New Testaments for use in the field, the war photographs Gute received from Berlin on postcards showing soldiers in every kind of garb, a blond beauty with his airplane, turbaned troops in Montenegro, a mustachioed German surveying a collapsed palace, fantastic armored Panzer trains—but then the waiter was asking if they'd care to move into the bar, the dining room had emptied, and the man was consulting his pocket watch and declaring he'd kept her too long. She wanted to cut off her tongue, or at least stick a knife in the prattling girl. As they passed through the archway to the marble hall, she pretended to notice the clock.

—I'm late, she said.

He apologized again for keeping her and then asked, tentatively, if he might impose on her with one small matter.

—What matter?

Just when one had escaped the witch's house, she always stuck out her arm with more gingerbread.

—I only wonder if you might do me the favor of meeting me again, later this week, any time that suits. Not here.

He smiled as if to say, *You and I have had as much stuffiness as we can stand.* The soaring columns beside them boasted their ancient lineage, pointing here to the lavish staircase, there to a room in rich leather, there to antique vases full of silk flowers. He sat down suddenly beside a table and opened its drawer as if he owned the place. Producing a pen from his inner pocket, he wrote a name and address on a piece of stationery.

—It's in Aldgate, he said, by—

He named two landmarks she didn't know. The place was a public house. He hoped she wouldn't mind.

—Thursday afternoon perhaps?

She couldn't think. He smiled again as though they were both suffering through it.

—No one else, he said. I promise.

She told him she couldn't come until the evening.

—I'll be there from four o'clock, he replied. You'll find me in the garden unless it rains, in which case I'll be steaming inside.

With effort he stood and, leaning against the table, took her hand.

—Thank you, Miss McDonagh. I won't see you to the door if you'll forgive me, but I thank you most specially . . . for today.

The sign outside the convalescent home declared it a sea-bathing hospital, and Jamie found Saltford-Kent on the terrace, reading in a bath chair. The man looked shrunken compared to the figure in photographs Jamie had seen, but he shook Jamie's hand with vigor and glared with the glare headmasters perfected, in their guilds, to stir cold fear in schoolboys.

—My replacement has arrived, the man declared.

He set his book aside, and Jamie saw the letter he'd sent requesting the interview and outlining the topics he wished to discuss. He realized that the speech he'd rehearsed, praising

S-K for what he had created and sustained at the school, would come across as patronizing claptrap. As if determined not to help him, S-K folded his hands and stared.

Instead of awkwardness, though, Jamie felt only detachment. This man, whom he'd imagined, feared, and resented since June, held no power over his future. Nothing the man said could decide Jamie's happiness or his anguish. The man could only give him information, or not, as he chose.

—Sir, Jamie said, you know what I'm up against. And you must know how ill-prepared I've been left, by the Board in particular.

S-K straightened in the chair:

—Overall means well, but he's wont to gloss over a great deal.

—Instead of giving me a proper briefing, he's left me to fend for myself, and I've scraped together little more than an elaboration in hearsay. It won't do.

—Indeed.

—With the greatest respect to you, sir—

—By which you mean none at all.

—Sir—

—Stop sirring me—

—The staff needs changing.

—More than you've already done?

Jamie hesitated at the reference to Mrs. Sparks.

—I'd like your help, he persisted, your frank and confidential help.

The man picked up the letter and then set it down again in aggravation:

—You had better call me Andrew.

—James.

S-K gestured to a chair, and Jamie sat.

—I know what you must be thinking of young Grieves, the man said, but you'll be making a mistake if you dismiss him.

—John Grieves?

—He's irregular. His politics are incoherent. He'll drive you mad with his schemes and notions, but he's worth gold. You won't see it at first, but trust me.

—I do, Jamie said.

S-K regarded him warily.

—But it isn't Grieves I want to be shot of.

—No?

And so he launched into the two housemasters he wished to jettison. Stagnation was the word he used to describe them. He tried to find the line between confiding his concerns and scandalizing the man, or worse, making him feel he was being criticized. When Jamie inquired about the other staff, S-K grew more expansive, conveying biographies of the Common Room. He recounted the history of the chapel, its stained glass, its organ damaged in a flood before the war, awaiting funds for repair. It appeared that religious life at the school had not always been as moribund as it seemed. Jamie's spirits lifted at the prospect of reviving it.

—You're reminding me of a dream I had, Jamie said, the night after visiting the school.

—Oh, yes?

—I dreamed I was announcing reconstruction of the chapel. It would be completed in three days, but as I was talking, I realized the absurdity of it all. Why would anyone rebuild the chapel when it was so beautiful? And who could rebuild anything in three days?

—Three days?

Jamie nodded.

—You aren't our Lord, the man said dryly, and I daresay whatever changes you attempt will take a bit longer.

Jamie blushed.

—But your heart's in it, S-K said. I'll give you that.

A tray arrived with cordial and greengages. Jamie discovered he was hungry.

—Have you not eaten lunch? S-K asked.

He admitted he hadn't.

—Breakfast?

—Not really.

S-K sighed and called for sandwiches.

—And some of those other plums from yesterday, if there are any. Now, James, I'm sure you're told this all the time, but you must guard your health more wisely. A headmaster must be fighting fit, term in, term out.

—I know.

—Take me through it, S-K said stretching out his legs. The whole day, your first glimpse of the Academy to the moment you accepted.

The narration took them through two plates of sandwiches, a saucer of plums, and a pot of tea. He did not tell S-K about the scene in Burton-Lee's study but presented the evening as a blur.

—Once you'd come to your senses, though, you could have told Overall you'd changed your mind. Why didn't you?

Jamie could only say that the day had knit him into the sleeve of the place. It was the best way to express his attachment, though he would not arrive, as S-K thought, a fresh commander. He would begin as one already written into the pacts between Burton-Lee, John, Wilberforce, and somehow his father. He'd no more stepped foot there than they had him cutting himself and making blood vows.

—That's a dramatic way of putting it, S-K said.

—I didn't mean—

—You aren't this emotionable with women, I hope?

—I beg your pardon?

—Are you planning to marry?

He said he was.

—When?

—I . . .

—They'll take everything if you let them, the boys.

At the station, he caught a train for Stoat's family place. Stoat had been pestering Jamie to visit for over a year, but Jamie had never got round to it since Stoat's home was so far from anywhere Jamie had ever cared to go. Arranging the visit to Scarborough, Jamie had looked for somewhere to stop the night, and his various railway timetables had revealed Stoat's place to be more or less on the way.

As the fields and platforms came and went, he turned over everything S-K had told him. He'd no intention of resigning his future to schoolboys, but behind S-K's remark was a truth: The era of free courtship was coming to an end. Even if his sisters introduced him to other girls (and they would), even if he took one to dinner or a concert, even if she revealed an alluring spark, how could he, a headmaster, enter into the kind of outpouring he'd had in all innocence with Amanda? *Marion.* He would never be that free or true again.

When at sunset he got down from the train, Stoat was waiting in a motorcar the likes of which Jamie had never touched. A sleek two-seater with an engine that hummed like sex, it had leather seats and a green top that folded down. Stoat called it the Volare, some poetic allusion Jamie assumed, and once Jamie had wedged himself into the passenger seat, Stoat announced his intention to *flog the old Volare fenders*. He looked suntanned and well, far healthier than he'd ever been at Oxford.

It was too loud to talk during the drive, and Jamie reminded himself of his resolution not to speak of her. Stoat had always been enthralled by the Amanda Affair, as he called it, but Jamie had never disclosed the marrow. He prepared himself to show interest in Stoat's latest romantic tragedy, whatever it was, and if Stoat wanted to gossip, Jamie had anecdotes galore from his afternoon with S-K.

Stoat's family home was extensive despite his referring to

it as *the old shack*—seventeenth-century, one wing closed for economies, a guest room that smelled of mildew. Stoat's parents, a Baron and Baroness, were addressed as Mumsy and Papa. Jamie was asked to call them the same. He couldn't refuse, but never could he pronounce such words, much less call Stoat by his real name as they did; he contented himself with *you* all around.

—What's this about leaving Marlborough? Stoat asked when they'd settled on the terrace with drinks.

Jamie provided a précis of his employment and a more lingering précis of his interview with S-K.

—He agreed about the two depraved housemasters? Stoat asked.

—I never said they were depraved, only . . . unsatisfactory.

—Same thing, Stoat said. The old congeon agreed they were no good yet had never tried to sack them himself?

—They were experienced.

—Good at their rackets, you mean.

—Rather.

—But why haven't you sacked them yourself?

Jamie tried to explain, one didn't dismiss a man without cause and through the post. Stoat quizzed him about what they taught and how long they'd been there, and he lingered over Jamie's account of their brown-nosing at the supper given in his honor.

—Jass, you've got to wake up, Stoat declared at last. Neither one of them is going to retire voluntarily, not now, not in a year, not ever.

—No?

—Get that other geezer to sack 'em, the Board chap.

—Overall?

—It's his fault the school's such a mess. He can jolly well dig it out, Stoat declared.

Jamie liked the idea. He liked it quite a lot, but aside from the arduous prospect of convincing Overall, there was the problem of replacements, who would have to be found, interviewed, and engaged in less than a month.

—Who do you know? Stoat asked.

Jamie had been thinking of it, of course. He told him of a Frenchman whose war memoir the press had published. They'd met in prison at Mainz, and after the war, he'd come to England for a woman. The last Jamie had heard, she'd gone back to her husband, leaving the Frenchman bereft.

—He'll jump at a post, Stoat said with feeling.

—How are Abelard and Eloise coming along, by the way?

Stoat had gone to Cambridge to finish a doctorate in medieval romance.

—Oh, I've done with all that.

—Back to Anglo-Saxons?

—Back to reality. I'm in the city now.

Jamie laughed:

—Don't tell me you've joined the host of gray-suited men tending the shrine of financial wonders?

—Guilty.

As Stoat described his new life, Jamie grasped that his—he couldn't honestly call him friend, though others would—his *fellow* from staircase six had taken, or been subjected to, a revolution in his life's purpose. Jamie had always assumed Stoat was even worse with finances than he was himself, but now he realized, from the *old shack* and green Volare, not to mention Stoat's throwaway remarks about currency, that his fellow was a lion by breeding and choice, and that he by contrast was the one lost, low-aiming, and disordered in his affairs.

—Any time, Jamie asked, for your former pursuits?

—Such as?

—Grooming the dark brides.

It had been Stoat's term for chasing girls.

—Oh, Stoat said dismissively, that.

He stubbed out one cigarette and lit another:

—I had a fundamental realization.

Stoat was famous for his fundamental realizations, as much for their delusion as their passion. He launched into the tale of a girl at Cambridge who had married a tutor. Stoat's tutor. He wouldn't say she was the reason he left his degree, but—

—The fact is I'm finished with romance, Stoat declared.

He sounded sincere, and relieved.

—I'm engaged to a darling girl, Florencia—

—Not your cousin?

—Second cousin.

—But you always said—

—She's grown up. The wedding's next summer, then we'll honeymoon on the Continent and live in town until we can find a place near her parents in Weybridge.

Jamie felt dazed.

—Oh, I know what I used to say, Jass, but everyone else is married or engaged.

After supper, they repaired to Stoat's rooms, where there were good cigars and even better brandy.

—What about Kepler? Stoat said apropos of nothing.

—The seventeenth-century German?

—The twentieth-century Scot. Young Shaw from staircase ten.

Vaguely Jamie remembered a hanger-on of the Set, a man much younger than they but only a year behind them, whom they called Kepler owing to his enthusiasm for astronomy.

—What ever happened to him? Jamie asked. Last I recall he was discovering new planets when he wasn't killing himself on the rugby pitch.

—Rowing was his sport, Stoat said, and he read physics, but in any case he took a post last year at Cheltenham.

—Ladies' College?

—Yes, Stoat said with a grin. Unfortunately they didn't learn much since all they did was stargaze.

—What?

—Fell in love with him, every single girl. Constant state of anxiety for the lad. One girl even took poison from unrequited love.

—She *what*?

—They had to ask him to leave. Top-hole reference, of course, brilliant scholar, lovely man, but for a girls' school too much *sex appeal*, as they say.

Jamie wondered if he should stop drinking for the night.

—What's he doing now?

—Oh, peering into the sky when the clouds part. Took the whole thing awfully hard.

—Breakdown?

—Shaw? Never. But he's off females. Snatch him up for your natural sciences. Safe as houses for a boys' school.

Jamie let Stoat refill his glass. There were times only brandy could make sense of the unexpected.

—But what about you, Jass? Not still bleeding from the Amanda Affair, one hopes?

—No.

—Thank God. I'd have to rethink our acquaintance.

He was jesting, perhaps.

—You know how it is, Jamie said trying to sound jaded, when you're locked up in a boys' school.

—And now you're going from one to another.

—Quite.

—But that's the thing, Jass.

Stoat was regarding him seriously:

—I know you live in a certain world—

—What *world*?

—One where the only women are those paid to look after you. As a result, you're naïve about private life.

—That is unbelievably steep!

—Shut up, Jass, I'm serious, and you need to be serious for

once in your life. Do you want to grow old in a bedsit with someone coming in twice a week to do for you?

S-K and his bath chair bruised his mind.

—You need to find someone you can stand and marry her. Any prospects?

—Perhaps.

—Well, you'd better un-perhaps one and propose before you get stuck into this place of yours. Where, again?

—Yorkshire.

—Jass! Do it now before she finds out. If you go up there without a wife, you'll die alone.

—A staircase with a broken stair, a stable with an old brown mare, silver sparkles everywhere.

The old rhymes came to her like fairies who found you. The girl's hair tangled, and you had to brush it lightly until the comb could follow. The words flowed as she brushed, and she wondered what else lurked inside her only waiting for a cue. Her mother always said, *Wait until you've children of your own*. She said it as a curse, a bitter *You'll see*. And she had always said, *I'll never have children*. By which she meant, *I'll never be like you*. Always tired, always pregnant, always wiping another selfish mouth, always tyrannizing them with her moods and commands and her sudden, inexplicable rules. *From now on*, her mother would say, and a new limit would be placed on their lives, a new pleasure squashed, a new freedom locked up in the walls of her control. She would never be like that, yet here she was brushing the girl's hair, reciting old rhymes, and coercing her.

—Sure, an enchantress would never do such a thing.

—I'm not an enchantress, and I *shall* do it.

She meant pick things from her nose and eat them.

She laughed off the girl's rebellion but then let the comb snag and was her mother again.

What was the use of pretending? Sure there were plenty of uses, first being it got you through the time. But at night they came to her in sleep, Jas and all their people, alive and touching her as each one did. Sometimes she woke touching herself, the wave already happening. She'd resolved at the chalet not to make the wave again, but sometimes she gave in and ended drowned in tears, which defeated the point. Last night in her dreams she had searched Jas out, sought him with candle through a house with many rooms, and when she found him, she woke into the wave.

The old man, for old he was, wanted to meet her at a public house. It would be easy enough not to come. She knew instinctively that if she didn't, he would not chase her, and whatever he'd wanted would be cast to the wind. Last night after the wave, she fell back asleep, back to the house with many rooms, and she knew that the old man was looking for her because he wanted to give her something. *The Bishop wants you*, a servant told her. She said she wouldn't treat with English bishops because they were tyrants and apostates, stiff-necked refusers of the one true church. The servant went away, and she knew she had won, but the mind inside the dream kept whispering to the candle, *don't step on the broken stair, don't pull the comb so hard through the hair.* And the mind inside the dream knew the man was calling with a father's tenderness. Her own father loved her for the help she gave, but the man in the house didn't need anything. He wanted her to come to him as a daughter ought, so he could love her and protect her and show her how to face the knife of the world.

It rained all the next morning, but nothing got cooler. When they went out, it was all she could do to stop them stomping in puddles and wetting their clothes.

—I want to be wet!

—You never know when you'll need to be dry. For want of a nail . . .

She told them of the kingdom that had been lost. Felicity quit stomping and pondered the tragedy, but Clive began why-notting. Why not use a piece of wire? Why not a screw?

—Why not take a plank of wood and splinter off a piece and use it as a spike?

There were wooden nails in the sideboard, he argued, so there was no reason kingdoms should be lost unless you never believed in them in the first place.

—I believe in Camelot, Felicity declared. And Father Christmas and Morgan le Fay.

They reached the post office, and after they chose postcards for their grandmother, she helped Clive with his address and Felicity with her message.

—Remember the loop on the top of the L.

—Lissy, Lissy come and kiss me.

—If you don't stop rhyming, Clive told his sister, I'll stuff your mouth with old socks.

—Socks socks, fox in a box.

—Marion, tell her to stop.

—Marion McDonagh, the flora and the fauna.

—Marion McDonagh? the post lady said.

—The flora and the fauna!

—There's something for you, I believe.

The woman shuffled through a box:

—There, I was right.

She froze in confusion and fear as the woman set an envelope on the desk.

—Oh, Marion!

—Marion!

—You never get post!

The envelope was written in block letters, stamp English.

They demanded to know what it was and what it said, but she stuffed it into her handbag and bought them each a barley stick.

—Letter letter, wetter wetter, watch out while I run to get her.

Her blood was rushing around like rivers after a storm as they escaped the post office and took refuge in the park.

—Park park, bark bark, lookout lookout in the dark.

She taught the girl an old skipping song to stop the senseless rhyming:

—*I am a little orphan girl, my mother she is dead, my father is a drunkard, and wouldn't buy me my bread.*

—I haven't got a skipping rope!

Hours stretched before them.

—You can do it without. Like this: *Ding dong the castle bell, farewell to my mother*. Hop, hop, toe and turn. *Bury me in the old churchyard, beside my eldest brother.*

—I'm not dead! Clive protested.

—You have to be!

—Try it again.

—*Ding dong the castle bell.*

—Right right, right right, left left, the other left.

Why was there a letter for her? She hadn't told his father where she lived, not even the neighborhood.

—Four each direction: *My coffin shall be white, six little angels by my side, two to kneel and two to pray, and two to carry my soul away.*

—I can do it, Clive said, watch me.

—It's *my* song.

—Try it holding hands.

Was he sending letters to post offices at random?

—Please, Marion, please!

They'd arrived at the Serpentine and wanted to put their feet in the water.

—We'll be good.

—You said that yesterday and went in to your waist.

—Please, Clive said, we'll just dangle our feet. I promise.

—Please, Marion?

—We've practically got heat stroke.

Felicity pretended to faint.

—If you spoil your clothes again, you'll spend all tomorrow on penmanship.

They threw their arms around her and then tore off their shoes and stockings.

She ought to sit at their side, but there was a bench far enough away that they couldn't see what she held in her lap. They couldn't see her finger tear the flap, couldn't see the page that fell out, torn from an exercise book.

The shape of his words like the touch of a finger, written long before she'd set eyes on his father.

> *3.1 If you're reading this, hope is real, not just a poem, not just a virtue, but living. I know, I know, there's always "even though," but listen, this is me. You know. You know. I don't bite (unless you ask). I can look the other way while we listen to the bird, you know the one, who sings without the words? Please, Ariadne, spin your web again. Dear, dear old you.*

She had to put her hat before her face. This was why you should never read in public. Her handkerchief soaked through, and she had to take the other one from her bag even though it held a half-sucked barley stick.

—Marion!

Felicity's hands wet on her arm:

—I need to spend a penny. Are you crying?

She blew her nose.

—Of course not. Hay fever.

She took her into the shrubbery and waited while she went.

Later, she bought them ices, and they rode on the top of an omnibus. Finally traffic thickened, and it was time to go home.

—I don't want tea. It's too hot.

—We'll sit in the garden after your bath. There'll be cold grapes.

—Without the pips?

Once they'd had their tea and come back inside, she put on a gramophone disc and set them drawing.

—Where are you going, Marion?

—You must never ask a lady when she's off to spend a penny.

She cringed each time she used the odious expression, but you had to call it something, and it was better than the nursery words Felicity had been using when she arrived. She took a sheet from Clive's exercise book and a pencil from the tin. *Turn back.* Just two words in the middle of the page. Mother's desk gave envelope and stamp. Clatter down stairs, latch, late sun like an oven, horse droppings, motors, heat, more heat, crossing the road to the pillar box that stood like a beacon before the chemist's shop; slot like a maw, envelope gone.

Did she mean the words on the page? She'd not composed them. They'd slipped off the pencil and she hadn't interfered. The acts of the last quarter of an hour, not premeditated but permitted, testified to a power she had thought long gone, one that had animated the cold Oxford night when she as Charlie had clambered through Stoat's window, slipped past the sleeping Stoat, tiptoed up the staircase to Jas's door, his Oak, and let herself in. He hadn't been angry to be woken but thrilled at her daring. They'd never spent the night in his rooms again (getting her out before dawn had been difficult enough), but the gambit set a standard for their audacity, and it published the truth about who she was and what he was willing to be.

Heat radiated from the pavement, and as she passed the Consumption Hospital, a tear fell on her arm. Moments later, the skies opened, and she dashed for shelter beneath a portico.

Umbrellas popped open, costuming the thoroughfare in a mantle of black. Was it possible for rain to make it hotter? A chubby woman stood beside her dangling a bag of shopping.

—Do you think we'll see a rainbow? the woman asked.

The children were drawing. No one knew she'd left the house.

—You're supposed to get a rainbow when it rains and suns together, the woman continued. Wouldn't it be glorious?

She'd only been absent a few minutes, but the rain was falling in angry crescendos that couldn't be soothed or distracted.

—The weather has shell shock, she said.

The woman giggled and went on about rainbows as the leeks bumped through the string bag and threatened to ladder her stockings. She was within her rights to go seven streets to post a letter, but that didn't mean ruin wouldn't follow. It took only an instant to trip with scissors, choke on grapes, to fall and hit your head in a way that erased the future. The rain lashed harder, but she dove into the needles, running nearly on tiptoe so she wouldn't slip. You wouldn't think you'd have to race against shipwreck when you'd left children listening to a violin concerto.

No one saw her slip in the house, kick off her shoes, and run up the service stairs. She could strip in a moment, throw on her dressing gown, kerchief her hair—

—What on earth is that . . . thing?

Outside her bedroom she froze. The voice was Felicity's, the shushing Clive's. By Mother's firm command, they'd never before ventured to her room, but now they'd left the schoolroom and were giggling on the other side of her door. Her mind raced through her belongings. She possessed nothing more scandalous than a corselette—except the cardboard box, but that she kept under the bed behind her case.

She threw open the door. They froze. The box was on her bed, its contents spilled across the blanket. Seizing their arms, she pushed them from the room, down the narrow stairs, along the passage, and into the schoolroom. Felicity began to cry. Clive rubbed his wrist where her fingernails had dug.

—Where did you go? he spluttered.

—None of your business.

—You were gone ages!

—Do you always go into my room when I'm out?

Felicity sobbed harder.

—Shut up! Clive hissed.

—How dare you?

—How dare *you*?

Her hand rang across his cheek, and Felicity fell silent. From the corridor came Mother's voice at the telephone. She shut them in the schoolroom and made for the bath. What was the word for a catastrophe you caused yourself?

An accident, Mary?

Worse than that.

—No.

Mary.

Mary!

You're that thrawn, are you?

Thought we'd give you up?

—No!

No is right, we never would.

Never, Mary.

Is it ruin you mean?

Like Jerusalem burned?

The prophet warned, but they wouldn't listen.

—Shut up!

Is it sack you mean, Mary?

Such a lovely family.

Why would you smash such a lovely thing?

Wrack it and wreck it.

Curse, you mean, Mary?

Downfall?

Bane?

—No! No, no!

Head, floor, until the ringing came.

—Marion? Dear?

Latch rattling.

—May I come in?

Battering, ice, splotches in the air.

Mary.

Mary!

Mary, Mary, Mary!

Rattling louder.

—Are you unwell, dear?

Fire in the looking glass.

—Marion!

Real voices, Mother's and the children's, arms around her, edge of the bath. Clive held her wrist and Felicity her knee as the room slowed its spin and then came to a stop.

—Marion, dear.

—What happened, Mummy?

Clive stared in fear and sorrow, like a knight who had failed her, or she like a bear that mauled him. Mother pressed a flannel to her forehead and said they'd put salt on her blouse.

—That tiny spot will come out in a trice. Go downstairs, children. Clive, take your sister.

Her ears emptied, pounding slowed. Mother didn't mention Clive's red cheek, and the children didn't speak of what they'd seen in her box. Later, Mother made her drink tea with brandy in it. A disgusting concoction, but one Mother swore by after a spell.

Stoat's Volare delivered him to the station, the LNER delivered him to King's Cross, and having worked off his nerves with a march from the station, he oozed up to the club in time to bathe before seeing his father.

When he found the man in the bar, Jamie thought he looked drained.

—I'm not sure I approve of this jaunt of yours, Jamie said. What does your physician say about hacking up to town?

—I'm taking things exceedingly slowly, his father insisted, and it's more peaceful here. No one hovers.

—The girls?

—Everyone.

His father's plans sounded vague, but he'd sent Wilberforce to the seaside with Beth & Co., and in a few days he intended to join them. He urged Jamie to take a week's holiday with the family.

—Fat chance, Jamie said. I doubt I'll get a full night's sleep until Christmas.

His father looked pained at his refusal, but once the gin-and-tonics arrived, the man sharpened, speaking with more strength and sparkle. Jamie reported on his jaunt to Scarborough and on his jaunt three days earlier to St. Stephen's to install Lewis and interview Miss Meyers.

—How very frenetic, his father said, though I suppose you're keeping the railways in business.

—I'm a walking, talking advertisement for the day return.

Jamie polished up the story of Lewis, omitting the wheelchair and the man's missing legs, and described Miss Meyers as keen. When he returned to the subject of the housemasters, his father encouraged him to ring Overall that very evening.

—One doesn't want to sound desperate, Jamie said.

—But it's your view that these changes are essential?

—Yes.

—And you've only four weeks to arrange them?

He nodded.

—Then there's no time to waste. You know what you're doing, and you're right.

He couldn't remember his father ever before uttering those words, to him or of him, but he recognized the pull of a turning tide.

—In that case, he said, I'd be glad of your help with one or two details.

—Such as?

Jamie returned to the subject of Kardleigh, dilating on the man's careers in town and on Jamie's dream, now hopeless, that he come to St. Stephen's as physician and complete his musical training at York Minster.

—That's your idea, is it?

It sounded harebrained spoken aloud. He shrugged.

—It's rather inspired, his father said. I could ring round if you like.

Jamie gathered himself. His father, whom he had expected just a month ago to thwart his every wish, had not only used his connections to send him Miss Meyers, but was now offering to exploit those same connections, which normally he protected jealously, to . . . what? Put him in touch with the Minster's organ master? Speak to the man himself? Prevail upon Bairstow to adopt as protégé the former director of a hospital for the shell-shocked?

A servant announced that their table was ready, but his father asked if they might have sandwiches and lemonade brought to the verandah instead. When Jamie asked for some cold plums, the servant looked askance but promised to inquire. They stepped outside, where the heat pressed and klaxons sounded and they dropped into wicker chairs.

—Everyone who can has fled to the seaside, Jamie complained. It's mad to imagine sorting anything out in August!

—Don't lose your nerve.

His father shifted out of the sun and opened his jacket.

—Now, the man continued, you said details plural. What's next?

—Matron.

—Ah.

They were interrupted by the arrival of the sandwiches. After pronouncing grace, his father began to eat in silence, methodically consuming two watercress triangles. They'd brought prunes instead of plums, so Jamie resigned himself to egg and cheese. The lemonade stung the back of his throat.

—St. Stephen's matron is a treasure of experience, his father said at last. You're going to need her.

—I know, but—

—She'll never be as devoted to you as she was to your predecessor—

—I sincerely hope *not*.

—Which is why she must be offered a second chapter.

Second chapter. The lemonade softened.

—Let her help you find your feet, his father proposed. By springtime, the school will be righted—

—That's optimistic.

—Realistic. And after Easter, the choir school will have announced a headmaster. She can come to Wiltshire, install herself in the Close, and take charge of domestic staffing.

Jamie gazed at his father, at a loss for words. In moments of fancy, he'd imagined the woman at the choir school, but he'd never spoken of it. Was his father employing the knowing, or was the notion simply obvious? As his father enumerated the benefits of the plan, for the choir school and for Matron herself, he spoke as he might in a Chapter meeting, as if Jamie were an equal whose ideas carried weight.

—Right, his father said. Next?

—Money, Jamie confessed.

His father's view, when he'd explained everything, was that he should negotiate with Overall while putting the screws to him over the staffing. The legacy from his mother could not be touched for two more years, and while his father was prepared to make him a loan, he suggested it might be better, in every way, if Jamie could secure the funds himself.

After his father had gone up to bed, Jamie approached the desk clerk.

—No letters, I'm afraid, sir.

Jamie rebuked the wooden track: men such as he did not cling to childish wishes.

—I need to place a telephone call, he told the clerk.

—Yes, sir.

Sending missives to six post offices on the off-chance that one might be collected was not how men conducted their affairs.

A butler answered the telephone, but when Jamie asked for Overall, the man starchily informed him that the Viscount was not at home. Jamie insisted that time was of the essence, that Overall had given his exchange when they'd last dined, that the Chairman of St. Stephen's Board would not wish to leave its headmaster standing at the door, as it were—

—Hold the line, please, sir.

Jamie held the line. Overall might play the vague aristocrat when it suited him, but he was tireless when it came to getting his way. Jamie hoped he'd recognize a fellow stubborn mule.

At last the extension clicked:

—Headmaster, said Overall warmly. To what do I owe the pleasure?

Jamie turned on the charm, answering a query from Overall's most recent letter and requesting an interview.

—I'm off to France at the weekend, Overall said.

—I need to see you before you go. It's essential.

If Overall was surprised, he didn't show it. He instructed Jamie to come the next day and to organize his arrival with the butler.

Buzzing with triumph, Jamie went for a walk, confining

himself to the lit edge of Green Park. He was not climbing the pitched rail of a sinking ship. He was not ruining his career and his happiness. He was merely facing a series of challenges, several of which he'd already overcome. He and his sisters used to play a game called Seven Quests, an elaborate entertainment invented before he was born. One of them, usually Agnes or Flora, would be the giantess, and everyone else formed the party that must complete seven quests or be swallowed by the giant, an ordeal that always left one sore. He'd never played giant to a party of his sisters, but once in later years he'd played it to Lucy and John. His reign lacked the epic feeling of the classic games, but it taught him the art of devising a course of increasing difficulty, no quests having been done before, none of them illegal by the standards of the household (or not much), for preference containing a theme. The giant presented one quest at a time, and if you failed it, that was the end for you, into the giant's mouth, a spectacle designed to intensify the resolve and fear of those who remained. Now quests were underway urgently and simultaneously, their outcomes more consequential than any his sisters could inflict. He had passed a boundary somewhere, and now he traversed a land where no rebellion, no play, no fun could be indulged. Aims mattered gravely; errors were irreversible.

There had been a time, he saw now, when he'd actually been as close as a person could come to free, his first year as an undergraduate, before meeting her, before discovering the Business. His days had consisted of reading, walking, chousing with the Set, and dabbling in novelties such as wide trouser legs and variety shows. Anyone who could carry a tune was pressed to join the college revue. *Oh, that's the way with every sailor. He will knock you in the perch and then leave you in the lurch.* The choreography had made them laugh so hard they collapsed on the floor. *They're all freemen from the seamen to the admiral of the fleet*! The evening had been a wild success, and he'd briefly wondered if he was cut out for the stage. That era, he now felt, had been his truest innocence even on the heels of the war. Contrary to popular belief—and he wanted to preach a sermon about this—there was no perfect innocence in childhood, no pure state from which they had been corrupted by friends or bullies, bad fathers or crime. Such a state did not exist, and when they longed for it, they were in fact longing for the ends of eternity, primal state and final state both. What they called innocence could only been seen in retrospect. You might, if you grew terribly experienced and alert, come to see when an Eden you'd inhabited was crumbling around you. A feeling would arrive like panic, but instead of thinking, *Oh no, another catastrophe*, you'd think, *There it goes, the innocence I didn't know I had.*

Would it be better if he'd never learned what became of her? At least then he could enshrine her in memory. The enshrining had happened quickly with his godfather. The dead couldn't answer back, couldn't say you were wrong, couldn't surprise you or disrupt your life with lunches or letters or telegrams. The dead were forced to be what you made them.

When he saw Overall's place (Tudor with Georgian additions), he regretted not bringing a dinner jacket. To be fair, he'd come on a day return, but after presenting his arguments to Overall, he realized he'd have to stay the night.

At first the man had tried to flatter him, brushing away his concerns about the two bad housemasters:

—I've every confidence in your ability to work wonders, my boy.

But Overall had used that line before, and Jamie wasn't having it. He attacked from another angle as Overall showed him the stables, from a third as they toured the orchard, and by the time they'd been served drinks under the hawthorn tree, Jamie was having to employ thinly-veiled threats of disaster.

Eventually, Overall announced his intention to lie down and informed Jamie dinner was at eight.

—We won't change, Overall said. Of course you'll stop the night.

Jamie was shown to a bedroom overlooking the kennels. Lady Overall, plump and genial, hailed him from the courtyard and insisted he come down to view her litter of terrier puppies. After Jamie had been thoroughly crawled over, licked, and nipped, he repaired to the bath. He brushed his suit vigorously before dinner, but even though they were forgoing evening wear (on his account surely), he felt shabby and resolved to make the appointment with his tailor on Monday. Perhaps the man would let him have a suit on credit; if not, he'd ask Beth for a loan.

At dinner, it became clear that Lady Overall had developed an interest in him. Her manner remained jolly and distracted, but she seemed to understand what was at stake.

—Tell me about these men you want to engage, she said brightly. Is it as difficult to find good schoolmasters as it is good servants?

Jamie described Kardleigh, wizard of the shell-shocked turned wizard of the organ, young Shaw, astronomer whose charisma unsuited him for a girls' school, and finally the Frenchman and poet, Henri. She quizzed him as one might a friendly witness, eventually drawing her husband into it. After the gooseberry fool, Jamie and Overall withdrew to the smoking room.

—All right, Overall said cutting the cigars, I'll bite. But I'm not sacking those housemasters until replacements are certain.

Jamie agreed the strategy was prudent.

—And if I'm being asked to gamble even more on this nightmare—

—Nightmare?

—Oh, you know the truth as well as I do, Overall continued.

But if this school is to thrive instead of, as you say, limping along until an even worse scandal closes its doors forever, not to mention what you didn't say, tarnishing the reputations of everyone who touches it . . .

Overall was nowhere near as oblivious as he seemed.

—If all that, then I really must audit your interviews with these men. I shan't interfere, but I mean to see for myself who's worth fighting for.

—What about your holiday?

—I'll follow on.

The next morning, Jamie telephoned round to arrange interviews with Shaw and Henri. Kardleigh proved trickier, but he agreed to dine at Overall's club. After a protracted journey back to town having mistakenly boarded the slow train, Jamie traipsed through the August haze towards his own club, lists multiplying like rabbits, desperate for a drink, a bath, and a wank, in that order.

—Sir, said the desk clerk.

An envelope slid across the pink marble surface.

They said of revolutions that they happen slowly, then all at once. His name scrawled in her wild, racing hand. Inside, blue pencil pressed so hard it left a mark. *Turn Back*!

He stood at the desk and composed his reply, six times for six post offices: *Never*!

Particularly fine, Professor Jay said of Charlie's composition. She flushed with pleasure and he bought her ice-cream and said she could have a head start on the men who chased her, and his finger was on her and the wave was close and a klaxon sounded and she awoke in the bed on the fourth story, sky already light, her hand where his had been, one impossible thing after another.

As Professor Jay, he had never said Charlie's compositions were fine, and though that was the point, of course, she'd always hungered as Charlie for his praise, even as she fashioned sloppy compositions to irk him. Their game, the Scene he called it, always felt real to her whether or not the costumes suited. The time little Mae told Uncle Jack she knew her father would fetch her home, and Uncle Jack told her gently that her father was gone, she'd worked herself so deeply into it that she'd burst into sobs of grief and it took him a long time to console her.

The Scene aimed ostensibly at one thing, but the more they played, the more it aimed at something else, though she couldn't even now say what. He told her once she had a talent for the stage. He meant it as a compliment, but she felt it as a slap. Scenes weren't the stage, she tried to tell him. They were reality. How could you call it theater when they'd no audience but each other? Yes, it was like playing as children, and Daniel had been very good at the make-believes they played, but this was because she and Daniel had a single mind so he could go as real as she did. There was a different realness you could live in a Scene because you didn't have to protect yourself as in life. You could play all the way into it because the worst was what you were reaching for, though sometimes it was too much, that woman in Wales for example. She'd played that woman because he said he wanted to go that far, and he never gave the signal that meant, *Find a way out*. He never gave it, but he was so cold and shaking at the end that it scared her like death. She said sorry later, more than once. Much later he said he'd like to see that woman again, but she knew she would never find her. Even at the time she had felt only a cold, detached puzzle: What to do to him next? How to get underneath that resolve? It was possible, she thought now, listening to the house stir and the street rattle with delivery carts, that the unfeeling of that woman *was* reality, and that people like that simply didn't have feelings as other people did.

When he first told her about the broader enterprise, which he called the Business, she'd felt it in her place of feeling, a first-class temptation, the way Artemis once described the desperate, beautiful soldier she'd let seduce her or the older man who bought her that dress of soie de chine. The men of the Business were to her like characters in literature, inwardly known but impossible to meet. After much writing back and forth with Jasper about the theory of the Business—and she could have published tracts to keep the press busy for months—they played their first Scene in a strange flat out near the Morris factory. There was a room with school desks, and she played Charlie to his Professor Jay. The action was short, simple, based on something real, and he proved as serious as Daniel, but unlike play with Daniel, no one interfered. Her stomach thudded even now remembering the excitement, not of the pretend drama but of the real thing with a real person, a boy not sharing her mind as Daniel had, but in a way (Daniel forgive her) better.

The alarm clock clanged, and her head ached when she sat up. She had to put on her long-sleeved blouse since the other was in the wash. She thought the pink on her forehead could be explained as sunburn, and the scab she covered with hair. She'd locked the cardboard box in her case and wore the key around her neck as she'd done at the chalet, and even though they had touched her locket in their lovely house on the lovely square, the Talkers had gone and the morning was new, dreams were only dreams, and she changed her knickers for fresh.

She should cut him off. She should put his letter to the candle, ditto the address of the pub in Aldgate. She must stop encouraging Mother's fear of foreign places, she must go abroad with them, and when they all returned, she must let Mother and Father write a lovely reference so that when Clive went to his school and Felicity to her nursery, she could take up with new children in a new square. She wasn't like Jane Eyre, weak, orphaned, stuck with a misanthrope. She could be governess to a king if she tried.

At breakfast, Felicity presented her a blossom she'd plucked off a weed. Clive fetched the unfinished crossword from the Sunday paper and offered to tell her any word she wanted. Mother asked if she'd like a glass of milk. She accepted the crossword, declined the milk, and tucked the blossom behind her ear.

—I've been thinking, Mother said turning to her husband, that Marion has been working *frightfully* hard.

Father regarded his wife over the part of the paper he'd been allowed to retain.

—We mustn't let her get overtired, Mother continued.

—Certainly not, said Father. Not with the Alsace in a fortnight.

—You must take the evening off, Marion dear. I shall take the children to Philomena's.

—I'm perfectly well, she assured them. It was only the heat.

—But what about your dear friend Diana? Wouldn't you like to visit her before . . . ?

Mother mouthed, *the baby*.

It was Thursday. She hadn't yet burned the address in Aldgate.

—As a matter of fact, Diana's been pestering me to come round.

—Don't say another word, Mother declared. You must take your leave the moment you return from the Center—

—It's the *Institute* today.

—The Center's *Saturday*, Mummy.

And so it was decided.

That afternoon a breeze picked up. She boarded a 'bus heading east and climbed the ladder to the open top. The air slid by like a cold pond.

She could toss the address over the rail and let the soot take it. If the man thought her a coward, who cared? She could even go to the pub and give the man a piece of her mind. She could tell him, *How dare you*? How dare he lure her to a club where his son had been staying and let her think they were alone? Had his son been surveilling them? First the club, now the other side of town, where alleys held men who'd sell you into white slavery. None of it mattered anyway because whatever his angle, her salvo would be the same. *How dare you*?

Yet, as the omnibus trundled along the river, through streets and quarters where people lived unaccountable lives, the beautifully written address for the Parliament Arms and the memory of the pen that wrote it stirred a first-class temptation. This man, this father, defied sense. He broke bans and bounds too many to count, yet his handwriting conveyed wisdom, as if madness were impossible so long as he were there.

A seagull swooped down for a biscuit left on a seat, gobbling it and then squawking away. Anyone, even the gull, would recognize the vanity of her errand. Hat tied beneath her chin, battered handbag, fingers picking a hangnail, this girl wandered in a fog of mistakes. Here she was wasting a free evening to kick at the shins of an old man steeped in a bad profession when what she ought to be doing was killing her pride, boarding a train to Oxford, and going to see Gute, the one man who'd always stood by her, who even now would break open the vodka at a word from her. After the war, when people rebelled against everything from stays to chaperones to bans on four-letter words, Gute attained his English citizenship. He began to carry his papers everywhere in a leather wallet he had made for the purpose. One night she asked him why he'd become English out of all the things he could be.

—My dear Amanda of Galway town.

They were lying in the garden behind the press, the only ones awake after a salon.

—A simple decision, Gute said. It was, you see, the excellent

English tobacco, beautiful in pipe or papers, excellent enough to make a person's blood flow always with the tilt of the earth.

A flutter of umbrellas opened atop the 'bus, and the driver called the name of her stop. As the skies opened, she tripped down the steps, leapt to the pavement, and dashed for the pub.

The Parliament Arms smelled like any public house except for the stocks set in jugs near the door, like vivacious daughters posed to brighten a household. Before she could shake out her hair, she saw him—armchair before an unlit grate, glass of bitter beside him, newspaper folded on his knee. He looked up and capped his pen, his face bright like Gute's on the moonlit grass:

—My dear Miss McDonagh, how good of you to come.

When he asked what she'd like, she told him lemonade but then wished for whiskey and couldn't undo the order. He gestured to one of the alcoves, the kind where you could speak closely as in your own parlor.

—Are you quite dry enough? he asked. Do you need a flannel?

She insisted she didn't, and he led her to the snug, offering her the seat one could easily escape. He'd arranged the moment, as he'd arranged the previous lunch, yet he settled into his seat not as a man intent on a goal, but as one with an afternoon to waste. He set his paper aside, open to the crossword. One mistake was snarling everything.

—It's catnip, she said.

—I beg your pardon?

—Thirteen across.

Surprise colonized his face, then pleasure.

—Why, you're a wonder, Miss McDonagh.

He looked like his son as she remembered him in the surf the last time they'd gone to Scotland. They'd taken the pup to the shore and waded into the sea, and he'd started to say something but stopped. His eyes glistened, and she had the sudden fear he was about to ask her to marry him. They'd talked of marriage in theory, and she'd always talked it down, insisting that she'd never submit to it again (or perhaps for the first time depending on the legitimacy of the so-called priest). Standing on the pebbles, icy water lapping their knees, he seemed to have glimpsed the future, but when she asked him what he meant to say, he said, *Not yet*.

His father's gaze settled on her fingers, which were fiddling with the clasp of her handbag. She set it aside and fetched the lemonade that had appeared on the bar. As she slid back into her seat, he let out a sigh, not of sorrow but of an ordinary day.

They began to speak of crosswords. He confessed he was terrible at them but worked them anyway to keep his mind sharp and his pride in check. He'd formed the habit earlier that summer when he had been, briefly, on his back. She showed her curiosity, and he admitted to a minor indisposition. They had brought him crosswords. He was avoiding the real story, yet his familiar strangeness, or his strange familiarity, made her heart beat deeper.

—Influenza? she asked.

—Touch of angina. The experience was salutary, not that one would seek it. All one's illusions of power, all one's distractions, gone.

The skin around his eyes sagged, but his irises stood out sharp like his son's.

—One feels one's unconquerable weakness.

—*Yes*.

His eyes focused on her, but she laughed lightly:

—When was all this?

—First of June.

—In the middle of the night?

—In a chapter meeting.

She reached for a joke but couldn't find one.

—Fancy, she said. Just as I was being engaged by my employer, you were . . .

—Collapsing before my staff and being carted away?

She heard it then, the hint of self-mockery so familiar in the one who had the same way of concealing a smile.

—But look at you now, she rejoined. Zipping up to town. Gadding about clubs and pubs. Doing crosswords. Entertaining governesses.

—Were you a reporter at that press of yours?

—Not in these trousers.

He smiled, and she leaned forward, wagging a finger:

—Don't try to change the subject. It's still my turn.

—Quid pro quo?

Her breath caught minutely at his mention of the game she had played with his son, but she pretended the lemonade had tickled her nose and laughed again. Relaxing slightly, he began to describe the hospital, gaining confidence with each detail as if he were accustomed to regaling but had not yet rehearsed this: the imprisoning sheets tucked tightly all around; the nerve-straining din of beds cranking up and down; the shiver-inducing application of margarine to every slice of bread; the relentless cut of disinfectant in the air. Thankfully his stay had been brief. His physician quickly declared him fit for discharge, which ought to have quashed the whole kerfuffle but for the interference of others. They mistrusted his physician, protested the discharge, fell over themselves concocting alternative arrangements, and in the end demanded he repair to Wight.

—Why?

—It's where they stash infirm clergy. One's meant to lounge in garden chairs eating porridge and loose custard for one's meat.

—Not even a fish or a handful of berries?

—Not even that.

Without specifying who *they* had been, he described his victory over their henpecking. He'd rejected Wight, promised to rest at home, and finally won release. Once home, however, inactivity had proved strenuous to the sane mind. Providentially, he had been called upon to assist with a project, one month of which had dispelled his torpor. Now said project was percolating at the seaside, and he was at liberty to attend to another concern here in town, across the way. He gestured to the window. His strength, he said, had never been better. All patients ought to be given projects.

She peered through the window. Building works surrounded the structure opposite, where gray brick transitioned into red at the level of the window sills. A cart rattled past with empty milk jugs.

—I'm afraid you'll have to explain, she said. I'm not good at guessing.

He hesitated, interrupting the rhythm of easy patter, so familiar and yet so differently graceful from the current that flowed through his son, that master guesser who understood so much without being told.

—The project is properly theirs, he said, not mine. You see the chapel, nearly completed.

—You're an architect as well?

—Only of follies. Friendship to the sisters is the limit of my abilities.

—Sisters? As in *nuns*?

—Anglican nuns. Don't look so scandalized. Their concern is the sick—

—How long have you been fraternizing with *nuns*?

He deployed the smile his son used to say, *lay down your arms*.

—I fell in with them years ago, when I was a young dean.

—And what's a dean in the English so-called church?

—Someone foolish enough to accept charge of a cathedral. Leaky roofs, imperious bishops, not enough money.

His wife had died, he said. His sister had moved in to help domestically, but he was taking the whole thing poorly.

—There was an abbot near the cathedral—Anglican, before your bristle—and my bishop ordered me to see him twice a week.

—See him how?

—Presumably, they were afraid I'd go off at the nail.

—You loved her?

—Very much.

He fell silent, and she turned her attention to the lemonade, wishing into the bubbles that he not speak of what she knew they both were thinking, the purpose behind the lunch and the pub, the reason he'd permitted her interrogation, the one they'd been discussing the entire time while speaking of other things.

—I'd always been certain we'd live to be a hundred, he said. To see our great-grandchildren wearing our eyes and smiles.

He flashed a rueful grin:

—The abbot quickly decided I—needed—a—project.

He tapped the table in imitation of an imperious cleric.

—And it happened that the sisters needed someone to hear their confessions.

—I thought you English didn't believe in confession.

—Oh, we do, though not quite as the Romans. *All may, some should, none must*, as the saying goes. In any case, what the sisters really needed was someone outside their house to listen to their concerns, and the abbess needed a friend as she developed their ministry. Nowadays I see them less often than I'd like. We correspond.

—What do they ask you, these nuns?

—Every kind of thing.

—Oh, Father, Sister Perpetua took all the sugar so I chucked her wimple down the cistern.

He smiled faintly.

—I suppose it builds you up, resolving the quibbles of holy sisters.

—None of them quibble.

—But they can't have asked you real things.

—Real things? Such as?

—*Such as*? How to open a bank account! How to patch a shoe! Why the English treat the world like mud, where are the rest of the unknown soldiers, what happens when you break a promise to God?

He glanced at his hands and then back to her.

—Break a promise how?

They weren't speaking of her. They were speaking of things.

—You know. Say a person makes a quid pro quo. If they break the quid, does God break the quo?

He studied the table like a map.

—We know, he said, that God keeps his promises.

—Even if people don't?

—That's the whole Old Testament, wouldn't you say, God's faithfulness to wayward Israel?

—Except when he has them killed and taken into slavery.

There was sadness in his eyes, but his mouth widened:

—He never promised deliverance from suffering.

—How convenient.

—He promises deliverance *in* suffering.

He broke her gaze, as if slipping from a room when one needed privacy. Beside him, secluded, she heard the questions he wasn't asking.

—I don't know why I came, she said.

—Neither do I.

She looked up from her hangnail.

—I mean, he continued, I'm on a lark as much as you.

Youth filled his face, as though she had conjured the recipient of her letter, and with the thirst that sprang beneath her tongue came a rush of fear.

—Just what do Anglican nuns do when they aren't being heretics?

—Oh, much the same as Catholic nuns. Only better.

—They scold better, do they?

—Probably not as well. These, my friends across the way, work alongside ordinary women, people such as you with employers and lives of their own.

—I thought they helped the sick.

—Also women and children, particularly women who find themselves with children and no husband, or women whose husbands are more life-threatening than life-supporting.

—Is *that* why you asked me here?

The way he blinked said her anger surprised him, that he didn't know what she meant, and then that she'd given herself away. When he didn't chase the knowledge, his delicacy felt more chivalrous than any way he'd treated her yet.

—To be perfectly honest, he said at last, I'd no plan in mind. Perhaps it was the delightful way you spoke of the press last time that made me wonder if you might wish for fresh acquaintances.

—I don't need friends.

—And if with all your governessing you might be persuadable, as they're in a pinch.

—Pinch?

—For volunteer teachers.

She nearly laughed.

—If you think you can lure me across town, witter about crosswords and wayward Israel, and then net me into a project with nuns, you're either mad or have a preposterous self-regard.

—Why not both?

—You can't shock me, Archie.

—Challenge?

—You'd like that.

She dug coins from her purse, but he only plunked them back inside and shut the clasp. It had been so long since she'd done what they were doing—Bicker? Joust? Play?

—I've two hours Saturday, she said, when the children are at the Center. Not a moment longer.

—Done, he said offering his hand.

When she shook it, he grinned. They donned their hats, and he moved to the door with more vigor than she thought he possessed. Outside, he gestured to a lane:

—Shall we?

Then they were crossing the road and passing through a gate and she'd missed the moment when she might have made for the omnibus halt. He assumed she was going inside, and as he pulled the bell at the brown door, she found she couldn't correct him without appearing afraid.

A woman admitted them. She wore ordinary clothing, blouse and skirt, and looked the age of Mother. Archie called her Elaine.

—And may I present my friend Marion.

Elaine extended her hand, looking pleased but unsurprised.

—I've told her about your tutoring shortages, Archie continued. She's a governess.

—Wonderful!

—I can't stay, she said.

—But you'll have a cup of tea, Elaine replied.

Then Archie had disappeared through a sliding panel, and Elaine was leading her through dim corridors to a kitchen, large and lit by high windows. Elaine proceeded to make the tea and describe the difficulties of providing lessons in August. Everyone who could had fled the city, she said, but the needs of their pilgrims did not vanish in the heat. Elaine took three digestive biscuits from a battered tin and set them on a plate, her voice bubbling about pilgrims, which seemed to mean the women they helped. Waiting for the water to boil, she described individuals as if Marion were a teacher about to accept a difficult class.

—You won't be alone, Elaine told her.

Their pilgrims came to the refectory for lessons, working singly or in pairs with their instructresses.

—Reading and penmanship and totting up.

The tea satisfied a place beneath her tongue, and Elaine was so beautiful, with her long eyelashes, her dark hair plaited back, and her face without a bit of makeup. Their pilgrims faced many troubles. Most had children, in hand or inside them, but the help they always needed was fending for themselves.

—Writing letters on their own behalf, keeping track of money, some are learning shorthand.

—I haven't got shorthand.

—There's a place we send them.

She explained about Felicity and Clive: she had only a few hours each week, and the omnibus—

—Oh, but you must bring them, Elaine said.

During their pilgrims' lessons, Sister Prue entertained the children in the courtyard.

—There's a boy one might call rough, but Prue has the measure of him. Now, let's see about your journey.

Elaine led her into a pantry on whose wall hung a map of London. After ascertaining the location of the Institute, the Center, and the lovely people's house, Elaine declared she must take the underground and proceeded to write instructions on the back of a shopping list. Diana had said you could get your throat slit on the underground, but Elaine claimed to take it every day. Safe as houses, speedy as thought.

Elaine was leading her back through the corridors when a sound squeezed her heart, a strain of music. She knew the piece, but never had it brushed her that way, like sun on her skin.

—Sister Laetitia's at the gramophone again, Elaine explained.

She heard it then, the timbre of a gramophone where moments before an orchestra had hummed from the heart of the priory.

—She's left the doors open. She isn't meant to, but no one's about, and it's cooler.

The piece came to an end, and the needle crackled.

—Nuns are allowed gramophones?

—Oh, yes, sometimes. And Sister Laetitia has a dispensation.

Elaine drew her down some steps to a passage that smelled of coal and sawdust. Through a doorway, a woman in black habit bent over a workbench, apron covered in shavings, sleeves turned up to her elbows.

—Could you lift the tone-arm? the woman said without looking up.

Elaine did as she asked.

—Have I missed the bell?

Elaine said she hadn't. Still she didn't look up from her work.

—This is Marion, Elaine said. She heard the music.

The woman turned to them, erect. Her face was older than Elaine's, almost gaunt, her eyes strained as though they could use spectacles.

—Marion.

Her name came slowly from the woman's lips and didn't sound ugly.

—Sister Laetitia is working on the chapel, Elaine said. One day we'll have choir stalls.

The woman brushed shavings from her work, revealing a hedgehog.

—You liked the music?

She said she liked the last piece.

—You know the story?

—The Mighty Hunter?

Sister Laetitia nodded:

—Nimrod. Elgar wrote it for his friend and publisher, Jaeger which means *hunter* in German. There was a time, Elgar said, when he had been at the point of giving up music altogether. Jaeger convinced him to carry on.

—It's so beautiful.

—Imagine if he'd stopped.

She had meant the hedgehog but said *Yes*. Then the bells

began to toll, and Sister Laetitia had to go to vespers and she had to find the underground and see if Diana was right or wrong about throat slitters. Elaine's instructions told her to stay on the line all the way back to the lovely people's house. If someone wanted to slit your throat, they'd have a job of it in the crowds, which reeked of cigarettes and hours in an office. Back above ground at South Kensington, her shadow stretched across the pavement as though a part of her had melted.

She heard the children bickering upstairs when she stepped into the vestibule. Cook was scolding them, and she saw Mother stretched across the chaise lounge, curtains drawn, arm across her face announcing a headache. She went up and stopped their barefoot chase through the corridor, dripping bathwater, towels scarcely covering them. Later, when they'd fallen asleep, when she'd mopped the bathroom floor and sponged herself off, as she lay on the tiles, as the light played across the ceiling, jumbled by the breeze through the leaves in the plane tree, strains of the gramophone still swished in her ears, punctuated only by the dripping tap.

How could music be described to one who hadn't heard it? Poetry couldn't do it. Possibly it couldn't be done. Jas used to say music was the most fundamental art, and to prove it he'd take her to concerts. Back then she wasn't up on music, but he taught her how the pieces were built and what they were called. He couldn't play or sing, but his face altered at certain points in the concerts, and sometimes tears appeared on his cheek. One time she had a bit of a tune stuck in her head, and even though she hadn't made a peep, he started whistling it. Another time, she was thinking of words from a song, rolling them around in her head and wondering if they could go in a poem, and he asked her a question that used another part of the same song.

—How's the gloom?

—Encircling.

—No kindly light?

When the spirit moved on the face of the waters, did it breathe sound into being? Like a hen brooding over welter and waste, waiting and waiting while order grew, did it draw music also from the deep? The piece on the gramophone he called *The Mighty Hunter*, the conceit being he himself was the hunter who'd tramped the earth and the Milky Way until he found her. He'd hunted her to her howls and caught her not with an arrow but with his mighty heart. She denied it (this was her role), but in his naked arms, she felt full and hungry at the thought of being hunted and kept of her own will. The music breathed at the start so you could barely hear it, but soon it sounded capital letters and took a feather to the seams of your heart, opening it so the walls were free as wings. It breathed in the past and it breathed in the future and when they heard it together in the recital hall, it breathed also between them. And now, echoing in her ears as it had in the workshop where that woman vowed in poverty carved hedgehogs for misericords, loving her creation as she loved the timid and sincere, the simple whiskered noses you'd find in any lane, now the voice of the hunter called as though she lived far in the future, when everyone flew in aeroplanes and it was nothing to rise above the clouds; he was long dead but the song found her in the gap above the clouds, proving the heart had been real, his heart, hers, the heart of the brooding maker.

If Archie was right—and no one said he was—if the Promiser kept his promises even if she broke every one, why could music not plait a rope to climb from this stifling crevasse? She was the last person to fall for superstition, and with only so many gramophone discs fit to be played by nuns, the odds were good for hearing it. Yet on this day that had thrown (on which *she* had thrown) all customary restraint over the edge of an omnibus, why as she made for the door after a cup of workman's tea and one slightly damp biscuit, why when she had almost escaped the nuns and their pilgrims, Archie and his wayward Israel, why had the mighty hunter cut open her heart with the feather of the brooding bird?

—The best adventures must be kept as perfect secrets, she told the children the next morning.

—I can keep a secret.

—Can you? No forgetting. No looks across the table?

—I'll promise in blood.

—Blood!

—That won't be necessary.

—Blood makes it real, Clive said. You know it does, Marion.

—What kind of blood? his sister asked.

—You cut your hand, and the blood is the promise.

Felicity began to cry.

—In Ireland they use tears, she told them.

And so they promised using blood from his hangnail and tears from the girl's cheek: they would never speak of where they were to go. They would use their noms de guerre, always and only. They would obey her perfectly, never let go of her hands as they descended into the underworld, giving their ticket to Charon, crossing the hot ventricles of Hades to the far side of the earth, where the exiled Tsar reigned and the bloody rebels knew nothing—

—Bloody, you said bloody!

—Father called the miners bloody.

—It's a naughty word!

—On the far side of Hades, who knows what words—

—Bloody hell!

—That'll do, Clive.

The underground excited them. They wanted to slide down the long handrails, and she had to hold their sticky hands tight when they came to the platform. Up and out, down the cockney street, through the gates to the brown door. Elaine let them in and then led them all to a shadowed courtyard, ringing with children's voices.

—Sister Prue, Elaine said to a girl in a habit, here are Morgan and Finn. They're Marion's.

Sister Prue took them both in her arms and kissed them. She was young and pretty enough that they let her. She took two boiled sweets from a pocket and pressed them into their hands, asking Felicity about the strawberries embroidered on her pocket—

—They're cherries.

And asking Clive whether he could help her repair a pole that had come loose—

—It needs a strong arm. Then we can play piggery-poke.

Elaine took her elbow, and they retreated through the passage until they came to a high, warm room with polished wooden tables.

A woman hunched at one, seeming young and old at the same time, her hair plaited so tightly it tugged the corners of her eyes. Elaine introduced her as Bess. Bess said little beyond a mumble, but Marion was given to understand she was there to learn totting up. Slate, pencils, and exercise books had been set on the table. Bess already clutched a cup of tea, and Elaine refilled it and brought one for Marion before vanishing. Bess added sugar to her own cup defiantly, as though someone would object. Marion wished she could roll down her stockings and take off her shoes.

—Don't you wish it would rain? she said.

Bess shrugged. She decided she would wait for Bess to speak. Little was more infuriating than people who wanted to jolly you along into something you'd no intention of doing. If Bess didn't want to tot up, what did it matter? Perhaps she'd only come for the tea. When their cups were empty, Marion refilled them. When Bess added three spoonsful of sugar, Marion did too.

—You're the fourth one 'as tried, Bess said at last.

Marion sighed and stretched out her legs:

—I'm not much good with figures myself.

With Elaine she'd spoken as she did to the children, governess London, clergyman's-daughter-standard, but now she let her accent slip across the water, back to her mother's kitchen, where bread was always baking (because someone such as she had kneaded it), children were always bickering, her mother always playing Mother Tara to anyone who'd believe her.

—They make it out to be murder, but you'd be surprised how little you need to get on.

Bess said numbers and money were invented by men to keep women under.

—That they were.

They kept your head straining, adding and taking away, bobs and farthings, remembering everything you had to pay and where you started, and still they never evened up, and before Thursday you'd have to do what you hated doing just so the tin lids'd stop squalling and sleep.

They talked lazily, grousing about men, men with money and men without it. Before anyone had touched a pencil, it was time for Bess to leave.

—See you tomorrow? she said.

Bess declared it all a waste of time.

—Sure, you won't make me drink tea on me own?

Bess said it would probably be impossible.

Marion returned the next day while the children were at the Center. In the refectory, two other women huddled at a table in the corner. Bess was sketching on the slate, her fingers covered in chalk dust. Marion peered into the biscuit tin and asked if they were the same as yesterday.

—Staler, Bess said.

Marion put one on the saucer with her cup and sprawled at the table as if on tea break from a grueling job. Bess had filled the slate with patterns, and as she grumbled about her wooden head with numbers, she hatched aggressively, wearing the chalk to a nub.

Marion commiserated. No one back home could do with any of it. Probably Bess had Irish in her.

—I 'av!

Bess claimed an Irish grandmother on her father's side, at least if you believed her mother that the man was her father.

—That explains it, Marion said. Irish blood'll addle any brain for figures. No fault of your own.

Bess said her brother could tot up.

—Boys all say they can, but who'd know?

Indeed it was a miracle anyone could calculate shillings and pence given the way Irish blood ran through nearly every vein.

—There is *one* thing you could try, she said. At least as a game it's good for a laugh.

Unless you'd memorized your pence tables and aliquots when you were this high, you could forget about fractions, but Marion showed her the tricks that seemed most like magic, and when it was time to collect the children, Bess could tell her, without writing anything, how much she'd need for forty pounds of cheese at two shillings seven pence a pound.

—Perhaps you've not much Irish after all. Oh—

Bess's face had turned red. Tears welled.

She said she was sorry, said she didn't mean it, but Bess dropped her head onto her arms and sobbed. The other women looked over.

—You'll get the rest, she said. Don't toss in the towel.

Bess sobbed louder, and the other women stirred from their table. The pilgrim slid onto the bench beside Bess and put an arm around her. The other woman, Sister someone, glanced questioningly at her.

—I must go, she said.

—No! Bess cried.

Sister someone took Bess's hand.

—I never fought, Bess sniffed. Never fought I could.

The pilgrim nodded.

—Always been so stupid.

—You ain't, the pilgrim said. Not no more.

—Never fought.

The sister took Marion's hand, too, and squeezed it:

—See you tomorrow?

—But . . .

The sister drew her away:

—Sometimes when they see what they can do . . .

—You mean she's crying because she's *happy*?

—Never fought I'd ever.

On the steps of the Center, Clive declared he had heat stroke.

—Nonsense. Let's get out of the sun.

—Can we go bathing in Alsace?

She said she didn't know.

—I want to swim in the sea.

—Today! Felicity demanded.

She did too.

—They haven't got the sea in Alsace, though, have they, Marion?

—There could be a lake.

—With snakes?

—Why can't we go to the *sea*?

—Can we stop at the river, just for a minute?

She promised them an ice if they made it to the post office before it closed. Half an hour later, they were dangling their feet in the Serpentine, ices melting down their fronts, and she held an envelope with his club's name letter-pressed onto the flap. Inside, a single sheet: *3.2 Never!*

She sat with Mother in her dressing room once the children were asleep. Father had an engagement, so the woman was teetering on the edge of despair the city was horrid, the heat infernal, people monsters, newspapers full of bile.

—But look here, she said folding back a column. This one isn't bad.

—I can't, Mother said. I cannot bear another nasty word.

—*Miss Gertrude Ederle, of New York, yesterday swam the Channel from Cap Grinez to Kingstown in 14 hours and 39 minutes. She is the first woman to do so and also beats the previous fastest time by almost two hours. She is eighteen years old.*

—First woman?

She read out the rest of the column. Mother gazed at the crown moldings:

—Americans are very queer. Imagine getting into the sea with all the things.

There was a way they could fight, because she didn't fear him and he didn't fear she would leave him. Was this what people meant by trust? She trusted no one, but when they argued, she knew she could strike all the way in and not let go until she was ready. Had their play established the foundation, or did something more elemental bind them together? Once she had growled in a voice that scraped her throat, *Don't touch me*! And he had pulled his hands away as though touching live wire. She'd fled the cottage (this was the second time in Scotland) and tramped the shore in the dark. When she finally returned, he gave her a wide berth. She gulped whisky and threw her arms around the hound, who whined at her return and thumped his tail against the settee. He said nothing, but later when she curled on the settee, head on her knees, he sat beside her untouching. The next morning when everything had evaporated, he said he'd never heard a sound like that before, and he looked as though he suspected demons.

They made you doubt yourself, they did. Her family. Priests.

Lovelace. The Frau. He was no different. Except really—battle between women and men aside—the sins she carried in her Gladstone bag weighed more than he could imagine.

When Father and Mother had both gone to bed, she raided Mother's secretary again.

> *7 August 1926*
> *Someone's got to say it—*

~

St. Edward the Martyr had a problem with mold, and even if they'd used incense, it wouldn't have covered it. The stained glass filtered out sunlight. The congregation filled barely a quarter of the pews. The whole depressing scene confirmed Jamie's suspicions of unfamiliar churches, and were it not for Kardleigh's invitation, he would never have ventured from his usual ecclesial haunts, especially not on a Sunday.

When the organ prelude began, the sound cooled the air. From his pew he could see only the back of Kardleigh's head, but the man looked to be stretching and dancing before the instrument as he conjured . . . the communion of saints? He hated his own thought. Mawkish ideas were the death of taste and truth.

The service managed to begin on time, and though the sermon was lackluster, it didn't offend him. Hymns proceeded at the proper tempos, and the singers standing in the loft with Kardleigh delivered the Te Deum and Jubilate with the precise simplicity of a monastery choir. The anthem, when it came, unlaced his composure almost from the first bars. It was out of season, but the sheer power of the nearly whispered opening bars—*Faire is the heaven, where happy souls have place*—filled him with the romance of autumn, shortening days, lengthening nights. He was used to hearing the piece at Michaelmas, its plainsong layers building imperceptibly to the arresting shouts of angels and archangels, its texture spreading until everything smelled sweet, more than enough air to breathe for all time, love found and secured, order restored so creation might flourish, all the promises of September, new terms, new years, new weather scudding across the sky. And he strained with a desire that could never be satisfied unless and until Kardleigh came where he was and gave them this, with any choir, even the smallest and newest. He needed it this Michaelmas and every Michaelmas, never failing, never muddying, and if Kardleigh would give him this, give them *all* this, then somehow a light could burn in the gloom, and John could be knit back, Wilberforce could be righted, and she could be . . . not tamed, never tamed, but joined, have places build around her and for her, for them, for the promise of the music to become true.

—You can play that thing after all, he told Kardleigh at the tea table after the service.

—The instrument's not bad, Kardleigh said, even if the place has seen better days.

Jamie asked about the singers and the anthem. Was it difficult? Kardleigh considered it advanced.

—Could you teach it to boys? In a fortnight?

—This again?

Kardleigh dropped his teaspoon in annoyance:

—I agreed to meet this Overall character, but only to scotch this fantasy of yours once and for all.

—Overall's tiresome. But that wasn't what I was wondering.

—Oh, no?

Jamie asked if he knew a certain organist currently at King's Cambridge.

—Only by reputation.

He asked Kardleigh's opinion of the King's organ. Kardleigh naturally expressed envy. Jamie asked if he could join him Thursday for lunch in Cambridge.

—I've business at King's, and they've promised to show me the organ.

—Are we on to bribes?

—A pleasant coincidence.

Kardleigh didn't believe him, but temptation had taken root. He agreed to check the hospital duty roster and see if he might extricate himself.

—How's Lewis working out, by the way?

—He sends me typed summaries daily and claims already to have organized the accounts.

—It's been how long?

—A week. It's freakish.

Kardleigh's mustache twitched:

—Told you he needed an outlet.

Jamie returned to the club to marshal his forces. He'd written John with the suggestion of visiting him in Saffron Walden. This John had energetically rebuffed: he made it a rule never to mix the private and the professional; holidays were short and he hoped still sacrosanct, he could not countenance contaminating his family (the word he used was *brushing*) with the monstrosities (the *teeth*) of St. Stephen's.

Was managing staff always like herding mules through a bog? What he needed was a bit of kismet, something to press the sails of his figurative boat and bring both John and Kardleigh to the same Cambridge restaurant on the same day. He couldn't see any further than that, and if some pest were to nag him with logic—did he imagine one lunch would convert Kardleigh and revive John's loyalty?—he would have no answer. When you'd run out of sure maneuvers, you had to resort to the double longs.

He stood at the club desk and composed a wire to John:

> NO WISH TO SPOIL HOLIDAY BUT MUST SEE YOU URGENTLY STOP LUNCH IN CAMBRIDGE THURSDAY STOP WILBERFORCE ON GOOD FORM STOP JAMIE

Cambridge was half an hour by train from Saffron Walden.

To refuse a simple lunch would constitute a move so hostile that Jamie doubted John had the nerve for it, especially given the parting shot.

—Sir, said the clerk.

It wasn't supposed to be possible to shock you the same way twice. Her hand, dated only yesterday:

> *Someone's got to say it—You're deranged. You refuse to understand a perfectly clear act. How many ways can there be to say no? A woman has crossed the English Channel faster than the fastest man. The world has changed.*

His mind raced in sleep, and again he woke halfway through the night, or realized he had been awake, rehearsing a tirade. Why really was she playing games with him? She'd opened his letters and replied twice, ostensibly in the negative. Why reply if you'd put it all behind you? And even if you harbored a grudge, what could justify refusing to meet for a simple drink? They hadn't lived the last four years so she could pretend he was some deranged former suitor. His mind tramped purgatorial circuits. Did she love someone else? Had she never loved him? Had grief for the dog damaged her psyche? Had she decided to hold him responsible for England's crimes against her people? Was it religion? She always claimed not to care about religion, and although he had begun to care quite a bit during their last months together, she didn't know it. She didn't know he'd resumed taking the sacrament out at the little church in Cowley. She didn't know the way its vicar had burned through the bracken of his ideas with a string of fervorinos. Religion had only come up seriously between them last Whitsunday when he'd been foolish enough to admit it was his favorite day in the church year. She'd made a snide remark, and he accused her of wretched prejudice. He couldn't say the truth, that the Old Boy had told him to sort himself out. He didn't know scripture half as well as he ought, but even he could see the regular pattern of history: the Lord sent warnings, many warnings in many ways, many chances to turn back to him, to one's senses and one's heart. But chances were not unlimited, and at a certain point if you persisted in rebellion, you got wrath. He couldn't tell her of the command to find her in the place where she was held (where she had taken refuge?). He had not yet combed the ramifications through his life or even his mind. He had changed nothing in his conduct, and he hadn't worked out how to broach the subject with her. So when she said the Holy Ghost was a vile lie, he felt it keenly. She said the English church, too, was a lie. It wasn't even religion but folly, and all the cathedrals and canons and dogma they discussed at his godfather's college, which was full of mollies who wished they were Catholic but would never submit to the Church, all of it was a self-aggrandizing praise of folly. She spoke in the passionate manner she used when they railed together against the world. Neither Wilde nor Swift was as keen in his barbs as she when the spirit moved her.

Though what spirit? All he had said was that he had a soft spot for Pentecost because of the way the wind had blown the gas away that time. He didn't say the unvarnished truth, that he believed the Holy Spirit had a special interest in him. He didn't say what he was thinking, *Wouldn't it be a novelty to go to The House and listen to the music on this Red Letter Day?* Instead he'd told her Pentecost was the feast day of poets, *Come Holy Ghost, our souls inspire and lighten with celestial fire—*

—Oh spleet, spleet, spleet!

She pulled her hand from his and stormed ahead along the river. Pollen swirled from the spicy-sweet trees, and he felt the urge to cry. When her anger had passed and they were walking together again, she asked if he'd gone back to it, meaning the church. He'd said he didn't know. Of course he knew, but he couldn't say it then. He was working on it!

Sometimes she would pose questions of an abstract nature, and he would muse on what followed, philosophically speaking, if one accepted a prime mover. Last winter he had inched into what followed theologically speaking, and she didn't balk. Then after Easter, when they returned to Applecross with the dog, something new began to happen. One morning apropos of nothing, she said she forgave him for Tim and Malcolm. That night it was different between them in the bed, and he wondered if soon he could broach the truth of what he had stopped fighting, of what he'd always known about the big truth. He had no idea how he'd fence with her Catholicism, but that was a problem for another day because first he had to discover what held her, and what she held, and then he had to open all his cupboards to her.

His father always told the truth naturally, without tension or apology. Gravity pulled things down and stuck them to the earth so they didn't fly away, and if you believed that, because you could see the effect if not the force itself, then was it such a scandal to say you knew the Holy Ghost was real? He'd seen and felt and *known* its effects, not just that night in no-man's-land but so many other times, including with her. How did they ever find each other, after all? Clichés didn't cover it. In the tempest of life and war, how had they come to that place with the poems and the drinks and the musical instruments?

He needed to face the true scope of the problem: even if he could convince her to meet him (and this had to be possible with a bit more pigheadedness on his part), he still had to tell her the truth and not lose her. People married with enormous secrets never told, but he couldn't. Not to her.

His reply came the day after she'd posted her second. He prefaced all his with a number, clearly a sequence, but if these were series three, wither one and two? They used to write each other in code, sometimes whole sentences using the first letter of each word. YDSOTBYC could still make her heart beat in her feeling place.

> *3.3 I can't wait to see your garrulous teeth bared. You can tyrant me all you like. I'll listen and never say a word. We can sit miles apart and never touch. I'll be waiting at the k-k-k-kitchen door.*

His closing line hit her like a scent swooshing through memory, resurrecting their joke about the stuttering song. Everyone knew the song, even the broken soldier they passed near the museum, yet that man's whistled strains and now the letter reminded her what it was to have someone know her mind and share her jokes. If not for the regulating claims of children, pilgrims, even Archie, who could say where her wishes might run?

Archie visited the priory every day. She couldn't swear to what he was doing there—listening to the sisters, or as Elaine reported, writing a missal with Mother Margaret and napping in the sanatorium—but she would find him each afternoon in the visitor's parlor holding a cup that he seemed rarely to sip and never to finish.

—Have you got any prayers for voles and badgers? she asked Monday afternoon.

—For their preservation or eradication?

—Multiplication!

She stretched across the settee, stopping just short of putting her feet on the cushion and said that if he was writing a missal, he had better put in prayers for the hedgehogs and owlets, the thistle-eating hares, all the creatures Sister Laetitia was chiseling from the wood. Freeing, she called it.

—What about the spirit brooding in the beginning? she asked. Didn't it free things from chaos?

She said she used to imagine a well in the sea that contained all the ideas that had ever been, and if she thought hard enough, she could force her mind into this well and poems would fill her. Now when she looked at those few surviving poems, their falseness grated.

—I wouldn't confuse naïveté with falseness.

Oh, but she'd not been naïve. They'd all been written after Lovelace and his sausage guts.

—You know, she said.

—I'm afraid I don't.

—Don't you?

He didn't answer. She pressed her knuckles to the ridge beneath her brows.

—Ought I?

—The point, she said, is that no one asks you to be a poet. And in the scheme of things, it's vanity.

—Unless you can't help it.

—Anyone can help it.

—Unless you find the true well.

—Don't tell me you write poems, Archie.

—For the good of the earth, I do not.

She smiled.

—Though what ought one to make, he asked, of Sister Laetitia?

Sister Laetitia who, she'd learned when she went downstairs to find out what the gramophone was playing yesterday, had never meant to be an artist. Sister Laetitia had only heard, as all the sisters heard, that the funds for the chapel would suffice only to close the roof and varnish the floor, that they'd have to borrow benches until more funds could be raised. Sister Laetitia had said not a word, but months later she'd asked permission to take woodworking lessons, and after twelve lessons the teacher had let her have some tools, and she'd gone down to the cellar, and started freeing hedgehogs, and it was all so beautiful that she still wanted to cry to think of it.

She posted her next reply from a pillar box in Aldgate. If he remembered the words that didn't need spelling, he'd find the code for the post office near the priory. The next day between pilgrim lessons, she went there. A card waited—one side the Peter Pan statue, the reverse a list of numbers she quickly deciphered as dates and times, a string of invitations.

She returned to the priory through the noisy, noisome streets, Nimrod in her ears. After helping two more pilgrims fill out forms for the Council, she went to the courtyard to collect the children.

—Where are yours? Sister Prue murmured. Finn? Morgan? Oh, there by the tunnel.

Felicity was clutching the arm of a ragamuffin girl (it was unkind to think that way, but the girl's face was dirty, her frock barely whole). Something dramatic had occurred, and Felicity was on the verge of tears, her lisp blossoming though she'd come so far in erasing it.

—Frantheth! she cried. Our babieth!

—Wot?

—They've dithapeared!

Prue stepped into the fray, crouching beside the girls, who claimed to have set their peg dolls in the metal tube they called the Tunnel and, moments later, to have found the tunnel empty, no person having been near. Felicity wept bitterly, angrily, while the other girl, Frances, suggested they hopscotch instead and sing *I am a little orphan girl.*

—Like wot you tort us.

But then Clive burst from behind the tube, covered in dust from having hidden himself:

—Your babies are mine! They shall come to my kingdom at the bottom of the sea!

It took sweets from Prue's pocket to restore peace and finally to detach Clive and Felicity, whom everyone called hers.

At the sweltering maw of the underground entrance, Felicity asked if they could travel to the bottom of the sea on the underground. She replied that they might if they took it far enough.

—May we, Marion? May we!

—How would we get to the bottom of the sea if we're only going sideways? Clive scoffed.

The roar of the underground covered their voices. Sweat trickled between her breasts, her frock stuck to her back, and the scent of her own body overpowered the odor of the woman pressed against her. His latest throbbed in her pocket, as sweet and deadly as temptations that mustn't be indulged.

She had collected at least some of his letters, but ever since his postcard, she'd ceased the children's visits to Kensington Gardens. Had she recognized him in his personnage de guerre?

> *3.5 A rare bird is rare, as Lucy says of Michael. Do you remember her suitor? They married last year. There was a flap, naturally. Michael isn't just RC, but the kind whose family has been since the days when you had to hide your priest in a wall. In other words, he didn't give it up for her. But Lucy insisted that a rare bird is rare, by which she means you can't expect to find a second extraordinary person after you've been lucky enough to find one, and in the end everyone was won over.*

Beth and Flora had never really been opposed to Michael, and he'd turned Agnes with flattery and homemade toffee. Their father made a show of opposition; he voiced his objections to Michael and insisted they be addressed, but everyone knew he would never deny Lucy.

Of course, because Lucy was Lucy and his family was his family, the rare bird credo would never be allowed to apply to Amanda. In a sane world, Lucy would have helped him. In a sane world, Michael would have provided a bridge, but the distance between the English Catholics Flynts and the Irish

Catholic McDonaghs, daughter runagate and avowed atheist, was farther than America. What would he have to give to hear her talk to him of the life they would have in their prairie log cabin amongst the fur traders and the buffalo in snow?

The day in Cambridge arrived before he was ready. He took an early train so he could make arrangements at the restaurant. The Man in the Moon that graced its placard regarded him inscrutably, as though it knew his longings and his fate but could promise no outcome with any certainty. The looking glass in the lavatory revealed an ingrown hair beside his ear, broken blood vessels he'd take for sunburn, and creases beneath his eyes, which themselves looked ready to sag. Had she seen then what he saw now, or had he deteriorated across the intervening months? He was turning twenty-nine in October, and each year as his birthday approached, he felt alarm at the number on the horizon. It was probably a blessing that you couldn't see things coming or who'd have the nerve to plod through a day?

When he arrived at the gates of King's, Kardleigh was waiting for him.

—Good news, Kardleigh chirped.

—Oh, yes?

The man wasn't one to gush, but he spoke brightly of a tutorial to which he'd been admitted with a much-sought composition tutor, a well-known composer—

—I didn't realize you were onto composition as well.

Jamie used his lightest tone, but as Kardleigh chattered on about oratorios, he began to sweat. At last, the King's man arrived in a flurry that betokened a head lost in organ pipes. Jamie left them to it.

The restaurant mercifully let him have the table early, and as he was settling his stomach with tonic, John arrived. Tall, smart, sunburned, and more imposing than his schoolmaster's summer suit would suggest, John caught his breath when he saw Jamie.

—So glad you could come, Jamie said.

John nodded, and Jamie began to speak breezily of the weather. Surveying the table set for three, John asked if Burton-Lee had arrived.

—Oh, Jamie replied, not Burton-Lee, but there's someone I'd like you to meet.

—I thought you said this was urgent.

—It is.

—I've only got an hour.

Jamie had the train timetable in his pocket, listing a string of returns John could take.

—Your family are well, I trust?

—If we could keep to the Academy, John said, I'd be very much obliged.

Jamie smiled as they took their seats. He declined the hock and asked for lemonade, remembering from the day at St. Stephen's that John was now a teetotaler. Judging by the subtle relaxation of his shoulders, John felt the courtesy.

—Did you know I went to Scarborough? Jamie said. S-K was more compos mentis than I expected.

John looked scandalized.

—You *saw S-K*?

Jamie launched into an account of his visit, deploying frivolity and a discursive style.

—Did S-K tell you to sack me? John demanded.

Jamie explained the man had done the opposite.

—Then who on earth is joining us?

The waiter brought a plate of toast with gentleman's relish and cucumbers.

—It's someone I knew in the war, Jamie said. Physician turned musician.

—I don't follow.

—If you'd just take your finger off the trigger, I'd count it a favor.

Jamie let his nerves show, spreading a thin layer of relish on the toast and nibbling it as he narrated his alterations to the St. Stephen's Common Room. John's bafflement drifted into admiration, bathing Jamie in a confidence he hadn't felt since—

—Sir?

The waiter announced that Kardleigh had arrived. Jamie stood for the introductions—Grieves (dazed), Kardleigh (exuberant)—and over the asparagus soup, Jamie kindled the conversation by eliciting a description of the King's organ. As Kardleigh spouted technical detail, John's aloofness faded. It emerged that John and Kardleigh were both Magdalene men, though of different eras. While the two discussed mutual acquaintances, Jamie's mind sparked with an unfamiliar current, like anger cut with fear. Jealousy? Was he jealous? Jealous of Kardleigh's regard for those head-in-the-air musicians, jealous of John's holiday family, jealous of the spoiled children who received her caresses and her love?

The cold poached salmon arrived, looking as magnificent on the platter as he had hoped when he arranged for it. The waiter served them, and Jamie steered the conversation back to Kardleigh's career, framing it as a blended vocation:

—Medicine and music. Aren't they nearly the same thing at the end of the day?

—It's a lovely idea, Kardleigh said, but entirely out of the question.

—You keep saying that.

—Wait, John said, *wait*. Are you actually trying to convince him to leave all this—

John gestured to include everything Kardleigh had said about the organ—

—And for *St. Stephen's*?

—I'm flattered of course.

—Has he told you everything?

—John—

—No games, Jamie.

John turned to Kardleigh:

—The place is a disaster. The founder's on his deathbed. A boy *did* die at Easter. The school is traumatized, demoralized, morally un-compassed, and suffers poor food and drafts twelve months of the year. Don't touch it with a barge pole.

—What keeps you there? Kardleigh replied.

—Who else would employ a red conchie like me?

Kardleigh habitually masked his reactions, but as the waiter served the new potatoes, he drummed the table like an organ console. John speared a potato. Jamie sipped his lemonade.

—Go back to the start, Kardleigh said at last.

John pretended bafflement, but Kardleigh persisted. When Jamie's father embarked on the professional interview, one knew it. Kardleigh's looked like friendly banter, but having been on the receiving end of it, Jamie knew it was pitched to elicit every essential. He addressed the French bean salad as Kardleigh collected John's biographical outline, one Jamie had been craving: John had indeed objected conscientiously to the war. He'd driven ambulances with Quakers. There had been a stint in Ypres, another in Verdun. He'd married, she'd died, he'd applied for the post at St. Stephen's. He supposed the Academy had provided a sort of retreat at first—he would call it counter-irritant—but subsequently he had chosen to remain. Seven years had come and gone; boys, having arrived in Eton jackets, departed men; food supplies had improved, the headmaster declined; the last two terms had been a nightmare.

—So, Kardleigh summarized, this St. Stephen's collects lost causes and broken toys, people such as you, these boys, Jass, and now me?

John began to choke, and when Kardleigh got up to thwack him across the back, the maneuver upset the lemonade. Jamie leapt out of the way, and then John, too, lurched to his feet, sending potatoes flying one way, French beans the other, crockery to the floor.

—Oh, well done, Grievous.

Jamie pretended sternness, but when he met John's eye, giggles seized him. It only got worse when waiters descended and John began to shake with laughter. Kardleigh played the adult, helping to pick up the shards, but for Jamie and John, each attempt at composure died with a glance, the way it had been when they were boys.

A blanket of clemency seemed to spread across the day, not bought or earned but given without asking. When the mess had been cleared and their glasses refilled, Jamie found his pulse steady, the task before him as solid as a cast-iron kettle. John was on his side as he'd always, always been, turning the conversation to elicit an account of Jamie's years and then to sketch for Kardleigh leading characters at St. Stephen's, including Wilberforce and a few other boys who fit the mold Jamie mentally labelled odd-but-worth-the-slog. As if playing along with a jest, John asked what Jamie imagined Kardleigh would do at the Academy with Matron in charge.

Like being bowled a perfect ball, Jamie described his scheme for her second chapter at the choir school. Kardleigh fell silent. A grin appeared on John's face.

—What a very efficient design, John drawled. One that could only have been concocted by you and your father.

He turned to Kardleigh, still amused:

—This is what you'd be mucking into, friend. Tyrannized by Matron for two long terms, training feral boys to sing, reviving your war hospital in our shell-shocked circle of hell. Barge pole, as previously discussed!

Kardleigh grimaced, but his gaze crossed Jamie's.

—No offense to the shell-shocked, John added.

Kardleigh nodded in a way that snagged memory, and as Jamie finished his meal in a Cambridge restaurant, he also lay in the iron bed assigned him at Kardleigh's hospital, the night after the fracas at the picnic, when Jamie had begged to be admitted to the asylum, the night Kardleigh had crouched by his pillow and whispered fiercely that he needed him, to stand in the gap, to take up arms against it, *it* being the illness of the world, every cruelty and injustice, every putrid corruption of power, every bland insistence that nothing was wrong. *If not us, then who*?

And he knew that when he had taken Kardleigh's hand that night, when he'd left the hospital, he had done more than snap out of an episode of madness; he had entered into a pact no less binding than the Covenant of the Pieces. He and Kardleigh had never again discussed that night, and Jamie had not thought of it the whole time he'd been courting Kardleigh—though how much simpler if he had! But now, the covenant was working on them both, and just as Kardleigh had once used it to recall him to the world, now he had invoked it without words to reel Kardleigh into his project. And as John chattered with irresistible charm, Jamie realized that what had happened to him on his first visit to St. Stephen's was happening now to Kardleigh. The man had eaten their meat, drained their tankards. He could never escape. Had he not already swept up their crockery?

The meal ended amicably, nothing having been ceded. On the way to the station, Jamie stepped into a shop whose window displayed sweets in spades and pails as if for the seaside. He rarely indulged in sweets, but fruit fizz sherbets seemed the only answer to the day. The effervescent lozenges dissolved on his tongue, conjuring those careless summers when everything was possible and life held only promise. On the train back to town, he tore a page from the newspaper abandoned on a seat:

> *3.7 Do you still rouge your lips? And is the scent you wear still borrowed from other people, or do you have your own*

now? I don't think I ever said it, but you could go as you are straight out of the bath and trounce every girl. I'm not sleeping in this heat, and when I do, it's like a fever. A day at the seaside, an hour on a cheap return, feet in the surf, no eyes, what if I sent you a ticket?

~

It had to stop, the blue-black script that made the past seem alive. Time did not turn backwards. And what could be more perverse than allowing him to write to her while she used his father as a salve, comforting herself with those eyes and cheekbones when the whole enterprise had rotted at the root, spawning gnats that would turn every leaf to mush?

—You've a queue, Elaine told her when she arrived at the priory. You're the most popular governess we've had.

—Very funny.

Oh, but she was, Elaine insisted. Word had spread, and now everyone wanted her help with their writing. Elaine had to ask three pilgrims to come again tomorrow.

—As it is you've got Lizzie, Allison, Susan, and Gwen.

—No Bess?

—She's disappeared before. You mustn't take it to heart.

—I ought to have gone slower.

—Nonsense.

Elaine slid open the refectory door:

—Here's Marion!

Her pupils had prepared her tea and arranged biscuits on a plate. The four women knew each other, and their patter enveloped her as they described what they needed to write. Elaine didn't know that Lizzie could never write a sentence that wasn't addled; that strictly speaking she wasn't teaching them anything but was composing letters for them to the entities they desired, mostly men who deserved a boot in the vitals.

—*Dear Mr. Turner*, she dictated to Lizzie. What do you want to tell him?

—Wish someone'd gut 'im wif a knife.

—*Esteemed Mr. Turner, I write in the hope that this finds you filleted with a stiletto behind the Jolly Candler*. What else?

—'E can take 'is intress an' stuff it.

—*Should you, sir, still move among the quick, I'm afraid I must inform you that the interest payments you require will not be forthcoming and that those previously received must suffice for you, in layman's terms, to stuff it*. New line. *Yours sincerely, Mrs. Lizzie Nolan*.

Their laughter rippled like rain melting snow and washing the sooty pavement white. They said she was an artist, a champion, a genie. They said no man would ever take an ell with her. They'd asked her already what happened to her man, and she'd told them dead in the war, which wasn't false if by *in* you meant *during*. They opined that only a dead man could have turned his back on a pair of tin lids like hers.

The afternoon sweated along, gossip, complaints, and later the comparison of marks. Lizzie showed off a six-inch scar on her scalp where someone had broken a bottle. Gwen displayed cigarette burns. Allison's torso was swollen in bruises.

—That there's why I brung 'er, Gwen said taking Allison's hand. To do somefink.

Did Allison want to make a police complaint? she asked.

What did she take her for? Allison protested. The women overlapped each other cursing Allison's husband, a smooth talking Bill Sykes minus the bulldog. Safe within the priory walls, they detailed what they would do to him given the chance. Allison looked caught between fear and hunger. Gwen proposed that Marion write Allison's landlord and insist the husband be barred from the flat.

—You write it, Marion. Make it sound like the law.

Gwen said Allison's man had been so bad last night that

Allison had finally agreed to meet Marion, even if it did mean treating with nuns. Now, at the suggestion of legal intimidation, Allison swelled with hatred, and then fear. The plan wouldn't work, Allison declared. The landlord was a fat pig who would talk and talk and never do nothing.

—No, Allison said. You write one to *'im.*

—To your husband?

—Gwenny'll take it down that flop 'ouse where he gone. And you—

She turned fiercely to Marion:

—You write it in your 'and.

—All right.

—You tell 'im, if 'e ever turns 'is fat boot down our lane again, I'll kill 'im.

—Oh.

—I got a knife, ain't I? An' if that don't take, I'll kill the kids. Bof of 'em.

She smiled reflexively, but Allison had the face of people past caring:

—Did it once didn't I?

—Oh.

—One come out last year, strangled it right off, told 'im it came dead and 'e believed it cause 'e never wanted it to start wif.

The others looked to her in support and expectation.

—It might not be wise to put that in writing, she said. It could be used, you know, in a court of law.

—So what if it is? Allison said. Just you write it. Write it *proper.*

—Any chance of a proper drink? she said at the parlor door.

Archie looked up from his crossword.

—It's like that, is it?

—Like that.

He abandoned his paper, retrieved his hat, and accompanied

her across the road to the Parliament Arms. Her skin felt fevered as he ordered himself a half-pint of best bitter, and for her a milk stout.

—I didn't write it, she said when they'd slid into the nook.

He gazed at her and sipped his bitter.

—Oh, I *can't* go round the houses and explain the whole thing. It's just that one of them wanted me to write something, and I didn't want to write it.

He nodded.

—You never said this would happen! You only said, *here are some nuns, help them with lessons.*

—And what is it that's happened?

—You know! The way you get to thinking the walls are enough, what with the nuns and the mighty hunter downstairs. And you're larking about, and their troubles aren't yours, and then it's like a riptide, someone's killed her baby and wants to do worse, and one of them is acting like it happens all the time and another is looking to you like you should stop it, and you try to back out but they won't let you, and before you make a decision, the one has stormed off to write it herself, telling you to go to hell—don't look like that because she meant it exactly—and even though you didn't do anything wrong, you didn't do anything right.

He straightened the mat under his glass:

—You were surprised to discover you weren't on neutral ground?

—What's that supposed to mean?

—Just what you described. No middle ground to take.

She hadn't condoned strangling a baby, but she hadn't condemned it either.

—It isn't truly possible to face two directions at once, he said. Those who try simply close their eyes to the master they're serving.

—Nothing's that simple. Not even you believe it. Real life is a sewer, and most of the time you don't know what to do until it's over, and sometimes not even then.

—It's certainly full of close places. One needn't face them alone, though.

—The closest ones are always alone! Top of a mountain in a snowstorm alone.

—Even there, he said, you're not forsaken.

—If you're trying to priest me, you can stop.

She didn't belong to his world. Every decision that mattered she'd taken half-asleep, not strictly doing what was worst, but permitting it and blurring her own vision to the point that she didn't think she knew what was happening. Runagates had no lasting home. They belonged nowhere that could be reached or endured.

He nodded to her glass, which was empty like his.

—Another round? he asked. I will if you will.

Her heart rate hadn't slowed, but she took the coin he'd set on the table and went to the bar.

—Another bitter, she said, and a Parkmore neat.

When she returned, he asked what she was drinking.

—They've only two Scotch whiskies and the other's vile, she said.

—I'm afraid I haven't bothered with scotch, he said, since Bo'ness closed. At this rate, we'll be following the Americans into prohibition.

She drained off her glass in one go, feeling the sharp heat in her nose.

—My dear.

Her stomach burned at the thought of the refectory, of the pistols it put in her hand and to her head.

—The sisters will never have me back after today.

He looked skeptical.

—Just as well! she continued with forced cheer. We're off to Alsace in a week.

—Alsace? France?

—Is there another?

—You're leaving England?

She explained the family's failure to secure an English holiday. She'd no notion what kind of place they'd have in Alsace, but Father had shown them ferry tickets at breakfast. He hadn't booked the return journey, but the children began school in six weeks.

—You aren't staying on with them?

She explained that this had always been the arrangement. Perhaps she'd even stop in Alsace. The western front was more her line than London.

—Now, now.

—Now, now yourself.

He mustn't think her abandoned to self-pity. Neither was she morbid or bereaved. People died every day for every reason. The world was in the business of dying, and really it amounted to a mercy when you saw what a slaughterhouse people made of their lives, every decision taken in ignorance, every inaction locking you into the opposite of what you loved. She'd never been naïve, not after everything she'd read, heard, seen, and lived. Even so, the world was so much worse than she had imagined possible.

—My dear—

—It isn't like that.

No one threatened her. The lovely family were benign. She enjoyed the children, cared for them. Letters even now awaited her, swinging open that garden gate again and again. *Oh you, my true love, tell me, tell me, tell me, do. Do you know the name of the rose, the rose, do you know my love, my love*?

—There are people, she said, whose lives are one disaster after another.

—Disasters they make or disasters visited upon them?

There were *people* who did not know how to act as human

beings, and such people not only were doomed to unhappiness but also doomed anyone who loved them. Once you'd knit a life so far, there was no unraveling. You were stuck with yourself. And if she opened the latch to him—

—To God?

—No! Are you deaf?

If she opened the latch to *him*—and she could!—things would be at first so true, as if she had lifted the spell cast by her whole dark island where politics and religion went with whiskey and smoke and hatred and death. She would be an English rose, but only for a time and then it would end up even worse than now, worse than it would be if she followed her short thread to the end, a routine of days and nights enough like a nun to be one without praying.

A cloth touched her hand. She pushed it away. She wasn't crying and never would cry before him, but if he wanted to show his collar, then he could look at her ugly face. She opened her handbag, retrieved her compact mirror, and wiped the place where the rouge had smudged.

—You're determined to go abroad? he said.

—Why shouldn't I?

His look conjured the bog of her fear.

—I can't very well refuse unless I mean to resign, and what then? Stuck in London, out six weeks' wages?

—What if a holiday could be found for the family in England?

—There are no places.

—But if there were. Could they exchange their tickets?

—No idea. But they'd insist on the seaside.

—Could it be a short distance from the seaside?

—By foot?

—Say motorcar.

—Father hasn't got one.

—Bicycle?

—Do you have something up your sleeve, or what?

—I don't know.

—Is it your natural reaction to pry into the holiday plans of strangers?

Her voice had a tartness she knew they were past.

—It's my natural reaction, he said, to throw a rope when someone's struggling in the current, especially when it's a friend and night is coming on.

—What *current*?

—A riptide.

Fear rinsed her skin; she wanted the lavatory and she wanted to walk home through the hot, fetid streets and the thick, wet air.

He let his thumb brush her handbag:

—I'd be unhappy if this were our last meeting.

She put her head in her hands and pressed her brow where it hurt. In the dark, a reverie gathered, like a poached egg collecting in the water: cottage down a lane, bicycles, the sea, Archie with his chair and flask, the children and their spades. Out in the sand, unseen and unheard, where no Irish priest would tread, there she could find out what his rope was made of.

—There are things, she said.

—I think there are.

—This is wrong.

—Would you permit me, he said, to ask a favor?

His words were formal, but his voice had the softness of a friend who knew you and answered your growls with good humor.

—You needn't grant it, he said lightly.

She was getting tangled in his words and his rope.

—I only wonder if you'd let me look into this holiday matter, just until tomorrow. You'll find me in the priory parlor after two, unless you'd let me ring you on a telephone?

—You won't find anything.

—Probably not, he said, but I'd count it an act of friendship if you let me try.

As the underground conveyed her back to Kensington, she began to feel like Marion McDonagh, governess, and as soon as she stepped into the house, Cook enveloped her in a cloud of domestic pique. Felicity had kicked up with Aunt Philomena at the zoo and sniped with Clive all evening. She'd refused her tea, wanted only strawberries and then eaten too many and been sick across the floor. Mother and Father would not return until late, and Cook couldn't be expected to hold the entire seasick ship down herself while poaching the chicken and pinching the pies too, now could she?

She approached the schoolroom with a certain eagerness for the woes of children she could console.

—Morgan le Fay, what's this I hear?

She peeked around the door and saw Felicity curled on the bare floor, Clive beside her with a book in his lap.

—She's got the grippe, Marion, and no one will believe her.

She knelt on the carpet and felt her face. Had they walked in the sun? She wished for the book beside the flour tin at home, the one her mother took down when one of them sickened for something. Soon she had them in the bath, lukewarm water with slices of lemon floating on top, beguiling away their complaints: the heat, their aunt, the heartbreaking pity of animals kept in cages. Later in the bedroom, she read to them, but when she tried to leave, Felicity cried again. Her own throat felt sore, so she began to tell them about the rain and the mist and sea chill back home, letting her voice slip into the tunes she'd forgotten and the sayings she didn't know she recalled.

—What *is* the truckely howl? Clive said.

—Oh, it's a thing old Mary knows, because Mary Lovelace once met a little truckely howl all the way out in the limeretty hillhockers, and this was long before the lepreshauny era, this was in the deep pondoon before the emerald isle was dropped—glunk glunk—in the water.

Water was coming down her own face because she was warm, sure, and because she hadn't ever told her—the one with his eyes—any of this; that child never got to hear of the deep pondoon or the truckely howl or any of the things she was meant to know, and she felt an ache where she'd carried her so long, even when she almost sent her to destruction.

If God *was*, and if he was the way they said, she would beg him to forgive her for even thinking it. Was she really the girl everyone saw, the girl of the new era? That girl had called herself the name with an A and worn a red knit hat. That girl was free and carefree; she'd left behind the miserable island where she'd almost gone mad from the truckely howl and the man who got his guts cut open in a privy. She left them all across the sea, left Daniel in the mud of France, and that was the end of the lepreshauny era. She came to England where the accents were clipped, the frocks gay, gin cheap, parties fast, printing presses inked and heavy, and she didn't care for anyone, least of all that English-come-lately who made her walk holes into the soles of her new shoes and wrote her those stories and showed her his secret English heart with its own words and rigors. She had a hound, and the hound died, and the Talkers closed in and she went to the chalet and, and, and . . .

She was not what the lovely people saw, and she wasn't any longer what the English boy saw. She was a woman who'd carried a child, someone who could sing of the limeretty hillhockers while almost in whispers hearing his voice, his voice and then Archie's voice, *Marion, Marion. What a beautiful name.* And now, she thought—not even in a whisper but beneath it where the truth crouched—it was possible there really was someone who had heard her wish that night, who received her promise, who was holding her child even now at his heart. It was possible she didn't imagine it. And it was possible she wasn't a modern girl at all but a woman like women in the past, wanting and needing what they had wanted and needed through the ages. And if that turned out to be true, she would never be able to show her face again. At home they'd say, *See, see we told you, not so high and mighty now, are you girl?* and at the press they'd say, *Oh, what an awful drip*, and Lovelace from the grave would say, *I always knew it and now you've admitted you deserved it all*, and *he*, what would he say? He wouldn't know her anymore because he loved the modern girl, the runagate, Amanda, Charlie, Aunt Agatha, and the rest. The last person he would ever want to know was this Marion from Galway town who lied to him and everyone, who was now in the heat of London in the great year 1926, an hour of light left in the sky, crying out a servant's window having sung sick children to sleep speaking like the Irish she was, and worse, *being* it and wanting to do it more and more with ones of her own, *their* own, and since she could never get that one back (*never?*), she could only beg the maker of the promise to give her another chance, two more, twelve, until she'd learned the talk and the grip and the limeretty truckely howl.

Friday, after Father left for the firm and Mother the hairdresser, she asked Cook for sandwiches and bade the children change into their lightest clothing. They took the mint-green line to the licorice-black line and emerged some time later near Hampstead Heath fairgrounds.

—Are we going to the *fair*, Marion?

They hadn't been to a fair since Felicity was a baby—

—I wasn't a baby. I remember!

And never in London.

—We shall go if we can give the Tsar's man the slip.

—Where is he, Marion?

—He's just vanished, but if we find a call box, we shan't have to worry.

—There's one!

She told them to stand guard while she rang Scotland Yard. Inside the box it was cooler, secret, cigarette-smelling. She gave the priory's exchange and dropped her coin in the slot.

The voice that answered was a sister by accent. She asked to leave word for Elaine. Would they let her know Marion couldn't come today?

—Elaine? Just a moment. Elaine, someone's—

She made a sound like the pips and rang off.

Outside, an omnibus belched fumes and Clive squinted down the road:

—I think I saw him, Marion. Was he wearing a red cap?

—Top hat, but never mind, I've spoken to the Yard, and they're sending someone to arrest him.

—Hooray!

—Is he a foreign spy?

—He certainly is.

—Ponies! Felicity cried as they rounded the corner. Ponies! May we ride them?

They made their way into the fairgrounds, which teemed with people even on a Friday morning. They rode the ponies twice. They went on the swing chairs and the boat swing and the carousel. They rode two merry-go-rounds and went down the slide that swirled round the tower. She ate the sandwiches and bought them lemonade and pineapple fizz, cotton floss and everything they asked to have. Felicity was sick twice, Clive once, and they laughed to tears and didn't mind being hot. On the underground journey home, office workers wilted in their seats, and everyone looked fit to snap.

She had given Archie the house exchange though at the time she'd no thought of spending the day at the fair. She had acted on instinct, knowing but not admitting that she could not return to the priory and the women desperate enough to kill. As she put the children in the bath, she could no longer repel the tense expectation of a telephone bell. He might ring any time, though surely he'd try before sitting down to supper—if he meant to ring at all. She had Cook bring the children's tea to the garden, where it was cooler and she could hear the bell.

Amid her watchfulness she grew aware of a lapse, one so basic that she'd lost the habit of guarding against it. The fluster in her stomach betrayed a secret hope that he succeed, that he find them a holiday in England, that the letters not cease. Such a hope, it need not be said, was vain. Feeble. Too late, she realized she ought never to have let him try. His effort had warmed soil and awakened seeds, but soon his failure would freeze the sprouts. She peered into the corridor where the clock swung its pendulum like the head of a lady teacher, saying tsk-tsk.

A brash jingle. She dashed inside.

—Kensington treble-six five.

—Miss McDonagh?

The pitch of his voice sounded higher through the telephone.

—Archie, she said, I've only a moment.

—I'll be brief.

There was a cottage in Dorset, half a mile from the sea. The people who were to take it had a change of plan, leaving the owner with an un-let cottage at the peak of the season. There were only two bedrooms, but if she were willing to sleep on a cot beside the children—

—Yes.

He told her the railway stop and the rent.

—A bargain for August. The owner was keen it not stand empty. You could have it in three days and stay for a fortnight.

She didn't know what Father would say, much less whether it would be possible to depart four days earlier than planned, but she took down the club's exchange so Father could ring and discuss particulars.

—I'll be there tomorrow morning until eleven.

—Right.

—Shall I see you in the afternoon?

Pineapple fizz burned up her throat. She said she didn't know.

—Ah, well. They'll be pained to lose you.

—I must ring off.

—So must I, he said. Is it Saturday tomorrow?

—From morning 'til night.

—I'm afraid my mind isn't everything it might be in this heat. But in honor of Saturday, I shall be at the priory after lunch. I always think a proper farewell soothes a myriad of pains, don't you?

The line went dead and she replaced the receiver, caught in cross-currents of rescue and rebuke. Returning to the garden, she suggested they climb the plane tree. The children sucked gooseberries sitting astride the branches, and she drank water like a traveler at a well. Soon, the caravan would depart and drag her into a future she couldn't see. In three days they might go to the seaside, three days meaning Monday, three days left of London and then she could bathe in the frigid water.

After the children had gone to bed, she sat in the drawing room to wait for Father and Mother to return from the theater. They possessed only one case of books, most of them poor, but she fingered the sets of Voltaire, Dickens, and Austen, whose pages had never been cut. It would be a service, surely, for her to take a paper knife to *Persuasion*; at least then someone other than herself might discover the most feeling epistle in English literature: *You pierce my soul*! She freed the edges, lingering over scenes that had blurred since she last read them from Gute's shelf. Memories blanketed the whole story, memories of the heroine's past, of dead mothers, dead loves, dead reprobate sons. Yet in the final scene of turning, Wentworth wrote to arrange a gift on behalf of a friend, a portrait painted for a dead love but now given to a new one, a woman herself recovered from peril, softened and deepened by pain. And as Wentworth wrote this letter, he also eavesdropped on Anne's conversation, in which she argued for women's more lasting affections and showed him what he had only been able to hope, that her feelings for him had not altered, that the past between them might yet be regrown, that the magic of *A Winter's Tale* might work upon their errors and follies to give them a second chance they never could merit.

—Marion, dear, you've sat up very late.

Mother and Father appeared in the archway.

—Is anything the matter? Father asked.

—The children?

They were well, she said. They'd been to the fair and had a splendid day. This evening she'd received a telephone call from a friend—

—Here? From dear Diana?

—What's the matter?

—Nothing.

The opposite, in fact. Her friend was a clergyman, acquaintance from Oxford. It was a terribly long story to tell at such an hour, but he'd rung about a holiday cottage.

—Cottage?

—Near the sea.

She'd imagined the conversation flowing more easily. Now she had to labor to make them understand.

—But what about the Alsace? Mother asked. We couldn't possibly back out now. Could we?

Her husband gave no response. Mother chattered along every byway: they couldn't possibly be so discourteous as to leave Father's colleague in the lurch, and she'd quite come to look forward to it, the exotic languages, the adventure.

—The train goes direct to Dorset in three hours, she told them. I thought you might prefer it to hacking across the Continent.

Train, ferry, further train or trains, horse-drawn dray. Unless a lorry could be found.

—Felicity was frightfully seasick, Mother recalled, that time on the yacht. Do you remember, Father?

Father remembered perfectly.

—She was even sick on the boat swing today.

—And what if you were needed at the firm? Mother continued. You could return to town in a trice from Dorset.

Father still made no comment.

—Oh, but it's too much to change now, Mother declared. We shall have your friend's cottage next year, Marion dear.

—It's only free the next fortnight, she said. But never mind! Alsace will be lovely. Felicity will manage the seas, and I'm sure the food won't be too foreign to eat.

Father stood as if to retire.

—Oh, but Father, are we making a mistake? Mother asked.

—Hmm?

—I mean . . . imagine the journey, the languages, foreign food and foreign lavatories. Do they all smell of garlic? And then imagine us thinking of a darling English cottage that dropped into our laps at the final moment and could have been ours, as we'd wanted all along.

—Hmm.

—Father, I really think we must grasp the nettle.

—Cancel Alsace?

—We'd never be able to enjoy it knowing what we might have had.

Father looked resigned, as if altering their plans would be less arduous than disobliging his wife.

—After all, we aren't French or German, and the thought of meeting anyone who'd killed an English soldier is too, too nasty.

The next morning, she left the children at the Center an hour early and continued on to the Aldgate post office. A brown envelope awaited her, containing an advertisement torn from Thursday's *Mail.* He always seemed to write on whatever was to hand: foolscap, telephone slips, club stationery. His expansive hand curled itself around the caption (*When the day is hot and the road is long, try a Bovril sandwich*) and around the girls in lawn chairs, their tennis racquets strewn beneath the table: *3.7 Do you still rouge your lips . . .*

Wentworth's letter turned the course of *Persuasion* and won the story's ultimate second-chance. She could never be an English rose whose roots went back and back, but if holidays could be found half a mile from the sea, could not the ceaseless leaving cease?

She traced the familiar streets to the priory. Elaine was relieved to see her and to hear she wasn't ill. She said she was leaving Monday, leaving London with her employers. Today would be her last visit.

—But how good of you, how *kind* and good, to come today and tell us goodbye.

The sisters embraced her. The three pilgrims who'd come specially for her help looked alarmed, but then a dull glaze came across their faces, as if disappointment were their native state.

—But I could help now, she said, if there's something you need to write.

They revived and explained their legal dilemmas and their battles with the wicked council. She told them what to write, and before anyone could grow sentimental, it was time for them to leave. The shops were closing, and there was Sunday dinner to supply.

—You'll say goodbye to Laetitia, won't you? Elaine said.

From the cellar, a Bach fugue echoed, the one Sister Laetitia had told her was both a puzzle and a set of wings. She listened from the archway, watching Laetitia stroke a column of wood and produce fresh curls. When the movement ended, she said she'd come to say good-bye, explaining as she had to the pilgrims.

Laetitia brushed off her hands and lifted the tone-arm:

—I never say good-bye. Only au revoir. Besides, you'll have to see what becomes of the chapel.

She shuffled among her tools and sawdust:

—I daresay it will be quite some time, but . . .

She extended her hand, revealing a wooden nut.

—Rub oil into it.

—It's very beautiful.

—An acorn's no different from a mighty oak. It only needs to grow.

She found Archie in the parlor pouring out the tea. He'd spoken with Father, he said. Everything was arranged, even a girl to do meals for them. She rolled the acorn between her thumb and finger.

—I am pleased to see you, he said, one more time.

—But we could meet tomorrow. Are you allowed drinks on Sundays?

He said he was going home in the morning.

—Oh.

—My family are expecting me, and there's a project that needs looking in on.

—More nuns?

—Not quite.

She glanced in alarm at the clock on the mantel. Soon she had to fetch the children. She'd expected tomorrow at least, and as he stirred sugar into his tea, she realized she needed longer, much longer. She needed drinks in the garden after everyone else had gone to sleep and the globe turned them round to the edge of the rising sun.

—I've smoked opium, she said. Have you?

She sounded desperate but didn't care.

—Twice, he replied.

—You . . . what?

—There was a craze at university. It didn't agree with me.

—Was it from a pipe with a hose like the Turks?

—Alas, no.

—What about laudanum?

—I'm afraid that was more troublesome.

She thought he could be blushing. He admitted to having once developed a fondness for laudanum and then having to undevelop it. She felt they were discussing a different person, not this elderly man, not her friend, not even the tyrannical father he played to his son at matinees. She told him she hadn't got on with laudanum. It made her queasy and she'd had to repair to the garden, even though it had been New Year's Eve and frigid, because she'd been afraid of spewing on Gute's Turkey carpet. Someone had given her what she thought was opium at the chalet, after.

—After?

—You can't expect me to tell you here in the daytime, in less than an hour!

Her throat seized.

—My dear.

She was choking—not weeping—stupid choked nottears . . . for *Lovelace* of all people, not the real man but the man she'd thought he was when she fell in love with him. She thought she'd forgotten that man, Professor she'd called him until that library twilight when he had run his fingertips over her wrist and asked her to call him Maurice. She had wished she could one day succeed where every other girl had failed and make him marry her and show her every day that same fleeting smile, and as their children grew up and she taught them to read, he would fill their home with books and life beyond their peasant shores, he'd take her to Venice to show her the watery city he'd described while teaching Dante, and their family would be beautiful like books. Religious people and poets—

—Not poets like I tried to be. Proper poets—

They were occupied with eternity. Now she wondered if eternity weren't another name for the whole of time. You were always inside it but locked in the present, barred forever from the past no matter how much you cried to return. All the past was unreachable whether ancient days—

—When they rode around in phaetons and wore enormous skirts—

Or just a year ago, all barred. And the other end of time was also barred even though you were always moving towards it, tomorrow and tomorrow until the last day.

—But *I* say . . . . D'you know what I say?

—What do you say?

—With all that as true, and it is true, isn't it?

—Yes.

—With all that . . . *nowness*, why shouldn't people follow their whims? Why shouldn't they mike off for a drink after supper? There must be someplace near that club of yours.

He let her see a smile and in his eyes a rogue flash, as if he, underneath his costume and office and age, were as much a miker-off as his son, as much a gambler and improviser, a balker of convention, a bull-stubborn mule who would have his way if it took years, someone professionally guarded and brazenly honest, someone who knew, perhaps, what she was just discovering, that there was no way out until they lost the endgame. That they were blind, deaf, and dumb and had only each other in the boat.

He wrote an address on a corner of newspaper.

—It's an hotel with a lounge, he said. If you mean it, I'll be there tonight after nine.

—Isn't it too late? I mean, oughtn't you . . . ?

—And here I thought you were the one person I could rely on not to fuss over my deuced health.

She arrived at the Center as their lessons were ending. Felicity's hair had come out of its knot, and Clive nursed a bruised shin.

—Look what I learned, Marion!

Felicity ran to her and then leaned forward into a handstand and a flip.

—That doesn't look like ballet.

—It's what they do in the circus. Just wait 'til Sister Prue sees!

And so she had to explain about the holiday.

—You mean we'll never see Sister Prue again?

—What about Frances?

Their distress at such an idea outweighed the pleasure she'd expected a seaside holiday to bring.

—It's a shame we haven't more time, she said.

—But we don't need more time! Clive declared.

He had learned the underground better than she thought. It was only a few stations from the Center to the priory, he announced. They could stop on the way home, and even though it was the opposite direction, it wouldn't take any longer. They must go now and tell Sister Prue goodbye.

—And I can show her my trick!

—We must bring a present.

—Chocolates!

She agreed to flowers, and half an hour later she was walking back through the gates she thought she'd left for good, tugging on the bell, and being admitted again by a surprised Elaine. Sister Prue was delighted to see the children and received the flowers with the solemnity Clive offered. She applauded Felicity's flip and listened to their description of the holiday-to-come.

—Swimming with mermaids!

—A bothy in a real pirate's cove!

She gave Felicity one of the peg dolls and Clive a black marble from the playground collection. When the door of the priory shut behind them, they'd reached the point of overexcitement that guaranteed a high-strung hour followed by a wall of tears.

—I want to pack my case tonight! Clive declared.

—So do I! May we? May we, Marion?

They were passing the post-office. Clive tugged her towards the door.

—I've already stopped in today, she said.

—But I must write Grandmother and tell her all the plans.

—I must write Grandmother, too!

—I need a stamp, Marion, and a card.

—So do I!

And so they stopped at the post office, where another brown envelope leapt like a biting snake. She put it in her handbag until the children were in bed. This was written on a page torn from a notebook, better paper than before but still ragged:

> *3.8 Remember the rings we bought to go on holiday? This weather makes me think of Whitby. Remember that cupboard of a room in the place by the quay? The bed was appalling, the walls thin as muslin. Remember the torment? Hearing the landlords blowing their noses in their squeaky bed, skulking around the ruins and being interrupted by that family with their sketchbooks? Sometimes I think it was a kind of torture to have Fishguard first, before we knew any better, and then not be allowed anything like it again. Being with you is like standing in the sun when all my bones need are light to grow.*

Had he forgotten Applecross, or was he avoiding mention of it? The weather there had been bland, mild gray days without rain. They'd stayed only a week. Nothing happened in the newspapers, at the press, at his college. He didn't ask her to marry him. Yet everything else, everything inside the cloud, even the ailing pup, all testified to lives in dramatic revolution, but one hidden inside an ordinary Easter on the far side of a pass that couldn't be crossed in the snow.

She'd always maintained that she was planning her own life and working the levers, but now she felt the weight of the hand that put everything into motion only to destroy it. Oh, she could hear the Catholics answering, and the Protestants, all the dapper theologians of Jasper's acquaintance. And she could hear the likes of Lina and the beautiful lady painter with the mind of a child bubbling words like Life, the Universe, Lady Fate, Goddess, all of which stood for the maker though none explained what ruled *him*—Mathematics? Reason? Chance? He treated people as parts in a machine whose only purpose was to execute his cold designs, but the one she had whispered to, in the water and the naming and the promise, he was different. He'd come without her asking even though she'd outraged him, denied him, slandered and rejected him across seas and years, guts pouring out, Talkers on high, her bitter tongue a knife. Still, when the time came and the baby stopped breathing and she put the water over her and said what she said, he was there as if he'd never left, there with her, *her* Marion and *her* Amanda, in the dark and the salt and the ocean trench where ships crumbled in the seabed. He was there, wind howling across the mountain, snow plastering the window. He was silent, but he held her, held them both. He accepted her promise and held it even now.

She could never explain these things. She couldn't repeat how she'd put her in the ground, how when the Frau returned—Some stretches of her life were like that, knife escapes and corpses. The next time the corpses would be worse, the flight longer and more desperate, which was another reason not to touch him again, even with letters, or he would end up—

Listen, you! You in the darkness, you of the promise, hear this now and tell the maker: Do not, not ever, take him. Do not strike him the way of Lovelace, of the pup, of little—Hear this. Leave him in the sun, not the desert sun but the English sun. Love him.

Though how could he stand in the sun without . . . ?

If she agreed to see him again, she would bring curses into his golden life, cutting him with the truth, and he'd be even more maimed than she because he wasn't used to maiming. But—and this was loud—if she left him alone, if she vanished herself for good, he would never again stand in the sun. This she knew suddenly, foreign and unwelcome. If she left, he would never become the full plump fruit the gardener had planted him to be.

Did the clearest decisions always feel like no choice?

She put on her better frock, brushed her hair, rouged her lips. The children were asleep, Mother and Father at a party. The underground map showed a way to the place Archie had written. She told Cook she was going out and then on impulse fetched her locket from its hiding place. She fingered it, riding the underground, but didn't open the circle. Arriving at the restaurant, she thought to put it in her handbag with the wooden acorn, but that would leave her neck bare, and she looked enough like a pauper clacking across the marble where women glided like languid nymphs in the latest fashions.

Sitting at a banquette and sipping from an old fashioned glass, Archie was pleased to see her. She ordered whiskey and set her handbag between them.

—It's worse than that, she said.

He didn't call her abrupt. He spoke as if they'd never stopped:

—Go on.

Four women in sparkling gowns clung to the arms of young men. A peal of laughter rang from the other side of the pillars. A man in a turquoise smoking jacket slid onto the piano bench and ran his fingers across the keys like water and glamor. A waiter set a glass beside her.

—It's a terrible burden, Archie said. That much is plain.

She said they all had burdens. Who was she to complain?

—Marion, he said, you've come all this way.

She pretended not to notice his using her name because it gave her a feeling that she didn't want to end.

—Every day you don't tell a thing, you move farther and farther from it, she said.

—Do you?

—You move farther and farther from the one you have to tell. Not telling is a lie, and you keep lying the longer you go.

—What would happen if you did tell it?

She screwed up her face to show what a stupid question that was. He swirled his glass and his ring tinkled the side:

—I could tell something too.

—Could you?

He shifted in his seat to look out at the room.

—I've an old friend, fellow man of the cloth. Bachelor, but there's a godson.

At first she thought the godson would be Jasper, but when he said the godson was American, she realized he was aiming at something else. He dwelt on minor details, sneaking up on the real story, or showing her how. The friend's godson had been at Oxford and while there had got a girl into trouble.

—Naturally my friend paid the girl's family and had the godson shipped back to New York.

—Did they love each other?

—There was no suggestion of it.

—Not that he'd know.

—Perhaps.

—I wish if you had something to say, you'd spit it out.

The sparkling women sipped their champagne.

—And I never said I wasn't a hypocrite!

—My dear . . .

The story after all was not about the godson. The story was about the advice the friend offered when his fellow clergyman found his own son mixed-up with a girl of whom the family disapproved. The friend encouraged him to steer the girl away from his son, to advise her in any direction, to pay her, lead her or push her, anything within his scope to effect.

—Is that what he did?

—It's what he tried, when he had her to his club.

—Some try! All he did was ask questions about publishing!

—He failed indeed, but then he tried again, or told himself he was trying.

—At a pub?

—But before he realized, it was too late and he couldn't do it.

—Why not?

—He didn't know.

—His son made threats.

—His son knew nothing.

—Knew?

—Knows.

—Don't lie to me, Archie. That one thing, don't do it.

He nodded to the waiter for another drink. She looked away to the dinner jackets and pearls.

—Well, he said, that's how the Holy Spirit works, isn't it? Forgive my being blunt, but its such a palaver to talk around it.

—I've no idea how it works.

—It gives you things you'd never choose and then grafts them to you. I mean imagine: one's son snatched away by a shipwreck in Yorkshire and a wild Irish girl. It's beyond absurd. Literally nothing according to plan!

—Pay the girl a ransom. Send the son—

—I wish you could hear what I'm saying, my dear. *Nothing was going according to plan*, but after the near miss—

—Near miss?

He tapped his chest.

—He'd begun to see that his plans were . . . undergoing a purgation.

—How near a miss?

—Evidently his days aren't done. But his ideas for them?

She bobbed in the sharp sea of what he was trying to say. He'd planned to push her off but had failed. Why keep seeing her, then? Why stay in London, dirty and hot, against medical advice? Why had he worked miracles to get the cottage and stop her crossing the channel?

—I don't understand whose side you're on.

—Sometimes I'm not sure myself.

—He's a grown man. You can't engineer his life forever.

—That's precisely what I'm trying to stop doing.

—Try harder.

He frowned. The turquoise jacket bubbled a fresh tune.

—I'd like something sweet, he said. What about you?

She told him she could murder a steak. He smiled, and then stopped himself from saying whatever he wanted to say.

—Why did you pretend to be my friend?

—I didn't, he said. I'm not. Pretending, that is.

—It won't work, you know, me and him.

—There are things you oughtn't to tell me.

She said she didn't plan to. She said she wasn't perverse enough to use a father as substitute for a son. But, she said, it wasn't fair of him to throw out his rope and make her think she could speak to him for herself, make her think she mattered regardless of his son, mattered to him, that he would pull her from the riptide.

—You matter immensely. What do you imagine I'm doing here—

He gestured to the tinkling room.

—At this hour, but answering your call?

He held out his hand, signet ring the same as his son's:

—This is the rope. The only one I've got.

She wanted to spit at the waiter who came to take the order and ask how she took her steak.

—Blue.

Archie asked for the elderflower jelly, and the waiter set a sharp knife beside her.

—Well, Archie said, quid pro quo?

His shadow of a smile wrapped her in at-home-ness, an almost-flirtation, as much dare as permission.

She unfolded her napkin and wrapped the knife inside it:

—At home, there were twins. And there were Irish twins.

He nodded as if her words made sense to him. Before she was born, there had been Mary, who died. Next came Joe, then herself, and, ten months later, Daniel. She was given her own name but perversely called Mary.

—A pet name, they said.

At first she liked it because it made her like Our Lady and like the other girls she knew called Mary. But then when she and Daniel were both six, their mother told them—Joe, herself, Daniel—about Mary, who had always been vague to them, and about another Mary, who had been Joe's twin born dead. *I never knew I had a twin*! Joe exclaimed to anyone who'd listen.

—He had a way of stating the obvious.

She had been confused and frightened, like when peril had its eyes on you.

—Two Marys dead? I mean.

What could come of reusing a bad name? Not that Our Lady had a bad name, or Mary McKenna or Mary Cuffe or Mary Columba, but Mary McDonagh and Mary McDonagh the second, and having to put up with a doomed ghost of a name being used towards her. She wanted to stand on the bench on her side of the kitchen table and gather the whole family together—Mama, Da, Joe, Daniel, Teddy, and baby Sheena and say, *Hear me, my people. Let's begin again. No longer shall you call me by the name of the dead but by this name: Amanda*!

—Did they?

—No, but my father started calling me Marie.

Only Daniel called her Amanda, but that was because he was her Irish twin and her mind twin. And now he couldn't call her that name or any other because he was dead and because she, in a moment of weakness, had done what she'd always sworn she would never do and reuse a name.

Was she dying or was she dead when the water hit her head and she said the words that named her? She had to think she was still on this side because otherwise the water and the naming and the promise weren't real, and she was lost to everlasting nothingness. There were ruins, but with time and money and sweat they could be built again. Debts could be paid, prison terms served, captivity escaped. Even wars came eventually to an end when there weren't enough boys to send into the bullets.

The child hadn't died because of the bargains she'd pursued, but she had nevertheless pursued them, and even though she knew how full-of-hell they were, she had entered into them. When it came to it, the maker stamped them null and void, which was a mercy in a way, though how could anyone call her burning up and drowning in air, turning blue then gray, how could it—

The napkin had come unrolled, and candlelight glinted off the knife, bright as a whistle showing her what she could do.

—Marion.

He didn't touch the knife. He only threw a net with the timbre of his voice.

—Understand this, she said. I know what's real, and I know he kills everything he creates.

Which wasn't to say they didn't deserve death. She more than deserved it, but—

—King David's child did nothing wrong. It died because of its father. After everything David did to Bathsheba and Uriah, he got to live but the little one—

Hers was flawless. The water hadn't been needed to wash her clean, but like the Red Sea to deliver her from the captivity her mother had arranged for her, naming her with her own name, speaking her into a promise that was true no matter what her mother believed, no matter what her mother poisoned.

Did the poisoning start when she learned what was inside her? Or did it go further back, listening to Lovelace, scorning her family, running away to the thief who pretended to marry them, all that and then calling Daniel to her with her mind and her heart, leading him into temptation—and if giving a brother reason to gut a man in a privy wasn't wrong, what was? How far back did the ruin go?

—All the way back, he said, to the beginning.

If she were the kind of girl who cried when she wished, she would have done it and her tears would have lured him from what she had just uttered. Instead, vileness stained the damask like blood from the meat they were searing even now. She let her head fall onto her arm, knife handle cool against her cheek.

—You didn't kill her. You named her. And you can say her name.

—What do you think I've been *telling* you?

—And I heard you. Marion?

She turned her head to expose an eye.

—What do you want?

What did she *want*?

—Right here and now.

Besides the complete rewinding of time?

—Everything I want is impossible.

—But if it weren't?

If the time weren't this time . . .

—I'd want you not to be his father. Not to be a clergyman. Only to be my friend.

—Only?

—Wholly.

Not that she deserved a friend. Not that she knew how to be one herself.

—And what is a friend, the kind you would want?

She didn't have a university mind. She had no patience for abstract things. She only knew what she'd never had, someone who knew you and stood by you in your awful, terrible mistakes.

—And your useless, un-deservable wishes.

—That's a good kind of friend.

—A castle in the air.

—Friends can be found in strange places, he said. And if you happen upon one, and he happens to know a thing or two about riptides—

—What do you know about holding the dead in your arms?

—More than you think.

Her stomach dropped; she couldn't reverse the conversation.

—Her name was Clara, he said.

She saw him holding a blue baby.

—The vow is only until death, but love is sometimes stronger.

He wasn't talking about his child, she realized, but about his wife, who she knew had died after his son was born. He spoke of twenty-eight years as if it were last week, how she'd come through the birth, how all had seemed well, how two nights later she had slipped through his fingers. An earthquake he'd never known, before or since, waking to a world poisoned by the one thing that couldn't be revoked. How in the eyes of others he had been a paragon of composure and grace, never wept where anyone could see, comforted his daughters, found a wet nurse for the infant, but how behind the mask he had raged and threatened the one who gave and took away, his deepest sorrow reserved for himself. How he had gone to the cathedral in the dead of night, crawled on his knees down the length of the nave, and offered the life of his son if only he could have her back.

The steak came, but she couldn't eat it. He asked again:

—What do you want?

—Do you think they've got any brown bread and honey?

He spoke to the waiter and then began to eat her steak. As he sliced and chewed each modest bite, she saw the darkened cathedral, his tears dripping on the stone floor, his desperation, his barbarity, his degradation before his God. His hands were trembling as he raised the fork to his mouth, as if eating might rebuild the man. Was it possible he had never told it before now? Last month he'd had a heart attack. Nothing was going according to plan. His ideas of the future had been yanked from the ground, and his life, she saw, must be now as much of a storm-smashed boat as her own.

If friends knew one another, they were friends. If friends stood by each other in their terrible mistakes and un-deservable wishes, they were friends. If friends depended on each other in trust? He had depended on her ear, and now he depended on her silence though he didn't say it, didn't need to.

He wiped his mouth after each bite as though it were his last.

—Tomorrow, he said, your friend will have to leave.

—I know, she said. But . . .

He dipped the meat in the blood that pooled.

—Tomorrow, he said, your friend must be a father to his son. Particularly if your aims are what they appear.

—I haven't aims.

—Truth, friend.

Her eyes strained in their sockets:

—Are you saying this is the last night, the last we can be friends?

—The last.

A cry cut her throat.

—*My dear.*

His hand never touched, but his voice gave succor. He began to speak of the naming, of the promise, both the promise she made and the promise from the water.

—You may have wanted it to be secret, but He never asks that. He means for his promise to shine in the world, a light to lighten.

—But . . .

—You must speak of her. You must knit her into your family. *Her* family.

His words a map if not a guide. He passed her a handkerchief, crisply pressed.

—It isn't fair to have one friend, *one* in your life and have it taken away!

—But it's necessary, isn't it, if you're to thread the needle you mean to thread.

—It's so much!

—Perhaps on the other side, it won't seem like much at all.

—He'll never forgive, he *shouldn't*—

—You don't know that.

—And I'm off Monday to the seaside with—how can I—how can he?

He looked as if to say, *There are trains.*

There was much, so much she needed to turn over with him. Could they not meet on holiday?

—Friends will the other's good, no matter the cost.

Her throat caught again, but he held her gaze. She had never been as perfectly sad, as perfectly sore, but also, somewhere, a window was blowing open, not to the past but to the one whose blue-black script caressed her heart even now. *If you're reading this, hope is real.*

—What will you tell him?

—I? he said. I'm not the one who has things to tell.

—So once tonight is over, it will be as if it never happened?

—Nothing can be undone. But once the curtain falls, it falls across everything shared in the trust of friendship. Oh, my dear, don't take on. This is good news. *Good* news!

The chucking in her throat and eyes chucked even harder.

—Is father-in-law so bankrupt an office?

~

He was always keeping himself in check even when others would say he'd abandoned every prudence. In check, he'd done the things he'd done, broken what he'd broken. If he ever chose to abandon restraint, he would sear eyes, drown hopes, drop minenwerfers into peace before anyone saw him coming. He thought she knew this about him.

He'd forced himself to stop looking for her letters every time he passed the club desk but instead to associate it with St. Stephen's, whose missives assailed him with the energy of sisters discovering a new craze. Lewis wrote daily regarding accounts, cooks, scullery maids, groundsmen, house matrons, and who knew so many people were required for the operation of a school? Miss Meyers had accomplished the refurbishment of his rooms, and Lewis assured him he would find her choices satisfactory. Jamie, for his part, had convinced Kardleigh to visit the school in September. He'd cast it as a consultation (a word native to Kardleigh in its medical context), the purpose being to take Kardleigh's opinion of the organ, the boys, and the prospect of a music program. Jamie wasn't sure Kardleigh believed the premise, but even pretending to believe was an improvement on refusal. How the school had gone from impossible to nearly ready to begin, he could not quite say.

Eating breakfast alone Monday morning, his father having departed the city, he felt at loose ends. His thoughts darted vainly like fireflies in a jar. Heartburn threatened. *Well, this is just your style, isn't it? Give me everything I ask except the thing I require most of all.* The damask tablecloth mocked his need, reminding him of his blessings and privilege. The waiter poured his coffee, usually a pleasure, now a bitter consolation. *You told me to fetch her from the maze. And now*? The Old Boy had no response.

You pretended to be the man you wished to be, and if you pretended with enough vigor, other people would believe you and eventually you might become that man. St. Stephen's would call for ceaseless pretending, beginning the first of September and continuing until his hair turned as white as his father's. Of course, he could quit. They might even sack him once they realized what a fraud he was. But if he were to be honest, to write with fine-tipped pen and indelible ink, he would admit his intention was to stay with St. Stephen's, to make the school better than it imagined it could be, full of men more subtle and supple than any others, not exalted like the so-called great schools but vividly *better*. And to do that, he could not play false. He needed full exercise of himself, not this locked existence. He needed the freedom of the cloud in Applecross, and behind closed doors, he needed to be held to account. Only she could do this. Only she could see entirely through him.

His father rang from the Rectory to say that the Minster's organ master had agreed to receive Kardleigh when he came to visit St. Stephen's.

—It will be an audition, his father said, not a social visit. The man's notoriously blunt.

—They'll get on like blue murder. Thank you, Father. Really.

—You can thank me by remembering your health. A few days at the seaside will do you the world of good. The children have taken quite a shine to young Wilberforce, by the way.

—Isn't it a bit much? Jamie asked. Holiday with a pupil installed as a member of one's household?

His father dismissed his concerns as over-scrupulousness. Jamie agreed to consider it.

That afternoon he returned to her familiar haunts but didn't see her. That evening he surveyed her house and found it dark. Next morning the curtains were drawn. He had to use every technique Kardleigh taught him to dispel the weakness, which at the sight of the shut-up house seized him like a cut-throat. It was still seizing him as he rang the club's service door still wearing his costume. The boy who admitted him looked alarmed.

—Will you sit down, sir? Have a drink of water?

He declined and retreated upstairs for a bath. Tim and Malcolm were all the way in Oxford, and even if he were unwise enough to write them, so long after giving up the Business and on the eve of his own headmastership, they wouldn't be able to help for days.

He had to face what had been too awful to contemplate: she'd left again, direction unknown. Dripping on the bathroom tiles, he felt himself losing ground. Was he going to have to ring Kardleigh in his capacity as physician? At this rate, he would have to ask the desk clerk to dial the number for him. He couldn't get all his buttons into their holes, but he managed to do up his trousers and throw a jacket over his disheveled self before descending to the lobby.

—Sir.

The clerk slid the evening mail across the desk. He did not mention Jamie's lack of a tie.

—I need to place a telephone call.

—Yes, sir.

—Directly.

—Yes, sir.

The clerk bore none of the kitchen boy's alarm but his gaze nevertheless fixed on Jamie.

—What?

The man released the envelopes, the kind of gesture that, years later, one looked back on. Time did not slow, but the script on the first . . .

You should drink a draft of Letheward and let it melt the past to steam. Consider this your last sentinel blast.

Wrapped in the page was another, smaller envelope. Correction, ersatz envelope like they fashioned at the press, designed as tamper-proof and the devil to open. His hands were not up to it.

—Allow me, sir?

He let the clerk unlock it and unfold the vital organs.

Cricket St. John, Dorset. 16 August - 1 September.

Of course nothing was simple, not even a snap decision to join his family on holiday. After ensuring his correspondence would follow him to the villa Beth was letting, he caught a train for Wiltshire. If he'd known a seaside wardrobe would be required, he might have brought something down from Yorkshire; as it was, he'd have to ransack the Rectory since there wasn't time to see his tailor.

The cupboard in his childhood bedroom contained the clothing of a university student, and in the case of his swimming costume, that of a schoolboy. The looking glass revealed that he was aging. The muscles in his chest had softened. His face was haggard. The old things, when he tried them on, did not make him look youthful, but overfed. He packed whatever fit him and, after negotiating three sets of railway timetables, arrived at the villa as the family were sitting down to tea. His nieces fell upon him, Beth and Robert plied him with food, his father looked irritatingly satisfied, and Wilberforce vacillated between ignoring him and blushing in his presence.

—Will you read to us at bedtime? asked Georgie.

—*The Secret Garden*, said Clara.

—My bed, my bed! demanded Tess.

—It's the first time she's had a grown-up bed.

—She's terribly excited.

—My bed!

And so the webs of Misselthwaite Manor ensnared him, and he read for too long, unable to remove himself from the warm pressure of his nieces' cheeks against his arm and his knee and his chest. He fell asleep that night sunk in a feather bed, dizzy from travel, unsure who he was. How long would it take her to receive his card? *Puggly Torn, Dorset, 20-30 August*. Should he have written more? The girl in her charge looked the same age as Georgie, the boy close to Clara. As for gangly Wilberforce, whom the girls clearly idolized, could he not be packed off with the children—his nieces and Amanda's charges—while he and she . . . How would it go? He'd grown used to her as an idea, a static memory, even an impossible object of desire, but he himself had changed since they last knew each other, in ways a verbal explanation couldn't bridge. He was no longer an Oxford man, though wouldn't a part of him always belong to that city, even when he'd grown decrepit, and wouldn't the banks of the Isis always hold her footprints and his, like the feeling in his stomach when she appeared at the door of the press, affixing her hat.

—Shall we, Miss McDonagh? he used to say offering his arm but implying more.

—Oh, the sky is clear.

She'd say this even when holding his umbrella, their shoes already wet.

—Let us not slip the occasion.

Sometimes on the doorstep she would kiss him and slip her tongue into his mouth, or she would slip her hand into his trouser pocket, or—these things belonged to that unreachable age when neither of them had ever been as old as they felt.

He couldn't think of a story that would weld their lives together again. Wasn't there a looking glass that could take them to a time when trees still covered the land, a time full of wolves and maids Marion, where they could vanish into tall forest towers? But even if there were such a glass, still they would carry everything they'd been. Nothing could undo where she'd gone and why, and it couldn't unmake the impression his fingerprints—not to mention those effortless good looks—had made on the poor hostage school that claimed him and depended on him and even now contained his hat rack and his tea set and the clothing of their people wrapped in brown paper at the bottom of his trunk.

~

The cottage smelled of mildew, but she'd opened all the windows and rustled the garden furniture into shape while Mother and Father unpacked their cases. She'd found bicycles in the shed and made it the project of the first afternoon to teach Clive to ride and Felicity to sit astride her handlebars. The next morning she had the children at the shore, Clive having fallen only twice on the way. Mother and Father insisted on staying behind at the cottage, whether to be free of the children or for their own purposes, no one inquired.

She lay on the sand as the children buried each other. Their chatter blended with the surf, stirring an ache for the kind of summers they had before she knew what time meant. Would she ever again be able to close her ears, let the sun scorch, and eddy away into dreams? It would require someone to guard her against everything the great torrent sluiced their way. He had wanted to be that, but she hadn't let him. She'd thought herself strong and wise to refuse to fall asleep while they picnicked in the meadow. *Let me keep the watch*, he'd said. She'd accused him of scheming to take advantage of her. *Oh*, he said smiling, *if I'm to take advantage of you, I want you fully awake.*

Her thoughts were more muddled than she wanted to admit. Archie had let her think him a perfectly sealed tomb, but as they were leaving the restaurant, he'd written a telephone exchange on the back of his hat check ticket:

—I'll be with Beth and the children. I can't speak for my son's arrangements, but my son-in-law has a motorcar, not far from where you'll be.

—Your son-in-law knows about me?

—He knows a friend needed a holiday cottage. He's remarkably discreet.

Outside, he'd put her into a taxi and paid the driver:

—I shan't disturb you.

—This is the end. I know.

—Nevertheless, if an old bishop could ever be of assistance . . .

She'd thought she understood, then, why he had found them the cottage, but now, salt and sun crusting her skin, she was no longer sure. She and the children had stopped at the post-office shop to buy ginger beer and packet crisps; a postcard had been waiting for her, and it gave the name of a village that the post lady said was some distance away, *halfway to Wool*, whatever that meant, leaving it to her to propose a rendezvous. A tearoom bustled next door to the shop, and she could ask Mother and Father for a free afternoon, but no shop sufficed for such a cataclysm.

He felt that soon he wouldn't be able to breathe. Three days had passed since his arrival. The postman pelted him with correspondence concerning St. Stephen's. The dining table pelted him with requests from his nieces, a deafening silence from his father, and the overshadowing reproach of unredeemed time. He'd gone so far as to climb out his dormer window to the roof just to escape the tempest. How could he ever give the enterprise—the enterprise of her—the full, undressed attention it required? Could someone not hold the world off, even for the span of a sunset, long enough to slip away and find her? They needed more than an hour, more than a day or even a fortnight, but they didn't have it. Life was perpetually vanishing, and it wouldn't stop until the candle was snuffed. The perfect moment was a mirage.

3.10 Something cuts when I try to write your name. Artemis-now-Diana tells me I mustn't use A— but must only call you M—. Is it really true? Here at the edge of this cliff, we either tell each other the truth, or kill each other in our hearts.

Here's an earnest: I followed you. You and the two children. You might have noticed the masked soldier with cigarettes? Please give me credit for superhuman restraint. I never spoke, never left word at your house on the square.

He put the letter in the morning post and sat down to breakfast with people who inhabited another world. They ate eggs and toast soldiers, spoke over one another, touched his shirt cuffs and his signet ring, his hair and the edge of his chin, but they could never know the balance of his heart. They occupied a summer's day that showed what perfect peace could be if you let it. The girls recruited Wilberforce for croquet, Beth watched, and Robert and his father read under the wisteria. Jamie devoted himself to his correspondence and three telephone calls; after lunch, Robert drove them to the seaside, and he threw his nieces around in the surf until they turned blue with cold. Just before tea, Wilberforce's father arrived, introducing a tension that Jamie compulsively smothered with jokes and charm. That evening, as the men were smoking in the garden, he found himself asking Wilberforce, in presence of the father, if he could count on him as a prefect in the new term. Not a single thing he was doing was well-considered. He left the house in the middle of the night and walked across the downs. The moon cast a shadow, and he could feel the sound of summer in its ancient fullness, its false promise, its nectar.

~

I knew it was you. Not exactly but still. Don't ask for the truth unless you can stand it.

~

Flower's Barrow, sunset? Path from the east. Please. If ever a word could make the time spin . . .

~

If aeroplanes could fly, and they did, and if as Gute had once claimed they took off against the wind, then the laws of creation might allow more impossible acts.

After supper, at the end of the grassy lane, Archie's son-in-law rolled up in a bullnose Morris. He introduced himself as Robert, slim fingers, soft voice, hair graying at the temples.

—Do you know Flower's Barrow? she asked. Path from the east?

He unfolded a map and, after consulting it, reversed into the road. He didn't speak, either from reserve or because driving with the top down made conversation difficult, but he drove placidly, slowing for rabbits, steering around hedgehogs, his right arm extended on the wheel. A memory stirred, something Jasper had told her about his brother-in-law—this one?—and aeroplanes during the war. Had he flown them? Something with aerial photography. What had Jasper said, and what had she imagined? Lanes twisted by, her hair blew into her mouth, and when they came over a rise, he held up his hand to shield his eyes from the sun.

—Summer's in its death throes, she said.

—I wouldn't be so sure.

He turned up a rough track and nosed towards a stile.

—I'll wait, he said. Down there?

He nodded at the shore, where fish and chips shops twinkled with lanterns. She hadn't thought far enough ahead to wonder how she'd get back, or indeed how far it was to Flower's Barrow.

—Are you sure you don't mind?

He ratcheted the handbrake:

—Tide's going out. Nothing like a walk to clear away the cobwebs.

Nothing was as she had imagined.

—Do you ever feel you're drifting with the current?

—Constantly, he said.

The sun was setting behind the peninsula.

—How many chances do you think we really get?

He gazed at the shore:

—As many as we can take, don't you think?

—Does the sun make a hiss when it touches the sea?

—It sounds, he said, like a piano sonata played with four hands.

She laughed.

—Go, he said. I'll be here. If the motor's empty, wait.

She got out and shut the door, like a spy dropped behind enemy lines.

The footpath was slimy though the sun had beat down all day. His destination, a waypost some half-mile off, wouldn't be visible until the last minute, at the last turn. A time came unwarranted to mind, mounds in no-man's-land, his men choking, staccato rifle fire, thinking, *This is how it ends, before you see twenty, drowning in air*, until, as he gagged and gasped, wind blew his sick into his collar. Now, gazing down at the surf that hammered the cliffs and rinsed lichen and sea urchins, he felt the wind again, carrying the scent of silage and saltwater. A skylark looped above him, and despite his fear (everyone else had died that night, his lungs were probably damaged for life, such an association should be seen as an omen), despite everything, he felt a curious balm he could only call coming-homeness. Such sentiment belonged to the simple-minded, yes and yes to the end of the book, but still the skylark rode the air, and the music was the music of return, of long shadows in a long summer twilight where it scarcely got dark and never got cold and the battles had ended and the heavy doors opened once again.

Let her be there when he turned the final turn. Let him find her. Let her stay. This was where words dried up and you had to hope in sighs too deep for hearing.

The cairn stood naked save a pair of munching sheep. The other track was hidden except its very start, there. She might be on it; she might not. A process blows the moon behind the clouds, he thought, and you couldn't rush the revealing, wish though you might, blow though you—

Hat. Ribbon. Face.

She scrabbled up the final rise, her skirt flapping with gusts he didn't feel. Was this how it felt to fall to your death? Before he was ready, she arrived, pulling herself in. The sun was in her eye, and although she could have stood in his shadow, she didn't.

—Have you got any water? she said.

He felt her voice where he always felt her, and although he'd imagined dropping to his knees and wrapping his arms around her waist, he maintained the distance she had set and reached into his pocket:

—Flask. Not water. Sorry, I should have thought.

He was wearing flannel trousers and a blazer that was too big for him. She could see perspiration on his shirt when his jacket flapped open. He moved to embrace her, but she reached out for the flask. His fingers brushed hers, relinquishing it, steel warm and full of whisky that tasted like the kind they used to drink. As she replaced the cap, a gust blew her middy top into her face, and she lost her balance. He caught her elbow, and she grasped the sleeve of his blazer as he held her there, not against her will but with it, waiting for her to pull closer, or away.

He smelled like her father. She hadn't even remembered how her father smelled but here, wearing someone else's blazer infused with someone else's tobacco, the whisky still on her tongue, his sweat—her father.

She stepped away and held down her skirt in the breeze.

—Tell me, she said, what we're looking at.

She turned to face the sea. He prized his gaze away from her and cast it across the coastline.

—That's Weymouth, he said, and Portland.

She retied the ribbon of her hat, and he pointed out the few landmarks he knew. Lulworth Castle, Hartland Moor. France.

—What else?

—Well . . .

How could he say the untouchable past, the unsayable words, the death of the old life and the birth of something new, whether better or worse they would decide?

—Can you see that cove across there, not the second but the third?

—Yes.

—That's where my friend Agatha once went bathing, without any bathing costume.

—Did she, the old trout?

—She wasn't old then. All the ladies did it. They'd go out a whole town of women and bathe naked as a needle.

—They must've got sand in all kinds of places.

—That was half the fun.

She didn't laugh, but he continued, inventing other locations—where Professor Jay capsized a sailboat, where That Man smuggled Champagne and Madeira, where Uncle Jack kept a cottage. She began to walk along the footpath, so close to the edge he didn't know how to take it. A cloud had screened the sun, but she kept hold of her hat, perhaps to stop him taking her hand.

She could feel his trailing steps as she strode towards the sunset. Ahead was a stile. She climbed it:

—What else?

He propped his arms on the wall beside her, looking up the hill:

—Six hundred miles that way, the moorland's wilder than this.

Surf hissed below, and she let her knee touch him.

—There's a school no one's heard of, and it's so desperate and full of fools that it let itself be dazzled by the fraudulent charisma—

He paused, letting her remember her own phrase.

—of a gadabout who's spent the last year frauding his way through his own former school.

She let more of her weight rest against his shoulder as he spoke in the third person, a self-deprecating account of the last fourteen months, his degree, his position, his father's near death.

—How near?

—Too near.

Gaining courage, he roamed into gossipy updates about his friends Stoat and Grady, and his horrid sister Lucy. He described the villa his eldest sister had taken nearby, the holiday party, their doings. He spoke of Archie, and a boy that could only be his *other project*.

—Is it normal to take pupils on a family holiday?

—Heavens, no. Nothing about St. Stephen's is normal. Not a single thing.

He was exercising restraint by not looking at her, but from the corner of his eye he caught that shy smile that came when she couldn't help it, the expression that made her seem a girl.

—I know what you think of public schools, and you're right in the main, but this place is different. It's deplorable. Right up your street.

She bumped him with her knee, the first true encouragement. He'd almost forgotten what it was to be fed. He gabbled about his father, how he had a line in messes, meaning he helped men in the midst of ordeals though until now only clergy and seminarians. She pulled away, and he didn't know what he'd said wrong.

The wall of the unsaid stretched into the sky until she couldn't see the top of it. She needed to get off the stile, go down the path, find Robert in his motorcar, and return to the cottage where the children would be waiting up for her.

—It's getting dark, she said.

—Not yet. Please?

He stepped away, his back to her, but one arm crooked behind.

—I haven't been alive, he said. Not truly. On the outside it's been everything you despise, effortless good looks, Edwin Drood shoving his way ahead, but . . .

He gripped his own shoulders.

—Please can I ask about the girl I knew before?

—She's dead.

He hugged himself tighter:

—That boy isn't.

The wind tousled his hair.

—He was cut up about the dog. Nearly as much as she. Had him buried in the garden of the press. Gutenberg allowed it, let him pay for a marker.

He stuffed his fists into his pockets.

—He knew what Rory meant to her, that girl, but still and all he didn't understand why she had to go. Or where. Or what she did, or why she came back.

She was standing behind him. He could feel the heat of her.

—There was something, she said.

He wanted to spill his thousand guesses, but he knew not yet, not yet. She spoke beside his ear:

—It hadn't happened in so long, she thought they were gone.

He let his hands fall to his sides, in case she came closer, in case, in case.

—He would fight anyone for her. He'd kill for her.

—These were a kind that couldn't be killed.

She stepped closer, he reached back.

—Whisper, he said. Nothing will hear, not even the truckely howl.

She gripped his hands, and they fell to the ground like a pair on a sled atop dried summer grass. He leaned back, her chin on his shoulder, whisper at his cheek:

There were Talkers. They sounded like a wireless in the next room. Two women, a man. Temperaments, accents, attitudes. Starting long ago before Lovelace, resuming after Rory. Only brute force silenced them, and only for a time. He'd never heard the like, yet he knew what she meant. The weakness never took that form with him, but in Kardleigh's hospital there had been men, many men.

—Did she go away because of—

—*Shhh*!

—the wireless programs?

Gute knew a spell, a song in another language that drew them off while she fled. Train, ferry, lady poet, funicular.

—Did the program play over there?

Halfway across the channel it stopped, but last week—

He pulled her arms around his waist:

—I know another spell.

—There is no lasting spell.

—You don't know that. And even if there isn't, we can listen together. We'll laugh. We'll laugh until they shrink, or until they're only hilarious.

Darkness was falling. She said she didn't want to twist an ankle going down the path. He mustn't come with her. He must return the way he'd come.

—You're shivering, he said.

He put his blazer around her shoulders.

—Tomorrow, he said. Please?

She told him where she took the children and how to find the path from the road. He looked as though he wanted to kiss her, but she turned down the path as quickly as she dared.

Later, in the cottage lane after Robert's motorcar vanished into the night, she felt the jacket as armor, smelling like him and like her father. Trees blocked the moon, and in the leafy darkness, eyes of creatures too eerie for a zoo watched her and whispered her coming. The sound hummed through the turf, under the sea, and back to the fairies who stole from her jars and had her in their sights from when she was this tall. She wore the pink-and-blue jacket of an Englishman, they hissed, and even now the bats whisked above the trees, her blood rushed through her veins, and his touch was already changing her.

—Marion!

—Marion!

—Shh, you'll wake Mother and Father.

—Did you see the truckely howl?

She said she had.

—What's that jacket?

—It belongs to the Elfin Prince.

—It looks like one Father has.

—That's part of the enchantment.

—We thought you'd never come back.

—We thought they'd stolen you to the underland.

—To the limeretty hillhockers.

—To the deep pondoon.

—They were waiting, she said, all along the lane, but they can't touch the Prince's mantle or anyone who wears it.

She brushed her hair but didn't wash her hands. Maybe she never would.

—Will you wear the mantle always?

She said she'd wear it tonight.

—And tomorrow?

—Mother and Father mustn't know.

—Would they sack you for having a paramour?

—Close your eyes, Clive.

—I want to meet this Elfin Prince. I'll tell you whether he's good or bad.

—We must see what tomorrow brings.

—Marion?

—Clive.

—Don't leave us.

The house was dark when he got back, but he could see an ember blinking like a red firefly. He rebuked the schoolboy guilt that rose inside him and crossed the lawn to the gazebo. As he approached, Robert extinguished his cigar and got up from the wicker armchair:

—I'm off to bed.

—Good walk? his father asked.

—Mmm.

—I'm headed in myself. There's something I've been meaning to give you.

He followed his father inside to his bedroom. A lamp poured yellow across the counterpane, and his father opened a drawer:

—You ought to have had it some time ago, I daresay. I hope you won't imagine I've been keeping it from you.

He set a small blue box on the bedside table. Jamie pressed the gold pin, and the box popped open revealing a ring with a small stone.

—Your mother's.

—What are you trying to say?

—I'm giving you what's yours.

His sisters remembered their mother vividly, and Jamie had learned to be somber when the shadows of remembrance closed around the Rectory.

—Thank you, he said solemnly.

Back in his garret room, he slid the ring onto his little finger as far as it would go. It struck him that he'd no firm idea of how proposals went. Whose permission was he meant to ask? Gutenberg sprang to mind, and he imagined himself drinking vodka with the man over the editing table, pleading his case. As for the proposing, three of his sisters had married, Stoat was engaged, but he'd never asked about the moment. If he had a living mother, would this be the kind of thing she told him?

She slipped out to the garden, hearing the song she'd heard when Daniel last appeared, in the corner of that room where she waited after Lovelace, waiting for word, when Dan was already dead. She dug in the plantings for a stone against the Talkers, a good sharp one in case it was needed. She knew she ought to use it now before they began, but she could still feel his fingers on her wrists where he held them to his stomach. He'd promised to laugh at the Talkers, but he didn't understand what he was promising. How could she make him see the one who had come from her very body, the one who had his eyes and suckled her and depended on her utterly, and then when she was choking, rather than do something, call anyone, shake her upside down (why had she never thought of that?), her only thought had been to take water from the glass and draw the shape with it, the shape of the tree where death had its hour. This is what she had done instead of anything else. And then when death had won and celebrated its majesty over everything good, then they had cut a hole in frozen ground and put her there alone. What words could show him? And who had the heart to slash his flesh and admit the curse that was everywhere, every time? People like Archie said the victory over death was already won, but she couldn't see it, couldn't comprehend it. Yet, if it really wasn't so, if the ice beneath the snow was the only, final answer, then what did anything matter? He said he would kill for her, but he didn't know what he was saying. Killing was easy. But hoping?

Eyes swollen, mouth full of thirst, she came inside and curled on the loveseat in the little parlor, blood thumping in her ears, too dread-filled to sleep. The opposite of hope was despair, but also nothingness, and both were better than the awful realization that you'd known the scent of hope but let it go by. Who would intercede when you were too far gone to help yourself? Who would look through the rain that fell like darts and ask the giver for the gift of hope? *No one can make you, but please.*

The villa had one bicycle with tires that held air. It got him to the path last night, and with a bit of luck and oil, it would get him to the farther path today. He wore his bathing costume under his trousers and packed a rucksack with towel and lunch. He thought there was enough to share if her charges weren't savages.

They asked her to time their foot races with the pocket watch Clive found at the cottage. She began a record in an exercise book as they drew start and stop marks in the sand.

—Do you think we'll see a selkie today?

She'd told them, earlier, of the maighdeann-ròin they used to watch for in Galway Bay.

—Are there only sea maidens or also sea men?

—Who can say for certain?

She saw him then, pushing a bicycle over the rise. He dropped it on the path and picked his way down to them, a rucksack on his back. The children clung to her when they saw him, Clive trembling with excitement or cold.

—Is he a sea man? Felicity asked.

—He looks like an agent of the Tsar.

Clive stepped in front of her, arms crossed, legs planted wide:

—I'll protect you.

—He's waving.

—Why has he sat down?

—He needs help with his shoes.

—Felicity, wait.

—You must use our noms de guerre, Marion. It's the rule.

It was the rule around strangers.

—Morgan, come back!

The girl was the size of his niece Georgie, her blonde hair a mass of ringlets. She scrambled up the dune and pointed at his shin:

—That's blood.

—Indeed.

—Did something chew you?

—A bicycle. And then the road.

He showed his palms. She shrieked, but it turned into a shriek of pleasure:

—Don't touch me!

He staggered forward:

—Help!

She shrieked again and darted away. He gave chase, gravel-scraped hands outstretched:

—Bloooood!

He wiped his shins and reached for the girl, catching her arm and smearing it red. She screamed again and ran her finger through it, presenting the red digit to her brother.

—The selkie got him! It chewed through his whole leg and he's going to die or faint.

He collapsed on the sand.

—Bring the salts and the vial!

—It's a *phial*, the boy insisted.

The girl climbed astride his chest, patted his cheeks, and tried to open his eyelid. He moaned.

—He needs the magic powder!

Sand sprinkled his forehead. He coughed and feigned awakening.

—I un-enchanted you. I'm a sorceress.

—Are you?

—Morgan le Fay. You were eaten by a selkie and there was blood everywhere but you're all right now.

—I'm much obliged to you, Mistress le Fay.

She giggled and gripped his ribs with her knees. Marion—so they both called her—appeared over the girl's shoulder.

—Morgan, you've got blood everywhere. Run along and rinse off.

The girl bounced on his stomach and then climbed off. He lay, pulse thudding beneath a glaring blue sky and her sunburned face.

He'd fallen from his bicycle, ripped his trouser leg, and left half his skin on the road. She'd never seen him with children. She hadn't thought there was so much more of him to discover.

—The girl's name is Morgan? he asked.

—Sometimes.

To his look she explained, nom de guerre.

—But why Morgan?

—Why not?

They joined the children at the tidemark. The boy made a point of placing himself between them.

—I'm going to swim with my face in the water today, the girl announced.

—You said that yesterday and were too scared.

—I wasn't.

—You were.

—Clive.

—*Finn!* I told you!

—I wasn't scared.

The boy stood up:

—Time me, Marion.

—Time me, too!

They bickered over the length of their race as she drew a new line in the sand and counted them off. When they dashed away, he took her cold hand and pressed it to his cheek. She didn't let him keep it.

—Aaah!

The boy crossed the line and demanded to know his time. When he'd recovered, Jamie drew the line again:

—This time don't let your fists cross your body.

He showed him how to pump his arms, how to start from a crouch.

—Will you go in the sea with me? the girl asked.

—I'll bury you in the sand.

—No! she cried with pleasure.

—Ten seconds faster!

Jas was wise enough to ignore Clive now, instead unpacking from his rucksack sandwiches, flask, a bag of penny cordials.

—You each may have one now and one after lunch, she told them.

—But there's lots in there. So many lots!

—Come with me, Clive told him.

—Can I come? Felicity asked.

—No! It's for boys.

The boy led him down the shore and over the rocks, promising a secret Jamie was enjoined with multiple oaths not to divulge. Jamie didn't know what to call him since two names had been used, but he decided that if pressed, he would use the boy's proper name. The children already struck him as too demanding; it was one thing to jest with them as he did his nieces, but he drew the line at being directed.

Just ahead, Clive ducked under a crag and vanished; Jamie followed, slipped, and landed in a cavern, sand beneath his feet. There the sea hushed, gently lapping their toes. The rock walls dripped, and he realized this was the kind of place people got trapped when the tide turned.

The boy scrambled up a ledge, reminding him unaccountably of John, lanky, dark, serious, though with more capacity for mirth.

—Are you sure it's quite safe in here? Jamie asked.

Clive clambered down holding a shoebox. Drawing Jamie to an alcove, he lifted the lid by degrees, revealing seaweed, rocks, and an angry, swollen spider.

—I wasn't supposed to look after it, Clive said. I was supposed to stamp on it.

Jamie admired the creature, listened to its provenance, its discovery in their holiday cottage, its secret adoption.

—It's going to have babies, don't you think?

Jamie supposed it might. Clive produced a knotted handkerchief, containing pear drops stuck together.

—I always save mine, the boy said, in my pocket, and then I wait until there's a treasure of them.

Jamie wondered why the boy was confiding in him, especially as he'd been so wary at first.

—Does Miss Marion know about your pirate's hoard?

—No! Clive said sharply. And you swore three times you wouldn't tell.

—I won't.

The surf thundered and sprayed down the slit where they'd come.

—Hadn't we better go back?

But Clive had disappeared into his vault, taking the spider and his cache of sorry sweets.

—That wasn't what I have to show you! he called.

—Oh, no?

The boy leapt back down, sure-footed as John had been at his age.

—Swear again, he said. Swear on your heart.

—I really think we ought to—

—Swear!

Hamlet's ghost had nothing on this one. Jamie hoped he'd never cross him in a school.

—I swear.

—Swear on your *heart.*

—On my heart.

—On your true love.

—My true love.

—If you ever, ever tell, your true love will perish in fire.

—All right.

—Say it.

He did. The boy's face flushed with sudden intensity. Jamie thought of the spider shut in its box, its murderousness and frustration.

The boy extended his hand to show a chain, a necklace.

—Where did you find that?

The boy scowled.

—You haven't nicked it, have you?

—Yes, Clive replied, I have!

Unlike the sureness he'd shown with the spider, the boy tremblingly pried the pendant open and disclosed a cutting of fine, fair hair, not long enough to be called a lock.

—People often put hair in lockets, Jamie said. You must put that back where you found it.

—No!

The boy thrust the locket forward, and Jamie saw the hair was stuck to the inside with a brownish smear.

—Yes? he asked in his best housemaster's tone.

—Don't you see?

—Let's say I don't.

—You *have* to. It's blood.

Jamie's scalp crawled.

—I don't think so.

—It is. I tasted it.

Jamie took the locket and snapped it shut.

—Where did you get this?

Clive gazed defiantly, jaw set.

—Have it your own way.

Jamie seized him by the elbow and pulled him to the ledge that gave to the surface.

—Up.

He emphasized his authority with a swat. As the boy vanished above, the sea rushed in at his ankles. Scraping his shin again, and his palms, Jamie crawled back up to the blazing, blinding sun.

—Give it back, Clive demanded.

—I don't think so.

—It's mine.

—It certainly isn't.

—I've got to put it back.

—The tide's coming in. You can't go down again.

—Not there. I'd never leave it there! I brought it in my secret pocket. The one in my pants!

Jamie had had enough, but the boy was proudly unbuttoning his shorts to reveal a small pouch in the waistband of his drawers.

—Very nice, Jamie said dryly.

—I need it. Please.

Jamie stepped around him and picked his way over the rocks until he could see her, wading with the girl in the surf.

—Please!

The boy grabbed his hand:

—She'll . . .

—Who?

—If she misses it, she'll . . .

The boy bit his lip. Jamie hadn't the patience for children, not truly, not ones you couldn't command.

—She'll go away even sooner, the boy said.

His ribs stabbed, and the charmed seaside day that had begun flying over his handlebars now skidded into—

—She keeps it in her bundle, and she doesn't know I know it. Once she had it in a box, but when we saw it, she gave us a smack, and then she hid it in her bundle and brought it on holiday, so it's *that* much. That much!

The boy was trying not to cry. Jamie took the necklace from his pocket, but before he let it go, he opened it again on the fraise-blonde lock. And he was hot and he was cold, knew and didn't know, feared and yet hungered for the final destruction.

He strode down the sand in the style she only just remembered, the way he must walk as a schoolmaster, with purpose. His trousers had come unrolled, and he was unbuttoning his shirt. She led Felicity out of the water and wrapped her in a towel.

—You're turning blue, my little selkie.

—Bury me in the sand. Bury me, Marion, and find me like treasure.

He was undressing as he approached, pulling off his shirt, unbuttoning his trousers.

—Come in with me, he said in an undertone.

She felt a wave of alarm at the sight of him stripping off in front of the children, but underneath he wore a swimming costume, one she in fact remembered. She suggested to Clive that he bury his sister, and the boy adopted a piratical persona, singing tunelessly of maps and rum.

They approached the surf together, and as they waded in, he braced himself against the cold and the salt on his wounds.

—You have to think of the great romances, he said.

—They all wind up dead.

—*You pierce my soul*!

Her breath caught, but she told him romance only worked

in stories, where each pairing was planned from the beginning, even Wentworth and Anne Elliot, who'd lost her bloom.

—We used to debate it, he said, whether history was inexorable.

—The Set!

—Dunham said juggernaut, but I said it only seemed that way looking back.

A wave was coming and she dove under, where the sand whispered and the wind couldn't blow.

He glimpsed her stomach beneath her costume, which floated as she swam. Kicking with the last of his breath, he caught her and lifted her above the surface. She blinked back water, hair dangling past her shoulders, lips red. They'd passed the breakers, and she turned back to check the children.

—I don't know what to call you, he said.

—Marion. Just Marion.

The name stabbed, but then he thought of the children saying it with love and abandon.

—Marion.

—James.

He groaned.

—Only my father calls me that, and only when he's cross.

—So, then?

His arms closed around her, and he hooked his chin over her shoulder.

—Please, he whispered, whatever it is, say it.

Her chest strained but you couldn't tell tears from the sea.

—Just to the wind. Please?

He pulled her legs around him, home to the hold she'd fled for so long and now in the sea where none could see, all the reasons, what were they? She shouldn't want, but here was one who wanted the same, whose arms were like a shell in the waves no one could contain. Here, inside, nothing could hear what she said to his ear, and if it sank like poison, if he thrust her away and swam back to the shore, if the candle was snuffed, then the sea could take her, she could breathe it, and then—

No one else would ever know the words she said.

—God! Oh, God, was she beautiful?

She wasn't even saying them, they were being said.

—Stopped breathing?

What spoke when you couldn't speak yourself?

—In the ground?

He wasn't letting go, but it was rending him.

—Really gone? But she lived? A real person?

He asked things more than twice.

—Was she beautiful? She had hair? Was it fine?

She'd never been able to imagine the words, but now she had to hold him as pictures formed in his mind.

—But she lived? Was she beautiful?

Held him as he learned to feel it as a man.

Even the knowing couldn't bring him into what she had lived, a tiny tincture of her grief all he could bear. He'd never carried a child, never touched her, only knew her through words as the world churned inside the welter of the deep. Had he always known, or had he only ever wished? To learn of her existence as he learned of her death shattered the shield he'd been clasping to defend himself against his true desire.

—I never want to be apart again. I want to know what you know, touch what you touch.

He wanted to live everything with her. He wanted children, not their people, but real, true, mortal and finite.

—Don't say we can have another!

—Never another Amanda. But there's still time. *Some* time. Please, God . . .

One more chance. Two. As many as they could take until the sun set the last time.

—You're shivering.

—So are you.

—Marion!

Clive was calling from the shore. He was hungry. They were thirsty. He wanted to swim but the waves were too big.

—In the midst of death, we are in life.

He said it like a quip.

—If you're going to quote theologians at me, this isn't going to work at all.

He grinned, a flash of Jasper Knox. She'd forgotten the way it made her feel, like the garden was new, everything invisible on your side.

—My father won't wear theologian, despite his pedantry, which is vast.

She dove under the breaker and he followed, catching her hand in the shallows. There the waves knocked them down, and they fought their way to land like staggering back from war.

—Marion!

Clive was waiting at the tideline.

—I'm starving of hunger!

—So am I! his sister called.

—You can't be hungry! You're buried treasure! What's the matter, Marion?

Clive took her hands and glared at Jamie.

—It's only the sea, she said, in my eyes.

—I don't want to put my face in the water! Felicity called.

She set out sandwiches and little cups of lemonade. Jamie poured tea while Clive unburied his sister and took her to rinse in the sea.

—Marion.

It wasn't as he'd imagined. How could he speak of marriage when they were speaking of death?

—I want to meet every death at your side. Every one from this day on.

He thought of his father, what the world would be without him.

—It's everywhere.

—I know.

The children returned, and she rubbed them dry, listening to their pirate prattle. He held his knees, like a sandcastle beneath a crashing wave.

—Your face is wet, Mr. Sebastian.

—Are you crying?

—It's the sun.

—Does it hurt, Mr. Bastian, where the blood was?

—No.

—But you're crying.

—Only because I'm happy.

—Why do grown-ups cry when they're happy and never when they're sad?

—Because, he said taking the girl onto his knee, grown-ups are under a terrible spell.

—From the truckely howl?

—From the lepreshauny truckely howl.

He asked them to fill his hat with sea shells.

—But only ones that are perfect and whole.

They darted along the sand, and he lay down beside her to watch the sky swirl.

—Come with me, he said.

He meant forward, into time.

—Side-by-side, whatever it brings.

She laced their fingers together, and the clouds broke and formed again, and everything was different and all was always the same, and the wind kept blowing it off until at last it wouldn't.

~

ACKNOWLEDGEMENTS

My grateful thanks:

Jennifer Gibbs, Jenny Turner Hall, Winsome Brown, Jean Wagner, Drew Keane, Kevin Salinger, Paul Thwaite, Miranda Reading, Amanda Gareis.

Alice Tasman, Michael Reynolds, Edoardo Andreoni, and everyone at Europa.

The Hawthornden Literary Fellowship (Scotland), the Danish Centre for Writers and Translators (Hald Hovedgaard, Denmark), Wildacres Retreat (North Carolina), the National Library of Scotland (Edinburgh), the War Poets Collection at Craiglockhart (Edinburgh Napier University), and the New York Public Library research collections.

About the Author

H. S. Cross was raised in Michigan and lived for many years in New York City. She has taught grades 2-12, and many of her formative experiences involved being semi-lost in the countrysides of England, Ireland, and Scotland. She currently lives in Savannah, Georgia.